Palo Alto City Library

The individual borrower is responsible for all library material borrowed on his or her card.

Charges as determined by the CITY OF PALO ALTO will be assessed for each overdue item.

Damaged or non-returned property will be billed to the individual borrower by the CITY OF PALO ALTO.

P.O. Box 10250, Palo Alto, CA 94303

GAYLORD

INVITATION TO MURDER

DARK HARVEST
Arlington Hts., Illinois · 1991

INVITATION TO MURDER

INTRODUCTION BY BILL PRONZINI

—All New Stories of Mystery and Suspense By —

Nancy Pickard	Teri White
Bill Pronzini	Andrew Vachss
John Lutz	William J. Reynolds
Carolyn G. Hart	Jan Grape
Joan Hess	Judith Kelman
Richard Laymon	William F. Nolan
Gary Brandner	Rex Miller
Billie Sue Mosiman	Barbara Paul
Kristine Kathryn Rusch	Loren D. Estleman

— Edited By —
Ed Gorman and Martin H. Greenberg

Trade Hardcover Edition ISBN 0-913165-65-4

Manufactured in the United States of America

FIRST EDITION

Dark Harvest / P.O. Box 941 / Arlington Heights, IL / 60006

TABLE OF CONTENTS

The publishers would like to express their gratitude to the following people. Thank you: Ann Cameron Mikol, Kathy Jo Camacho, Stan and Phyllis Mikol, Dr. Stan Gurnick PhD, Luis Trevino, Raymond, Teresa and Mark Stadalsky, Tom Pas, Bob Lavoie, and Bill Pronzini.

And, of course, special thanks go to all the contributors for their fine stories, and to Ed Gorman and Marty Greenberg for the effort it took to get this one together.

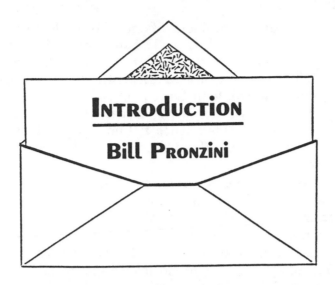

INTRODUCTION

Bill Pronzini

The best ideas are usually the simple ones.

Case in point: this anthology. Each of the eighteen contributors was given the same ultra-basic plot element—*the body of a young woman is found in her apartment*—and asked to write a story in which that element plays some sort of pivotal role. The contributor was to make use of the component as he or she saw fit: as a starting place, or included somewhere in the body of the story, or saved for the end; as a case of murder, suicide, accidental death, even a supernatural or unearthly happening; as an event that happens on stage or off, in the past or present or future. No restrictions, no taboos. Any type of story, at any length up to 10,000 words, with any tone or slant or message.

What could be simpler?

Cunningly so. The editors, clever fellows that they are, knew that few writers can resist such a subtle tweaking of the imagination, or such freedom to improvise.

The result, predictably, was eighteen unpredictable stories as disparate as the authors selected to write them. None is like any other in style, content, or the use to which the given plot element is put. There are private eye and police investigations, psychological thrillers, quiet (and quietly amusing) cozy-style tales, *noir* journeys down the mean streets, exercises in cauld grue, and a number of less easily definable delights.

INTRODUCTION

Equally diverse is the lineup of contributors. Represented here are bestselling crime writers (Loren D. Estleman, Andrew Vachss, Rex Miller, Judith Kelman), bestselling horror writers (Richard Laymon, Gary Brandner), well-established and critically acclaimed mystery writers (Nancy Pickard, John Lutz, Joan Hess, Teri White, William T. Reynolds, Carolyn G. Hart, Barbara Paul), a multi-skilled scribe best known for his science fiction (William F. Nolan), and three talented newcomers (Jan Grape, Kristine K. Rusch, Billie Sue Mosiman).

If any anthology ever warranted the descriptive term "mixed bag," it is *Invitation to Murder*. And a most appetizing mixed bag it is. You may not like every story, but you won't find a poorly conceived or poorly written one in the bunch.

Remember the basic plot element as you read each entry: The body of a young woman is found in her apartment. When you've finished reading all eighteen, ask yourself what you'd have done with that element if you had been one of the selected contributors.

What story would *you* have written?

—Bill Pronzini

The Dead Past

Nancy Pickard

At first, she was only a new name in the appointment book of the psychologist, Paul Laner, Ph.D.:

"March 3, Tues., 12:10 Ouvray, Elizabeth."

Then she was a lovely girl in the doorway of his office, young and slim, pale as a ghost, wearing grey trousers and sweater, and her platinum hair caught up at the sides of her scalp with translucent plastic barettes. Her beauty, Laner thought at the time, was the stunning natural kind that is formidable to look upon, and which instantly forms a wall that other people have to scale in order to reach the person behind it. According to the form she had filled out for his receptionist, Elizabeth Ouvray was nineteen years old. Laner, at forty-five, was old enough to be her father, and he felt at least that much more mature than she as he stared at the nervous, ghost-like girl in his doorway.

Indeed, like a ghost who was afraid to materialize, she hesitated, her head down, eyes averted. She looked to him as if she wished she were invisible. Her hair, parted in the middle, hung down from the barettes like curtains pulled over her face.

"Come in," he said.

She glanced up at him, and smiled stiffly, slightly, as if any facial expression was an effort. Instinctively, Laner wanted to put his hand under her elbow and lead her gently into his office, but he didn't. The doctor was careful not to touch her, not only because Elizabeth Ouvray looked as if she would flee at the slightest overture, but also because the hand of a male counselor on a female client could be so easily misinterpreted. A comforting pat on the shoulder, a gently intended squeeze of the hand could get even a well-respected psychologist like him into serious trouble.

She scooted past him without speaking, leaving in her wake a lemony scent that made his jaws ache. Saliva pooled on his tongue, and he swallowed. She was, easily, the best looking patient to walk through his doorway in his twenty-three years of professional counseling. He thought it poignant that a woman so blessed in her physical appearance should appear to feel so cursed. Following that thought, Laner experienced such an immediate and intense desire to find out *why* she felt cursed that he experienced a mild sexual arousal.

"Down boy," he commanded his libido. "Sublimate."

Behind her back, he smiled to himself. It pleased him that after all this time in his career he could still get excited about the human mysteries that awaited his unraveling.

"Sit anywhere you like," he suggested to her.

He observed her as she made the difficult and meaningful choice that faced every new client: whether to sit on the couch in the corner farthest away from him, or the Windsor chair midway between the couch and his desk, or in the rocking chair beside his desk. She finally chose the latter—not, he thought, because she was self-confident enough to sit that close to him or because she craved intimacy, or even because she had a bad back. Rather, he suspected, it was because she felt safer there than she would have felt all the way across the room by herself. The doctor couldn't help but make an instantaneous diagnosis in layman's terms: *fear*—stark, staring, trembling, not-quite-raving fear. This clearly neurotic young woman was afraid of her own shadow.

Laner smiled inwardly at his own Jungian pun.

He felt a warm surge of hope for this new patient and an even warmer surge of self confidence. Eagerly, almost buoyantly, he crossed the room and sat down at his desk, facing her. Sensing that small talk would not relax this patient who had yet to utter a word to him, he launched right in.

"How can I help you, Elizabeth?"

She didn't hesitate, but said in a soft voice, "I'm afraid."

Laner was surprised at her directness. But taking that as a cue, he proceeded to be extremely direct and clear with her, himself.

"What are you afraid of, Elizabeth?"

"*Everything.*" She didn't smile when she said it.

"All right. Tell me one thing that frightens you."

"Coming here."

"Yes, everybody's nervous the first time."

Laner purposely cultivated a fatherly appearance in order to put his clients at ease. He knew that when she looked at him she perceived a nice, middle-aged man with frizzly grey hair, a bushy moustache and beard, bright, intense blue eyes and a tactful, sympathetic smile.

He presented that smile to her. "What else?"

"I'm not *just* nervous," she protested, as if he had belittled her complaint. Her near-whisper had a defensive, annoyed edge to it. *What was this?* he wondered. Was she proud of her neurosis, (many patients secretly were) or did she already have resources of courage and independence with which to defend herself? That would be a hopeful sign for her prognosis, he thought.

"I believe you," he said quickly. "What else scares you, Elizabeth?"

"People," she said, and he was inwardly amused to see her look suspiciously, even furtively at him. "Strangers."

"I see. What else scares you?"

"Oh God, you name it!" she burst out. "I think I'm really crazy. I must be crazy to be so frightened all the time."

"Nobody is afraid for no reason, Elizabeth," he told her. "My experience tells me that we will discover that your fears are the natural, if perhaps rather exaggerated, effects of certain causes. Our job will be to uncover those causes, so that we may eliminate the effects of them. You understand what I'm saying?"

"Yes, but it sounds too . . . easy."

"Would it make you feel better if I assure you that it probably won't be easy?" He smiled at her. "We often find that the greater the fear, the more deeply buried the cause. I will help you, Elizabeth, but I can almost guarantee that it will not be in one easy lesson."

"You'll help me?"

"I will," he said firmly, and was delighted to see the relieved expression in her eyes, and the slight relaxation of her tense body. "Tell me, Elizabeth, do you feel scared all of the time?"

"Yes! Every minute. All the time."

"Right now?"

"Yes!"

"How does that affect your life?"

There was anguish in her eyes. "It ruins it."

"How does it ruin it?"

"I don't want to be around anybody. I don't want to go out, I don't want to go anyplace. I don't date. I've never had many friends. I was in college, but I quit, and now I just get up in the morning, I go to work, I go home, and I stay at home until it's time to go to work in the morning."

"Not much of a life," Laner commented, gently.

She began to cry. "No, it's not much of a life."

He encouraged her to weep the sadness out. In truth, at that point, he foresaw a long and difficult therapy, but he was not for a minute afraid of failing her.

*　　*　　*

First, the psychologist attempted conventional therapy, fully expecting it to work.

He began by administering psychological tests, which served to confirm his original hypothesis that Elizabeth was deeply neurotic due to abnormally deep-seated fears of undetermined origin. Or, as he commented privately to his wife, "The poor girl's scared shitless."

Twice weekly, he asked probing questions and Elizabeth reacted, sometimes calmly, sometimes decidedly not. But none of them was the *right* question; none of her answers was *the* answer. Sometimes Laner felt she was telling him the truth; other times, not.

"Tell me about your mother, Elizabeth," he said.

"She raised me by herself."

"Where was your father?"

"Pretending I didn't exist."

"Tell me how you felt about school, Elizabeth," he suggested. "... about God, Elizabeth ... about men ... tell me about your dreams, Elizabeth ... your daydreams, your fantasies. Tell me, Elizabeth ..."

Over time, it became clear that she was not getting better. Instead, to his dismay, she grew progressively worse. Her appearance disintegrated. Laner grieved at the loss of her remarkable beauty, at her frightening weight loss, at the acne that ruined her beautiful skin, at her humped, defensive posture, and the sad, grey cast to her eyes.

"I've quit my job," she announced one day.

She lost her insurance, and couldn't pay his fee.

Laner adjusted his sliding scale to compensate, until finally he was treating her for free, something he had always sworn he would never do for clients because it would increase their dependency on him and destroy one of their main motivations to change.

"You're taking this case awfully hard," his wife finally said. What she really meant, he knew, was that he was taking it too personally. "Watch it, Paul," his colleagues warned, "you're becoming obsessed by this case." Their comments infuriated him, although he couldn't deny them. But he couldn't quite believe them, either.

It was not conceivable that Dr. Paul Laner could so miserably and completely fail to help one of his patients. No one, he thought, would be able to comprehend it, least of all him. "I'm a *good* psychologist," he kept telling himself; in fact, the peer recognition he had achieved over a long career suggested that many considered him to be a great one. But the doctor began to sleep less well, and to be aware of vague, unpleasant stirrings in his chest and abdomen. He did not need a psychiatrist to diagnose: anxiety.

He was not yet ready to call it fear.

But that's what he was: afraid, terrified that Elizabeth Ouvray was dying before his eyes, a little more every week, incrementally every session. He could not even be sure that his "treatment," his reknowned methods of analysis, were helping to keep her alive. It was even possible that he was—mistakenly, unintentionally, horribly— speeding the painful process of her death.

*   *   *

At the beginning of the final month of his treatment of Elizabeth Ouvray, Dr. Paul Laner tried hypnosis for the first time. It was not a mode of treatment he particularly condoned, believing as he did in the more conventional forms of therapy. Indeed, he had to cram a quick refresher course on hypnosis with a younger, more holistically-inclined psychologist of his acquaintance.

"Let your scalp relax," he began the first time, using his deepest, most soothing and mellifluous voice, and feeling faintly ridiculous even saying the words. Elizabeth lay on her back on the couch in the corner of his office, her skeletal hands folded over her stomach, her eyes closed.

He was seated beside her right shoulder.

"Allow even your hair to relax . . . relax your forehead, feel your forehead grow smooth, smooth . . . relax your eyebrows, eyelids, let your eyes fall back in your head, feel your eyes relax, feel them relax . . . relax your cheekbones . . . your lips, relax your tongue, let your jaw relax . . . relax the back of your neck, and now your throat . . . feel how relaxed your whole head is, your whole neck and throat . . . now let that feeling of complete relaxation slide down into your shoulders . . ."

When Elizabeth was visibly relaxed and breathing easily, he led her through a series of non-threatening questions and answers. Then he said, "Let's go further back now, Elizabeth, to a time when you were just a little girl. Now, while you are absolutely safe and secure in the present, I will ask you to go back to a time in your childhood when you were afraid. Remember, Elizabeth, that whatever it was that frightened you then, cannot hurt you now. The past is over. It is safe for you to remember what frightened you. When I count to three, you will remember something that frightened you when you were a little girl. One, two, three . . ."

"I'm in my bedroom," she said immediately.

Laner stared, surprised. This had the sound of something new, something previously uncovered.

"How old are you in this bedroom?"

"I don't know. Young. I'm really young."

"Look around the room, Elizabeth. What do you see?"

"Oh!" Suddenly, her voice was like a child's. "It's our first little apartment! I'm two."

Good grief, Laner thought, can this be true?

"Are you two years old?"

"Yes."

"Is it night time?"

"Yes."

"Your mother has put you to bed?"

"Yes."

"Are you alone in the bed?"

"No."

"No, Elizabeth?"

"Tubby."

"Your teddy bear is with you."

"Yes."

"And you feel . . . how do you feel?"

"Scared! I'm awake. I don't know why I'm awake. It's dark! Where's Mommy? Mommy? There's a noise! Mommy!"

Laner's own heart was beating rapidly, but he leaned forward to calm her.

"You are safe from the noise, Elizabeth, it cannot hurt you, I will not let it hurt you. Are you calling out for your mother?"

"Yes. No! I thought I was! But I'm not, I'm too scared, oh, what is that, who is that? *Mommy!*"

The last word burst from Elizabeth's throat as if it had broken loose from paralyzed vocal chords. She remained lying on the couch, but her head and shoulders strained upward, her eyes bulged beneath their lids, and she breathed in ragged gasps.

"It cannot hurt you, Elizabeth," Laner said, hoping he did not sound as unnerved as he felt. "Tell me what you see, tell me what it is that frightens you so."

"A face!" Elizabeth began sobbing, quick, keening sobs that sounded like a frightened child's. She was trembling all over, and his own hands were shaking. "He's got a flashlight. He's got curly hair. He's got a mean face, oh, it's the meanest face I ever saw! He's looking down at me, he's angry at me, he's going to hurt me!"

"Does he hurt you, Elizabeth?"

"Oh!" Her sobs caught in her throat, as if she were startled. "He's gone! Mommy's here and she's holding me . . . a burglar," she said next, in a wondering voice. "I can hear Mommy saying that. Shhh, Mommy says to me, it's all right, baby girl, it was just a dream, it was only a bad dream, that's all it was, forget all about it now, go back to sleep, it didn't happen, it never happened, it was only a bad dream . . ."

Soon after that, Laner brought Elizabeth up out of the hypnotic trance. She remembered nothing of what had transpired, so he told her.

"A *burglar*?" She was still as wide-eyed as a child. "That's where my nightmares came from? But my mother only meant to protect me."

"I'm sure that's true, Elizabeth."

"She told me it was only a dream . . ."

"And it became a recurring nightmare."

19

"Is that why I'm frightened of strangers, too?"

"What do you think, Elizabeth?"

She smiled tentatively. "I think maybe it is."

He thought maybe it was, too. In fact, he was positive of it. And he felt sure that now that Elizabeth had at last delved far enough into her subconsious to uncover the source of her fears, she would begin to recover.

But she did not.

*   *   *

She began to report horrifying nightmares.

At their next session, she reported a continued terror of strangers, along with her many other fears. Indeed, she looked as if she had slept even less that week than before. She reported that the headaches and muscle cramps that Laner suspected were a consequence of malnutrition had increased in frequency and intensity. He had been on the verge of hospitalizing her before; now he felt he surely must. But what an admission of failure on his part that would be! Still, how much worse it would be if she died when simple medical procedures like an IV might keep her alive.

The psychologist's own sleep was not much better than hers. "She looks awful," he thought, "and what am I going to do now?"

*   *   *

He decided to hypnotize her again.

"All right," she said, dully.

Again, he relaxed her, although it took a long time, as he was anything but relaxed himself. Again, he led her through safe and easy memories, then back through the traumatic memory of the burglar, and then . . .

"Go further back now, Elizabeth, back as far as you can go to the first, the very first frightening thing that ever happened to you . . ."

"Please, I won't tell anyone!" she cried.

"What?" Laner was confused at the sudden and dramatic change in her voice and tone. "Where are you?"

"In my bedroom. Oh my God, please don't do that. I swear to you that I never told anyone, I won't tell anyone, I swear it."

"Elizabeth, how old are you?"

"Twenty-two."

What? Laner thought—twenty-two? But she was only nineteen in the present, in the here and now. What was going on?

"Where are you?" he asked again, trying to orient himself as much as to orient her.

"I'm sitting here on the edge of my bed, and I'm begging him, begging him . . ."

She began to sob convulsively.

"Begging him to do what, Elizabeth?"

"Begging him not to kill me. I won't tell anyone. I swear I won't. Please, please . . ."

She screamed, and Laner jumped back in his chair.

"Elizabeth," he said slowly, "who are you?"

"Susan Naylor," she whispered, "I am dying . . ."

Oh my God, he thought, my God, my God, what is this, what is this that is happening here?

This time when he brought her out of hypnosis, he did not tell her what she had said and done. He could hardly credit it himself. How could a 19-year-old patient suddenly "become" a different, even an older woman entirely? Could this possibly be an example of past-life regression such as he had read about (and disbelieved) in some medical journals? Could it be a form of ESP? If he wrote it up as such, he'd be laughed out of his practice. The psychologist sent her home, canceled all of his appointments for the rest of that day and secreted himself in a secluded recess of the medical library at a near-by hospital. For the rest of that afternoon, he read every case study he could locate that even slightly resembled the strange events that had transpired in his office.

He found no reassuring answers.

Near dinnertime, he called his wife.

"I'll be late," he told her. "I have to see a patient."

* * *

21

Elizabeth Ouvray lived in the second-floor rear apartment of a brick fourplex in a shabby neighborhood. It was twilight and getting cool outside by the time he rang her doorbell.

"Dr. Laner?" she said, when she saw him.

She was pale, exhausted-looking, shaking, and so was he.

"May I please come in, Elizabeth?"

"I'm . . ." She looked as if she were trying to come up with some good reason to turn him away. He suspected he was the first person to enter her apartment in a very long time. "I . . . all right . . . yes."

The doctor followed her into her living room, which was starkly decorated with furniture so nondescript it could have been rented. He sat down in the middle of her couch, but Elizabeth remained standing, propping herself against a wall as if it alone gave her the strength to remain upright.

"Elizabeth, today . . ."

"I don't want to know!"

"You're aware then, that something happened . . . something unusual . . . during hypnosis?"

"I think so . . . yes."

"Elizabeth, who is . . . was . . . Susan Naylor?"

The doctor held his breath, hoping she'd come up with some explanation, some conscious recognition of the name that would explain how a 22-year-old dead woman's memories got into Elizabeth Ouvray's brain.

She looked blank. "Who?"

He felt like crying. It wasn't only her life that was at stake here. His reputation, his 23-year counseling career, was about to go down the tubes because this insane young woman had memories she had no logical reason for having!

"I'm sorry," she whispered.

Laner was appalled to realize he had actually spoken his thoughts aloud to her. He felt desperate enough to suggest, "I want to hypnotize you again, Elizabeth."

"Right here, Dr. Laner? You mean now?"

"Please," he said softly, gently. "Please."

* * *

22

She said she'd be most comfortable seated at the table in the kitchen, and so she led him there. She faced the chrome door of the refrigerator as he attempted one more time to relax her into a deep trance state. The contorted reflection he saw over her shoulders was of an old man who looked as if he had just been told that his favorite grandchild had been run over on her tricycle. The haggard woman reflected in the chrome bore little resemblance to the blonde beauty who'd walked through his office door at a time that now seemed so long ago.

When she appeared to be deep in trance, he made the hypnotic suggestion: "You are now Susan Naylor," and then he stood back to see what might happen next.

It was instantaneous.

"*No!*" she screamed, loud enough for the neighbors to hear. "*Please, no! Get away from me! Don't hurt me, I won't tell anyone! Please, don't hurt me, don't hurt me!*" She lurched to her feet, knocking the stool over, still screaming, "*No, no, no!*" When she turned toward the doctor, she was holding a butcher knife. "*Please don't kill me!*" she screamed—over and over, as she stabbed him in his throat.

* * *

When the police arrived at the urgent summons of several of the neighbors, they found Elizabeth, weeping and bloody, still holding the knife with which she had killed Dr. Paul Laner. Her blouse was torn, revealing her ripped bra, and the zipper of her jeans was broken so that she had to hold it together with one hand.

"Tell us what happened," a detective, a woman, urged her. "Your neighbors reported hearing your scream for help."

"He was my psychologist," Elizabeth whispered. "I trusted him. And he came here tonight, and he tried to rape me. I'm so afraid all the time, of everything, that's what he was treating me for, he knew how horribly afraid I am of men, and when he attacked me, I . . . I . . . killed him."

On the way to the hospital, she whispered to the policewoman, "Somebody told me that Dr. Laner got into trouble years ago with another female patient, but he was so good to me that I didn't believe it. Do you think it could be true?"

*   *   *

"It's true," the policewoman called her at the hospital to say. "At least I think it's true, although it was only a rumor at the time. It makes sense though, considering how obsessed even his wife and his colleagues admit that he was about you. What I've learned is that when he was just starting out, twenty-three years ago, there were rumors that he had an affair with a patient, supposedly as a part of her treatment, and that she had a child by him. Lousy bastard, abusing his power like that. They said she was blonde, like you, only 22 years old, and very beautiful."

"I'd like to hear her name," Elizabether whispered.

"Naylor, Susan Naylor," the policewoman said, and then, because she heard Elizabeth moan, she added sharply, "What's the matter?"

"Nothing."

"There was a rumor that she was going to file a paternity suit," the policewoman continued, "but before that could happen she was murdered. Susan Naylor was stabbed one night by someone who broke into her apartment."

"Oh God," Elizabeth breathed. "They didn't catch him."

"Nope. They interrogated Laner, because of the rumors. But their only witness was the baby, Susan Naylor's two-year-old little girl. And the only word they got out of her was 'burglar.' Poor little thing. After her mother's murder, she was taken by her grandparents. Do you think Laner was her father? I'll bet you the bastard was, and I'll bet you he killed her mother to keep his precious reputation intact." The cop laughed. "At least, that's my wild theory, what do you think of it?"

"I think you're right," Elizabeth whispered.

"Well, you get to feeling better, okay?"

"I will now."

"What?"

"Bye."

*   *   *

"Bye."

The policewoman's hand lingered on the receiver after she hung up the phone. On her desk lay the old homicide file from which she'd been quoting to Elizabeth.

Elizabeth.

The child's name was Elizabeth.

"I think you're right," the policewoman whispered to herself. When no one was looking, she slid a few pages out of the file and slipped them into her morning newspaper, which she folded in half and dropped into her wastebasket.

La Bellezza Delle Bellezze

A "Nameless Detective" Story

Bill Pronzini

1.

That Sunday, the day before she died, I went down to Aquatic Park to watch the old men play bocce. I do that sometimes on weekends when I'm not working, when Kerry and I have nothing planned. More often than I used to, out of nostalgia and compassion and maybe just a touch of guilt, because in San Francisco bocce is a dying sport.

Only one of the courts was in use. Time was, all six were packed throughout the day and there were spectators and waiting players lined two and three deep at courtside and up along the fence on Van Ness. No more. Most of the city's older Italians, to whom bocce was more a religion than a sport, have died off. The once large and close-knit North Beach Italian community has been steadily losing its identity since the fifties—families moving to the suburbs, the expansion of Chinatown and the gobbling up of North Beach real estate by wealthy Chinese—and even though there has been a small new wave of immigrants from Italy in recent years, they're mostly young and upscale. Young, upscale Italians don't play bocce much, if at all; their interests lie in soccer, in the American sports where money and fame and power have replaced a love of the game itself. The Di Massimo bocce courts at the North Beach Playground are mostly closed now; the only place you can find a game every Saturday and Sunday is on the one Aquatic Park court. And the players get older, and sadder, and fewer each year.

There were maybe fifteen players and watchers on this Sunday, almost all of them older than my fifty-eight. The two courts nearest the street are covered by a high, pillar-supported roof, so that contests can be held even in wet weather; and there are wooden benches set between the pillars. I parked myself on one of the benches midway along. The only other seated spectator was Pietro Lombardi, in a patch of warm May sunlight at the far end, and this surprised me. Even though Pietro was in his seventies, he was one of the best and spryest of the regulars, and also one of the most social. To see him sitting alone, shoulders slumped and head bowed, was puzzling.

Pining away for the old days, maybe, I thought—as I had just been doing. And a phrase popped into my head, a line from Dante that one of my uncles was fond of quoting when I was growing up in the Outer Mission: *Nessun maggior dolore che ricordarsi del tempo felice nella miseria.* The bitterest of woes is to remember old happy days.

Pietro and his woes didn't occupy my attention for long. The game in progress was spirited and voluable, as only a game of bocce played by elderly *'paesanos* can be, and I was soon caught up in it.

Bocce is simple—deceptively simple. You play it on a long narrow packed-earth pit with low wooden sides. A wooden marker ball the size of a walnut is rolled to one end; the players stand at the opposite end and in turn roll eight larger, heavier balls, grapefruit-sized, in the direction of the marker, the object being to see who can put his bocce ball closest to it. One of the required skills is slow-rolling the ball, usually in a curving trajectory, so that it kisses the marker and then lies up against it—the perfect shot—or else stops an inch or two away. The other required skill is knocking an opponent's ball away from any such close lie without disturbing the marker. The best players, like Pietro Lombardi, can do this two out of three times on the fly— no mean feat from a distance of fifty feet. They can also do it by caroming the ball off the pit walls, with topspin or reverse spin after the fashion of pool-shooters.

Nobody paid much attention to me until after the game in progress had been decided. Then I was acknowledged with hand gestures and a few words—the tolerant acceptance accorded to known spectators and occasional players. Unknowns got no greeting at all; these men still clung to the old ways, and one of the old ways was clannishness.

Only one of the group, Dominick Marra, came over to where I was sitting. And that was because he had something on his mind. He was in his mid-seventies, white-haired, white-mustached; a bantamweight in baggy trousers held up by galluses. He and Pietro Lombardi had been close friends for most of their lives. Born in the same town—Agropoli, a village on the Gulf of Salerno not far from Naples; moved to San Francisco with their families a year apart, in the late twenties; married cousins, raised large families, were widowered at almost the same time a few years ago. The kind of friendship that is almost a blood tie. Dominick had been a baker; Pietro had owned a North Beach trattoria that now belonged to one of his daughters.

What Dominick had on his mind was Pietro. "You see how he sits over there, hah? He's got trouble—*la miseria.*"

"What kind of trouble?"

"His granddaughter. Gianna Fornessi."

"Something happen to her?"

"She's maybe go to jail," Dominick said.

"What for?"

"Stealing money."

"I'm sorry to hear it. How much money?"

"Two thousand dollars."

"Who did she steal it from?"

"*Che?*"

"Who did she steal the money from?"

Dominick gave me a disgusted look. "She don't steal it. Why you think Pietro he's got *la miseria,* hah?"

I knew what was coming now; I should have known it the instant Dominick starting confiding to me about Pietro's problem. I said, "You want me to help him and his granddaughter."

"Sure. You a detective."

"A busy detective."

"You got no time for old man and young girl? *Compaesani?*"

I sighed, but not so he could hear me do it. "All right, I'll talk to Pietro. See if he wants my help, if there's anything I can do."

"Sure he wants your help. He just don't know it yet."

We went to where Pietro was sitting alone in the sun. He was taller than Dominick, heavier, balder. And he had a fondness for Toscanas, those little twisted black Italian cigars; one protruded now from a corner of his mouth. He didn't want to talk at first but Dominick launched into a monologue in Italian that changed his mind and put a glimmer of hope in his sad eyes. Even though I've lost a lot of the language over the years, I can understand enough to follow most conversations. The gist of Dominick's monologue was that I was not just a detective but a miracle worker, a cross between Sherlock Holmes and the messiah. Italians are given to hyperbole in times of excitement or stress, and there isn't much you can do to counteract it — especially when you're one of the *compaesani* yourself.

"My Gianna, she's good girl," Pietro said. "Never give trouble, even when she's little one. *La bellezza delle bellezze,* you understand?"

The beauty of beauties. His favorite grandchild, probably. I said, "I understand. Tell me about the money, Pietro."

"She don't steal it," he said. "*Una ladra,* my Gianna? No, no, it's all big lie."

"Did the police arrest her?"

"They got no evidence to arrest her."

"But somebody filed charges, is that it?"

"Charges," Pietro said. "Bah," he said and spat.

"Who made the complaint?"

Dominick said, "Ferry," as if the name were an obscenity.

"Who's Ferry?"

He tapped his skull. "*Caga di testa,* this man."

"That doesn't answer my question."

"He live where she live. Same apartment building."

"And he says Gianna stole two thousand dollars from him."

"Liar," Pietro said. "He lies."

"Stole it how? Broke in or what?"

"She don't break in nowhere, not my Gianna. This Ferry, this *bastardo,* he says she take the money when she's come to pay rent and he's talk on telephone. But how she knows where he keep his money? Hah? How she knows he have two thousand dollars in his desk?"

"Maybe he told her."

"Sure, that's what he says to police," Dominick said. "Maybe he told her, he says. He don't tell her nothing."

"Is that what Gianna claims?"

Pietro nodded. Threw down what was left of his Toscana and ground in into the dirt with his shoe—a gesture of anger and frustration. "She don't steal that money," he said. "What she need to steal money for? She got good job, she live good, she don't have to steal."

'What kind of job does she have?"

"She sell drapes, curtains. In . . . what you call that business, Dominick?"

"Interior decorating business," Dominick said.

"*Si.* In interior decorating business."

"Where does she live?" I asked.

"Chestnut Street."

"Where on Chestnut Street? What number?"

"Seventy-two fifty."

"You make that Ferry tell the truth, hah?" Dominick said to me. "You fix it up for Gianna and her goombah?"

"I'll do what I can."

"*Va bene.* Then you come tell Pietro right away."

"If Pietro will tell me where he lives—"

There was a sharp whacking sound as one of the bocce balls caromed off the side wall near us, then a softer clicking of ball meeting ball, and a shout went up from the players at the far end: another game won and lost. When I looked back at Dominick and Pietro they were both on their feet. Dominick said, "You find Pietro okay, good detective like you," and Pietro said, "*Grazie, mi amico,*" and before I could say anything else the two of them were off arm in arm to join the others.

Now I was the one sitting alone in the sun, holding up a burden. Primed and ready to do a job I didn't want to do, probably couldn't do, and would not be paid well for if at all. Maybe this man Ferry wasn't the only one involved who had *caga di testa*—shit for brains. Maybe I did too.

2.

The building at 7250 Chestnut Street was an old three-storied, brown-shingled job, set high in the shadow of Coit Tower and across from the retaining wall where Telegraph Hill falls off steeply toward the Embarcadero. From each of the apartments, especially the ones on the third floor, you'd have quite a view of the bay, the East Bay, and both bridges. Prime North Beach address, this. The rent would be well in excess of two thousand a month.

A man in a tan trenchcoat was coming out of the building as I started up the steps to the vestibule. I called out to him to hold the door for me—it's easier to get apartment dwellers to talk to you once you're inside the building—but either he didn't hear me or he chose to ignore me. He came hurrying down without a glance my way as he passed. City-bred paranoia, I thought. It was everywhere these days, rich and poor neighborhoods both, like a nasty strain of social disease. Bumpersticker for the nineties: *Fear Lives.*

There were six mailboxes in the foyer, each with Dymo-Label stickers identifying the tenants. Gianna Fornessi's name was under box #4, along with a second name: Ashley Hansen. It figured that she'd have a roommate; salespersons working in the interior design trade are well but not extravagantly paid. Box #1 bore the name George Ferry and that was the bell I pushed. He was the one I wanted to talk to first.

A minute died away, while I listened to the wind that was savaging the trees on the hillside below. Out on the bay hundreds of sailboats formed a mosaic of white on blue. Somewhere among them a ship's horn sounded—to me, a sad false note. Shipping was all but dead on this side of the bay, thanks to wholesale mismanagement of the port over the past few decades.

The intercom crackled finally and a male voice said, "Who is it?" in wary tones.

I asked if he was George Ferry, and he admitted it, even more guardedly. I gave him my name, said that I was there to ask him a few questions about his complaint against Gianna Fornessi. He said, "Oh Christ." There was a pause, and then, "I called you people yesterday, I told Inspector Cullen I was dropping the charges. Isn't that enough?"

He thought I was a cop. I could have told him I wasn't; I could have let the whole thing drop right there, since what he'd just said was a perfect escape clause from my commitment to Pietro Lombardi. But I have too much curiosity to let go of something, once I've got a piece of it, without knowing the particulars. So I said, "I won't keep you long, Mr. Ferry. Just a few questions."

Another pause. "Is it really necessary?"

32

"I think it is, yes."

An even longer pause. But then he didn't argue, didn't say anything else — just buzzed me in.

His apartment was on the left, beyond a carpeted, dark-wood staircase. He opened the door as I approached it. Mid-forties, short, rotund, with a nose like a blob of putty and a Friar Tuck fringe of reddish hair. And a bruise on his left cheekbone, a cut along the right corner of his mouth. The marks weren't fresh, but then they weren't very old either. Twenty-four hours, maybe less.

He didn't ask to see a police ID; if he had I would have told him immediately that I was a private detective, because nothing can lose you a California investigator's license faster than impersonating a police officer. On the other hand, you can't be held accountable for somebody's false assumption. Ferry gave me a nervous once-over, holding his head tilted downward as if that would keep me from seeing his bruise and cut, then stood aside to let me come in.

The front room was neat, furnished in a self-consciously masculine fashion: dark woods, leather, expensive sporting prints. It reeked of leather, dust, and his lime-scented cologne.

As soon as he shut the door Ferry went straight to a liquor cabinet and poured himself three fingers of Jack Daniels, no water or mix, no ice. Just holding the drink seemed to give him courage. He said, "So. What is it you want to know?"

"Why you dropped your complaint against Gianna Fornessi."

"I explained to Inspector Cullen . . ."

"Explain to me, if you don't mind."

He had some of the sour mash. "Well, it was all a mistake . . . just a silly mistake. She didn't take the money after all."

"You know who did take it, then?"

"Nobody took it. I . . . misplaced it."

"Misplaced it. Uh-huh."

"I thought it was in my desk," Ferry said. "That's where I usually keep the cash I bring home. But I'd put it in my safe deposit box along with some other papers, without realizing it. It was in an envelope, you see, and the envelope got mixed up with the other papers."

"Two thousand dollars is a lot of cash to keep at home. You make a habit of that sort of thing?"

"In my business . . ." The rest of the sentence seemed to hang up in his throat; he oiled the route with the rest of his drink. "In my business I need to keep a certain amount of cash on hand, both here and at the office. The amount I keep here isn't usually as large as two thousand dollars, but I—"

"What business are you in, Mr. Ferry?"

"I run a temp employment agency for domestics."

"Temp?"

"Short for temporary," he said. "I supply domestics for part-time work in offices and private homes. A lot of them are poor, don't have checking accounts, so they prefer to be paid in cash. Most come to the office, but a few—"

"Why did you think Gianna Fornessi had stolen the two thousand dollars?"

". . . What?"

"Why Gianna Fornessi? Why not somebody else?"

"She's the only one who was here. Before I thought the money was missing, I mean. I had no other visitors for two days and there wasn't any evidence of a break-in."

"You and she are good friends, then?"

"Well . . . no, not really. She's a lot younger . . ."

"Then why was she here?"

"The rent," Ferry said. "She was paying her rent for the month. I'm the building manager, I collect for the owner. Before I could write out a receipt I had a call, I was on the phone for quite a while and she . . . I didn't pay any attention to her and I thought she must have . . . you see why I thought she'd taken the money?"

I was silent.

He looked at me, looked at his empty glass, licked his lips, and went to commune with Jack Daniels again.

While he was pouring I asked him, "What happened to your face, Mr. Ferry?"

His hand twitched enough to clink bottle against glass. He had himself another taste before he turned back to me. "Clumsy," he said, "I'm clumsy as hell. I fell down the stairs, the front stairs, yesterday morning." He tried a laugh that didn't come off. "Fog makes the steps slippery. I just wasn't watching where I was going."

"Looks to me like somebody hit you."

"Hit me? No, I told you . . . I fell down the stairs."

"You're sure about that?"

"Of course I'm sure. Why would I lie about it?"

That was a good question. Why would he lie about that, and

about all the rest of it too? There was about as much truth in what he'd told me as there is value in a chunk of fool's gold.

3.

The young woman who opened the door of apartment #4 was not Gianna Fornessi. She was blond, with the kind of fresh-faced Nordic features you see on models for Norwegian ski wear. Tall and slender in a pair of green silk lounging pajamas; arms decorated with hammered gold bracelets, ears with dangly gold triangles. Judging from the expression in her pale eyes, there wasn't much going on behind them. But then, with her physical attributes, not many men would care if her entire brain had been surgically removed.

"Well," she said, "hello."

"Ashley Hansen?"

"That's me. Who're you?"

When I told her my name her smile brightened, as if I'd said something amusing or clever. Or maybe she just liked the sound of it.

"I knew right away you were Italian," she said. "Are you a friend of Jack's?"

"Jack?"

"Jack Bisconte." The smile dulled a little. "You are, aren't you?"

"No," I said, "I'm a friend of Pietro Lombardi."

"Who?"

"Your roommate's grandfather. I'd like to talk to Gianna, if she's home."

Ashley Hansen's smile was gone now; her whole demeanor had changed, become less self-assured. She nibbled at a corner of her lower lip, ran a hand through her hair, fiddled with one of her bracelets. Finally she said, "Gianna isn't here."

"When will she be back?"

"She didn't say."

"You know where I can find her?"

"No. What do you want to talk to her about?"

"The complaint George Ferry filed against her."

"Oh, that," she said. "That's all been taken care of."

"I know. I just talked to Ferry."

"He's a creepy little prick, isn't he."

"That's one way of putting it."

"Gianna didn't take his money. He was just trying to hassle her, that's all."

"Why would he do that?"

"Well, why do you think?"

I shrugged. "Suppose you tell me."

"He wanted her to do things."

"You mean go to bed with him?"

"Things," she said. "Kinky crap, *real* kinky."

"And she wouldn't have anything to do with him."

"No way, Jose. What a creep."

"So he made up the story about the stolen money to get back at her, is that it?"

"That's it."

"What made him change his mind, drop the charges?"

"He didn't tell you?"

"No."

"Who knows?" She laughed. "Maybe he got religion."

"Or a couple of smacks in the face."

"Huh?"

"Somebody worked him over yesterday," I said. "Bruised his cheek and cut his mouth. You have any idea who?"

"Not me, mister. How come you're so interested, anyway?"

"I told you, I'm a friend of Gianna's grandfather."

"Yeah, well."

"Gianna have a boyfriend, does she?"

". . . Why do you want to know that?"

"Jack Bisconte, maybe? Or is he yours?"

"He's just somebody I know." She nibbled at her lip again, did some more fiddling with her bracelets. "Look, I've got to go. You want me to tell Gianna you were here?"

"Yes." I handed her one of my business cards. "Give her this and ask her to call me."

She looked at the card; blinked at it and then blinked at me. "You . . . you're a detective?"

"That's right."

"My God," she said, and backed off, and shut the door in my face.

36

I stood there for a few seconds, remembering her eyes—the sudden fear in her eyes when she'd realized she had been talking to a detective.

What the hell?

4.

North Beach used to be the place you went when you wanted *pasta fino*, expresso and biscotti, conversation about *la dolce vita* and *il patria d'Italia*. Not anymore. There are still plenty of Italians in North Beach, and you can still get the good food and some of the good conversation; but their turf continues to shrink a little more each year, and despite the best efforts of the entreprenurial new immigrants, the vitality and most of the Old World atmosphere are just memories.

The Chinese are partly responsible, not that you can blame them for buying available North Beach real estate when Chinatown, to the west, began to burst its boundaries. Another culprit is the Bohemian element that took over upper Grant Avenue in the fifties, paving the way for the hippies and the introduction of hard drugs in the sixties, which in turn paved the way for the jolly current mix of motorcyle toughs, aging hippies, coke and crack dealers, and the pimps and small-time crooks who work the flesh palaces along lower Broadway. Those "Silicone Alley" nightclubs, made famous by Carol Doda in the late sixties, also share responsibility: they added a smutty leer to the gaiety of North Beach, turned the heart of it into a ghetto.

Parts of the neighborhood, particularly those up around Coit Tower where Gianna Fornessi lived, are still prime city real estate; and the area around Washington Square Park, *il giardino* to the original immigrants, is where the city's literati now congregates. Here and there, too, you can still get a sense of what it was like in the old days. But most of the landmarks are gone—Enrico's, Vanessi's, The Bocce Ball where you could hear mustachioed waiters in gondolier costumes singing arias from operas by Verdi and Puccini—and so is most of the flavor. North Beach is oddly tasteless now, like a week-old mostaccioli made without good spices or garlic. And that is another thing that is all but gone: twenty-five years ago you could not get within a thousand yards of North Beach without picking up the fine, rich fragrance of garlic. Nowadays you're much more likely to smell fried egg roll and the sour stench of somebody's garbage.

Parking in the Beach is the worst in the city; on weekends you can drive around its hilly streets for hours without finding a legal parking space. So today, in the perverse way of things, I found a spot waiting for me when I came down Stockton.

In a public telephone booth near Washington Square Park I discovered a second minor miracle: a directory that had yet to be either stolen or mutilated. The only Bisconte listed was Bisconte Florist Shop, with an address on upper Grant a few blocks away. I took myself off in that direction, through the usual good-weather Sunday crowds of locals and gawking sightseers and drifting homeless.

Upper Grant, like the rest of the area, has changed drastically over the past few decades. Once a rock-ribbed Little Italy, it has become an ethnic mixed bag: Italian markets, trattorias, pizza parlors, bakeries cheek by jowl with Chinese sewing-machine sweat shops, food and herb vendors, and fortune-cookie companies. But most of the faces on the streets are Asian and most of the apartments in the vicinity are occupied by Chinese.

The Bisconte Florist Shop was a hole-in-the-wall near Filbert, sand-wiched between an Italian saloon and the Sip Hing Herb Company. It was open for business, not surprisingly on a Sunday in this neighborhood: tourists buy flowers too, given the opportunity.

The front part of the shop was cramped and jungly with cut flowers, ferns, plants in pots and hanging baskets. A small glass-fronted cooler contained a variety of roses and orchids. There was nobody in sight, but a bell had gone off when I entered and a male voice from beyond a rear doorway called, "Be right with you." I shut the door, went up near the counter. Some people like florist shops; I don't. All of them have the same damp, cloyingly sweet smell that reminds me of funeral parlors; of my mother in her casket at the Figlia Brothers Mortuary in Daly City nearly forty years ago. That day, with all its smells, all its painful images, is as clear to me now as if it were yesterday.

I had been waiting about a minute when the voice's owner came out of the back room. Late thirties, dark, on the beefy side; wearing a professional smile and a floral-patterned apron that should have been ludicrous on a man of his size and coloring but wasn't. We had a good look at each other before he said, "Sorry to keep you waiting—I was putting up an arrangement. What can I do for you?"

"Mr. Bisconte? Jack Bisconte?"

"That's me. Something for the wife, maybe?"

"I'm not here for flowers. I'd like to ask you a few questions, if you don't mind."

The smile didn't waver. "Oh? What about?"

"Gianna Fornessi."

"Who?"

"You don't know her?"

"Name's not familiar, no."

"She lives up on Chestnut with Ashley Hansen."

"Ashley Hansen . . . I don't know that name either."

"She knows you. Young, blonde, looks Norwegian."

"Well, I know a lot of young blondes," Bisconte said. He winked at me. "I'm a bachelor and I get around pretty good, you know?"

"Uh-huh."

"Lot of bars and clubs in North Beach, lot of women to pick and choose from." He shrugged. "So how come you're asking about these two?"

"Not both of them. Just Gianna Fornessi."

"That so? You a friend of hers?"

"Of her grandfather's. She's had a little trouble."

"What kind of trouble?"

"Manager of her building accused her of stealing some money. But somebody convinced him to drop the charges."

"That so?" Bisconte said again, but not as if he cared.

"Leaned on him to do it. Scared the hell out of him."

"You don't think it was me, do you? I told you, I don't know anybody named Gianna Fornessi."

"So you did."

"What's the big deal anyway?" he said. "I mean, if the guy dropped the charges, then this Gianna is off the hook, right?"

"Right."

"Then why all the questions?"

"Curiosity," I said. "Mine and her grandfather's."

Another shrug. "I'd like to help you, pal, but like I said, I don't know the lady. Sorry."

"Sure."

"Come back any time you need flowers," Bisconte said. He gave me a little salute, waited for me to turn and then did the same himself. He was hidden away again in the back room when I let myself out.

Today was my day for liars. Liars and puzzles.

He hadn't asked me who I was or what I did for a living; that was because he already knew. And the way he knew, I thought, was that Ashley Hansen had gotten on the horn after I left and told him about me. He knew Gianna Fornessi pretty well too, and exactly where the two women lived.

He was the man in the tan trenchcoat I'd seen earlier, the one who wouldn't hold the door for me at 7250 Chestnut.

5.

I treated myself to a plate of linguine and fresh clams at a ristorante off Washington Square and then drove back over to Aquatic Park. Now, in mid-afternoon, with fog seeping in through the Gate and the temperature dropping sharply, the number of bocce players and kibitzers had thinned by half. Pietro Lombardi was one of those remaining; Dominick Marra was another. Bocce may be dying easy in the city but not in men like them. They cling to it and to the other old ways as tenaciously as they cling to life itself.

I told Pietro—and Dominick, who wasn't about to let us talk in private—what I'd learned so far. He was relieved that Ferry had dropped his complaint, but just as curious as I was about the Jack Bisconte connection.

"Do you know Bisconte?" I asked him.

"No. I see his shop but I never go inside."

"Know anything about him?"

"*Niente.*"

"How about you, Dominick?"

He shook his head. "He's too old for Gianna, hah? Almost forty, you say—that's too old for girl twenty-three."

"If that's their relationship," I said.

"Men almost forty they go after young woman, they only got one reason. *Fatto 'na bella chiavata.* You remember, eh, Pietro?"

"*Pazzo!* You think I forget '*na bella chiavata?*"

I asked Pietro, "You know anything about Gianna's roommate?"

"Only once I meet her," he said. "Pretty, but not so pretty like my Gianna, *la bellezza delle bellezze*. I don't like her too much."

"Why not?"

"She don't have respect like she should."

"What does she do for a living, do you know?"

"No. She don't say and Gianna don't tell me."

"How long have they been sharing the apartment?"

"Eight, nine months."

"Did they know each other long before they moved in together?"

He shrugged. "Gianna and me, we don't talk much like when she's little girl," he said sadly. "Young people now, they got no time for *la familia*." Another shrug, a sigh. "*Ognuno pensa per sè*," he said. Everybody thinks only of himself.

Dominick gripped his shoulder. Then he said to me, "You find out what's happen with Bisconte and Ferry and those girls. Then you see they don't bother them no more. Hah?"

"If I can, Dominick. If I can."

The fog was coming in thickly now and the other players were making noises about ending the day's tournament. Dominick got into an argument with one of them; he wanted to play another game or two. He was outvoted, but he was still pleading his case when I left. Their Sunday was almost over. So was mine.

I went home to my flat in Pacific Heights. And Kerry came over later on and we had dinner and listened to some jazz. I thought maybe Gianna Fornessi might call but she didn't. No one called. Good thing, too. I would not have been pleased to hear the phone ring after eight o'clock; I was busy then.

Men in their late fifties are just as interested in '*na bella chiavata.* Women in their early forties, too.

6.

At the office in the morning I called TRW for credit checks on Jack Bisconte, George Ferry, Gianna Fornessi, and Ashley Hansen. I also asked my partner, Eberhardt, who has been off the cops just a few years and who still has plenty of cronies sprinkled throughout the SFPD, to find out what Inspector Cullen and the Robbery Detail had on Ferry's theft complaint, and to have the four names run through R&I for any local arrest record.

The report out of Robbery told me nothing much. Ferry's complaint had been filed on Friday morning; Cullen had gone to investigate, talked to the two principals, and determined that there wasn't enough evidence to take Gianna Fornessi into custody. Thirty hours later Ferry had called in and withdrawn the complaint, giving the same flimsy reason he'd handed me. As far as Cullen and the department were concerned, it was all very minor and routine.

The TRW and R&I checks took a little longer to come through, but I had the information by noon. It went like this:

Jack Bisconte. Good credit rating. Owner and sole operator, Bisconte Florist Shop, since 1978; lived on upper Greenwich Street, in a rented apartment, same length of time. No listing of previous jobs held or previous local addresses. No felony or misdemeanor arrests.

George Ferry. Excellent credit rating. Owner and principal operator, Ferry Temporary Employment Agency, since 1972. Resident of 7250 Chest-nut since 1980. No felony arrests; one DWI arrest and conviction following a minor traffic accident in May of 1981, sentenced to ninety days in jail (suspended), driver's license revoked for six months.

Gianna Fornessi. Fair to good credit rating. Employed by Home Draperies, Showplace Square, as a sales representative since 1988. Resident of 7250 Chestnut for eight months; address prior to that, her parents' home in Daly City. No felony or misdemeanor arrests.

Ashley Hansen. No credit rating. No felony or misdemeanor arrests.

There wasn't much in any of that, either, except for the fact that TRW had no listing on Ashley Hansen. Almost everybody uses credit cards these days, establishes some kind of credit — especially a young woman whose income is substantial enough to afford an apartment in one of the city's best neighborhoods. Why not Ashley Hansen?

She was one person who could tell me; another was Gianna Fornessi. I had yet to talk to Pietro's granddaughter and I thought it was high time. I left the office in Eberhardt's care, picked up my car, and drove south of Market to Showplace Square.

The Square is a newish complex of manufacturer's showrooms

for the interior decorating trade—carpets, draperies, lighting fixtures, and other types of home furnishings. It's not open to the public, but I showed the photostat of my license to one of the security men at the door and talked him into calling the Home Draperies showroom and asking them to send Gianna Fornessi out to talk to me.

They sent somebody out but it wasn't Gianna Fornessi. It was a fluffy looking little man in his forties named Lundquist, who said, "I'm sorry, Ms. Fornessi is no longer employed by us."

"Oh? When did she leave?"

"Eight months ago."

"Eight *months?*"

"At the end of September."

"Quit or terminated?"

"Quit. Rather abruptly, too."

"To take another job?"

"I don't know. She gave no adequate reason."

"No one called afterward for a reference?"

"No one," Lundquist said.

"She worked for you two years, is that right?"

"About two years, yes."

"As a sales representative?"

"That's correct."

"May I ask her salary?"

"I really couldn't tell you that . . ."

"Just this, then: Was hers a high-salaried position? In excess of thirty thousand a year, say?"

Lundquist smiled a faint, fluffy smile. "Hardly," he said.

"Were her skills such that she could have taken another, better paying job in the industry?"

Another fluffy smile. And another "Hardly."

So why had she quit Home Draperies so suddenly eight months ago, at just about the same time she moved into the Chestnut Street apartment with Ashley Hansen? And what was she doing to pay her share of the rent?

7.

There was an appliance store delivery truck double-parked in front of 7250 Chestnut, and when I went up the stairs I found the entrance door wedged wide open. Nobody was in the vestibule or lobby, but the murmur of voices filtered down from the third floor. If I'd been a burglar I would have rubbed my hands together in glee. As it was, I walked in as if I belonged there and climbed the inside staircase to the second floor.

When I swung off the stairs I came face to face with Jack Bisconte.

He was hurrying toward me from the direction of apartment #4, something small and red and rectangular clutched in the fingers of his left hand. He broke stride when he saw me; and then recognition made him do a jerky double-take and he came to a halt. I stopped, too, with maybe fifteen feet separating us. That was close enough, and the hallway was well-lighted enough, for me to get a good look at his face. It was pinched, sweat-slicked, the eyes wide and shiny— the face of a man on the cutting edge of panic.

Frozen time, maybe five seconds of it, while we stood staring at each other. There was nobody else in the hall; no audible sounds on this floor except for the quick rasp of Bisconte's breathing. Then we both moved at the same time—Bisconte in the same jerky fashion of his double-take, shoving the red object into his coat pocket as he came forward. And then, when we had closed the gap between us by half, we both stopped again as if on cue. It might have been a mildly amusing little pantomime if you'd been a disinterested observer. It wasn't amusing to me. Or to Bisconte, from the look of him.

I said, "Fancy meeting you here. I thought you didn't know Gianna Fornessi or Ashley Hansen."

"Get out of my way."

"What's your hurry?"

"Get out of my way. I mean it." The edge of panic had cut into his voice; it was thick, liquidy, as if it were bleeding.

"What did you put in your pocket, the red thing?"

He said, "Christ!" and tried to lunge past me.

I blocked his way, getting my hands up between us to push him back. He made a noise in his throat and swung at me. It was a clumsy shot; I ducked away from it without much effort, so that his knuckles

44

just grazed my neck. But then the son of a bitch kicked me, hard, on the left shinbone. I yelled and went down. He kicked out again, this time at my head; didn't connect because I was already rolling away. I fetched up tight against the wall and by the time I got myself twisted back around he was pelting toward the stairs.

I shoved up the wall to my feet, almost fell again when I put weight on the leg he'd kicked. Hobbling, wiping pain-wet out of my eyes, I went after him. People were piling down from the third floor; the one in the lead was George Ferry. He called something that I didn't listen to as I started to descend. Bisconte, damn him, had already crossed the lobby and was running out through the open front door.

Hop, hop, hop down the stairs like a contestant in a one-legged race, using the railing for support. By the time I reached the lobby, some of the sting had gone out of my shinbone and I could put more weight on the leg. Out into the vestibule, half running and half hobbling now, looking for him. He was across the street and down a ways, fumbling with a set of keys at the driver's door of a new silver Mercedes.

But he didn't stay there long. He was too wrought up to get the right key into the lock, and when he saw me pounding across the street in his direction, the panic goosed him and he ran again. Around behind the Mercedes, onto the sidewalk, up and over the concrete retaining wall. And gone.

I heard him go sliding or tumbling through the undergrowth below. I staggered up to the wall, leaned over it. The slope down there was steep, covered with trees and brush, strewn with the leavings of semi-humans who had used it for a dumping ground. Bisconte was on his buttocks, digging hands and heels into the ground to slow his momentum. For a few seconds I thought he was going to turn into a one-man avalanche and plummet over the edge where the slope ended in a sheer bluff face. But then he managed to catch hold of one of the tree trunks and swing himself away from the bluff, in among a tangle of bushes where I couldn't see him anymore. I could hear him—and then I couldn't. He'd found purchase, I thought, and was easing himself down to where the backside of another apartment building leaned in against the cliff.

There was no way I was going down there after him. I turned and went to the Mercedes.

It had a vanity plate, the kind that makes you wonder why somebody would pay $25 extra to the DMV to put it on his car:

BISFLWR. If the Mercedes had had an external hood release I would have popped it and disabled the engine; but it didn't, and all four doors were locked. All right. Chances were, he wouldn't risk coming back soon—and even if he ran the risk, it would take him a good long while to get here.

I limped back to 7250. Four people were clustered in the vestibule, staring at me—Ferry and a couple of uniformed deliverymen and a fat woman in her forties. Ferry said as I came up the steps, "What happened, what's going on?" I didn't answer him. There was a bad feeling in me now; or maybe it had been there since I'd first seen the look on Bisconte's face. I pushed through the cluster—none of them tried to stop me—and crossed the lobby and went up to the second floor.

Nobody answered the bell at apartment #4. I tried the door, and it was unlocked, and I opened it and walked in and shut it again and locked it behind me.

She was lying on the floor in the living room, sprawled and bent on her back near a heavy teak coffee table, peach-colored dressing gown hiked up over her knees; head twisted at an off-angle, blood and a deep triangular puncture wound on her left temple. The blood was still wet and clotting. She hadn't been dead much more than an hour.

In the sunlight that spilled in through the undraped windows, the blood had a kind of shimmery radiance. So did her hair—her long gold-blond hair.

Goodbye Ashley Hansen.

8.

I called the Hall of Justice and talked to a Homicide inspector I knew slightly named Craddock. I told him what I'd found, and about my little skirmish with Jack Bisconte, and said that yes, I would wait right here and no, I wouldn't touch anything. He didn't tell me not to look around and I didn't say that I wouldn't.

Somebody had started banging on the door. Ferry, probably. I went the other way, into one of the bedrooms. Ashley Hansen's: there was a photograph of her prominently displayed on the dresser, and lots of mirrors to give her a live image of herself. A narcissist, among other things. On one nightstand was a telephone and an answering machine. On the unmade bed, tipped on its side with some of the contents spilled out, was a fancy leather purse. I used the backs of my two index fingers to stir around among the spilled items and the stuff inside. Everything you'd expect to find in a woman's purse— and one thing that should have been there and wasn't.

Gianna Fornessi's bedroom was across the hall. She also had a telephone and an answering machine; the number on the telephone dial was different from her roommate's. I hesitated for maybe five seconds, then I went to the answering machine and pushed the button marked "playback calls" and listened to two old messages before I stopped the tape and rewound it. One message would have been enough.

Back into the living room. The knocking was still going on. I started over there; stopped after a few feet and stood sniffing the air. I thought I smelled something—a faint lingering acrid odor. Or maybe I was just imagining it . . .

Bang, bang, bang. And Ferry's voice: "What's going on in there?"

I moved ahead to the door, threw the bolt lock, yanked the door open. "Quit making so damned much noise."

Ferry blinked and backed off a step; he didn't know whether to be afraid of me or not. Behind and to one side of him, the two deliverymen and the fat woman looked on with hungry eyes. They would have liked seeing what lay inside; blood attracts some people, the gawkers, the insensitive ones, the same way it attracts flies.

"What's happened?" Ferry asked nervously.

"Come in and see for yourself. Just you."

I opened up a little wider and he came in past me, showing reluctance. I shut and locked the door again behind him. And when I turned he said, "Oh my God," in a sickened voice. He was staring at the body on the floor, one hand pressed up under his breastbone. "Is she . . .?"

"Very."

"Gianna . . . is she here?"

"No."

"Somebody did that to Ashley? It wasn't an accident?"

"What do you think?"

"Who? Who did it?"

"You know who, Ferry. You saw me chase him out of here."

"I . . . don't know who he is. I never saw him before."

"The hell you never saw him. He's the one put those cuts and bruises on your face."

"No," Ferry said, "that's not true." He looked and sounded even sicker now. "I told you how that happened . . ."

"You told me lies. Bisconte roughed you up so you'd drop your complaint against Gianna. He did it because Gianna and Ashley Hansen have been working as call girls and he's their pimp and he didn't want the cops digging into her background and finding out the truth."

Ferry leaned unsteadily against the wall, facing away from what was left of the Hansen woman. He didn't speak.

"Nice quiet little operation they had," I said, "until you got wind of it. That's how it was, wasn't it? You found out and and you wanted some of what Gianna's been selling."

Nothing for ten seconds. Then, softly, "It wasn't like that, not at first. I . . . loved her."

"Sure you did."

"I *did*. But she wouldn't have anything to do with me."

"So then you offered to pay her."

". . . Yes. Whatever she charged."

"Only you wanted kinky sex and she wouldn't play."

"No! I never asked for anything except a night with her . . . one night. She pretended to be insulted; she denied that she's been selling herself to men. She . . . she said she'd never go to bed with a man as . . . ugly . . ." He moved against the wall—a writhing movement, as if he were in pain.

"That was when you decided to get even with her."

"I wanted to hurt her, the way she'd hurt me. It was stupid, I know that, but I wasn't thinking clearly. I just wanted to hurt her . . ."

"Well, you succeeded," I said. "But the one you really hurt is Ashley Hansen. If it hadn't been for you, she'd still be alive."

He started to say something but the words were lost in the sudden summons of the doorbell.

"That'll be the police," I said.

"The police? But . . . I thought you were . . ."

"I know you did. I never told you I was, did I?"

I left him holding up the wall and went to buzz them in.

9.

I spent more than two hours in the company of the law, alternately answering questions and waiting around. I told Inspector Craddock how I happened to be there. I told him how I'd come to realize that Gianna Fornessi and Ashley Hansen were call girls, and how George Ferry and Jack Bisconte figured into it. I told him about the small red rectangular object I'd seen Bisconte shove into his pocket—an address book, no doubt, with the names of some of Hansen's johns. That was the common item that was missing from her purse.

Craddock seemed satisfied. I wished I was.

When he finally let me go I drove back to the office. But I didn't stay long; it was late afternoon, Eberhardt had already gone for the day, and I felt too restless to tackle the stack of routine paperwork on my desk. I went out to Ocean Beach and walked on the sand, as I sometimes do when an edginess is on me. It helped a little—not much.

I ate an early dinner out, and when I got home I put in a call to the Hall of Justice to ask if Jack Bisconte had been picked up yet. But Craddock was off duty and the inspector I spoke to wouldn't tell me anything.

The edginess stayed with me all evening, and kept me awake past midnight. I knew what was causing it, all right; and I knew what to do to get rid of it. Only I wasn't ready to do it yet.

In the morning, after eight, I called the Hall again. Craddock came on duty at eight, I'd been told. He was there and willing to talk, but what he had to tell me was not what I wanted to hear. Bisconte was in custody but not because he'd been apprehended. At eight-thirty Monday night he'd walked into the North Beach precinct station with his lawyer in tow and given himself up. He'd confessed to being a pimp for the two women; he'd confessed to working over George Ferry; he'd confessed to being in the women's apartment just prior to his tussle with me. But he swore up and down that he hadn't killed Ashley Hansen. He'd never had any trouble with her, he said; in fact he'd been half in love with her. The cops had Gianna Fornessi in custody too by this time, and she'd confirmed that there had never been any rough stuff or bad feelings between her roommate and Bisconte.

Hansen had been dead when he got to the apartment, Bisconte said. Fear that he'd be blamed had pushed him into a panic. He'd taken the address book out of her purse—he hadn't thought about the answering machine tapes or he'd have erased the messages left by eager johns—and when he'd encountered me in the hallway he'd lost his head completely. Later, after he'd had time to calm down, he'd gone to the lawyer, who had advised him to turn himself in.

Craddock wasn't so sure Bisconte was telling the truth, but I was. I knew who had been responsible for Ashley Hansen's death; I'd known it a few minutes after I found her body. I just hadn't wanted it to be that way.

I didn't tell Craddock any of this. When he heard the truth it would not be over the phone. And it would not be from me.

10.

It did not take me long to track him down. He wasn't home but a woman in his building said that in nice weather he liked to sit in Washington Square Park with his cronies. That was where I found him, in the park. Not in the company of anyone; just sitting alone on a bench across from the Saints Peter and Paul Catholic church, in the same slump-shouldered, bowed-head posture as when I'd first seen him on Sunday—the posture of *la miseria.*

I sat down beside him. He didn't look at me, not even when I said, *"Buon giorno,* Pietro."

He took out one of his twisted black cigars and lit it carefully with a kitchen match. Its odor was acrid on the warm morning air—the same odor that had been in his granddaughter's apartment, that I'd pretended to myself I was imagining. Nothing smells like a Toscana; nothing. And only old men like Pietro smoke Toscanas these days. They don't even have to smoke one in a closed room for the smell to linger after them; it gets into and comes off the heavy user's clothing.

"It's time for us to talk," I said.

"Che sopra?"

"Ashley Hansen. How she died."

A little silence. Then he sighed and said, "You already know, hah, good detective like you? How you find out?"

"Does it matter?"

"It don't matter. You tell police yet?"

"It'll be better if you tell them."

More silence, while he smoked his little cigar.

I said, "But first tell me. Exactly what happened."

He shut his eyes; he didn't want to relive what had happened.

"It was me telling you about Bisconte that started it," I said to prod him. "After you got home Sunday night you called Gianna and asked her about him. Or she called you."

". . . I call her," he said. "She's angry, she tell me mind my own business. Never before she talks to her goombah this way."

"Because of me. Because she was afraid of what I'd find out about her and Ashley Hansen and Bisconte."

"Bisconte." He spat the name, as if ridding his mouth of something foul.

"So this morning you asked around the neighborhood about him. And somebody told you he wasn't just a florist, about his little sideline. Then you got on a bus and went to see your granddaughter."

"I don't believe it, not about Gianna. I want her tell me it's not true. But she's not there. Only the other one, the *bionda.*"

"And then?"

"She don't want to let me in, that one. I go in anyway. I ask if she and Gianna are . . . if they sell themselves for money. She laugh. In my face she laugh, this girl what have no respect. She says what difference it make? She says I am old man—dinosaur, she says. But she pat my cheek like I am little boy or big joke. Then she . . . ah, *Cristo,* she come up close to me and she say you want some, old man, I give you some. To me she says this. Me." Pietro shook his head; there were tears in his eyes now. "I push her away. I feel . . . *feroce,* like when I am young man and somebody he make trouble with me. I push her too hard and she fall, her head hit the table and I see blood and she don't move . . . ah, *mio Dio!* She was wicked, that one, but I don't mean to hurt her . . ."

"I know you didn't, Pietro."

"I think, call doctor quick. But she is dead. And I hurt here, inside" —he tapped his chest—"and I think, what if Gianna she come home?

I don't want to see Gianna. You understand? Never again I want to see her."

"I understand," I said. And I thought: Funny—I've never laid eyes on her, not even a photograph of her. I don't know what she looks like; now I don't want to know. I never want to see her either.

Pietro finished his cigar. Then he straightened on the bench, seemed to compose himself. His eyes had dried; they were clear and sad. He looked past me, across at the looming Romanesque pile of the church. "I make confession to priest," he said, "little while before you come. Now we go to police and I make confession to them."

"Yes."

"You think they put me in gas chamber?"

"I doubt they'll put you in prison at all. It was an accident. Just a bad accident."

Another silence. On Pietro's face was an expression of the deepest pain. "This thing, this accident, she shouldn't have happen. Once . . . ah, once . . ." Pause. "*Morto,*" he said.

He didn't mean the death of Ashley Hansen. He meant the death of the old days, the days when families were tightly knit and there was respect for elders, the days when bocce was king of his world and that world was a far simpler and better place. The bitterest of woes is to remember old happy days . . .

We sat there in the pale sun. And pretty soon he said, in a voice so low I barely heard the words, "*La bellezza delle bellezze.*" Twice before he had used that phrase in my presence and both times he had been referring to his granddaughter. This time I knew he was not.

"*Sí, 'paesano,*" I said. "*La bellezza delle bellezze.*"

Open and Shut

John Lutz

"Now's not the time to lie to each other," Bruce said. "We're all glad she's dead."

His two brothers stared at him morosely but without shock. Bruce had always been the one who'd spoken his mind, and often it was the collective mind of the three Creighton brothers.

The three men standing over the body in the tastefully decorated apartment living room looked nothing alike. Bruce was stocky and dark, even swarthy. Martin was tall and fair and had about him the look of a paranoid accountant whose books seldom balanced, which in fact he was and they didn't. Henry was medium height and slender, a handsome man often described as dapper. Looking at the courtly Henry, one wondered where his top hat and walking stick had been mislaid.

"We're glad she's dead," Henry admitted, "but not so glad you should have said it."

Bruce looked at him with dark contempt, as if to say he wouldn't mind so much if Henry joined their sister Deborah, whose corpse they were discussing.

"Well, *I'm* sorry she's dead," Martin said, "because now we won't know why she called us here to talk to us."

That was something Bruce hadn't yet considered. He nodded, and the brothers stood silently, thinking and staring down at the late Deborah. She'd never been even close to attractive, but in death she appeared peaceful and almost beautiful. Dignified, certainly, which she'd always been in life. Stuffy and dignified beyond her twenty-three years. Now she lay on her back on the Persian rug in the center of her living room, her arms primly folded across her meager chest, her eyes open and seemingly fixed with disdain on some object on the ceiling. An obvious priss even in death.

It was Martin who spoke first, having reduced the situation to mathematics and reached a sum. "We all stand to profit," he said succinctly.

Deborah had been the only one of the four Creighton offspring who hadn't squandered a share of the fortune left by their father, who'd made his pile in the textile dying business that had died with him. Within five years the brothers were struggling, practically penniless, while Deborah's invested inheritance had somehow increased five fold. Now the brothers were about to inherit again, this time from their sister. Their financial future appeared rosy, except for the phone call last night.

"Are you forgetting her intention to alter her will?" Henry asked.

"She only *said* she was planning on altering it," Martin pointed out. "She could hardly have had time to change it yet. That's probably what she wanted to talk to us about. Anyway, I doubt she was going to cut us out altogether."

Bruce snorted. "I don't doubt it a bit. Deborah'd gotten stranger the last few years, in case you hadn't noticed. Got involved with charities—why for God's sake I don't know. She knew she had a bad heart, so I suspect she was going to leave everything to some medical research foundation or hospital involved in heart treatment. Just like her to forsake her kin, the heartless bi—"

"Speaking of what you suspect," Bruce interrupted, "has it occurred to anyone that we're bound to be suspected of her death?"

Martin glared down at his sister, still angry with her for what he assumed she'd planned to do with his rightful inheritance. "Why should we be suspected? Why should anyone? It's obvious she died of a heart attack, even though she was only twenty-three. Everybody knew she had the Creighton heart defect; she'd already had two mild coronaries."

"I'm sure an autopsy will prove it was her heart," Henry said confidently.

"*Wait* a minute," Martin said. "I see what Bruce means."

"Of course she died of a heart attack," Bruce said, "but a heart attack's easy to provoke, and we all knew she had the family's chronic and potentially dangerous heart problem." He bent down and touched Deborah's bare arm. "She's still warm. She hasn't been dead long at all, and we were seen entering the building and coming up in the elevator. Willy the super even said hello to us."

Martin looked disbelievingly at Bruce. "You don't think the police will suspect us of causing her death? Not *really?*"

"Certainly they will," Martin said. "They always look to family first in a murder case."

"But it wsn't murder!" Henry insisted.

"The police don't know that," Martin said. "Don't imagine the police won't be out to get us. It's their nature as well as their job."

"Consider our motives," Bruce said. "She probably informed Wellmore she was going to change her will. If Deborah had lived even a few more days, time enough to get to Wellmore's office, we would have lost our inheritance, hundreds of thousands of dollars." Wellmore was Harold Wellmore, of Smathers, Hankering, and Wellmore, the law firm that had handled the elder Creighton's will and managed Deborah's finances.

The irony of their position sank in on the brothers. It was possible, of course, that their sister's natural death would be ruled just that — natural. But it was also disturbingly possible that their motive and proximity to the fresh corpse would cause the law to build a very tight if circumstantial case against them. It was common knowledge that they all knew about her dangerously weak heart.

"We're in a world of trouble," the paranoid Martin proclaimed, having had time to mull over the assets and liabilities of the situation.

Henry, whose kidneys always failed him under stress, suddenly stepped over Deborah and sprinted for the bathroom.

Bruce rubbed his broad, swarthy chin and looked thoughtful. He was the most resourceful of the brothers, the leader in times of peril. This was such a time, and he knew the others were waiting for some signal from him. For the moment, though, he was stumped.

The toilet flushed, and a minute later Henry reappeared. He was so pale he might have passed for a dapper corpse himself had he stretched out beside Deborah. Deborah was dressed rather spiffily, as if she'd planned on going out somewhere after meeting with her brothers. She and Henry would make an attractive couple there on the floor. For a second the thought occurred to Bruce that another sibling's death would increase his soon-to-be fortune by a third.

Soon-to-be fortune if the police's impending suspicions could somehow be directed to channels leading away from anyone named Creighton.

Henry said, "I stubbed my toe. The bathroom's full of tools."

"What?"

"Deborah's washbasin faucet was leaking," Martin said. "She mentioned it on the phone last night. I guess Willy the super was working on it."

"Wrenches," Henry said. "Willy left wrenches on the floor under the washbasin. And some kind of little blowtorch."

Bruce thought about Willie Bently, the energetic, potbellied little handyman made to look older than his forty-five years by alcohol. Amiable, disorganized Willy. "It's Willy who can place us at the scene of Deborah's death," Bruce said.

"Ah!" Martin said after only a few seconds, with an early inkling of what Bruce was about to suggest. Bruce might be more clever and decisive than his brothers, but their minds worked in much the same patterns.

"Suppose we make it seem as if Willy committed the murder?" Bruce said.

Martin and Henry thought that one over.

"But Deborah wasn't murdered," Henry pointed out again.

"We can make it seem that she was, by striking her on the head with Willy's wrench. Handyman working on plumbing, makes pass at rich tenant, is rejected, loses temper. Happens all the time."

"Does it?" Henry asked.

"Often enough, anyway."

"One thing," Martin said. "The police will know Deborah was hit on the head *after* death. Forensic medicine and all that. The wound probably wouldn't even bleed, despite the fact she's still warm. You know, the heart's stopped pumping. That's really her only problem."

"Deborah's heart stopped pumping years ago, as far as we were concerned," Henry said.

Bruce held up a hand palm out, quieting the other two and taking charge firmly now. "It won't matter if the head wound was inflicted after her heart stopped," he said. "The police will think her heart attack occurred during a struggle, before Willy whacked her with the wrench, or maybe he thought she was only unconscious and he struck her so she couldn't accuse him when she came around. It'll still be murder."

The three brothers looked at each other. Bruce was devious and daring, but he'd never gone quite this far.

"Put it to a vote?" Martin said.

They nodded simultaneously. Two out of three would have sufficed, but the decision was unanimous.

"Okay, we need to work fast," Bruce said. "No one will be able to place our arrival here to the minute, and Deborah hasn't been dead very long. We can say she was alive when we left her. Let's do what's required and get out of the apartment as soon as possible."

What was required didn't take long. Bruce used his handkerchief to bring Willy's heaviest pipe wrench in from where it was lying beneath the washbasin in the bathroom. While his two brothers looked on dispassionately, he turned Deborah's head slightly and without difficulty, pleased to note she hadn't been dead long enough for rigor mortis to set in. When her head was cocked at just the right angle, so it would appear she'd been struck standing up, he dealt her a powerful blow behind the right ear with the wrench. Martin winced at the sickening hollow sound the wrench made when it struck flesh and bone, but that was the only reaction. Henry merely looked on and adjusted a French cuff.

After placing the wrench beside the body, Bruce stood up and stuffed his handkerchief into his pocket. "It'll look like Willy panicked and ran after he killed her," he said.

"He didn't run far," Martin said. "He's still in the building."

Bruce smiled. He wasn't one to move drastically without having reasoned far ahead. "Remember a few months ago when Willy was here to make some electrical repairs and Deborah was asking him about his mother in Seattle?"

"I think so," Henry said.

Martin nodded. "How does that figure into what *we're* doing?" he asked.

"Let's leave here and find a public phone and I'll show you," Bruce said.

As they walked out of the apartment, he called goodbye to Deborah, in case any of her neighbors might be listening. For the purposes of his plan, Willy hadn't yet killed her.

Willy was nowhere in sight as they left the building and walked down the block. They'd all taken public transportation to see Deborah, as none of them could by now afford owning and operating a car.

If everything worked out as planned, it could be said that Deborah's death had occurred just in time.

Bruce had been in the drugstore in the next block and remembered the phone booths along the back wall near Hardware. The store had only a small counter where prescriptions were filled. The rest of it was devoted to shelves of everything from picnic supplies to cheap shirts.

Trying not to attract attention, the brothers casually strolled among the aisles of pet supplies and motor oil to the three old-fashioned wooden phone booths on the back wall. An elderly woman was talking in one of the booths with the accordian door open, but as they approached she hung up the phone and left, barely glancing at them.

Bruce squeezed into the middle booth and scanned the directory. He punched out the number of a major airline, talked for a few minutes with a reservationist, then said he'd call back.

Then he consulted the phone directory again and pecked out another number with his forefinger, thinking that for Willy Bently it was the finger of fate. He waited. His brothers stood within earshot.

"Willy Bently?" Bruce inquired, when the phone at the other end of the connection had been answered. Henry and Martin exchanged surprised but not alarmed glances. Their fates and Bruce's were the same, and it was by now habit to count on Bruce to save them.

"This is Saint Augustus Hospital in Seattle, Mr. Bently. I'm afraid your mother's been injured in a fall down some stairs. When she was conscious she asked us to contact you." Bruce was silent for a long moment. Then: "She's critical, I'm afraid." And in a more somber tone: "I think it would be a good idea if you got here soon as possible, Mr. Bently. It's not an exaggeration to say that any hour might be her last. I see. Fine, we'll be expecting you. If fact, you'll be met at the airport. Our man will be holding up a sign saying Saint Augustus."

Bruce was smiling as he hung up. "Willy's going to be on the next flight to Seattle," he said. "Which leaves in about an hour." He glanced at his watch. "I would have preferred a slightly later flight; he'll barely have time to pack."

The brothers strolled leisurely back toward Deborah's apartment, then stopped walking about half a block from the building and pretended to study shoes in a display window. Shoes they'd soon be able to afford. They'd all be relieved to see portly and unsuspecting

Willy leave for the airport in plenty of time to make his flight.

Only a few minutes passed before a cab pulled to the curb in front of the apartment building. Two brief blasts of the taxi's horn drifted back to them.

Willy emerged from the building on the run, carrying a small suitcase, a garment bag slung over his shoulder. He shook his head at the cabbie, who started to get out and help him with his bags. Then he hurriedly tossed his luggage into the back of the cab and climbed in after it. Through the rear window the brothers saw him lean forward to give instructions to the cabbie. The taxi's back bumper dropped low and away it sped, belching a haze of exhaust and heading for the airport.

"What if the flight had been sold out?" Martin the worrier asked, when the cab had turned the corner.

"I checked when I called the airport," Bruce told him smugly. "There were plenty of seats available."

"You think of everything," Henry said.

"I do," Bruce said.

"What did we talk about with Deborah?" Martin asked.

"She phoned us last night and said she'd been having chest pains," Bruce said. "We were concerned and decided to visit her today to make sure she was all right, which she was. She assured us she'd had no more pain and would see her doctor tomorrow."

"You *do* think of everything," Martin said.

Bruce nodded. He was sure he had this matter completely in hand. Evidence of Willy's guilt had been planted, Willy had fled the scene of the crime, and, when arrested in Seattle, he'd concoct some bizarre story about a hospital calling him with news of his mother's illness. The brothers had sound and simple stories that supported each other. The time element didn't quite work out, but it was highly unlikely anyone, including Willy, could swear to the exact time when Deborah's brothers had arrived at the building and then left, and the police wouldn't be able to know her time of death exactly either. After all, we were dealing in minutes here, not hours.

In a little while, Bruce would make an anonymous call to the police about overhearing a woman scream in Deborah's apartment. The ball would be rolling then, and Bruce was sure it would become an eight-ball and stop a hair's thickness away from Willy Bently. None of the brothers would be suspected of murder, because it would be established that Willy had killed Deborah, or at least intended to, heart attack or not. Tough luck for Willy, but the brothers saw no reason to take the chance that Deborah's heart attack might not be deemed natural, that they might be accused of provoking it or administering some untraceable stimulant. This would work out much better, not to mention more profitably, for everyone but Willy. Bruce was confident. All the brothers were confident.

They smiled the Creighton smile, a shifty, crooked arcing of thin lips, then went their separate ways to return home and wait for the police to contact them.

*   *   *

No problem. The police, the news media, described Deborah's murder as an open and shut case. Open and shut like a trap, Bruce thought, when he read about Willy Bently in the *Post-Gazette*. Willy had been arrested in Seattle and promptly extradited. He was charged with murder, and his arraignment was Friday. A guilty verdict was almost guaranteed by the prosecutor, who'd soon be running for reelection. The country's mood being what it was, Willy would probably be put to death by lethal injection, and all speculation about Deborah's death, even by Willy's family, friends and attorneys, would cease. The trap set by the brothers had led to the larger trap set by society for people of Willy's ilk, whose habits and circumstances made them such convenient avenues of explanation.

In the three days since the brothers had walked into Deborah's apartment and discovered her body, everything had moved fast and in precisely the direction planned by Bruce. He really had thought of everything. Apparently.

There'd been a few uneasy moments when Homicide detectives had taken the brothers' statements. But the Creightons had discussed their interrogations afterward and were sure nothing had been said that didn't ring true or might be attributed to anything more than the stunned disbelief of the aggrieved family.

The funeral was over even before Willy's arraignment. Now came the reading of the will. Bruce had to congratulate himself; everything was going even more smoothly than he'd imagined.

The brothers gathered Thursday afternoon in Wellmore's office, in the tall glass and granite building that housed the Smathers, Hankering, and Wellmore Legal Firm. Harold Wellmore, a tall, fiftyish man with a hawkish face and a shrewd glint in his eye, stood behind his wide cherrywood desk and opened the yellow file folder containing Deborah's will. Slightly behind him and off to the side, leaning against the wall, was a young man he'd introduced as James Hoyt, there to witness the reading. Wellmore's longtime secretary, Jane Vianna, was also present, dressed primly and seated on the black leather sofa near the window. The Creighton brothers sat in small black-upholstered chairs facing Wellmore's desk, somewhat like schoolboys called to task in the principal's office. Only they weren't there to receive a reprimand, even for feigning a murder; they were there to inherit their respective fortunes.

The office smelled like money and was quiet. Only the faint hum of traffic from Nineteenth Street five stories below filtered in through the double-glazed windows and thick purple drapes. Wellmore, tall and elegant, if a bit stuffy, in his gray three-piece suit and conservative plain blue tie, cleared his throat.

"Might we get on with it?" Bruce asked, only because he assumed impatience might be expected of him. Actually he was enjoying this moment and wouldn't mind if it were drawn out to an hour.

But Wellmore glanced at his secretary, then said, "Of course," and fitted rectangular wire-rimmed half glasses to the bridge of his narrow, predatory nose. Very deliberate and in no big hurry. Such a dry person. That was how Bruce thought of cautious, conservative people like Wellmore, and like Deborah, juiceless people who took few chances and had no lust for what life might offer.

"First of all," Wellmore said in his precise dry voice, "I must point out that on top of Deborah's will in this folder is a letter from her I received in the mail yesterday."

Bruce's heart jumped and he edged forward in his chair. In the corner of his vision he could see Martin and Henry, on either side of him, also tense their bodies and sit forward. "Letter?" Bruce said. His voice was higher than usual.

"Suicide note, actually," Wellmore said.

Bruce felt a cold vacuum expand in him. While he was sure his expression remained calm, his mind darted this way and that, seeking explanations, possibilities, a way out of a trap whose method and dimensions it could now only sense. Martin started to stand, but Bruce clutched his elbow and not so gently pulled him back down in his chair.

Wellmore, who'd known the brothers for years, stared coldly at

Bruce and said, "The autopsy revealed that Deborah died of a drug overdose. Her letter confirms this. I won't read it verbatim, but it says that she was in love with someone she could never marry—she doesn't go into the reasons. She saw suicide as the only way out."

"Deborah in love?" Henry gasped. He seemed to find the fact remarkable. Bruce certainly thought it unlikely. Deborah was always so . . . well, she was plain and unromantic, had the Creighton sense of the practical. Dry.

Bruce figured it was time to play dumbfounded. "But Deborah was murdered, wasn't she? Struck on the head?"

"She was struck after she was already dead," Hoyt, still leaning against the wall, said casually. Bruce looked up at him. The man didn't have the eyes of a lawyer, he decided. They were flat, accusatory eyes. Policeman's eyes.

"This is Homicide Lieutenant James Hoyt," Wellmore reintroduced Hoyt.

Bruce glanced from Henry to Martin. Stay calm, his look said, I've got this under control. And he still was confident. There was no way the police could link them to the sham murder. No way. And whoever this secret lover was, he'd have a legal battle on his hands now instead of Deborah, if she had already changed her will. If Wellmore thought some damned fortune hunter—

"We can't charge anyone with murder, obviously," Hoyt was saying in his monotonous cop's voice. "And quite possibly we can't even bring serious charges of fraud against whoever fractured your sister's skull with that wrench and tried to make her death seem like murder."

"I thought Willy the super struck her," Bruce said. He was feeling his confidence swell. The surviving Creighton family was safe; even Lieutenant Hoyt had just admitted it.

"The super struck no one," Hoyt said. "We have a pretty good idea as to the identity of the guilty party—or parties—but there simply isn't enough evidence to bring charges. That happens in a lot of crimes. Too many, in fact. And that's a shame."

"Deplorable," Bruce agreed. He didn't like the way Harold Wellmore was staring at him, the way a bird might gaze at a worm.

"I suppose you can guess the rest," Wellmore said, looking now from one brother to the other. "Deborah had mentioned to me that, in her newfound happiness and generosity, she'd planned to revise her will, but apparently depression overcame her before she had a chance to carry out her intentions. Her original will is still in effect, unfortunately. It provides each of you with only one dollar, for reasons of legality in case the will might be contested under state statutes. The bulk of her estate, worth approximately two million dollars, goes to her lover."

"Two million!" Bruce sat back, astounded by the size of the estate.

"So *read* the will!" Martin blurted out. "I demand it! We have a right to know this man's name!"

Wellmore sighed. "It would be in your best interest if I didn't actually read the will," he said. "Better for all concerned if you don't know the identity of Deborah's lover."

"That's absurd!" Henry objected. He flicked lint from the shoulder of his threadbare but custom-tailored suit, as if brushing away Wellmore's advice.

"Why shouldn't we know the man's name?" Bruce asked, sensing unexpected depths to this matter.

"Deborah had a secret vice," Wellmore explained. "She was a compulsive gambler. And an extremely lucky one." He glanced at Hoyt, as if asking him to elaborate.

Hoyt said, "During the course of her gambling, your sister made some friends that you three, and the police, would consider undesirable. Her lover and beneficiary's name is one you might recognize from having read the newspapers. We can't prove anything, but we know he fulfills a certain dangerous and deadly function for his clients, many of whom are members of organized crime."

"Dangerous and deadly function?" Martin said, obviously puzzled. He couldn't imagine Deborah getting mixed up in any way with someone connected with organized crime. A man involved in something dangerous and deadly. Though upon reflection he wasn't amazed that she'd led a secret life. Why shouldn't Creighton deviousness run in her blood as well as his?

"I don't want to go out on a legal limb and flatly warn you about this man," Hoyt said. "About the service he allegedly performs for his clients."

The vacuum in Bruce's stomach grew cold. "He's a hit man," he said. "A professional killer." He looked at Hoyt. "Is that right?"

Hoyt shrugged. "Allegedly. But as I said, there are plenty of crimes we know about but can't prove."

Wellmore smiled slightly, Bruce was sure. "I wouldn't sue this man to challenge Deborah's will," the attorney advised again. "You'd lose even if you won. That's why I didn't give you his name, for your own protection. And Lieutenant Hoyt here can pass the word that you still don't know the man's identity. That will give you an added measure of safety."

"Measure of safety?" Bruce asked. "Protection? Why would we need that?"

"After we release Willy the super," Hoyt said, "it'll be only a matter of time before this man reaches his own conclusions about your sister's death, and what happened to her after her death. And why. He might not accept the idea of suicide." He stared directly at Bruce. "He's a top-notch pro-fessional. No one has ever successfully hidden from him, even under the witness protection program. Nothing stops him."

Bruce heard phlegm crack in Martin's throat as he swallowed.

"Whoever broke open your sister's skull has nothing to fear from the legal system," Hoyt said, "but we in law enforcement often speak of a higher justice, cleaner and more complete than the court's."

Wellmore leaned like a carnivorous bird over his desk. "I'm legally bound to tell you the man's name if you insist," he pointed out.

"No!" Henry almost shouted. "I don't want to know! And make sure he *knows* I don't know!" He leaped from his chair and bolted toward the door.

"That's my intention," Hoyt reminded him, just as the door closed. "For whatever good it will do."

Martin stood up, said nothing, and followed Henry.

Bruce continued to sit in his chair, returning Wellmore's cool stare. He finally decided the trap was sprung tight. It encompassed all three brothers and there was no escape. Wellmore's cunning legal mind had made sure of it.

He and Wellmore exchanged faint smiles, Wellmore's of triumph, Bruce's of reluctant yet admiring submission. Then Bruce stood up and walked from the office, already considering countries where he might live cheaply and anonymously.

When the brothers had left, Wellmore looked at Hoyt. He said nothing, but handed him a thick white envelope.

Hoyt nodded and left the office.

"I'm going home for a while," Wellmore said to his secretary Jane.

"I'll adjust your schedule and patch through any important calls," she told him. Then she smiled and stood and left him.

*   *   *

Wellmore drove his Jaguar sedan north, out of the city, to his large house with a view of the river. Milly, the live-in nurse who took care of his wife Arlene, met him at the door.

"Wasn't expecting you so early, Mr. Wellmore."

"I had some cancelled apointments," he explained, "so I thought I'd spend the spare time at home. Catch up on some work here in the study."

Working at home wasn't Wellmore's usual style. Milly gave him a curious look, then said, "Mrs. Wellmore's in the sunroom."

Wellmore walked through the house to the spacious, many-windowed room with a river view. Arlene was sitting in her chair staring out at the snaking water, a half dozen sailboats, a string of barges moving downriver beyond them. She comprehended none of it. She slowly turned her head and looked at Wellmore, not recognizing him.

During the past six years her Alzheimer's disease had robbed her of memory and personality, and much of her reason, leaving Wellmore to break under the strain of caring for her and watching her decline.

And he would have broken had it not been for Deborah. Only Deborah had understood, had provided the comfort and relief that kept Wellmore sane and whole. It was a romance that must stay in the shadows for as long as Arlene was alive, which could be many years. There was no way to know for sure what glimmering facts, what pain, might penetrate her degenerating mind. Deborah had realized that from the beginning, but she couldn't give up what they'd found, couldn't leave Wellmore.

And though he'd tried, he couldn't leave her. Their love had been a trap.

Finally, she'd been the one who'd broken.

He'd struggled to give her everything possible under the circumstances, shrewdly investing her inheritance, sometimes in ways not totally legal but immensely profitable. An attorney in Wellmore's position knew people, learned of matters confidential and potentially profitable. Now he'd bent his ethics this final time for Deborah. The fortune in her account would go not to her uncaring and greedy brothers, but to the various heart disease charities she'd felt so strongly about.

Wellmore stood for a long time with his hand resting lightly on his wife's shoulder, staring out at the endless rolling river. He didn't bother holding back his tears, knowing Arlene wouldn't notice he was sobbing.

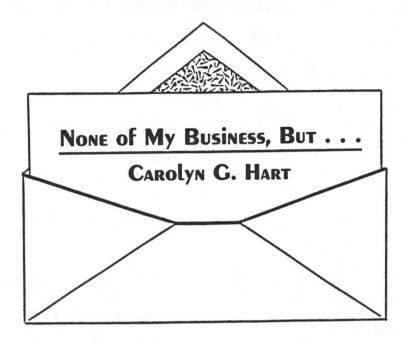

NONE OF MY BUSINESS, BUT . . .

CAROLYN G. HART

I listened to the heavy thumps on the stairs. They must be taking the body down. I had left the front door ajar. Not because I was curious, but simply because I knew I would have to talk to the police. At that point, I had no intention of getting involved, other than offering what information I had. As far as I was concerned, Mollie Epsley was a budding virago who would have been a fullblown bitch by age thirty. That had been easy enough to figure out in the two weeks she'd lived in the apartment next door. In my judgment, her lissome blonde beauty wasn't a mitigating factor, though it blinded most men to her defective character. Women, of course, see through that kind of female with ease. As for Calvin Bolt, he was a poor excuse for a man, willing to endure any kind of abuse so long as Mollie let him stay around. And he was an M.I.T. graduate with a thriving electronics firm! But, as we all know, business acumen isn't necessarily transferable to the bedroom. And vice versa.

So I had no personal interest in either of these creatures. I was merely prepared to cooperate as a good citizen must when peripherally involved in a case of homicide. Actually, I had only one consuming interest at the moment, and that was to meet my deadline. My fall had been about as fractured as Lavinia's leg, but what can you do when your oldest friend, both in years and events, falls down dew-slick marble library steps and ends up in a body cast and traction and desperately needs someone to complete her semester courses? If you are Henrietta O'Dwyer Collins, you arrive one midnight in a sleepy college town in the depths of Missouri and find yourself the next day explaining the 5Ws and H to several classes full of embryonic journalists who think news is the equivalent of sound bites. It was my pleasure to disabuse them of this concept. When they found out I'd covered wars, revolutions, and earthquakes, they tried to con me into regaling them with my adventures.

I am rarely connable.

I do, however, have an intensity of character which served me well during my reporting years, but which has always been a drawback otherwise. When I take on an assignment, I give it my all. Whether it requires pursuing reluctant principals, staking out a love nest, researching land titles, tracking down eyewitnesses, or—in Lavinia's case—teaching idiot-box refugees basic reporting skills, I will go to any lengths to succeed.

When I took over Lavinia's classes, I thought it would be a simple task. Suffice it to say, it was not only not simple, the challenge of eliciting decent prose from the couch potatoes became a time consuming obsession, with the result that my editor had gone from plaintive pleas to angry rumblings, and I *had* to get the finished draft of Istabul Transfer in the mail post haste.

That's why I was up and working at a quarter to midnight Monday night and heard yet another episode in the drama of Mollie and Calvin.

I had no idea at the time that it was the final episode.

Nor did they, of course.

It was the usual. Mollie had only lived next door for two weeks, but, believe me, it was the usual. Slamming doors. Shouts. Screams of fury.

There is quite a difference between screams of fear and screams of fury. Mollie Epsley worked herself into a towering state of rage several nights a week. The object of her scorn, of course, was the hapless Calvin. Unfortunately, the walls were thin enough that I could hear only too well the substance of every argument. Monday night she was focusing on his lack of virility, which she described colorfully enough to satisfy an Ambrose Bierce fan.

I was writing at fever pitch, my CIA heroine escaping the clutches

68

of the evildoers via a rope ladder dangling from the parapet of an Adriatic villa, when the entire wall behind me trembled.

I turned and glared at it.

More thumps.

Books, probably. Glass would break and there was no sound of splintering.

Mollie's voice rose, gut ugly, into a vicious screech. "If you can't get it up, then get the fuck out of here. Do you hear me! Get out!"

Instead of telling her to go to hell, he begged, "Mollie, don't. Please, don't." It was more than his usual whine, it was a sob. There was another crash, and he cried out in pain. Blinded either by tears or emotion, he must have stumbled into a chair. Mollie erupted into derisive laughter. "Going to claim a war wound? Better be careful or you'll fall down like an old lady. Maybe you are an old lady!"

My eyes slitted like a cat's. I take strong exception to derogatory comments linked to age.

The stairwell reverberated with Calvin's blind rush down the steps.

Then it was silent, except for an occasional slam or bang in the next apartment and Mollie's continued cursing. The dear child hadn't quite got it all out of her system yet.

I tried to concentrate on the glowing green letters on my monitor.

My eyes felt like over easy eggs that had overed too many hours before, and my heroine, Eileen Cameron, dangled limply in the purple night, awaiting my inspiration. But I couldn't get past Calvin's sad plea to Eileen's brisk resourcefulness.

"Damn."

I shoved back the chair and stalked out to the kitchen, because the drama had yet to play out. In a little while, Calvin would return and there would be a loud and teary rapprochement, ending up with squeaky bedsprings that played hell with my concentration. So I did some slamming and banging of my own en route to producing a cup of hot chocolate. I have always delighted in life's sensual pleasures, so I added a dollop of whipped cream and a handful of Toll House chocolate bits and determinedly closed my mind to the recent episode and concentrated on Eileen. The scene began to take shape in my mind: Instead of dropping to the ground and thereby falling into the hands of the bearded and turbaned watchman, Eileen enters the second floor bedroom window of the prime minister's mistress and—

That's when he began to scream.

I tipped over the mug of chocolate—thank God I was at the kitchen table and not at the word processor where my precious manuscript pages rested—and hurried out to the landing.

Calvin Bolt clung to the doorframe of Mollie's apartment, his face contorted in an agony of grief. He made a high whistling sound, eerily like the shriek of a tea kettle, as he struggled to draw breath into shock-emptied lungs.

I knew it was going to be bad.

It was.

I looked past him just long enough to take it all in. Mollie's once-voluptuous body arched backward over the red-and-green plaid couch, shiny blonde hair spread like an open fan. My gaze riveted just long enough on that swollen, bluish face, the eyes protruding, the tongue extended, a classic case of strangulation. I drew my breath in sharply, then turned back to Lavinia's apartment and the phone. As I made my report, Calvin blundered past my open front door and headed blindly down the stairs.

The police, in the form of a fuzz-faced patrolman, arrived within minutes and directed me to remain in Lavinia's apartment until further notice. "And don't worry, ma'am, we've got an alert out for Bolt and a guard downstairs."

"I'm not at all worried."

I didn't work, of course. Although I had no personal liking for either Mollie Epsley or Calvin Bolt, I don't like death. Especially unnecessary, premature, violent death. Nobody my age does. Surviving this long in a world fraught with perils is as much an indication of stubborness as it is of chance.

I'd seen a lot of death over the years, starting when I was younger than Mollie. It was, in fact, during the war that I had seen victims who had died like Mollie, garroted with a thin, fine wire, the twisted ends poking out from the fleshy trench. I not only saw such victims, in the course of duty I—but that is a closed chapter and one I prefer not to recall.

I continued to consider the method of Mollie's murder. In the 1940s, in Occupied France, it was the method of choice for OSS and SOE agents when a Nazi had to be removed, quickly, quietly, efficiently. It was quite out of the ordinary in this the Year of Our Lord Nineteen Hundred and Ninety.

I drank coffee, fought off the perennial desire for a cigarette, and thought about the night's events. By the time a gentlemanly knock sounded on the apartment door, I'd reached some conclusions.

The man in the doorway wasn't fuzz-faced, but he didn't look old enough to be a police lieutenant. However, I've reluctantly begun to accept the fact that the world is now run by children, doctors who could pass for Eagle Scouts, lawyers who've never heard of Clarence Darrow, copyeditors unaware of the identity of the Former Naval Person. I have not, however, accepted the premise of these youthful upstarts that anyone over sixty is superannuated. So we got off on the wrong foot right from the start.

He gave me a reassuring nod and spoke in a deliberately gentle voice. "Mrs. Collins? Mrs. Henrietta Collins?" He had sandy hair, an unremarkable build, a polite, noncommital face, and weary eyes.

"Yes." I don't like the cellophane-box approach, so I may have snapped it.

"Lt. Don Brown, Homicide. I know it's very late and this has been an upsetting experience, but I would appreciate it if I could talk to you for a few minutes. I'll be as brief as I can. It all seems pretty clear cut."

"Indeed?"

He heard the sharp edge in my voice and that surprised him. Those weary eyes widened, and he really looked at me. I caught a glimpse of my reflection in the hall mirror. I like to be comfortable when I work. I was barefoot and wearing baggy blue sweat pants and a faded, oversized yellow t-shirt emblazoned with the Archie Goodwin quote, "Go to hell. I'm reading." Otherwise, I looked as I had for many years, dark hair silvered at the temples, dark brown eyes that had seen much and remembered much, a Roman coin profile, and an angular body with a lean and hungry appearance of forward motion even when at rest. Lt. Brown glanced at Lavinia's living room, a recreation of Victoriana that should have been aborted, then back at me.

"I'm a guest. Come in." I led the way, gesturing for him to take the oversized easy chair, the only comfortable damn seat in the place, and I dropped gingerly onto a bony horsehair sofa.

He glanced at his notepad. "Sure. This is Mrs. Lavinia Malleson's apartment. She teaches at the college and you've taken her place for the semester. Right?"

"Yes."

"Now, Mrs. Collins, if you could tell me what happened here tonight, ma'am."

I went through it, quickly, precisely, concisely. When I reached the part about Mollie's taunts at Calvin, he wrote furiously and carefully didn't look toward me. But he was frowning as I neared the end.

"You heard Ms. Epsley—the victim—you heard her *after* somebody—you think Calvin Bolt—went downstairs. Are you sure it was her?"

"Certainly. She had a lighter step. Besides she was still swearing. Look, she started raising hell with him about a quarter to twelve. It went on for maybe ten minutes, her yelling, him whining, then he left. And she was still banging around after he went down the stairs. The usual pattern."

Brown's sandy brows knotted. "How much later was it when he found her and yelled—or acted like he found her?"

So that was his perception. My daughter, Emily, has often warned me against what she perceives as unfortunate bluntness on my part.

But facts are facts.

"Not an act, Lieutenant."

He had the gall to give me a patronizing smile. "Now, ma'am, I know this has been a shock and it's hard for—" and I swear he went on to say "—a nice little old lady like you to believe anybody you know could've done such an awful thing. But Ted Bundy was downright charming and—"

"Lieutenant, only a fool could think Calvin Bolt committed that murder."

His face flushed a bright red. Not an indication of a very stable blood pressure.

"Ma'am, murder is my business. Think about it: The neighbors report screams, followed by someone running downstairs, at approximately five minutes before twelve. Your call, reporting the body, came in at twenty past twelve. From your own testimony, the victim had engaged in a violent quarrel with the suspect. Now, it's pretty obvious he staged the discovery of her body for the benefit of witnesses. When you went to call the police, he got scared and beat it. Well, he won't get far. We've got cars out hunting—"

With the artistry of television, the fuzz-faced patrolman burst in. "They picked him up, Lieutenant, down on the bridge over the river. Grabbed him before he could jump."

They left in a flurry of excitement.

Which meant I didn't get a chance to complete my report to Lt. Brown, how tonight had been the repeat of the other soap opera episodes, right up to the final moment. Nor did I have the opportunity to share with him my conclusions, so his later claims that I was deliberately uncooperative are absolutely unwarranted.

I cleaned up the hot chocolate mess and poured a glass of sherry. I do like Lavinia's taste in sherry. Cream, of course. As I sipped, I came to the regretful decision that I had no choice.

It was up to me to find Mollie Epsley's murderer.

I am not a woman to shirk my clear-cut duty.

*   *   *

"Henrie O!" Lavinia's voice rose in dismay Tuesday morning. The familiar nickname is special to only my oldest and dearest of friends. It was coined by my late husband, who always claimed I packed more twists and surprises into a single day than O. Henry ever thought about investing in a short story. Rather gallant of Richard, I always thought. "Oh, Henrie O., are you all right!"

"Of course I am," I replied briskly and perhaps a little irritably. Lavinia does have a tendency to bleat. "It wasn't nice, but the point is, Lavinia, the damn fool police have arrested that pathetic Calvin, and he didn't do it. So, I need some facts."

That settled Lavinia down. Lavinia is quite good with facts. Despite her motherly, meatloaf appearance, she was a top financial reporter in Chicago for many years. I made a sheaf of notes.

That was how I spent the day, gathering data, a good deal of it on the victim.

Mollie Epsley was twenty-seven. Never married. Which didn't surprise me, despite her remarkable blond loveliness. She'd finished high school, attended a secretarial school, and refined her skills at a paralegal institute. She was by all accounts very quick, very competent, and very overbearing. She found it difficult to hold jobs, and I didn't have any trouble finding out why. As the office manager at one law firm snapped, "She wouldn't mind her own business. Always poking and prying, wanting to know too much about people. And the more they tried not to tell her, the more determined she was to know."

This sounded promising. "Did she try to use her knowledge for gain?"

The office manager quickly backed off. "Oh, no, nothing like that. She loved to gossip. She liked to know things about people and tell the world. Especially things that would make them uncomfortable. She was a nasty, spiteful woman."

I would agree to that.

Calvin came off as one of life's losers.

"Just a damn sap," his cousin said sadly. "No guts. No sense. But believe me, Mrs. Collins, he would never hurt anyone. He would have been better off if he had lashed out now and then. But he didn't, and I'll never believe he could strangle anyone. I don't care how awful she was to him."

So Calvin was ineffectual and pathetic, but neither of those qualities translated to violence. However, a cousin's testimony and my opinion wouldn't sway the lieutenant. No. I had to come up with some hard facts if Calvin were to be saved.

Some of my legwork had already been accomplished by Judi Myerson, an enterprising reporter for the local newspaper. She hadn't written the lead story on the murder. That belonged to the police reporter, Sam Frizzell. I scanned it, but it didn't tell me anything I didn't know. After all, I'd been right on the spot. But Judi, probably a young reporter, was assigned to do a sidebar on the Scholar's Inn apartments and the residents' reactions to the murder. I could tell she'd put heart and soul into it and come up with very little. But that's what interested me. Judi'd rung every bell in the apartment house and had found no one who really knew Mollie.

That was important. Not a surprise—she'd only lived there two weeks—but important.

Of course, I didn't spend all my time on the telephone. I sallied forth several times.

My first outing would have appeared desultory to any observer. It was early October, a nice time of year for a walk. Of course, anyone my age (most damn fools think) can walk only a short while and that at a limited pace. So it was easy for me to wander about the grounds of Scholar's Inn. (It was interesting to speculate upon the motives of the businessman who chose that name. Was it prompted by wistfulness or stupidity?) The apartment house was built as a quadrangle. A tiled pool and patio occupied the center area.

Three locations suited my hypothesis, a clump of patio chairs near the back of the pool, the parking area just past the back gate, and the laundry facilities. Each provided a clear view of Mollie's apartment windows, and each was within earshot.

74

It had rained most of Monday, steadily, persistently.

A little rainwater still glistened on the webbed patio chairs. I studied the patch of earth where the chairs sat. No impressions, no footprints.

The parking area was asphalted. Now, at midday, most of the slots were empty. The residents of Scholar's Inn worked or attended college, for the most part. Many were students and many of those led what I would term irregular lives. Up late. Out early. Arriving and departing on no set schedule. Part of the background noise to the apartment was the muted thud of slammed car doors. At all hours. Not, then, a likely spot for surveillance. Especially not on weekend nights.

That left only the laundry room. As usual, the door to the laundry area was ajar. I stepped inside. A sign in bold red print enjoined: NO SMOKING. Added to it, across the bottom, in thick black printing was the message: AND THIS MEANS YOU, BOZOS. A tiny smile touched my face. I was on the right track.

Bud Morgan, the custodian, was an ex-smoker. He reviled all smokers, and the laundry facilities were within his domain. He exercised his power. Tenants who wished for unruly toilets, etc., to be repaired made it a point to respond to his directives. No resident dared smoke in the laundry room or was unwise enough to drop errant butts at will on the grass or walks. But that angry black scrawl indicated someone was flouting his orders. And the offense must have occurred recently. The addendum had occurred since my last visit to the laundry room three days ago.

Bud was going to be furious. Several mounds of ash spotted the green cement floor. The smoker had stood close to the doorway with its excellent view of Mollie's apartment. But there were no butts on the floor.

I glanced around, then bent to my left to peer into the empty steel drum beside the door that served as a trash receptacle. There was only a little trash. Someone had thrown away an empty box of Tide. A mound of dryer fluff was draped over it. Leaning over, I gently poked at the debris. On the rusting bottom of the drum, I found a single pink baby's sock and four cigarette butts. Unfiltered Camels.

I considered calling Lt. Brown. Truly I did. But I could imagine his reaction. So what if I had found four cigarette butts in a trash can! My leap from the cigarette butts to a stranger on the premises, stealthily staking out Mollie's apartment for several nights in a row—

witness Bud's vituperative addition to the NO SMOKING sign—would be a hard one for the sandy haired lieutenant. Of course, it had to be that way. Someone knew that Mollie goaded Calvin night after night. Someone knew the pattern and had taken advantage of it. When a murder is necessary, how delightful to position it after the victim has engaged in a violent quarrel. However, I could see that the weary lieutenant might have difficulty in positing all of this from Calvin's sad sack personna and four cigarette butts. So, after due thought, I followed standard investigative procedures. I used separate envelopes for each item and listed the date and location of the discoveries. I used eyebrow tweezers for retrieval, of course. If finger-prints existed—on the cigarette butts—I certainly was careful to preserve them.

Further, I had satisfied the major requisite of my reconstruction. I had found the area where the killer had waited, listening to the customary quarrel and anticipating Calvin's departure.

It didn't take long to track down Mollie's closest friend. She didn't have many. She corroborated my conclusion that Mollie was unacquainted with her neighbors. A neighbor would have had no need to observe from the laundry room.

I had by this time a shadowy picture of the killer and an inkling of motive.

Don—Lt. Brown—later insisted I could have had no such ideas at this point in the investigation.

Nonsense.

It was all quite simple.

Mollie's murder—despite her blonde beauty and her troubled relationship with Calvin—had nothing to do with sex.

Simple garroting with no physical disfigurement is not customary for sexually motivated killers.

Garroting from behind with a fine wire (as opposed to manual strangulation) is not customary modus operandi in crimes commit-ted under emotional stress.

Rather, the manner of her death indicated premeditation and calculation, the opposite of impulsive violence. This was unmistakably an execution. And the method hinted both at the perpetrator and at the motive.

A quiet, effective means of silencing an enemy.

The murderer was either a former OSS officer, a member of the French Resistance, or someone who knew a great deal about that period. The murderer smoked. The murderer was swift, competent, and dangerous. And the murderer counted Mollie as an enemy.

Three more phone calls and the facts began to pile up. Secreted among them, I felt certain, was both the name of a murderer and the reason for the deed.

Mollie had been temping for two weeks at the law firm of Hornsby, McMichael, and Samuelson.

In Mollie's three previous temp engagements (Jetton and Jetton, Foster, McCloud and Williams, and Borden, Frampton, and Fraley) there was no employee with whom she had contact who was of the appropriate background (served in Intelligence during World War II or possessed a great deal of knowledge about that period). Besides, all of the other law firms had non-smoking offices.

It was a different matter at Hornsby, McMichael and Samuelson.

Horace Hornsby didn't smoke. Now. He'd been dead for twenty-five years. He was, when alive, partial to Cuban cigars. Sinclair Samuelson didn't smoke. He was the yuppieish youngest partner, a tri-athlete who flung himself from pool to bicycle to track before and after work.

Marvin McMichael smoked. McMichael was a distinguished veteran of the European theater in World War II. A colonel at war's end. In the OSS.

My final visit of the day, just before closing time, was to the law offices of Hornsby, McMichael, and Samuelson. I wore a black dress I'd found in a back corner of Lavinia's closet, a dyed black straw hat (God, where *had* she bought it?) adorned with a limp spray of fake violets, and black orthopedic shoes. (Lavinia's closet is full of frightful surprises.) The right shoe pinched my foot abominably so I listed to starboard.

I windowshopped next door, gazing intently at an astonishing assortment of porcelain elephants. Small towns have the enchanting quality of offering a potpourri of offices and shops along a main street. Observation would have been difficult in a huge city building.

My patience was rewarded a few minutes before five. I had no difficulty in recognizing Marvin McMichael. The morgue attendant at the newspaper had been very helpful and McMichael's image from innumerable photo-graphs was firmly fixed in my mind.

He didn't notice me, pressed close to the curio shop window, but I saw him clearly. He was taller than average, with a lean athletic build and a noticeable shock of thick white hair. His muted gray plaid

Oxxford suit was a perfect fit. Iron gray brows bunched over cold gray eyes. He had a distinguished, if severe, face with chiseled features, a smooth high forehead, beaked nose, thin-drawn lips. He walked briskly, head high, shoulders back, striding down the street with all the arrogance of a Roman senator.

I looked after him speculatively for a moment, then turned and entered the office. As I approached the secretary, I checked my appearance in the ornately framed mirror over the goldleaf side table. For a moment, I didn't even recognize the apparition in black. What a hoot.

My voice quavered just a little as I addressed a young woman whose hair looked as though she'd been on the receiving end of a hundred volts. "Hello, I'm Matilda Harris and I'm here to get my niece's things. I called to let you know I was coming." I dabbed a scented handkerchief to my eyes. Unfortunately, I'd dabbed on too much of Lavinia's cologne—I never use the stuff—and I almost strangled. It came out to the good, however, as Frizzy Hair, beneath her sleek exterior, was goodhearted and kindly. She rushed to get me a glass of water and by the time I could breathe, we were on excellent terms, sitting side by side on a brocaded bench.

"Oh, you must be Mollie Epsley's aunt. Oh, Mrs. Harris, we are all *so* sorry. It's such an awful thing to happen. No one's safe anymore. And to think it was her lover who killed her! I'd never have believed it, from what she said about him."

Calvin's arrest had been reported, of course.

I sighed heavily. "We never know what will happen in life," I observed darkly. Not, by the way, a tenet I accept. It's quite easy to know what's going to happen, especially when unstable elements combine. "And it's so very sad," I continued lugubriously, "because Mollie was enjoying this job so much. She told me just the other night—such a dear girl—so good to telephone her old aunt—that this was one of the most challenging work experiences of her life."

Frizzy Hair blinked. "But Mr. McMichael almost fired her—" She clapped a red-taloned hand over artistically carmined lips.

"Oh, that." I tsked. I crossed mental fingers and heaved a sigh. "Sometimes Mollie just didn't use good sense."

"I couldn't believe it," the receptionist said, her eyes wide. "I'd *told* her Mr. McMichael always kept that drawer locked and she said every lawyer needed a good secretary to keep things straight and she was going to put the files *she* was in charge of in first class shape."

"A locked drawer always was a challenge to Mollie. Couldn't keep her out of them when she was a little girl. She always had to see inside everything! But I'm sure she smoothed it over."

Frizzy Hair nodded, but her light brown eyes were faintly puzzled. "I guess so, 'cause she was at work Friday just like nothing had ever happened. But Thursday night, I heard them going at it." She shivered. "His voice was like an icicle down your back. I didn't hang around to hear anything after he told her she was fired." She looked nervously over her shoulder. "Mr. McMichael left for the day just a few minutes ago. I don't know that he'd like for me to talk about the cabinet. See," she confided, "he doesn't know I overheard any of it. It was after work last Thursday. I'd forgotten my car keys. I'd taken them out of my purse earlier to poke out that little aluminum thingymubob when the ring came off my Tab can." She led the way into a small office. "Let me tell you, I got out of here in a flash when I heard him talking to her. I couldn't believe it when she was here Friday morning, just like nothing had ever happened."

Mollie's work area was nicely appointed, a golden oak veneer desk and standing beside it a wooden filing cabinet. Through a connecting door, I could see the sumptuously decorated office of Marvin McMichael, senior partner. Mahogany desk. A massive red leather chair. Red and blue Persian rug. A ten by eight foot wall painting, an impressionist's swirl of brown and gold and rose, of a polo player at full gallop.

I'd tucked a grocery sack into the absurdly large crocheted handbag I'd also borrowed from Lavinia. I sat down behind the desk, pulled out the sack, shook it open, and, with little mews of distress, began to empty out the few personal effects Mollie had left behind from her two week's occupancy: a package of Juicy Fruit, a plastic bottle of Tylenol caplets, three emory boards, a plastic rain hood, a comb, a hairbrush, some loose change, several coupons, and an ad for a white sale. I added a Kleenex box from the lower right hand drawer and a pair of lowheeled shoes. I sighed again, cradled the shoes in my lap, and looked mournfully at my guide. "If I could just sit here for a few minutes. A silent reverie. I feel so close to Mollie here."

The receptionist looked at me uncertainly, darted a glance at the open door to McMichael's office, and said slowly, "I don't know. I mean, I guess it's all right. He's left for the day."

"Just for a few minutes. For Mollie's sake."

"Oh, well, sure. I mean, yeah, I understand," and she backed out into the hall.

I was on my feet and crouched beside the locked cabinet before the door closed behind her.

Funny how you don't lose some skills. I picked that lock in a flash and eased out the drawer.

Empty.

As I'd expected.

It didn't take more than a minute and a half to determine that there was no locked receptacle of any kind in McMichael's office.

That didn't surprise me either.

But I had some ideas about where the contents of that filing cabinet might be.

At the appropriate time, I would share my conclusions with Lt. Brown.

*   *   *

An envelope of silence surrounded me as I walked through The Sahara. Obviously, the clientele of this dimly lit watering hole rarely shared the ambience with elderly women clothed entirely in black. I would have stopped at the bar for a sherry, but my time wasn't my own.

I found the phone booths near the restrooms. The first booth was occupied. I stepped into the second. I already had the numbers committed to memory.

The first call was short, if not sweet. McMichael, after a long, thoughful silence, was coldly, cautiously responsive. I was more relaxed as I dialed the second number and my eyes scanned the booth, absorbing some of the au courant graffiti: Safe Sex Saves Lives, Cocaine Kills, and X Exxon. Since my mind, yesterday and today, was going back in time, I remembered some from the war years: Kilroy was Here, Uncle Sam Needs You!, and V for Victory. Autres temps, autres moeurs.

"Brown, Homicide."

"Lt. Brown, Henrie Collins here. I would appreciate it if you could join me. I've made an appointment with Mollie Epsley's murderer."

Don Brown reminded me just a bit of Richard. Very difficult to manage. He didn't want to meet me at the door to the men's room of The Sahara.

But he did.

He didn't want to ride on the backseat floor of my Volvo to the Scholar's Inn.

But he did.

I didn't tell him the name of the murderer until we had successfully crept up the back stairs to the apartment.

He'd glared at me. "That's ridiculous. Why, he's been an elder in his church, worked with youth groups for years."

That didn't surprise me at all. I said so. Lt. Brown glared again.

And he most especially did not want to recline beneath Lavinia's dining room table, well hidden by the lace tablecloth which hung to the floor.

But he did.

*   *   *

The knock came earlier than scheduled.

That didn't surprise me.

McMichael would have scouted the area as soon as it was dark, to be certain he wasn't walking into a trap. But there were no official looking unofficial cars and no brawny young men lurking in this residential neighborhood.

As I opened the door, I backpedaled, I hope gracefully.

"Come in, Mr. McMichael. You are a little early."

He stepped inside. Tonight his noticeable shock of thick white hair was hidden beneath a tan rain hat. A spear of light from Lavinia's Tiffany lamp illuminated his face. Cotton wadded between gum and cheek subtly distorted his face, but nothing could disguise that beaked nose and those thin lips. There was no trace of elegance in his shiny rayon raincoats. I would have wagered the farm that it was a longforgotten item from a back closet of the firm.

"Your telephone call wasn't clear." His voice was thick. It's hard to move the jaw when impeded by cotton, but the tone was as cold as ice-slick cobbles on a winter street. He stepped inside and unobtrusively nudged the door shut with his elbow. His hands were stuffed in the pockets of the cheap raincoat.

I walked into the living room, putting several feet between us, then turned to face him. "To the contrary," I replied pleasantly. "It was eminently clear. Or you would not have come."

"What do you want?"

I didn't permit my face to reveal my satisfaction. Lt. Brown was sure to be listening with ever increasing attention.

"Oh, to have a little talk with you." I made a vexed noise. "I would offer you a cigarette, but I don't have your brand."

The tightening of his facial muscles emphasized the protrusion of his cheeks.

"Camels, I believe," I continued cheerfully. "But perhaps you don't wish to smoke right now. We do have so much to discuss. I find crime an interesting subject, worthy of study. As I'm sure you do, Mr. McMichael. And to have murder occur so close to you—actually to an employee of yours."

"The police have arrested the murderer," he said harshly. "The case is closed." He took a step toward me.

"Yes, I know. Poor Calvin. I do feel he needs help. So I'm sure you won't mind explaining to the police how you found Mollie last night—and how you left her."

Another step. His shoulders hunched. I could imagine the cool feel of the thin wire against his fingers in the pocket of that coat.

"There's nothing to connect me to her. Nothing."

"I saw you. And I know why you came."

That stopped him for an instant.

"Mollie snooped. Lots of people know that. When the police find out how she opened that locked cabinet at your office—" I paused, looked at him inquiringly. "I suppose you thought that was the safest place to keep it. You certainly didn't want that kind of material at home. For years your mother, old Mrs. McMichael, lived with you. And you've always had a housekeeper. Josie's her name, isn't it? She's a bit of a tartar. You couldn't have unexplained locked drawers in her house! I suppose, too, it was convenient to keep that material there. You often work such late hours."

He came closer, step by step.

"You never expected your safe world to be invaded by someone like Mollie Epsley. A snoop. A sneak. A loud-mouthed virago. And once she'd seen the contents of that cabinet, she had to die, didn't she? But you wanted to be sure you killed her without a breath of suspicion attaching to your firm. So you followed her. I've checked your record, you know. SOE in France. A colonel, by war's end. You know how to follow people—and how to kill. I spotted the wire at once. Do you know, that was your only mistake. That and smoking in the laundry room and positioning the crime so that poor Calvin

82

took the rap. Rather ugly, don't you think? I doubt, however, that you spend much time empathizing with others. You watched Mollie's apartment Friday night and Saturday night, too, I imagine. And the pattern came clear. A quarrel. Calvin running out into the night. And, always, a good twenty minutes before he slunk back. Enough time for murder. More than enough. I doubt it took you more than five minutes at the most."

He was almost to me now.

In the dining room, I saw the lace tablecloth switch.

McMichael lunged for me.

I suppose, despite his own agility, he'd relegated me to the class of a helpless old woman.

When he made his move, I wasn't, of course, still standing where he expected. As I landed on my feet, after vaulting over the horsehair sofa, I watched him whirl to face me.

His face was suffused now, an ugly purple.

"Yes, you old bitch. I killed her—just like I'm going to kill you!"

*   *   *

Youth does have its innings. McMichael was no match for Lt. Brown, who executed an excellent rugby tackle, although he occasionally rubbed his right shoulder the next morning as we drank a fresh pot of coffee. I did glance at my watch at one point. I had to be in class in another twenty minutes.

"Okay," he admitted finally. "I see how you got there. The murder was just like a war-time execution and that let out Calvin. If he'd lost it, he would have slammed her up against a wall, choked her with his hands."

"Correct. Poor Calvin would never have come up behind her and looped a wire over her head."

"Yeah. I should have seen it. But how the hell did you get from there to McMichael?"

It was all so simple, but I did manage to keep that tone out of my voice. After all, the dear boy had been handy in a pinch.

"Once I tied it to the war, that limited the murderer to someone of my own age or someone with a deep knowledge of World War II and Intelligence training. I combed through personal friends of Mollie's. No one fit. I backtracked over her most recent jobs. No one fit. I came to her final employer—and there was McMichael. I expected to find the murderer among people she had dealt with very recently. Whatever she'd learned, she hadn't broadcast it yet. I imagine she was enjoying her power, teasing him, as a cat toys with a mouse. That would have been her style. But she'd come up against a desperate man."

Lt. Brown finished his coffee. He gave me a peculiar look. "Okay. I can see all of it. But how the hell did you know she'd discovered actual physical material that he would kill to keep secret?"

I poured us each another cup. A quarter to nine. Time enough.

"It had to be something that on the face of it was so illegal or so heinous that anyone seeing it would immediately be shocked to the core."

"You were right," he said grimly. "I got a search warrant this morning and in the trunk of his car—"

"You found pornographic pictures that he'd taken over the years of children he'd molested at church camps and in youth groups with whom he worked."

I suppose the witches of Salem must have elicited similar stunned responses in somewhat different circumstances.

"My God," he breathed. "You're right. My God. Sure glad you're a lawabiding citizen."

I smiled pleasantly and reached for my briefcase. As we walked downstairs—I en route to my class, he, I presume, to the station—I will admit I enjoyed his admiring sidelong glances.

And no, I didn't tell him that I'd picked the lock on McMichael's Mercedes in his garage Tuesday evening before I made my phone calls at The Sahara. Obviously, the hidden material could as easily have been cocaine or a stash of cash.

It is good to encourage reverence for one's elders among the young.

DEAD ON ARRIVAL

JOAN HESS

The girl's body lay in the middle of my living room floor. Long, black hair partially veiled her face and wound around her neck like a silky scarf. Her hands were contorted, her eyes flat and unfocused. The hilt of a knife protruded from her chest, an unadorned wooden marker in an irregular blotch of blood.

For a long, paralytic minute, all I did was stare, trying to convince myself that I was in the throes of some obscure jet lag syndrome that involved a particularly insidious form of hallucination. I finally dropped my suitcase, purse, nylon carry-on bag and sack of groceries I'd bought on the way from the airport, stuck my knuckles in my mouth, and edged around the sofa for a closer look.

It was not a good idea. I stumbled back, doing my best not to scream or swoon or something equally unproductive, and made it to the telephone in the kitchen. I thought I'd managed to avoid hysterics, but by the time Peter came on the line, my voice was an octave too high and I was slumped on the floor with my back against a cabinet door.

"There's a body in the living room," I said.

"Claire? Are you all right?"

"No, I am not all right, but I'm a damn sight better than that poor girl in the living room, because she's dead and I'm going to scream any minute and you'd—"

"I thought you were in Atlanta at that booksellers' convention until Thursday?"

"Well, I'm not," I said unsteadily and perhaps a shade acerbically. "I got home about three minutes ago, and there's this body in the living room and I'd appreciate it if you'll stop behaving like a nosy travel agent and do something because I really, truly am going to lose control—"

"Get out of there," Peter cut in harshly. "No! Go downstairs and wait until we get there."

I dropped the receiver and gazed down the hall at my bedroom door, Caron's bedroom and the bathroom door. All three were closed. I looked up at the back door, which was bolted from the inside. I listened intently for a sound, a faint intake of breath or the merest scuffle of a nervous foot. Or a bellow from a maniacal monster with a bad attitude and another knife.

It took several seconds of mental lecturing to get myself up, out of the kitchen and back through the living room, where I kept my eyes on the front door with the determination of a dieter passing a bakery or a mild-mannered bookseller passing a corpse. I then ran down the steps to the ground floor apartment and pounded on the door in a most undignifed fashion. I was prepared to beat it down with my fists if need be when the lock clicked and the door opened a few inches, saving me countless splinters and an unpleasant conversation with the miserly landlord.

"Mrs. Malloy?" said a startled voice. "I thought you were in Atlanta for another couple of days."

The apartment had been rented a few weeks earlier to two college boys with the unremarkable names of Jonathon and Sean. I hadn't bothered to figure out which was which, and at the moment I still wasn't interested.

"I am not in Atlanta. Let me in, please. There's been an—an accident upstairs. There may be someone hiding up there. The police are coming. I need to stay here."

"The police?" he said as he opened the door and gestured for me to come in. Jonathon (I thought) was a tall boy with blue eyes and stylish blond hair. At the moment his hair was dripping on the floor like melting icicles and he was clutching a towel around his waist. "I was taking a shower," he explained in case I was unable to make the leap unassisted. "Police, huh? I guess I'd better put some clothes on."

"Good idea." I sank down on a nubby Salvation Army sofa and rubbed my face, fighting not to visualize the body ten feet above my head. In my living room. Partly on the area rug.

"I'll tell Sean to get you something to drink," Jonathon continued, still attempting to play the gracious host in his towel.

He went into one of the bedrooms, and after a minute the other boy appeared. Sean moved slowly, his dark hair ruffled and his expression groggy. "Hi, Mrs. Malloy," he said through a yawn. "I was taking a nap. I stayed up all night because of a damn calculus exam this morning. Jon said the police are coming. That's weird, real weird. You want a glass of wine? I think we got some left from a party last weekend."

Before I could decline, sirens whined in the distance, becoming louder as they neared the usually quiet street across from the campus lawn. Blue light flashed, doors slammed, feet thudded on the porch, and voices barked like angry mastiffs. The Farberville cavalry, it seemed, had arrived.

Several hours later I was allowed to sit on my own sofa. The chalk outline on the other side of the coffee table looked like a crude paper-doll, and I tried to keep my eyes away from it. Peter Rosen of the Farberville CID, a man of great charm upon occasion, alternated between scribbling in his notebook and rubbing my neck.

"You're sure you didn't recognize her?" he said for not the first time.

"I'm very, very sure. Who was she? How did she get into my apartment, Peter?"

"We checked, and the deadbolt hasn't been tampered with. You've said several times now that you've got the only key and the door was locked when you came upstairs."

I leaned back and stared at the network of cracks in the ceiling. "When I got to the porch, I had to put everything down to unlock that door. I then put the key between my lips, picked everything up and trudged upstairs to my landing, where I had to put everything down again to unlock this door. It was locked; I'm sure of it."

"Caron doesn't have a key?"

"No one else has a key—not even the landlord. He had someone put on the deadbolts about five years ago and told me that I'd have to pay for a replacement if I lost my key. I considered having a copy made for Caron, but never got around to it. The only key is right there on the coffee table."

We both glared at the slightly discolored offender. When it failed to offer any hints, Peter opted to nuzzle my ear and murmur about the stupidity of citizens dallying in their scene-of-the-crime apartments when crazed murderers might be lurking in closets or behind closed doors.

The telephone rang, ending that nonsense. To someone's consternation, Peter took the call in the kitchen. Luckily, someone could overhear his side despite his efforts to mutter, and I was frowning when he rejoined me.

"Her name was Wendy, right?" I said. "I can't think of anyone I've ever known named Wendy. Well, one, but I doubt she and a boy in green tights flew through an upstairs window."

"Wendy Billingsberg, a business major at the college. She was twenty-two and lived alone on the top floor of that cheap brick apartment house beside the copy shop. She was from some little town about forty miles from here called Hasty. Her family's being notified now, and I suppose I'll question them tomorrow when they've had a chance to assimilate this. It's even harder when the victim is young." He looked away for a moment. "Wendy Billingsberg. Perhaps she came into the Book Depot. Try to remember if you've seen the name on a check or a credit card."

I did as directed, then shook my head. "I make the students produce a battery of identification, and I think I'd remember the name. I did look at her face when they—took her out. She was a pretty girl and that long black hair was striking. I can't swear she's never been in the bookstore or walked past me on the sidewalk, but I'm almost certain I never spoke to her, Peter. Why was she in my apartment and how did she get inside?"

Peter flipped through his notebook and sighed. "The medical examiner said the angle of the weapon was such that the wound could not have been self-inflicted, so she wasn't the only one here."

"What about the two boys downstairs? Have they ever seen her before, or noticed her hanging around the neighborhood?"

"Jorgeson had them look at the victim and then interviewed them briefly. Neither one recognized her or offered any theory concerning what she was doing in your apartment. Could she have been a friend of Caron's?"

"I don't think so," I said, then went to the telephone, dialed Inez's number, and asked to speak to Caron.

She responded with the customary grace of a fifteen year-old controlled solely by hormonal tides. "What, Mother? Inez and I were just about to go over to Rhonda's house to watch a movie. Aren't you supposed to be in Atlanta?"

"Yes, I am supposed to be in Atlanta," I said evenly, "but I am not. I am home and this is important. Do you know a twenty-two year-old girl named Wendy Billingsberg?"

"No. Is that all? Inez and I really, really need to go now. Rhonda's such a bitch that she won't bother to wait for us. Some people have no consideration." Her tone made it clear there was more than one inconsiderate person in her life.

I reported the gist to Peter, who sighed again and said he'd better return to the police station to see if Jorgeson had dug up anything further. He promised to send by a uniformed officer to install a chain until I could have the lock rekeyed, and then spent several minutes asking my earlobes if I would be all right.

We all assured him I would, but after he'd gone, I caught myself tiptoeing around the apartment as I unpacked groceries and put away my suitcase. The front door had been locked; the back door had been bolted from the inside. The locks on the windows were unsullied except for a patina of black dust from being examined for fingerprint. They were not the only things to have been dusted, of course. Most of the surfaces in the apartment had been treated in a similar fashion, and had produced Caron's prints all over everything (including the bottle of perfume Peter'd given me for my birthday), mine, and one on a glass on the bedside table that had resulted in a moment of great excitement, until Peter suggested they compare it to his. The success of this resulted in a silence and several smirky glances.

Wendy and her companion had not searched the apartment. There was no indication they'd gone further than the living room. Why had they chosen my apartment—and how had they gotten inside?

An idea struck, and I hurried into the kitchen and hunted through junky drawers until I found the telephone number of my landlord. I crossed my fingers as I dialed the number, and was rewarded with a grouchy hello. "Mr. Fleechum," I said excitedly, "this is Claire Malloy. I need to ask you something."

"Look, I told you when you moved in that I didn't want any damn excuses about the rent. I ain't your father, and I don't care about your financial problems. I got to pay the bank every month, so there's no point in—"

"That's not why I called," I interrupted before he worked himself into an impressive fettle. "I was hoping you might remember the name of the locksmith who installed the deadbolts several years ago . . ."

"Yeah, I know his name. You lose the key, Mizz Malloy? I told you then that I wasn't going to waste money on a spare."

I wasn't inclined to explain the situation at the moment. "No, I didn't lose the key. I was thinking about having a deadbolt installed on the back door—at my expense, naturally. My daughter and I would feel more secure."

Fleechum grumbled under his breath, then said, "That's all right with me, as long as I don't have to pay for it. But you'll have to find your own locksmith. My deadbeat brother-in-law put in the deadbolts, due in part to owing me money. He cleared out three, four years ago, taking his tools. My sister had everything else hauled off to the dump. I'm just sorry that sorry husband of hers couldn't have been in the bottom of the load."

"And no one knows where he is now?"

"No one cares where he is now, Mizz Malloy, including me. Last I heard he was in Arizona or some place like that, living in a trailer with a bimbo. Probably beating her like he did my sister. You want to have locks installed, do it."

He replaced the receiver with an unnecessary vigor. I put mine down more gently and regretfully allowed my brilliant idea to deflate like a cooling souffle. Mr. Fleechum's brother-in-law had been gone for three or four years. It seemed unlikely that he had made an extra key, kept it all that time, and then waited until my apartment was empty for a few days so that he could invite a college girl over to murder her.

I was still tiptoeing, but I couldn't seem to shake a sense of someone or something hovering in the apartment, possessing it in the tradition of a proper British ghost in the tower. I went so far as to stand in the dining room doorway, trying to pick up some psychic insight into an earlier scene when two people had entered the room and one had departed.

I tried to envision them as burglars. They'd have been seriously disappointed burglars when they saw the decrepit stereo system and small television set. But why choose my apartment to begin with? The duplex fit in well with the neighborhood ambiance of run-down rental property and transient tenants. There were people downstairs, single boys who were likely to come and go at unpredictable hours and have a stream of visitors.

Okay, Wendy and her companion weren't burglars and they hadn't come in hopes of filching the Hope Diamond and other fancy stuff. The girl had come to see me, and her murderer had followed her, bringing his knife with him. She hadn't known I was out of town—and why would she, since she didn't know me from Mary Magdalen?

A knock on the door interrupted my admittedly pointless mental exercise. It also knotted my stomach and threatened my knees, and my voice was shaky as I said, "Who is it?"

"Jorgeson and Corporal Katz, Mrs. Malloy. Katz is going to put up the chain so you'll feel safe tonight."

I let them in. Katz immediately busied himself with screwdrivers and such, while Jorgeson watched with the impassiveness of a road-crew supervisor. I subtly sidled over and said, "Have you turned up anything more about the victim?"

"The lieutenant said not to discuss it with you, ma'am," Jorgeson said, his bulldog face turning pink. "He said that you're not supposed to meddle in an official police investigation—this time."

"Oh, Jorgeson," I said with a charmingly wry chuckle, "we both know the lieutenant didn't mean that I wasn't supposed to know anything whatsoever about the victim. I might be able to remember something if I knew more about her. What if she'd been a contestant in that ghastly beauty pageant I helped direct, or been a waitress at the beer garden across from the Book Depot? You know how awkward it is to run into someone you've seen a thousand times, but you can't place him because he's out of context. When I saw this Wendy Billingsberg, she was decidedly out of context."

Jorgeson's jaw crept out further and his ears gradually matched the hue of his face. "The lieutenant said you'd try something like that, ma'am. As far as we know, the victim didn't have any connections with any of the locals. She attended classes sporadically and pretty much hung out with the more unsavory elements of the campus community."

"Ah," I said wisely, "drugs." When Jorgeson twitched, I bit back a smile and continued. "Peter's right; none of the druggies buy books at the store or hold down jobs along Thurber Street. Was she dealing?"

"I'm not supposed to discuss it, ma'am. Hurry up, Katz. I told those boys downstairs to wait for me."

Katz hurried up, and within a few minutes, Jorgeson wished me a nice day (and hadn't it been dandy thus far?) and led his cohort out of my apartment. I waited until I heard them reach the ground floor, then eased open my door and crept as close to the middle landing as I dared.

Jorgeson, bless his heart, had opted to conduct his interview from the foyer. "Wendy Billingsberg," he said in a low voice. "You both sure that doesn't ring a bell? She was a business major. Either of you have any classes in the department?" There was a pause during which I assumed they'd made suitable nonverbal responses. "She lived in the Bellaire Apartments. You been there?" Another pause. "And she used to be seen on the street with a coke dealer nicknamed Hambone. Tall guy, dirty blond ponytail, brown beard, disappeared at the end of the last semester, probably when he caught wind of a pending warrant. Ever heard of this Hambone?"

"Hambone?" Jonathon echoed. "The description doesn't sound like anyone I know, but we're not exactly in that social circle. What's his real name?"

"We're still working on that," Jorgeson said. "What about you? You ever heard of someone named Hambone?"

"Nope," Sean said firmly. "Look, Officer, I was up all night studying. I've already told you that I didn't see anyone and I didn't hear anything."

"Neither did I," Jonathon said with equal conviction. "I went out for a hamburger and a brew at the beer garden, then came back and watched some old war movie. Fell asleep on the couch."

"What time did you leave and subsequently return?" Jorgeson asked, still speaking softly but with an edge of intensity.

"Jesus, I don't know. I went out at maybe ten and got back at maybe midnight. You can ask the chubby blond waitress; she's seen me enough times to remember me."

"The medical examiner's initial estimate is that the girl was killed around midnight, with an hour margin of error on either side. It looks like the girl and her friend managed to sneak upstairs while you were out and your roommate was studying in his bedroom. You didn't notice anyone on the sidewalk when you came back?"

After a pause, Jonathon said, "Well, there was a couple, but they were heading away from the duplex and having a heated discussion about him forgetting her birthday or something. I didn't pay much attention, and it was too dark to get a good look at them. Other than them, I don't think I saw anyone during the last couple of blocks. There was a guy going around the corner the other way, but all I saw was the back of his head."

"Did he have a ponytail?" Jorgeson said quickly.

"I just caught a glimpse of him. Sorry."

I heard the sound of Jorgeson's pencil scratching a brief note. "And you didn't hear anything?" he added, now speaking to the other boy.

"No," Sean said, "I've already told you that. Nothing."

"That's enough for the moment," Jorgeson said. "Both of you need to come to the station tomorrow morning so we can take formal statements. In the meantime, if you think of anything at all that might help, call Lieutenant Rosen or myself."

The front door closed. The downstairs door closed. Shortly thereafter, two car doors closed. I closed my door and tested the chain Katz had installed. It allowed the door to open two or three inches and seemed solid enough until I could get the lock rekeyed, which was pretty darn close to the top of my priorities list. Breathing, number one. Deadbolt rekeyed, number two.

I went into the kitchen, made sure the bolt on the back door was still in place, and started to make myself a cup of tea while I assimilated the latest information so graciously shared with me.

Wendy was known to have consorted with a dealer. He'd vanished, and no doubt preferred to remain thus. She'd run into him, recognized him, and threatened to expose him. She found a way into my apartment and ended up on the living room floor. I again checked the bolt, then turned off the burner beneath the tea kettle and made myself a nice, stiff drink. I went back into the living room, checked that the chain was in place and the deadbolt secured, and sat down on the sofa, wondering if the emergent compulsion to maintain security would be with me for weeks, months, or decades.

I put down my drink, checked that the chain and deadbolt had not slipped loose, and went into the kitchen to call a locksmith and pay for an after-hours emergency visit. And after a moment of revelation, found myself calling someone else.

Half an hour later I went downstairs and knocked on the boys' door. Jonathon opened the door. His expression tightened as he saw me, as though he expected another bizarre outburst from the crazy lady who cohabited with bats in the upstairs belfry.

"Hi," I said in a thoroughly civilized voice. "I realize it's been an awful day for all of us, but I'm not going to be able to relax, much less sleep, if I don't have the locksmith in to rekey the deadbolt. He said he'd be here in an hour. I just thought I'd warn you and Sean so you wouldn't come storming out the door."

"Sean's sacked out under the air conditioner, so he couldn't hear a freight train drive across the porch. I'll see if I can get through to him, though. We're both pretty rattled by all this. Thanks for telling me, but I think I'll wander down to the beer garden and soothe myself with a pitcher. Two pitchers. Whatever it takes."

I went back upstairs, secured the chain and the deadbolt, and sat down to wait. Ten minutes later I heard the front door downstairs close and footsteps on the porch. So far, so good. I turned on the television to give a sense of security to my visitor as he came creeping up the squeaky stairs, the key to my door in what surely was a very sweaty hand.

To my chagrin, it was all for naught, because he walked up the stairs like he owned them (or rented them, anyway) and knocked on my door.

"Who is it?" I said with the breathlessness of a gothic heroine.

"It's Sean, Mrs. Malloy. I wanted to talk to you for a minute. There's something that occurred to me, and I don't know if it's important enough to call the police now."

"Sorry," I said through the door, "but I'm too terrified to open the door to anyone except the locksmith. Go ahead and call Lieutenant Rosen; I'm sure he'll want to hear whatever you have."

I listened with increasing disappointment as he went downstairs and into his apartment. A window unit began to hum somewhere below.

"Phooey," I said as I switched off the television and did a quick round to ascertain all my locks were locked. I was brooding on the sofa several minutes later when I heard a tell-tale series of squeaks. A key rustled into the keyhole. As I stared, fascinated and rather pleased with myself, the knob of the lock clicked to one side, the doorknob twisted silently, and the door edged open. I went so far as to assume the standard gothic heroine stance: hands clasped beside my chest, eyelids frozen in mid-flutter, lips pursed.

Then the chain reached its limit, of course, and the door came to a halt. A male voice let out a muted grunt of frustration, but became much louder as the police came thundering upstairs. Once the arguing and protesting abated, I removed the chain and opened the door.

Jonathon had been handcuffed and was in the process of being escorted downstairs by Jorgeson and Katz, among others. Peter gave me a pained look and said, "I was about to remove the evidence from your lock when you did that, Claire. Why don't you wait inside like a good little girl?"

"Because I'm not," I said, now opting for the role of gothic dowager dealing with inferiors. "I happen to be the one who figured out the key problem, you know."

"You happen to be the one who swore there was only one key for the deadbolt. That's what threw me off in the first place."

"Don't pull that nonsense. You heard me say that I used the same key downstairs as upstairs. It was perfectly obvious that my door, the boys' door and the front door are all keyed the same. Fleechum, the prince of penury, saved himself big bucks. Once I told the boys that a locksmith was coming, both of them realized they'd have to have their deadbolt rekeyed, too. Sean was puzzled, but I'm afraid Jonathon was panicked enough to try something unpleasant."

"It would have come to me at two in the morning," Peter said. "I would have sat up in bed, slapped my forehead, and called Jorgeson to rush over here and test the theory."

"Then I'm delighted that your sleep will be uninterrupted."

"When I get some, which won't be anytime soon. Now we've got to see if anyone at the beer garden noticed Wendy recognize her old boyfriend and follow him back to his apartment. Sean wouldn't have heard any discussion, but he might have had problems with a corpse in his living room the next morning. Did you tell the boys you'd be in Atlanta until Thursday?"

"I asked them to collect my mail."

"So Jonathon, a.k.a. Hambone, figured he had a couple of days to do something with the body. Unfortunately, you returned."

"Unfortunately, my fanny! If I hadn't come home early, he might have had a chance to take Wendy's body out in the woods where she wouldn't have been discovered for weeks. Months. Decades. And don't you find it a bit ironic that you sent me downstairs—to the murder's apartment—when I discovered the body?" I was warming up for another onslaught of righteous indignation when Peter put his arms around me.

"And why did you come home early?" he murmured.

"Because every now and then I like being told that I'm a meddlesome busybody who interferes in official police investigations," I retorted, now warming up for entirely different reasons. "No one in Atlanta had anything but nice things to say about me."

"Are you saying you missed me?"

"Jorgeson, you fool," I said. "I missed Jorgeson."

I wondered if his soft laugh meant he didn't believe me.

Invitation to Murder

Richard Laymon

A story. Gotta have a story. Time's running out.

The week in Hawaii wouldn't be any vacation at all with a deadline looming.

You've got tonight and tomorrow, pal. Otherwise, you'll be scowling into your Mai Tais, worrying your damn head off.

Shane booted up the word processor, typed the date, and got started.

"Ed wants a story for his *Invitation to Murder* anthology. Every story in the book must have something to do with a 22 year old female being found dead in her apartment. That's the anthology's unifying premise."

Oughta be a cinch. A million ways you can go with that.

Has to be tricky, though. I need a nifty reversal for it.

Can't be a who-dun-it. Not from me. He'll probably get plenty of those from the mystery writers. From me, he'll expect horror or a thriller. It has to be a grabber. There'll be names a lot bigger than mine in that book. I don't want to look like a slouch.

Gotta come up with something hot.

Hot. Christ, it's hot in here.

West L.A. usually cooled off at night. But this was one of those periods that seemed to come around a couple of weeks each summer when the daytime temperatures hit the upper nineties, the cooling sea breeze took a hike, and the heat lingered on through the night. Even with the windows open, the still air in the apartment felt stifling. Shane's T-shirt and shorts were already damp and clinging with sweat.

A long, cool shower would feel great.

Come up with a plot first. A shower can be your reward.

All right. Shouldn't be all that difficult.

Shane stared out the window and tried to concentrate. A gimmick. A reversal. Okay.

"Idea. A guy picks out this gal. She's 22, of course. And a knockout. He'd got the hots to mess around with her. One fine night, intending to rape her, he breaks into the gal's apartment. Only to find her stretched out on the floor, dead. Murdered. Neat. But then what? Is the killer still in the apartment?"

Shane stared at the computer screen, read the amber lines again and again.

How does it end? What's the twist?

Nothing came.

Forget it.

"I like the idea of a guy obsessed with a woman. Maybe he's alone in his hot apartment. Goes out on the fire escape for some fresh air."

I wish I had a fire escape. Or a balcony, for godsake.

"Just across from his building is an old, abandoned apartment house. Condemned, maybe. But while he's out there trying to get cool, a beautiful young woman appears in a window of that creepy old place. The most beautiful woman he has ever seen."

All right! Now we're cooking!

A sudden blare of raucous music shattered Shane's thoughts. Shit!

Was it coming from outside? Yeah, but it also seemed to be driving straight through the wall.

Standing, Shane leaned over the computer screen and touched the wall. It *vibrated* like the head of a drum.

Goddamn modern cheap apartment houses!

Calm down, calm down. Just ignore it.

What if it goes on all night?

It won't.

Forget about it.

Guy on fire escape trying to get cool. Gal appears in window across the alley. "The lighting is bad," Shane typed. "No electricity, of course, since the building is condemned. He sees her by firelight. Candles. Can't make her out very well. In fact, all he can really see is her gorgeous face, her shimmering blond hair. They talk. She has sultry voice. Invites him over. He's reluctant to go. Worried. Who is she? What's she doing there? He REALLY wants her, but he's hesitant about venturing over there. It's a lousy neighborhood. Weirdos around. Only that evening, he'd run into a bag lady at the mouth of the alley between the two buildings. A real hag.

"Reluctantly, he declines to go over. He's about to go back inside his apartment to avoid further temptation when the woman lifts a couple of candles onto the window sill. She is visible from the waist up. She is naked. She fondles her breasts and again asks him to come over.

"He goes. Spooky stuff while he searches the alley, finds a broken door, and enters. Makes his way through the dark corridor, up a creepy staircase. (Give him a flashlight.) Goes along the second story corridor to the door of the apartment across from his. The door is ajar. A glow of candles from inside. He enters.

"And finds a body sprawled in a corner of the room. He shines his flashlight on it. The body is that of a female (22, of course). Her clothes are strewn around the floor. She had no face, no hair. From shoulders to waist, she is a mass of gore.

"Out of the shadows steps another woman. Naked. Wearing a mask of the dead gal's face. Withered old arms and legs. But with a fresh, young torso tied in place with a harness of twine. She hobbles toward the guy, caressing the full, perfect breasts she'd taken from the corpse.

"She cackles, tells him he's such a hunk. Tells him that she knew, from the way he'd reacted in the alley earlier, that she couldn't hope to have him—he's too picky to be interested in someone like her. So she borrowed good looks from a gal she caught walking past the alley.

"He stands there stunned as she comes closer. 'Ain't I pretty now? Ain't I a knockout?'"

Shane grinned at the screen.

Terrific! That story'll be prime Shane Malone: creepy, perverse, sexy, with a touch of black humor. And nice thematic touches about lonliness, desperation, the dubious merits of physical beauty. It'll blow Ed's socks off.

But what if it's too much? Ed had explained that he didn't want stories that were too extreme.

This is pretty damn extreme. That old babe's wearing a dead gal's tits.

A *vest of tits.*

Shit! Harris used that in *Silence of the Lambs.* A goddamn best-seller! Everyone'll think I stole it from him. He got the idea from Gein, no doubt. Gein really did it. But still, they'd figure I copied Harris's gimmick.

Shane sank back in the chair and gazed at the computer screen. And gazed at it.

That idea's dead in the water. Gotta come up with something else.

The music was still blaring.

It hadn't really gotten in the way, though. Shane had hardly been aware of it once the story idea began to flow. But now . . .

What kind of cretin plays music that loud?

Who the hell *is* playing it? The noise was obviously coming from 210. That apartment had been empty for the past month.

Somebody must've moved in while I was at work.

Some fucking lunatic.

Just block it out. Ignore it.

A twenty-two year old gal is found dead in her apartment. Need a twist.

How about something from the point of view of a young woman?

Damn that racket!

"Open with gal walking alone through city streets. Nervous about being out so late. Maybe she thinks someone is following her. She's spooked, quickens her pace. At last, she gets to her apartment building. Unlocks the foyer door, enters. She's safe at last. Relieved, she climbs the stairs to the second floor. The door of her apartment is ajar. She looks in. Her roommate, a 22 year old gal (of course), is dead on the floor. And the killer, crouching over the body, grins over his shoulder at the main gal, lurches up and rushes her."

Rushes her. Then what?

"She whirls away and runs . . ."

Shane glared at the wall. That music!

Am I the only person in the whole damn place it's driving nuts?

This *is* Saturday night. Maybe everyone's out—gone to the movies, gone to visit friends, gone to parties.

Was the creep in the next apartment having a party? Didn't sound that way. No voices, no laughter, no sounds of anyone moving around. Just that blasting music.

Shane stood up, leaned over the computer screen, and pounded the wall. "Hey! Could you please hold it down in there? I'm trying to work."

The volume of the music lowered.

"Thank you."

"Get fucked!" shouted a female voice from the other side of the wall. Then the music blared, even louder than before.

Shane's heart thudded.

Calm down, calm down.

I oughta go over and clean that bitch's clock for her!

What I oughta do is calm down.

What about complaining to the landlord? Right. That moron. Dudley. A dud, all right. I'd get nothing but grief from him. If he's even home. Saturday night. Probably out somewhere, pursuing his hobby—"bagging babes" as he liked to put it.

What about calling the cops?

Oh, that'd be a neat move. If they do come over and give that bitch a warning, I'll have a real enemy on my hands. No telling what kind of shit she might start pulling.

What about taking the shower?

Come up with a story first. That was the deal.

Shane blinked away some sweat and read the last few sentences on the computer screen.

"Okay. The gal finds her roommate dead. The killer leaps at her and she whirls aways and runs through the doorway. Runs down the corridor, shouting for help. Nobody comes out to help. The killer races after her with his knife."

What next?

That bitch! Told me to get fucked!

Pound on the wall again? Lot of good that would do. She'd probably turn the music up even louder—if that's possible.

"The guy hot on her tail, she pounds on an apartment door. It swings open. She rushes in. Trips over a body. Sees another body slumped against a wall.

"Neat idea. Suppose the . . ."

Sweat stung Shane's eyes. Nothing within reach to wipe them dry.

My shirt.

The T-shirt came off. Though damp, it did a fine job mopping the sweat away. There *was* a breeze from the window. Very slight. But it felt good. Shane tossed the shirt to the floor, sighed, and studied the computer screen.

". . . killer has murdered everyone in the whole building? But why would he do something like that? Just because he's nuts? Suppose he's the owner and there's rent control and he wants to get rid of all his tenants so he can convert the place into condos?"

Stupid.

"Forget him killing any other people in the building. His targets are the two gals, nobody else. He lived in the apartment next to theirs. He decided to knock them off because he just couldn't stand them always playing their fucking stereo too damn loud!"

Oh, man, I'm getting nowhere fast.

Too noisy! Too hot!

The breeze was better than nothing, but hardly cool enough to stop sweat from running down Shane's face and sides and chest.

This might easily qualify as the most miserable night of my life. Thanks a lot, Ed. And *you*, you bitch!

Shane kicked the wall, then hunched down sideways and picked up the T-shirt and attacked some tickling runnels of sweat.

I'll *never* come up with a decent idea. Not with all this racket. Not with all this heat making the sweat pop out as fast as I can wipe it off.

So take the shower.

Yeah!

Feeling better already, Shane hurried to the bathroom. Its shut door muffled the maddening beat of the music. And the sounds of water splashing into the tub obliterated the noise completely.

Maybe I'll just stay in here. Never come out again.

You left the computer on, stupid. Good move. Hope it doesn't explode or something. That'd be a fitting finale for this misbegotten night.

Hey, I'd have a good excuse for Ed. Sorry, afraid I can't do that story for you. My computer blew up.

Peeling the shorts down, Shane scowled at a haggard twin in the full-length mirror: short hair clinging in wet points; specks of sweat under the eyes, above the upper lip; tanned skin gleaming as if it had been slicked with oil; untanned skin, hidden from the sun by swimsuits, that looked white and felt clammy.

Oughta get some air conditioning in this dump. Maybe buy one of those window units.

Sure. With what?

With the $5,000 advance I got for *The Black Room?*

That was reserved for Hawaii.

In two days, I'll be soaring out over the Pacific. Away from all this. Hawaii. Beaches. Soft breezes. Mai-tais. Maybe meet someone nice . . .

The bod's not half bad. Trim and firm. The tan looks pretty good, and nobody'll see the white. Not unless I get lucky.

Shane smirked at the face in the mirror, then stepped to the tub, climbed in, swept the curtain shut and turned on the water. It gushed from the spout. Nice and cool. A tug at the little knob on top of the spout sent it raining down.

Wonderful!

Maybe I can pick up some kind of air conditioning unit with the money I get from Ed.

Have to write the story, first.

Have to think of *an idea* first.

How about a twenty-two year old babe gets offed in the shower? Some kind of a twist on the *Psycho* thing. Maybe the gal in the shower turns out to be a guy. Right. Only then we've got a *male* dead. Has to be a female.

Besides, it's stupid. Everybody would say I was ripping off Bloch. I could say it's not a rip-off, it's a *homage*. That's what everyone else calls it when they swipe somebody's stuff.

Shane sat down on the tub's cool, slick enamel.

Think think think.

Eyes shut, legs crossed, the deliciously cool water pattering, sliding, caressing.

I could almost fall asleep.

You can't.

Think! Twenty-two year old gal found dead in her apartment.

What if she's a bitch who deserved to die? A nag. Always at her husband. And her husband's a cripple in a wheelchair. Totally at her mercy. One fine night, she steps out of the bathroom after taking a shower and he zaps her.

How does he zap her?

With darts. That's his only fun in life, throwing darts. And she's always giving him shit because he mises the target sometimes and puts little holes in the wall.

Maybe the bitch hid his dart board. And that was the last straw. She steps out of the bathroom, maybe onto a sheet of plastic he's spread on the carpet to catch the blood, and whammo! Nails her with some darts in the face.

Not half bad.

Smiling, Shane stretched out along the bottom of the tub.

Now we're getting someplace!

Could you kill someone with a dart? Probably. A good hard shot right to the forehead. Penetrates the skull. Pokes the brain. And maybe he puts one in her eye.

Bull's-eye!

Make her a lesbian, you'd have a nifty play on words: bull's-eye, bull dyke.

No. The pun's going too far. Pushing the ludicrous.

But nice and sickening, a dart jabbing into her eyeball.

Anyway, she winds up dead. Twenty-two year old gal dead in her apartment.

And the perp is a cripple in a wheelchair. So he needs help disposing of her body. So he phones his best friend, and invites the guy to come over for a game of darts. The friend is reluctant to come. Doesn't want to face the guy's shrew of a wife. Guy says, "That's okay, she's out."

Out, all right.

This is great.

So the friend shows up, finds the bitch dead on the floor. He's shocked, but not especially upset. He needs some convincing, but finally agrees to help get rid of the body. He's afraid he might be seen if he tries to carry it out through the apartment building, but there's a balcony over the alley. So he and the crippled guy lower the body with a rope.

How about giving it a toss, instead? More fun that way.

Either way, it ends up in the alley. And the friend goes down, planning to drive it away. But the body isn't there. He can't find it anywhere. He goes back up to the apartment.

The two guys are discussing what to do, when suddenly they hear voices. Shouts. They go to the balcony and look down. Half a dozen creepy, ragged derelicts are gathered in the alley, all of them gazing up at these fellows. "Give us another one! We want another!"

What did they do with her? Eat her? And they're still hungry, and if the boys don't throw down seconds for them, they might just come up and help themselves.

So then what?

Shane sat up, shivering.

Too much time under the cold shower? Or am I shivering with excitement because of the story?

Hell, it's not that good. But it's not that bad.

Is it good enough?

Shane turned off the water, groaned at the muffled sound of the music, but climbed out of the tub and pulled a towel off its bar.

Just don't think about the damn noise or that slimy scum-sucking bitch next door. Think about the story.

Is it really the end of the story when we figure the bums want more? Maybe the guy in the wheelchair could push his friend off the balcony. But then what? It would sure be the end if I tell the story from the friend's point of view. But that way, how would I work in the neat business of the cripple darting his wife to death?

Dry, Shane draped the towel over its bar and opened the bathroom door. The music pounded in.

"Shit!"

At least the apartment no longer felt like an oven. Probably as hot as before, *I'm* just cool. Won't be for long, though, especially if I let that music get to me.

Shane put on a fresh pair of running shorts and a short-sleeved shirt, left the shirt unbuttoned so air could get in, and sat down in front of the computer.

Stick with the idea of the wheelchair guy? Cannibalism. Derelicts. I've used both those things a lot lately. And the ending isn't all that terrific.

The story seems okay until the bums show up in the alley. But if I get rid of them, where did the body go?

Walked away? She's dead, for Christsake. Make it a zombie story, and she comes stumbling back up, seeking vengence.

Crapola.

Damn it! The story hadn't seemed half bad while while I was under the shower—and couldn't hear that bitch's music. With that noise messing up my head, maybe *nothing* will seem any good.

I oughta go over there and break her face. Or break her stereo, even better.

No, just be polite. Explain the situation. Ask her nicely to turn the volume down.

The thought of it made Shane's heart pound.

Chicken.

You've gotta do it. Otherwise, you'll just sit here getting more and more steamed and you'll never accomplish anything.

Do it!

Heart hammering, mouth dry, Shane got up from the chair and walked to the door. Paused to button up.

Shit. I don't want to do this.

Opened the door.

She might be nice. Who knows? Nice, sure. She told me to get fucked.

Stepped into the corridor, left the door open, and walked on shaky legs to the neighbor's door. Knocked.

Bitch probably can't hear me through all that noise.

Knocked again.

The volume of the music dropped. "Yeah? Who's there?"

"It's me from next door."

"What do you want?"

"I'd just like to talk to you for a second."

"Yeah?"

Shane heard a metallic click.

"If you came over here to give me shit about . . ." The door swung open. The woman's glower softened. So did the tone of her voice as she said, "Well, now. So you're my new neighbor, huh?" She made a little toasting gesture with her cocktail glass, and said, "Pleased to meet you, neighbor."

Shane managed a nervous smile.

Jeez, the gal was practically naked. All she wore was a black negligee. It had spaghetti straps. Its low front exposed the tops of her breasts. Its skirt was hardly long enough to reach her thighs. And Shane could see right through the gauzy fabric.

Any gal who would open the door in an outfit like that must be weird or half-polluted. Maybe both. Her eyes looked a little red. From the booze, or had she been crying?

"I'm Francine," she said, holding out her hand.

Reluctantly, Shane shook it. "I'm Shane."

"Nice to meet you. Come on in, why don't you?"

"Oh, I don't want to intrude."

"Please?" A smile twitched on her heavy lips. "Come on in and have a drink, okay? Hey, it's my birthday. Nobody oughta have to be alone on her birthday, huh?"

Shane suddenly felt a little sorry for the woman. "I guess I can come in for a minute. But no booze. I'm trying to work."

"Sure, sure. How about a Pepsi?"

"That'd be fine, thank you."

Francine shut the door, gestured with her glass toward a sofa, and headed for the kitchen area.

Shane sat at one end of the sofa.

This is not bright. Francine's obviously a bit mental. But not really a bitch. After this, she might be willing to cooperate and keep the music down.

The stereo and its twin speakers were on the floor, right up against the same wall that Shane faced when sitting at the word processor.

If the wall weren't there, I could've knocked them over with my feet.

No wonder the noise had been so bad.

The turntable was empty. In front of the stereo were stacks of cassette cases.

"How do you like this heat?" Francine called.

"I don't."

"My last place was air conditioned."

"This close to the ocean, you usually don't need one. Just for a couple of weeks each summer . . ."

"Makes me wanta scream."

She came back, a full glass in each hand. A strap had slipped off her shoulder. When she bent down to hand the soda to Shane, that side of her negligee drooped, exposing her entire breast.

On purpose?

What've I gotten myself into, here?

She stepped by, and lowered herself next to Shane. Turning sideways, she rested an arm across the back of the sofa, brought up one leg and hooked its foot behind her other knee.

Shane glanced down. The negligee was hardly long enough to conceal Francine's groin.

Man oh man.

"Here's how," Francine said, and gulped some of her drink.

"Happy birthday."

"Happy. It's been the shits till now."

"Birthday's can be that way."

"See how *you* feel when you hit the big two-two."

"Already did," Shane said.

This gal is twenty-two! Talk about your coincidences and ironies of life!

"You don't look any older than nineteen," Francine said.

"Neither do you," Shane lied. The gal looked closer to thirty.

"You're just saying that."

"No, it's true."

A corner of Francine's mouth curled up. "Do you think I'm attractive?"

Her dark hair was mussed, her face a little puffy and red. Though she looked older than her age, she was beautiful. No denying that. And she certainly had a body.

"Sure," Shane said. "Of course you're attractive."

The other corner of her mouth trembled upward. "You're not bad, yourself. I'm so glad you came over. I was feeling so down in the dumps you just wouldn't believe it."

"It hasn't been a banner night for me, either."

"I guess I'm partly to blame, huh?"

"Well, it's all right."

She took another drink, then set her glass on the table. "I'm sorry I yelled at you." She leaned a little closer. Her fingers began to caress the back of Shane's neck. "Can you forgive me?"

"Sure. No problem. But I'd better . . ."

Her other hand, wet and chilly from the glass, squeezed Shane's thigh. "Doesn't that feel good? Nice and cold?"

"Look, Francine . . ."

"You have such lovely blue eyes."

"I'm really busy tonight. I have to get back to my work."

"Do you? Do you really?" The hand crept higher, fingertips slipping under the leg hole of Shane's shorts.

"Hey!"

The hand retreated. Francine stared into Shane's eyes.

"You want me," she said. "I know you want me."

"I don't. Really. Thanks all the same."

There was pain in the woman's eyes. Loneliness. Despair.

"I'm sorry, Francine, but . . ."

With a noise that seemed partly growl, partly whimper, she hurled herself onto Shane. The Pepsi glass went flying.

"No! Get off!"

Lips. Wet, sloppy lips. A sour reak of gin. Hands plucking feverishly at buttons, yanking open Shane's shirt. Grabbing, caressing, squeezing.

I don't believe this. God, I don't believe this!

The mouth and hands suddenly went away. Shane, slumped on the sofa, hips pinned down by Francine's weight, gasped for breath as the frenzied woman arched her back and peeled off her negligee.

"Don't. Please."

"You love it." Hunching down, she pushed a breast against Shane's mouth.

And tumbled off as Shane bucked and twisted.

Her back struck the edge of the coffee table. Her head pounded it. The table skidded, capsizing her glass. Then she flopped off and dropped to the floor.

She lay there facedown, sprawled between the table and the front of the sofa.

Shane scurried over the end of the sofa. Stood. Stared down at Francine. Felt a hot surge of shame and revulsion. Whirled away, doubled over and vomited.

Shouldn't have shoved her. Oh, God, shouldn't have shoved her.

Why didn't I just let her do what she wanted?

Shane backed away from the mess on the carpet, and gazed at Francine.

What if she's dead and I killed her?

Who says she's dead. Probably just unconscious. That's cheap movie stuff, people getting shoved during a struggle, falling, dying from a little bump on the head. She'll probably wake up in a few seconds.

When she does, I don't want to be here.

Watching the body, Shane knelt beside the coffee table and picked up the Pepsi glass.

Anything else with my fingerprints?

Probably just this glass.

Don't take it! Jesus! That's like admitting she's dead, admitting your guilt.

But Shane kept the glass. Rushed to the door. Wrapped a hand in a shirttail before turning the knob. Checked the corridor.

Empty. Silent.

Stepped out, swung the door shut, and walked fast.

She can't be dead. But if she is, there's no way they can pin it on me. No physical evidence. The vomit! They'll know somebody else was there. But they won't know who. They'll end up deciding it was an accident. She was drunk, she fell and hit her head. They'll check her blood alcohol level during the autopsy, realize she was polluted, and . . .

There won't be an autopsy! She's okay.

What if I'm locked out?

But the door was still open. Shane lunged in, locked the door and leaned against it, gasping.

Safe.

God, *why* did I have to go over there!

She's all right. Just a little knock on the head.

Shane pushed away from the door, staggered over to the desk, and dropped onto the chair. The music came softly through the wall.

Turn it up, Francine. Come on, make it blast.

On the computer screen was Shane's last sentence. "He decided to knock them off because he couldn't stand them always playing their fucking stereo too damn loud!"

No no no no no!

"Shane?"

Little more than a whisper through the wall.

"Francine?" Rising from the seat. Heart thumping. Relief like a flowing warmth. "Francine, are you okay?"

"Fuck you."

"I'm sorry you got hurt, but . . ."

A blast pounded Shane's ears. White dust and flecks exploded from the wall a foot to the right. Something zipped by.

In the wall was a hole the size of a dime.

She shot at me!

"Francine!"

The next shot punched Shane in the chest.

Twenty-two year old female found dead in her apartment.

Oh, shit.

Shane dropped onto the chair, saw blood hit the computer screen, the keyboard—then stared down at the spurting hole between her breasts.

DARKE STREET

GARY BRANDNER

Detective Sgt. Dan Mulvehill felt like hell. His head ached. His joints creaked. His back hurt him where the twenty-year-old bullet was still lodged up against the spinal cord. The breath whistled in his chest from climbing the single flight of stairs. And he felt a cold coming on. Mulvehill was 59 years old, two weeks away from retirement. He felt 79, and two weeks away from death.

Looking down at what lay on the bed didn't make him feel any better. Alive she must have been stunningly beautiful. Hell, even dead she was something. Smooth, delicately tanned skin, lustrous black hair, full red lips, a body to roil any man's juices. Mulvehill felt a twinge of guilt at the emotions the girl's body stirred within him. He coughed into his fist and got businesslike.

"Cause of death?"

Jaime Ruiz, the young assistant medical examiner, looked up from the body. "No visible trauma. I'll have to wait till we get her on the table."

"Can you make a guess?"

Jaime looked down at the dead girl, back at the detective. "Wouldn't even try. She might as well be asleep. Heck, just look at her."

Mulvehill looked. A soft smile curved the girl's lips. Her hands lay relaxed, palms up, at her sides. Her body . . .

"Uh, can you . . . cover her?"

Jaime pulled the sheet up over the nude young woman. "One point of interest—she seems to have had sexual intercourse shortly before she died. Very shortly."

Mulvehill tried not to visualize the last scene of the girl's life. He turned away and looked around the small, cluttered bedroom. Like the rest of the apartment, it was scrupulously clean. It occupied the second floor of an old house in Los Angeles's Hancock Park district. The furniture was old, but well cared for. The walls were covered with prints, framed photographs, calendar plates, needlepoint. Every available surface held figurines, vases, more photographs, ceramic animals, potted plants, satin cushions, crocheted doilies. Handbraided rugs were scattered over the floor. Goggle-eyed tropical fish looked back at him from a bubbling glass tank.

Nothing in the place seemed to belong with the young woman who lay dead in the bed. In the closet were dark, long dresses, sensible shoes, small hats, woolen coats—all from a generation or two earlier. Only the boat-neck sweater, white jeans, and Reeboks next to the bed obviously belonged with the dead girl.

A uniformed officer approached Mulvehill. "I've got the downstairs neighbor out in the living room, Sergeant. A Mrs. Kaufman. You want me to bring her in?"

Mulvehill glanced back at the sheet covering the full-breasted form on the bed. "No, I'll talk to her out there."

Golda Kaufman was a sturdy woman with steel gray hair and bright little eyes that were magnified by bifocal lenses. Mulvehill gestured her to a chair and lowered himself into another facing her. As they talked Mrs. Kaufman tilted her head back to focus on him through her glasses.

"She seemed like such a nice girl. Only two weeks she's been here, but so open, so friendly. I felt like I knew her for years already."

"What was the girl's name, Mrs. Kaufman?"

"Sarah. Such a pretty name. It suited her."

"Sarah what?"

"That's all she told me. I never thought to ask her for a last name. It didn't seem to matter."

Mulvehill shifted his focus. "How well did you know Mrs. Esterhaus, the woman who lived in this apartment?"

"Helena? We were like sisters. No, even closer than that. My own sister I wouldn't trust like I did Helena. Poor darling, her arthritis was getting so bad she could hardly make it up and down the stairs any more. It's a blessing she isn't here to see this happen in her own home."

Mulvehill consulted a notebook. "You told the officer Mrs. Esterhaus left on some kind of a trip."

"Like a miracle it was. She won a cruise around the world in one of those magazine sweepstakes things. We used to laugh about how nobody we knew ever won anything. Then two weeks ago she tells me she's a winner. She's leaving right away. I couldn't be happier if it was me."

"Yes, that was pretty lucky," Mulvehill said, making a note.

"And lucky too she should have somebody as sweet as Sarah to stay in the apartment and water the plants and feed her birds. I'd have done it for her gladly, but it was a favor to Sarah too, Helena said. Gave the girl a place to stay while she was going to school. And now she's . . . she's . . ."

Mulvehill spoke up as Mrs. Kaufman started to snuffle. "School?"

"Acting lessons she was taking. Out every night almost. So lovely, she'd have made a wonderful actress." Mrs. Kaufman raised the bifocals to dab at her eyes.

"Did you know any of Sarah's friends?"

"She never talked about anybody. Like I said, she was only two weeks here."

"Did she have any visitors? A man, say, like last night?"

"I wouldn't know. What do you think, I sit at the window watching who comes and goes. I got my own life."

"I'm sure you have. Thanks, Mrs. Kaufman." Mulvehill hoisted himself painfully from the chair to indicate that the interview was ended.

Trevor Wilkes, Mulvehill's partner met him at the bedroom door. Young, square-jawed, sharp-eyed. Mulvehill saw himself of 25 years ago. For Wilkes' sake, he hoped the young policeman would be in better shape than he was 25 years from now. The kid didn't know how lucky he was. The young ones never did.

Wilkes held up a zip-sealed plastic bag. It held three items: An empty glass vial, a pair of men's glasses, and a leather case for the glasses.

"This stuff looks fresh. The glasses and case were on the table next to the bed. The medicine bottle we found in the bathroom. Everything else, except for the girl's clothes, seems to belong to the old woman who lived here."

"Mrs. Esterhaus."

"Right. CID will go over the place, but I want to get these things into the lab right away. The ME's wagon is downstairs for the girl."

Mulvehill nodded absently. He grasped the glass vial through the plastic and squinted to read the label.

"Paul's Potions and Palliatives." He exchanged a look with the younger detective, who answered with a shrug. *"Seventy-seven Darke Street.* Ever hear of Darke Street?"

"Doesn't ring a bell. Does it say Los Angeles?"

Mulvehill shook his head. "No city. Check the L.A. and Orange County Street Atlas. Try other cities in California, then spread out."

"Right."

Wilkes took the baggie with him and strode off toward the stairs. Mulvehill went back into the bedroom. He turned the sheet down for a last look at the beautiful young face, then gently recovered her. He felt old, old, old. He limped stiffly back out of the apartment and down the stairs.

*　　*　　*

The little frame house in the Silver Lake district had been just right for Dan Mulvehill and his wife. Now alone he rattled around in it like a marble in a cigar box. For six years he had planned to move into something smaller, but never got around to it.

He took the bottle of Wild Turkey down from the kitchen shelf, looked at it with affection, stroked the label, and put it back. It was not worth the worsening morning headaches. Hell of a thing. One by one the pleasures of life had been taken from him. After Fran died he had gone a full twelve months without really missing sex. When he finally tried it with one of the cop groupies from The Trail's End, it hadn't worked. Next his lungs rebelled and he had to quit his unfiltered cigarettes or cough himself into fragments. Now he couldn't even drink. So in two weeks he retired. To what?

The morning matched his mood—gray, damp, and oppressive. Mulvehill managed his usual breakfast of instant coffee, black, and drove the dented old Dodge down the freeway to the Los Angeles Police Building. He was grumbling through his stack of paperwork at mid-morning when Jaime Ruiz stopped by his desk. The young medical examiner's assistant carried a styrofoam cup of decaffeinated coffee and a thick glazed donut. He talked through a mouthful of donut.

"You can write off the dead brunette," he said. "There were no signs of violence of any kind on the body. No evidence of toxic substances in the blood or stomach contents."

"What *did* kill her?" Mulvehill asked.

"Her heart stopped beating."

"Is that morgue humor?"

Jaime swallowed the last of his donut, took a noisy gulp of coffee. "Hey, if we stopped to grieve over every cold one, we'd all wind up psycho. If you want my unofficial opinion on the cause of death, I'd say old age."

Mulvehill stared at him. "Are you nuts? I saw the girl, remember?"

"You saw the exterior. Her internal organs were a mess. Heart, lungs, liver . . . They belonged in a woman eighty or more years old."

"Is there some diesease that could that?"

"A couple of them. But they'd leave her shriveled and old looking on the outside too. Nothing I learned in med school explains this one."

It was late afternoon and the sky was heavy with the threat of rain when Trevor Wilkes strolled back from the forensics lab and tossed the evidence packet on his desk. Mulvehill spilled out the empty vial and the glasses, now inside their leather case. He looked up at the younger man. "Learn anything?"

Wilkes tapped the vial with the tip of a ballpoint pen. "Contents zero. No trace of anything. Latent prints of the dead girl. The address zero. The only Darke Street west of the Mississippi is in Custer, South Dakota. No address there close to Seventy-seven. No establishment that sounds anything like Paul's Potions and Palliatives."

"What about the glasses?"

"We did better there. The owner is Alan Esterhaus. Same last name as the old lady who lived in the apartment. Occupation computer programmer. Home address 6976 Calle Verde in West Hills."

"That was fast. What happened, you luck out and pick the right optometrist on the first try?"

Wilkes grinned. "Better than that. The guy had a business card tucked inside the case."

"Nothing beats solid police work."

"I hear it's not Homicide's baby, anyway. Jaime Ruiz says natural causes."

Mulvehill balanced the glasses in his palm. "All the same, I'd like to talk to Mr. Esterhaus." He pocketed the glasses. "I'll deliver these to him myself tomorrow."

* * *

The storm hit full force that night. A spectacular play of lightning danced over the Santa Monica mountains, and thunder rumbled down through the canyons. Rain slashed the windows of Mulvehill's bungalow. His joints ached and the old bullet sent painful tremors up his spine.

Sleep was out of the question. Reading hurt his eyes. Television was glutted with hyperkinetic sitcoms. His old records only reminded him of Fran and happier days. Mulvehill limped to the closet and shrugged into his battered raincoat. He left the house and shuffled across the wet grass to the garage. The Dodge started reluctantly and Mulvehill backed out to the street and drove off into the storm. He made an effort to send his mind some-where away from the pain and the lonliness.

For half an hour he drove aimlessly, staying away from the freeways and the more traveled streets. His headache worsened from the strain of squinting against the glare of lights off the wet asphalt. He found himself on a narrow street of low, featureless buildings. The street lamps were dim and widely spaced. Only a forlorn Seven-Eleven store seemed to be open for business. There was no business.

As Mulvehill slowed for an intersection he peered up to read the name on the blue and white sign.

Darke Street.

"What the hell?" He sat there for a moment staring up at the street sign as the rain lashed the Dodge. Then he popped the car into gear, turned right and cruised slowly along close to the curb, studying the store fronts.

They were all dark, except one tiny shop where a light showed faintly from inside. Mulvehill stopped the car and got out. He was not surprised to find the corroded metal numbers bolted to the heavy door: 77. A wooden sign, meticulously hand-lettered in old English print read: *Paul's Potions and Palliatives.*

The proprietor was small and bent. He peered at Mulvehill over half-glasses. The detective showed him the empty vial. The little man nodded.

116

"Yep, that's one of mine."

"Can you tell me who bought it?"

"A nice old lady, couple of weeks ago it was. I don't bother with names, if that's your next question. People come in and want to buy, I sell. They don't ask my name, I don't ask theirs."

"What was in the vial when you sold it?"

The proprietor tilted his head to read the label. "Popular number. Youth."

"Youth?"

"That's what I said. Sell a lot of it."

"Wait a minute, are you telling me you're selling some kind of a magic rejuvenating potion here?"

"I didn't say magic. Youth. That's what I said."

Mulvehill looked at him narrowly. "There's got to be a catch."

"'Course there is. Nobody can sell real Youth. I don't pretend to. My potion gives you the look, the feel, the fun of being young. But inside you're as old as you ever were. My potion doesn't make your life one day longer. Maybe a lot shorter. I don't promise what I can't deliver."

"The woman you sold this to . . . could her name have been Esterhaus?"

"Told you, I never ask."

Mulvehill peered around the dim interior of the shop. There were no bright displays, no advertising posters, no posted prices. Not even a cash register in sight. Nothing but dusty shelves on which stood a variety of containers.

He assumed his official police voice. "Do you have a license to operate here?"

The bent little man was unperturbed. "Nope. Never figured I needed one."

"Well you'd better start thinking about it. There are state laws and some pretty stiff city ordinances about who can sell what in Los Angeles."

"Do tell."

The man's calm was unnerving. "I don't know that you're doing anything illegal here, mister, but you'd better believe I'm going to check you out. And if you don't have the proper permits, I'll be back."

"Any time."

The bent little man smiled at him and peered over his half-glasses. Mulvehill nodded decisively, as though something had been accomplished, and left the shop.

He drove slowly home through the rain. The strange little man and the musty shop filled his thoughts. By the time he was in bed and sleep finally came Mulvehill was half-convinced he had imagined the whole encounter.

The rain continued the next day. Los Angeles needed it, so everybody said. There had been two years of near drought. Still, Mulvehill wished it would stop. All of his aches were worse when it rained. His house smelled musty and his life seemed emptier than usual.

It was late afternoon before he could get away from his desk to drive out to West Hills. Alan Esterhaus lived in a two-story redwood and fieldstone house on a street of similar houses, each with a generous patch of bright green lawn an a three-car garage. Esterhaus was a mild man of 37 who looked extremely uncomfortable as he sat across from Mulvehill in the spacious living room. His wife, a trim blonde woman in the family photograph on the piano, was at a garden club meeting. Their two boys watched a violent cop show in the den.

Esterhaus fingered the glasses nervously. They were a match to the pair he was wearing. "As soon as I missed them I knew you'd find me. I should have come in on my own. I should have reported it to somebody when it happened." He looked up at Mulvehill as though he expected to be whipped. "When I saw that the girl was dead I panicked. I've never done anything like that before, Sergeant. Not with anybody. And then to have her die like that . . . It's been driving me crazy for the last two days."

"I can imagine. You say you didn't know your grandmother had gone on away on a cruise?"

"She never said anything to me. I didn't call her as often as I should have. Hadn't been to see her in maybe six months. Then, this time I thought I'd surprise her, and the girl answered the door. I never even found out her name. I . . . I just lost all control. I've never seen anyone so beautiful. And when she asked me in, well, one thing lead to another. The next thing I knew we . . . we . . ., well you found her. I'm sick with shame about the whole thing."

"Your grandmother's name was Helena," Mulvehill said. "Did your grandmother have a middle name?"

"W-what's that?"

The detective repeated the question.

"Yes. She never used it, but her middle name was Sarah. Why do you ask?"

Mulvehill studied the young man, who sat shifting nervously in his chair. "No reason," he said. "Just curious."

"What's going to happen to me now?"

"Unless there's some new development . . . nothing."

"You mean . . . This is all there is?"

"As far as I'm concerned. There's no evidence that you committed any crime. How you deal with your conscience is up to you." There was no point, Mulvehill decided, in giving this troubled man one more terrible guilt to live with. He levered himself out of the chair and lumbered out the door.

On the front walk he met the blonde woman he recognized from the family photograph inside. She smiled at him. Her smile was enough like Fran's to make him hurt deep in his throat. He touched the brim of his rain hat and continued out to his car.

The rhythmic *shnick, shnick* of the windshield wipers had a hypnotic effect as Mulvehill drove back toward the city. A cluster of red lights up ahead told him an accident had clotted the freeway. Unwilling to sit alone in the rain, he turned off at an unfamiliar ramp and drove through strange streets. He was only a little surprised when he recognized the row of sad, faceless buildings and the lonely Seven-Eleven.

He slowed at the intersection and turned right without hesitation. He had an appointment to keep. On Darke Street.

Pretty Boy

Billie Sue Mosiman

I knew I never should have gotten involved with a pretty boy. Grandma married a pretty boy much to her distress. He was vain, she said years after his death. So vain about his clothes and his tortoise shell comb set, so *vain*, she said in her creaky old woman's voice, that when he came down with pneumonia he wouldn't let her call a doctor for it was improper anyone should see him disheveled and incontinent in the cherry four-poster bed. Being pretty, Grandma concluded, had killed my grandfather before his time.

But I didn't think about these admonitions when I met Bobby Tremain. There are some experiences in life that defy common sense and the validity of good advice.

It was the winter of 1967 and I had come to Louisville by way of Atlanta where no one wanted to hire a nineteen-year-old college dropout. They didn't much want to hire me in Louisville either so I took a job selling candy behind the counter at Stewart's Department Store. The boyfriend who had come to Atlanta to drive me to Louisville, where he attended television repair school, worked in the mail room of Stewart's. I figured he could stand it, I could stand it.

It was Christmas season and he was busy wrapping gifts and mailing them worldwide. I was busy eating all the chocolates I could stuff into my mouth when the other sales girls weren't looking. Swiping candy kept my appetite abated and stretched my paycheck considerably.

I was content with my job until Christmas Eve. Customers flocked to the counters ordering last minute gifts of filberts, pounds of pistachios wrapped in red foil, boxes of fancy mints and divinity and bridge mix chocolates. I hadn't a moment to filch a lemon drop, my feet hurt, it had begun to snow hard and my walk home to an apartment on Chestnut Street promised to be a miserable cold one. As if all this were not punishment enough for my sins of minor theft, Jerry, the boyfriend working in the mail room, wandered up to the counter during this mad rush and handed me a small black felt ring box.

"Marry me," he said.

Just that. No preamble, no romance, just 'marry me.'

"I'm busy, Jerry. Please."

"Open it. This isn't a joke, I promise."

"Miss, could you wait on me? I'd like two pounds of walnut fudge and a pound and a half of the pecan. Could you wrap it?"

I gave the fudge-hog in the mink a look insuring she wait another minute. Beyond that and I'd hear from her was the look she returned. After all it was Christmas and her time was more valuable than mine.

"I can't accept it. You know that, Jerry." I pushed the little box back across the shiny glass counter top. "I'm busy, I have to go."

While weighing and wrapping the fudge I glanced twice at where Jerry stood with his hands hanging at his sides staring at the jewel box. I hadn't meant to be so cold about it, but what did he expect? He knew I didn't love him; I didn't love anyone. Besides, he was a year younger than me and his parents would kill him if he got married. Just because I let him drive me from Atlanta to Louisville didn't mean we should spend our lives together. What was wrong with his head?

The day after Christmas I began looking for another job. Stewart's was too far to walk and too close to Jerry. Across the street from my apartment house stood Louisville General Hospital. The building was a solid piece of craftsmanship, the best looking architecture within four blocks. My apartment house, a sleaze bag resort for the poor and semi-stupid nineteen-year-old like myself, was a red brick dwarf compared to the soaring many-storied structure of Louisville General. If I found a job at the hospital I could come home for lunch, save a dollar or two. That was my main interest, saving money. I had big plans Jerry knew nothing about. I was headed for the golden West, for San Francisco and the famed Haight-Ashbury district where flower children danced through one long carnival night. But I could never get there if I didn't save traveling money and a stake to sustain me when I arrived.

My first interview with the personnel director of Louisville General went poorly.

"How old are you?" he asked, looking over the rims of his glasses. He had to be forty if he was a day. I could usually charm old farts.

"Nineteen."

"Where are your parents, your family?"

"They live in upstate New York."

"Why don't *you* live in upstate New York then?"

"Why should I? I'm nineteen."

"Hmmm." He pondered this winsome bit of logic a moment. "Aren't you afraid to live on your own?"

"No."

"Where do you live?"

"Across the street. I have an apartment. I could be here anytime you needed me. It's quite convenient."

He pushed the glasses up his nose and sniffed as if he could actually smell the stained linoleum covering of the apartment lobby floor, the dust coating the plastic plants, the mustiness of the worn red diamond-patterned hall runners. "Don't you think that's a dangerous place for a young girl to live alone?"

"It's fine. It's cheap. No one bothers me. I play gin rummy with a couple down the hall."

"Umm hmmm. And what do you know about hospital work?"

I sat forward and put forth my most earnest face. "I don't know anything, but I'm willing to learn. I thought I'd do well in the admitting department. I can type and file and do anything I'm trained to do. I know I don't have work experience, but I'm quick; I catch on fast." I paused when I saw a ghost of a smile creeping onto his lips. He was not taking me seriously and that was unfair. "Best of all," I concluded, "I live right across the street and I can come work anytime you need me."

I thought I'd convinced him despite the smug little smile, but finally he shook his head and said, "You shouldn't be in this city alone, a girl as young as you. You've no experience . . ."

I stood, realizing I had been dismissed. But I had not given up.

I knew what I wanted—out of the candy department and away from Jerry's lovesick gaze—and I was determined to have this job. The director was vastly underestimating my ability to suffer patronizing attitudes. I could take it until the cows came home if that's what he wanted. He had not seen the last of me.

I waited two days. In preparation I quit my job at Stewart's much to Jerry's chagrin. ("What are you doing? How can you leave me this way?") I camped in the secretary's office until she let me see the personnel director a second time.

"You again."

"Oh yes. I'm free now. I quit my job and I can start here anytime you like."

He sighed, propped his glasses higher on the bridge of his nose. "Young lady . . ."

"I know I don't have any qualifications, but you won't find a more eager and able learner. I've had two years of college; I know how to learn."

"We really don't . . ."

"I'll take the scummiest job you have open. If you want, I'll make beds, scrub floors, clean toilets, anything. You have to give me a chance. And I live right across the street, I can . . ."

"Come anytime we call. Yes, you've mentioned that."

I smiled. I was earnest and young and winning. How could I miss? Still it took two more trips into the director's office to convince him he couldn't do without my services in Louisville General. I imagine I simply wore the man down, but that is youth's prerogative. Older people cannot fly in the face of unabashed enthusiasm and energy. It tires them.

I had not been working in the admitting department two weeks before I met the pretty boy. The admitting supervisor had me going into the wards to verify insurance information. Most of the patients had no insurance to verify. Seven out of every eight hour stint I spent interviewing welfare mothers with new babies. I don't know why the hospital thought these women had changed their ways, succumbed to middle-class values, and carried hospitalization now when most of them had been in these wards delivering babies only the year before. But I was not to question procedure. I was to ask my silly questions about income and insurance and write down the answers.

In my second week on the job I entered the men's ward for the first time. A patient had come in the night before through emergency and I was to verify the insurance on him. My papers said he was twenty years old and he had been shot in the leg.

Shot? Now wasn't that an interesting injury? It beat gallstones and the maternity ward all to hell.

I wandered through the big open ward blushing at the whistles and hoots coming from the beds. Men of all ages sat up on their pillows, swiveled their bodies at my passing, and generally had a good time making me uncomfortable. "Bobby Tremain?" I called out above the din. "Where is Bobby Tremain?"

"I'm right here," came a deep male voice behind me. "I'm Bobby."

I turned and was at once awestruck by his beauty. Blond, curly haired, features chiseled fine and noble as the face of Jesus in the Pieta I had seen in the New York World's Fair. From what I could see beneath the sheet he also possessed the physique of Michelangelo's David. I must have appeared dumfounded because Bobby cocked his beautiful head and said, "Well? Did you want me?"

The way he said *want me* sent shivers running. Did I want him? Oh yes, absolutely, I wanted him clothed or unclothed, bedridden or healthy, in his hospital bed in full view of thirty men or alone on a deserted mountain top before the eyes of heaven. A terrible thing for him to ask, did I want him.

I managed to move to his bedside. "Hi . . . I'm supposed to . . . uh . . . ask you some questions . . ."

"Ask away." He punched the pillow behind his neck. Overhead pulleys held his right leg in traction, the massive cast covering it from groin to toe. He winced when he moved and even his grimace was an appealing sight. For the first time in my life the maternal instinct flared. I wanted to mother and protect, take a stranger into my arms and soothe away the pain. That emotion should have alerted me. You don't mix mothering with sexual attraction. Not if you have two years of college under your belt, something you'd think would make you immune to psychological transgression.

"Oh, this?" he asked, noticing my stare. He lightly slapped the blinding white cast on his thigh. "It looks like I'll have to wear this baby for months. I guess I'd better get used to it."

"Who shot you?" This was not on the questionnaire, but it was of the uppermost importance to me. I already felt my anger building at whoever committed the desecration of a perfectly Adonis-like creature.

"Cop. Cop did it."

"No."

"Yep. But I guess I deserved it. I was running away."

"Why?"

"I was scared."

I nodded my head. Of course he had been scared, poor baby, who wouldn't be scared of a cop? Everyone trembled when confronted with people who carried guns. "What had you done?"

He smiled, casting a silver net of shivers over me again. There was something menacing in his smile, enough menace to make it fascinating, mesmerizing. "I didn't do anything," he said. "I swear it was all a mistake."

To anyone else, to someone older and less naive, to someone more worldly wise and cynical, his words would have condemned him from the outset. Criminals always swear innocence. It's to be expected. But I was not fully mature or wise to the ways of the world. I was a girl on the lam from parental authority, heading for the hippie revolution that had bypassed middle America, and I believed when people spoke, they spoke the truth. What profit a lie? To a stranger? A girl come to verify insurance? What profit that?

"You see I was driving with an expired license. A cop car pulled up behind me with his lights on and I panicked. He said later I was speeding, but I don't think I was. I knew, though, I'd get in trouble about the license so I did something dumb. I tried to get away."

"You shouldn't have."

"Don't I know it! It was the dumbest move in my life. I got it into my head that I'd outrun him and get home. I turned down streets and took a wrong turn somewhere and got lost."

"You could have stopped."

"Not by then. You don't know cops. You run from the bastards and you're in deep shit. Well, this wrong turn led to a deadend. I did have to stop then. I was cut off. I got out of the car and in the glare of the headlights, I ran up a hill to a high fence. I was climbing over when he shot me." He shrugged as if to say that's life, you win a few, you lose a lot, big damn deal, it happens all the time.

My outrage boiled over. "Just for climbing on a fence? Didn't he say 'halt' first or anything?"

Bobby, having enlisted my sympathy, shook his head.

"He just started shooting without even warning you first?"

Bobby nodded, eyes shyly downcast.

"Oh, you should get a lawyer and put that cop in jail. He had no right to shoot like that. He might have killed you." The thought of Bobby Tremain dying, hanging from a fence in the dark with bullet holes in his back made me sick with fury. How dare a trigger happy cop shoot down such a pretty boy just because he panicked over an expired driver's license! It was obscene. It was the establishment bulldozing down the youth of America. You couldn't do anything you believed in, you couldn't change the system, you couldn't save yourself and the future from the bloodsuckers. It was a travesty.

It was also love. Now I had an inkling of what Jerry felt for me. I lived, breathed, dreamed Bobby Tremain. Every day at the hospital I used my ward-hopping privilege to look in on him. I brought him magazines and candy bars from the hospital gift shop. I plumped his pillows and held the water glass to his fine lips. I told him how I had never been farther west than Texas and how I yearned to see the Pacific ocean. How it was like a narcotic and I was a junkie, just had to make it out West before I died from the cold sweats and the hot tremors.

"How will you get there?" he asked.

"I'm saving my money. I have a hundred and twenty dollars saved so far."

"That's not a bad sum," he said. "That would buy gas."

"Oh, I'm going by bus. I want to see Salt Lake City and Reno. Besides, I don't have a car."

"I do," he said and my head went faint. Was this a proposal we travel together? If I supplied expenses would he take me in his car? I feared to hope. Bobby was too beautiful for me. Angels do not consort with fragile, flawed earthlings.

Bobby remained in Louisville General six weeks. He confided he must go to court and face charges the day he was to be released. "They're going to hang me," he said. "That cop'll make sure of it."

"What about your parents, didn't they hire a good attorney?"

He laughed and turned away his head. "I don't have parents. Not so you'd notice. I left home when I was fifteen. I haven't seen them since so I'm on my own in this deal. They'll railroad me into prison where I'll never see daylight again."

"You can't let that happen, Bobby."

He turned back to me, eyes brimming, the sky blue of the irises thunderhead dark and troubled. "I have a car," he said. "It was impounded, but a friend of mine got it out for me. I've always wanted to see the land west of the Mississippi."

I trembled in ecstasy at the thought of having Bobby all to myself even though I was not ready to abandon Louisville and my good job yet. What would Jerry say? What would my supervisor and the personnel director say? Then there was the fact I would be abetting a felon or something along those lines. All I knew about cops and the law came from television. I *did* know that what Bobby proposed meant flight from justice and without me and the money I had saved, he couldn't do it.

"I don't know, Bobby . . ."

He caught my hand where I stood next to him and drew me down toward the bed. In front of God and the whole men's ward he kissed me to the accompaniment of catcalls and shrill whistles. I was signed, sealed, stamped, and delivered. Just exactly what Bobby wanted.

"Meet me here at six in the morning," he whispered. "A court appointed officer is coming for me at ten. I have to get out before then. We'll have to be very quiet about it."

"But your hospital bill . . ."

"Let the state pay it. That's what they're good for."

You don't listen to pretty boys, that's what my grandmother told me. You don't listen to silky promises from the cunning lips of an angel in disguise. Even Lucifer was pretty. The prettiest. And look what he is responsible for, she said.

These thoughts plagued me all night while snow swirled down from a night sky onto Chestnut Street. The one window in my first floor efficiency apartment was barred and looked out on a narrow alley. On the other side of the alley stood a fence and on the other side of the fence reared an ancient structure that housed the Juvenile Detention Center. Cries and howls from my unfortunate neighbors often startled me awake in the night where I lay in the dark imagining the horrors taking place mere feet away from my window.

The snow had stopped by five in the morning. I sat on the ratty brown sofa with two suitcases parked next to me. This was a momentous decision, maybe more important than the decision to quit college or to take up Jerry on the offer of a ride to Lousiville.

The apartment, bare and depressing before, now bore down my spirit with the full weight of its poverty. There was a long uneven rip in the linoleum starting at the bathroom door and zigzagging to the foot of the sagging double bed. Roaches marched in hordes across the white porcelain sink counters, unafraid of interference. Pine wood shelves, once painted black but now peeling, separated the dining alcove from the living-sleeping room. The shelves were barren of the odd decoration, the few books of poetry I owned, the bunch of dried flowers Jerry had brought to show he was a good sport when I landed the job at the hospital.

What was I giving up by leaving with Bobby? Nothing but an experiment in low living, Friday night gin rummy games with the out-of-work couple down the hall, Saturday night forays to the YWCA where we all sat around sipping tepid Cokes and listening to the latest bad folk singer strum and sing of the times they are a'changin.

I craved more excitement than Louisville offered. I wanted to taste the adult life, get myself into corners and out again, pay my own rent, buy my own navy blue pea coats for Kentucky winters, talk myself into better jobs. And I wanted Bobby. How I wanted Bobby.

It was in Reno that I left him. I knew I had to by the time we drove across the Utah line toward Salt Lake City. It wasn't just the pistol he'd secreted in the car pocket. That scared me, but I could have found a way to understand it. No, it wasn't just that. The angel was tarnished as greening brass. Outside the sterile hospital atmosphere, Bobby let down his guard and showed a cruel, hateful, manipulative side. On the outskirts of Reno he was complaining how his leg hurt and how my excited chatter got onto his nerves.

"Do you always blabber on this way?" Sarcasm dripped from his voice. It coated the air inside the car, turned it as frigid and disgusting as frozen vomit. I cringed against the door. "Don't you ever shut up? God, you'd think you had something to say."

Yes, I thought I had. It's possible I was wrong about that the way I'd been wrong about Bobby.

On a dim side street we took a room from a smirking hotel manager and fought in the rickety elevator about whose fault it was we stayed in fleabag hotels. The room, the only one in the city we could afford, overlooked a shadowed, windswept shaft cornered by the backsides of three smog-grayed buildings. Bobby had been too tired from the trip for making love, even once, and I thought perhaps the glorious event might occur in this tawdry room and make it a magical, special place. Something had to happen to save me from jumping into the shaft. But Bobby was ill-natured as a dog in pre-heat and continued to rag me about everything.

"Who needs to go to San Francisco," he bitched. "Anyplace will do. Why not L.A.? I should go to Hollywood."

"Hollywood's phony."

"And you think your pukey friends hiding out in Haight-Ashbury are for real?"

"Bobby don't." We had already been over this particular terrain before. Hippies to him meant acid heads, free love, and panhandling. He wanted nothing to do with riffraff. He was about enlightened as some of my southern redneck relatives.

"I'd have some kind of chance in Hollywood. I have the looks to get into the movies."

He was right about that, but at this point I could have told him he didn't have the personality. Hollywood might be shark-infested, but as far as I knew they hadn't yet found interest in mean-spirited gila monsters.

"Bobby, love me. Make love to me." I expected the logistics to be difficult considering the leg cast, but any sort of impossible maneuvering was preferable to listening to Bobby bitch. The more he opened his mouth, the more I loathed him, the more I wished I were back at Louisville General with my clipboard and my wards to wander.

"Is that what you want?" he asked. "Is that all you've ever wanted from me? One good fuck?"

I wilted under his gaze. "I only want you to love me, Bobby."

"Love!" He let go a splutter of breath, exasperated. "What do you know about love? What do you know about anything for that matter? You really bought that story I told you, didn't you?"

"Don't tease me."

"I won't tease you. I won't tell you what a fucking dunce you are. What a damn brainless dummy you are."

"Bobby, please."

"I won't tell you that cop shot me because I drew on him. I won't tell you if he hadn't shot me in the leg, I might have splattered his idiotic brains all over the sidewalk. No, I won't tell you anything truthful because you'll believe any lying bullshit I feel like making up."

"You wouldn't kill a cop."

He laughed and of course it was true, he would do it, he would kill if pressed to it, he would destroy like the avenging angel he was if he felt the slightest whim. He was right. I was a fucking dunce. I was the biggest fucking dunce ever came down the fucking pike.

"What are you doing?" he asked.

"I'm getting my suitcase."

"What for?"

"I'm leaving now, Bobby. I don't have to take this anymore."

"Hey, wait a minute. What is this bullshit?"

"It's goodbye shit, that's what it is." I was at the door. Bobby lay disadvantaged where he had fallen onto his back on the bed when we entered the room. He struggled to get the cast to the floor and lever himself onto his feet.

"Don't you dare walk out that door. It's my car. *My* car, you bitch!"

"And it's my money, Bobby. I worked months for it. It's my dream, this trip. It was your escape and I was stupid enough to provide it for you. But it's my dream. I've done all I mean to ever do for you." I had the door open and one foot in the hallway.

"I'll find you if you dump me here." He was onto his feet and tottering, reaching for the cane he used where it leaned against the arm of a busted-spring chair. It all pressed down then, swallowing the two of us in a murky cloud. The window facing the airshaft. The gloom, the faded rose bouquet wallpaper, the smell of urine spilled and soaked over a period of years, the old bad scent of dried semen, the stench of despair, of dreams trounced and smashed and lying without pity upon the floor.

"You mean you can try to find me. You won't, though. If I were you I'd be careful running red lights and skipping out on hotel bills. Which is what you'll have to do here because I'm not leaving you a penny, Bobby, not a penny."

"Aw, don't be that way. I was just kidding ya. My leg's hurting, that's all, I was outta my head, baby. I'm in a bad mood but I wanna apologize. You don't believe that crap I said, do you? I made it up, really, come here, baby, let me do to you what you want, let me make a little . . ."

"Goodbye Bobby." I was into the hall. He approached the door, his face red and livid with splotches. He was not so pretty now. He was not at all pretty. How could I have been so blind as not to see? "By the way," I said, making for the elevator while he painfully followed, leaning against the aged wallpapered wall for support, the heavy cast clumping along the floor. "I threw away your goddamned pistol in Salt Lake. I found it and threw it in a garbage can at a service station."

"I'll . . ."

The elevator door slid shut before he reached me. The chugs and clangs of the cables rang in my ears as I descended to the lobby floor. "Goodbye, Bobby," I whispered. "I wish I could say it had been fun."

There weren't many pretty boys in Haight-Ashbury. It's hard to be pretty when you're stoned and vacant-eyed. LSD trips do not make for pretty. The ones I found there I left as pickings for other, weaker girls. Someone should have told them not to get involved. Pretty boys either die stubbornly of pneumonia or they do crime like crime wants to be done. Either way they aren't worth the bother to spit on.

Bobby found me two months later. I didn't think he could, but the street talked. That's what the street did best in Haight-Ashbury in 1967, talk and sell shit.

Someone told him I'd crashed with a girl everyone called "Petunia," Pet for short. She had a two-room dump on the ground floor of a dilapidated, condemned building just three blocks off the main drag. The only working toilet was on the second floor and the way it worked was we poured a bucket of water into it. Bathing, when it was done, came from the same bucket. But the pad was free, who was going to complain?

I was nearly bummed out with the hippie crowd. That's what you said then — bummed, crashed, talking shit in the pad. I thought hippiedom would be fun, the sex fantastic, the drugs more than adequate. The truth was the people in the midst of this revolution were crazy as hell, the sex, when you could get it, was listless and uninspiring, and the drugs gave me ultra-paranoid dreams where ten-foot tall cats tried to scratch out my eyeballs. So much for the Golden West and the counterculture movement. Just one more demonstration of bad taste.

Pet was a sweetheart, though, and even if she slept all day and hallucinated all night, she was good people. If the hippie heart was to be found, she had it cornered. I needed clothes, she went scavenging and brought back brocaded vests, silk pants, rich, colored scarves. I got hungry, she disappeared and returned loaded down with a feast extraordinaire, everything from pizza to chicken soup and sardines, to plums so purple and ripe they made your mouth run water just to look at them. I don't know how she did it, but she knew how to supply our two rooms with everything but electricity. And she was working on that.

Sweeping long dishwater blond hair from her sleepy, hooded, brown eyes she said, "Babe, I got connections. We'll have a free line into the power company by week's end."

Pet came from San Diego. "That pit of vipers. Sailor lech types and Chicano macho types. You can have it."

She was going nowhere. "This is the best place on earth. This is where God settled in."

I tentatively put forth the traitorous notion that we were floating through life and maybe should rejoin the establishment, get a job, get a *real* apartment, make some honest cash.

Pet gave me a pained look and took up her place on the three stacked mattresses that lay on the floor. "Get smart, babe. You don't want straight time. It's slow poison and you know it."

At that point I wasn't sure she was right. Poison, yeah, it was out there in three-piece suits and nappy haircuts, but wasn't there a middle ground somewhere? Couldn't you play the game and still win? Stealing from the electric company wasn't my idea of making remarkable social progress.

That was the day and the dying conversation we were having when Bobby showed up.

He loomed in the open doorway, grinning an evil, twisted smile. "Found you," he said quietly.

"Friend of yours?" Pet asked. "He's pretty."

So she thought so too. But she didn't know Bobby Tremain.

He wore faded jeans and a ripped black tee-shirt. The cast was gone, but he leaned a little sideways against the door as if the leg was still a problem.

"Hello Bobby. Goodbye Bobby."

"You won't get rid of me so easy this time. I come for my car."

"You come for revenge. I know you, Bobby."

"Hey now, cool out," Pet said, climbing off the mattresses and going to where Bobby leaned. "Whatchu wanna fight for, babe? How about a few tokes, get you mellowed out?"

"You get away from me, you pothead," he said.

Pet held up both hands. "Hey, fine. *Sae la vie*, man, and all that good shit, you know what I mean?"

"My car," he repeated, his gaze boring into me.

"I had to sell it, Bobby. So get another one." Saying this did not give me the satisfaction I thought it would.

He moved past Pet and limped across the room. He stood much too close and I could smell the danger coming off him like a cologne too heavily splashed on the skin. I couldn't look him in the eye. A trill of fear finger-walked up my spine. I didn't remember him being this big, this overwhelming. Maybe the cast had made him seem vulnerable. Without it, he was gargantuan, a nightmare, a reject from one of my last doped out visions of cats and bells and Pepsi cans that said things like, "Pardon me while I kiss the sky." He blocked the light from the grimy windows. I backed away, slowly, oh so carefully.

"Leave me alone, Bobby."

"I'm going to kill you."

I sucked in my breath because I knew this was the truth, the unvarnished, absolute truth. Grandma hadn't told me pretty boys might be homicidal. But then how would she know?

Pet laughed nervously. "Listen, man, that's a little stringent for somebody taking your car, don't you think? What if I see if I can get you another car? I might be able to do that if you're sweet."

Bobby turned faster than I thought he would be able to. "Sweet, my dimpled ass! Now you get outta my face, you understand? This ain't got nothing to do with you, but if you want, I'll just make this a twosome. Two for the price of one, are you getting my drift, little honey?"

Pet changed color. She was creamy California sun beige and turned white as cottage cheese. Her small mouth pinched down tight as a lid on a catsup bottle. Her eyes blazed with more formidable emotion than I'd ever seen from her before. I didn't know if she was impressing Bobby, but she sure as hell impressed me. This was warrior territory and Pet had on her paint.

"Out," she commanded, pointing to the door. "You get out."

Bobby threw me a dark glance before limping past her to the hall entry. "Later, baby."

When the front entrance door slammed, I was finally able to breathe, but not too easily.

"Hell, where'd that freakzoid come from? That the one you left in Reno?"

"That's him. He wanted to shoot a cop. I think we better believe his threats."

"And what? Decamp my place? Move in with some heads? Uh uh, he don't scare me *that* bad. I've run into bad and he ain't it."

"Pet, I don't think you understand. Bobby's the devil. He's after me and if you get in the way, he'll get us both. You heard him."

"I *heard* him, the sonofabitch, but he won't make me run." She drew her skinny self up and stalked to the mattresses. She reverently took up a dope pipe from the scratched bedside table and tapped crumpled fragrant leaves into it.

"Maybe you better go," she said after she had the pipe glowing, the smoke sucked into her lungs. She closed her eyes.

"If I leave and he comes looking, he'll hurt you, Pet. I swear he will."

"You let me worry about Pretty Boy. I got friends, you know, who'll watch out for me. But I think you oughta go. You been wanting to cut out anyway. This is the perfect time, babe."

She was right, of course. I had to get away. If I wasn't around maybe he would come for me, leave Pet alone. But what if he didn't? How would I live with that?

"I'll take off tomorrow," I said, sighing. I pushed aside the tie-dyed curtains over the stained sink. "Right now I'll make some tea. I can't stop shaking, he's so goddamned *big* . . ."

"Bucket's upstairs," Pet said dreamily. "Upstairs is the bucket. Right by the toilet, where it is, you know, that's where the water is, in the bucket, the fucking bucket's big as the fucking toilet bowl, holds plenty . . ."

"Yeah, Pet. I know. Go to sleep."

And she did. Sweetheart Petunia of the blond-brown hair, the heart of gold, the soul of a warrior, the friend in need, the space cadet who know how to live free . . . almost free.

Pet slept the rest of the day, as was her custom, and woke around ten p.m. to go tooling the street while I packed my meager belongings.

She returned at midnight babbling about electricity and how the current *flows*, man, how it surrounds you everywhere in a city. "It's in the wires," she said, her eyes darting around the peeling walls. "And there's wires everywhere."

I agreed as to how there were a lot of wires, yes, but it was nothing to get uptight about and what had she taken, exactly? It didn't seem to be sitting too well with her whatever it was.

"Oh," she waved a hand around the air, "just a little sumpthin special, sumpthin I think I'm gonna like . . . ummmhmmm . . . like pretty fucking good . . ."

"One of these days I'm gonna FLY, sweet honeychile mine!" She leapt into the air, transported into a jet-glide fantasy. It took me an hour to get her down and onto the mattress. She tossed and turned in the dark and made me hold her while she shook with cataclysmic episodes of sudden trembling.

So small. Only three years older than me, Pet seemed much younger, more innocent and trusting that I had ever been. Which was saying a great deal considering the mess I'd made of my heretofore young years.

I held onto her for dear life and thought about what would happen to her when I left on the morrow. Here I thought she'd been protecting me, providing me with a way to live, when all the while it was I who had been her pillar, her Gibraltar. This was not the first time I'd coached Pet through the throes of a drug-induced delirium. Before it was just something I did without thinking about it. It was what we all did for one another. But if I weren't here who was going to hold on to Pet and keep her from flying so high the clouds would forever claim her?

Well, I'd make her go with me, that's what I'd do. I'd kidnap her if I had to, get her out of this madhouse, away from the free-floating anxieties and the paranoid dream world. Away from the singing wires and the pills and the tabs of stuff and the smoke, away from the Bobby Tremains.

Pet stopped convulsing and snored peacefully, her mouth open and smelling of an apple she must have snatched from a food-vendor earlier. I drowsed, but held onto Pet's hand to give us both security in the black quiet hours before dawn. I didn't like those hours, especially on nights Pet needed watching.

At first I thought I was dreaming when I heard a door creaking on its un-oiled hinges. Bobby's silky voice ("I'm back.") brought me partially awake. I sat up in bed, trying to untangle the Indian woven spread from around my legs, fighting with the material, fighting off the deep sleep trance that had hold of my mind.

"Wha . . .? Who's there? That you, Bobby?"

Pet slept on. I gripped her right arm and buried my nails in her tender flesh. She did not respond. Whatever she'd taken was enough to put her out for the longterm. *Oh Pet. Oh Pet, please wake up. Jesus, Pet, don't crap out on me now . . .*

"She can't help you."

I could see him as deeper shadow sneaking across the room, hunched, lurching sideways, something in his hands, something with a long handle, a baseball bat, an axe, something bad, real bad.

"Bobby . . ."

"You took my fucking car."

Halfway across the room.

"Bobby, I'll pay you back."

"You dumped me in fucking Reno."

Three-fourths of the way across the room.

"Bobby, c'mon, you gotta listen to me, I was crazy about you, don't you know that, don't you know how you treated me?"

Halted.

What was the handled thing? How bad was it? If I threw up my arms, could I stop the damage?

"You break my fucking heart," he said.

"Bobby, you don't want to do this. You're just mad, I admit you've got reason to be mad," I lied breathlessly. "But didn't I get you out of the hospital, out of Louisville? Didn't I help you escape prison? Didn't I? Doesn't that count?"

"It took me two months to track you down," he said. His voice was just all wrong, all wrong. I'd never heard him sound so calm, so utterly insanely calm. Tundra would double freeze from this voice.

I shook Pet violently. She groaned and turned onto her back. *Oh Pet, oh Pet, why did you get drugged out tonight?*

"I'm sorry, Bobby, honest I am. If I had it to do over again, I'd never take your car."

"And leave me stranded. Had to sneak out of that goddamned room. Had to *panhandle* like some fucking hippie buddy of yours to get coffee money. Had to *hitchhike* outta Reno. Had to *walk* in the fucking rain and wind in Sacramento. You want to make up for that?"

"Yeah, Bobby, I do. I mean I will, just tell me what I can do, okay? We don't have to be enemies. We don't, we just don't."

At the foot of the mattresses.

Baseball bat. That's what it was. He was going to bash my head in, that's what he was going to do. Fuck *me*, Bobby Tremain was Death and grimmer by far than the Reaper could ever hope to be.

"Bobby . . ."

"Get outta the bed."

"Sure, sure, right away." I scrambled from beneath the covers and judged my chances of getting around him and to the open door. They weren't good. They were so bad to be nearly non-existent. Bobby was just too big, he took up too much room, his arms were too long, the bat too heavy, the world too goddamned unfair. I was going to die for paying back in kind? I was going to end up a bloody mass of brain and teeth in a Haight-Ashbury condemned apartment house? While Pet slept oblivious and woke to find her drug dreams have invaded the real world? In Bobby's inelegant parlance, what kind of shit was this?

It's hard to believe it when you're about to die. You try to think of anything, but that. You do little calculations of your chances and weigh them in your favor. You pray, I don't care if God left you high and dry when you were in the cradle. You think up great excuses, beautifully exaggerated lies, and make yourself believe they're working. Because if they aren't, the alternative isn't even thinkable.

Bobby came toward me and I squeezed shut my eyes against him. He was Raw Hide and Bloody Bones from my Alabama childhood, he was the Swamp Thing, he was Frankenstein's monster and the faceless intruder who came to people asleep in their safe homes. He was a force of Nature against which there is no recompense.

"No, Bobby, please."

He gently moved me aside so he could stand next to the side of the bed I'd just vacated. His touch made me jangle and jump like a rabbit in a cage. "Bobby . . . don't . . ."

"I won't," he said softly and then lifted the long spear of dark in both hands and crushed Pet's skull with one fast heavy downward stroke.

"JESUSJESUSOHMYGODNONONONO!"

I was behind him and I had his arms and he was off balance and toppling, we were both falling and the floor came up, smacked us hard, and I screamed in his ear, screamed and screamed in his filthy, horrible, inhuman ear. We rolled, I scratched at his face, at his eyes, his nose, his mouth, his neck, his chest, his arms. I screamed and he screamed and the night bloomed napalm lights as he struck me and I struck back hard as I could, hard as I knew how, hard as my frenzy allowed. The bat skittered under the bed, the bloody weapon was lost, and Bobby was scooting for it, frantic to have possession again, so he could bash me, so he could do to me what he'd done to a poor, sleeping, totally innocent dreamer. His legs flailed to free himself from the lock I had on his body, and I heard it -*crack*- the way you hear thunder erupting on the edge of a blast of ozone from a bank of storm clouds. His leg, broken again, shattered I hoped, splintered to a million pieces, like . . . like . . . Pet . . . like . . . Pet . . . shattered, splintered, broken.

Smashed. Beyond redemption.

Hit him, hit him, that's all I could think, hit him until he stops, until he vanishes, until he's gone, until he's dead, dead, dead and gone.

Three street loungers, guys hopped up on something or other, stumbled into the foyer led on by our screaming. They tottered into the melee, only sober enough to take Bobby from my fury and hold him while the police came for him and the ambulance came for what was left of Pet.

"Man," one of my rescuers kept saying. "Man, this is shit-for-brains, this is bad, dude, this is sick and revolting, you sonofabitch, how'd you think you could do this, don't cry, you fucking whiner, we don't care if your leg hurts, we *hope* it hurts, by God, we hope it fucking *kills you,* man!" Then he kicked him. And kicked him some more before the cops showed.

Well, it didn't kill him. Left him further maimed, but it was the state who killed pretty Bobby Tremain. Not literally. He died in a prison riot, shot right through his gorgeous heart, was the report. Sometimes, like really, there's a little justice out there in the lousy establishment, you know what I'm telling you?

I heard in later years Jerry married a jockey and set up his own television repair shop in Cairo, Illinois.

I drove through Louisville recently to show my teenage girls where I had lived and worked on Chestnut Street. The hospital had been razed to the ground. Only the cement steps remained leading up to a flat grassy expanse open to the sky. The sleazy apartment house was gone too and in its place stood a one story modern office building. Even the detention center was gone. It was as if none of it had ever been, as if 1967 had been but a fantasy. But lots of people from that year feel that way. You ask them, find out.

"I met a boy in that hospital," I told my daughters as we drove slowly past what had been and was no more. "He was the prettiest thing, but . . ."

"Boys aren't pretty, Mom. Boys are handsome or good-looking or cute. *Girls* are pretty."

They have a lot to learn, my young feisty children. But I doubt if warnings will do a bit of good. At least that has been me and my grandmother's educated experience.

You can't persuade a girl to stay away from a pretty boy. You can't tell a woman there aren't any heavensent angels walking this mean earth.

The Life and Deaths of Rachel Long

Kristine Kathryn Rusch

The fifth time she died, she took the guitar with her. She went down in a haze of smoke and ash, bullets and flames.

And this time, not even the music remained.

*   *   *

My mother claims my grandmother was a good Christian woman, but I disagree. The woman I remember spoke of walk-ins and souls too strong to die. She said that she and my grandfather had "unfinished business" and would meet in another life. The year before she died, I asked her what would happen if she didn't get another life. "I guess I'll just have to be a haunt, Devon," she said, "and wait for your granddaddy's soul to reappear so's we can settle things in right and proper fashion."

My grandmother's beliefs made more sense to me than my mother's good Christian ones. Perhaps that's why I'm the one to chronicle Rachel Long's life and deaths. I'm one of the few with the foundation to understand the entire story.

*   *   *

The first time she died, she died alone in her apartment: the Emily Dickinson of modern folk music. Someone had strangled her, squeezed the songs out of her talented throat. No one seemed to know who or why she was. It was an enterprising neighbor—the same one who called the cops—who found the sheet music shoved in the belly of her stringless guitar.

The stuff of legend is always difficult to trace. A few years ago, I located a computer record of the first death certificate, a brief newspaper article about violence on the lower South Side which mentioned her, and a photograph of the sheet music. Nothing else remains.

*　　*　　*

The first time I saw her, I was nearly thirty. My second wife had just left me, and I spent my nights in bars, nursing one drink and the pain in my heart. In the mornings, I saw shadows like charcoal smears under my eyes and frown lines digging into the corners of my mouth. I sold cars then: twelve-hour days at minimum wage unless some sucker came in and took a vehicle off my hands. Days that consisted of cigarette smoke, stale coffee and boredom, punctuated by moments of upbeat salesmanship and cold calls. Not quite the life for a B.A. in Business, but I was good at sales, and I had two alimony payments to make.

I don't know what made me go to the Wild Hall. I hadn't been there since college and it hadn't changed in those eight years. The stage was still tiny: one raised platform with room for a stool, two amps and a mike. The scarred wooden tables clustered together like kittens on a frosty morning, and the patrons—young and old—wore ripped denim, long hair, and no makeup. I had dressed down that night, stone-washed jeans and a wrinkled shirt, but I still wished I had a hat to cover the stylish cut that curled around my ears. The Hall served beer and wine, and as I took my Guinness, I noted that the conversational din had an energy I hadn't heard in years. The place smelled of pot, popcorn, and clove cigarettes, and that too seemed a welcome change of pace.

I found a wobbly chair in the back corner, no candle on the table, far away from the lights, and waited for the entertainment. I didn't have to wait long.

She was a tiny woman—five feet and a hundred pounds on a good day. Her face had a Vogue model's anorexic beauty and her skin had that lovely dark cream color that suggested a large percentage of white blood. She clutched an accoustic guitar to her chest as if she were hiding behind a lover, but she scanned the audience with the calm of an old pro.

"Good evening," she said. Her voice was husky with hints of some kind of southern drawl. "I'm Rachel Long. I'd like to sing for you."

The cries of the small crowd almost drowned out her last words. She swung into a fast-paced piece with a guitar part that made the instrument sound like a three-piece band complete with drums. I knew something about guitar; had fancied myself a bit of a talent until I found out that I had more of a knack for promotion of any type. I couldn't have played this piece, not even in the days when I practiced for eight hours at a stretch. This kind of music belonged to someone born with strings against her fingers and songs within her mind.

The crowd clapped and stomped with the beat, already so familiar with her music that they didn't have to listen to it, they just had to feel it. I had to strain to hear her husky voice croon the lyrics because all the people around me sang too.

And the songs . . .

I didn't think anyone wrote songs like that any more.

Simple songs of simple injustices: the shooting death of a young black man on the South Side; lament for a rape committed in Carster's Park; ode to mine workers dead in a collapse caused by company negligence; a song to the earth; a song for peace; and a love song about two people who treated each other with warmth, respect and more than a little understanding.

All the while, I tapped my fingers and rocked with the beat, wishing I knew the lyrics that I too could sing along.

When the set ended, and she melted from the stage, I took my warm mug of Guinness, downed a bitter sip and congratulated myself for surviving a whirlwind. She had stripped me down to my idealistic nineteen-year-old self, the one who believed that protests could save the world, that each person who ate the right foods, recycled the right products and refused to pollute the environment would make a difference. The self who got drunk on his twentieth birthday when he realized that he had to survive in the cruel, cruel world, and that somewhere, somehow, he had to choose between principles and getting ahead. Several hundred commissions and two wives later, he

143

doubted if he made the right choice.

I left a tip on the table and staggered out of the Hall into the fresh clean air of the spring night. A car went by, tires swooshing in puddles left by a recent rain. I shivered in the damp chill, wanting to go back inside, but knowing that I didn't dare. I couldn't afford to be politicized, to see the life that I had built, to see the emptiness of the world around me. A world that consisted of an expensive bachelor's apartment in an all-glass high rise overlooking the lake, a job I didn't much like, and evenings spent in bars listening to people make music of the kind my fingertips once owned.

I went back the next night, and the next, each time staying longer and listening for the meanings behind the words, singing along before I could catch myself and shut off the voice.

I was there every night for the next two weeks — until the night she died.

*   *   *

I had a date that night, a pretty young client who wandered away from my Geo Storms and bought herself a Mazda instead. We had dinner, a drink or two, and I found myself talking about the Wild Hall, about music, about politics. I asked her to join me, to hear Rachael Long, and my date shook her head. She liked pop music and hated politics; she would rather go home. I dropped her off without kissing her — odd because dipping into pretty women on the first date had become an addictive challenge for me. I found myself driving to the Wild Hall, to clove cigarettes, Guinness beer, and my nineteen-year-old ideals.

Rachel was already on stage when I arrived and the only table remaining was a tiny one to her left, tucked against the rough wood wall. I sat there, clutching the cold beer stein against my fingers, and listened to the music wash through me. Her words seemed to have more power than usual — or perhaps I later embellished the memory, thinking the added power in her words gave her death some meaning. I don't know. I do know that she was singing a new song, a song about love, togetherness and change, when a bang echoed through the room.

I looked around, not sure what had caused the sound. People were ducking, screaming, diving under tables. A man in the back

144

stood, a gun clutched in both hands. The light from nearby candles caught his eyes, glittering with a half-crazed passion. His hair was unwashed, his beard tangled and matted. I dove across the room, past cowering people, and overturned chairs, absorbing details as I went. I had to get to him before he shot Rachel, before he stopped her beautiful voice —

and then I realized that she wasn't singing. And he was no longer shooting. He was staring straight ahead, like a man awakening from a nightmare, and slowly, ever so slowly, he lowered his gun.

I turned. Rachel was sprawled backward across the stage, guitar cradled against her side like a newborn baby. The spotlight illuminated the blood on her chest and face. Her sightless eyes caught me for what seemed like an eternity. It wasn't until the sirens echoed outside that I realized the darkness between her chin and shoulders was not a shadow; it was more blood, covering all that remained of her throat.

*   *   *

The papers named him Neil Stebbons, a homeless alcoholic with no previous history of violence. He had stolen the gun from a pawn shop the week before and had waited at the Wild Hall for "the right song, the right lyric." The national press didn't touch the story, but locally Stebbons dominated the news for nearly nine months, even after his guilty plea eliminated the need for a trial.

I haunted music stores and folk concerts, searching for a voice like hers, a message like hers. I brought out my guitar and found myself picking at it for at least an hour per day. Wife Number One remarried and my alimony payments decreased. I got a new job selling books for a local textbook company at less base pay, but with room for advancement. I also had a travel budget, and by the time Stebbons disappeared from the local press, I had started marking out my sales territory, all across the Pacific Northwest. Someone gave me a bootleg tape (made on a handheld recorder) of one of Rachel's final concerts and I played it continually as I drove.

One night in Seattle, after a frustrating meeting with the buyer for the university's bookstore, I crawled into a dark, dingy bar, the kind of place I had thought existed only on film. Cigarette smoke gave the air a bluish haze and the smell of whiskey had seeped into the old polished wood. I was going to get plastered — roaring, stinking, outrageously drunk—so that I could forget the emptiness that had moved into my stomach on the night I first heard Rachel Long. Sometimes I blamed her for my declining commissions, for my lack of sleep, for the way my hands lingered over my guitar, searching for answers to questions I had never asked before. I hadn't liked the complacent life I lived before I went to the Wild Hall, but at least I lived it instead of agonizing over it.

I sat on the stool near the bar and ordered a particularly fine brandy, figuring that if I was going to drink, I would do it with style. Two snifters later, the lights dimmed even more and a spotlight haloed a tiny stage I hadn't noticed before. Someone had moved the piano to one side and covered it with a stained green cloth. The spotlight focused on an empty stool, and I fancied that Rachel Long would sit in it and sing to me one final time.

I turned away from the stage, unable to bear the thought of another musician trying to fill Rachel's shoes. My finger caressed the rim of my glass, making a small hum. Mixed with that and the scattered applause, I heard the words that I wanted to hear: *Good evening. I'm Rachel Long. I'd like to sing for you.*

I swiveled so fast that I spilled my brandy. She stood on stage, a little thinner than I remembered, and not quite as beautiful. She clutched the guitar like a lover and the sounds it made sent shivers down my back.

"Who is she?" I asked the bartender.

He shrugged. "They hired her this morning. All they told me was someone was going to sing tonight."

I picked up my brandy and took a table closer to the stage. She sang all of the songs I had on my tape, in the same order and with a similar precision. Then she shuddered once, lifted her eyes to the light, and began playing the song she was singing when she died.

I had had enough. I pushed my chair back and ran out to the street. The air was fresh with the scents of a recent rain. A homeless man slept against a trash can, his body half-hidden under a soggy cardboard box. Rachel sang about the homeless. She sang about the way people mistreated each other, about the way they should love and care for each other.

I was drunk. I had to be. I wandered down the street to my car and drove back to the hotel. The next morning, I left Seattle early, decided to forfeit my commission and return to the quiet, familiar emptiness of my home.

*   *   *

I set my guitar aside, placed the tape in an old box, and focused on my job with renewed vigor. Wife Number Two remarried and my income rose. After three promotions, I bought my own house. I became West Coast Regional Head of the Sales, and the only thing that impressed my sales team (besides my sales record) was my talent for tall tales and my staunch refusal to drink.

The women changed too. Instead of one night stands, I established a girlfriend in each of my major stops. None of these women were the ice-blonde beauties I used to prefer. Sharon, in San Francisco, was part Cherokee. Amita, in Seattle, was from India. Rose, in Los Angeles, was Eurasian. They were all exceptionally thin, and their voices were soft and musical.

I was at Amita's when I saw the news in the *Seattle-Post Intelligencer*:

> SINGER DIES IN BARROOM BRAWL
> (Tacoma)—Popular folk singer, Rachel Long, died Sunday night after a crazed fan stuck a knife in her throat during a fight. The violence erupted shortly after seven in Pete's Tavern while Long performed her first set of the evening. Andrew Slescher, a regular attendee of Long's performances, argued with an unidentified patron over the lyrics of one of Long's songs. The argument turned into blows. Patrons tried to stop the fight, but Slescher slipped free, ran to the stage, and stabbed Long in the throat. No other patrons were injured.
>
> Long was a popular attraction at Pete's Tavern, where she began singing nearly a year ago as a complete unknown . . .

I set the paper down and leaned on Amita's cutglass dining room table. The room's honey and roses scent suddenly became cloying. Amita stood across the room, long and luxurious in the satin robe I had bought her for her birthday.

"Something wrong?" she asked.

147

I opened my mouth to tell her, then thought about how the words would sound. "An acquaintance of mine died," I said.

"I'm sorry," Amita said, with all the sincerity of a check-out clerk bidding good day. She grabbed the large silver pot from the center of the table. "More coffee?"

I nodded and closed the paper. My hands were trembling just enough for Amita to ignore them. I promised myself that as soon as I left the house, my investigation of the entire strange incident would begin.

* * *

The newspaper accounts were clear enough: Rachel Long, budding folk musician, murdered in her Chicago apartment; Rachel Long, budding folk singer, murdered in an Oregon nightclub; Rachel Long, popular folk singer, murdered in a Seattle-area bar. I felt as if I looked hard enough, I would find a Rachel Long in every city in the country.

I even read books on folk music to see if Rachel Long was an historic mythic figure, the kind that young musicians would emulate and try to become. In all my research, I found nothing. Nothing except for one odd fact:

The man who found Rachel's body in her Chicago apartment was named Neil Stebbons.

* * *

By the time I took over a dying rep's route in northern Idaho, I had started playing Rachel's tape again. I was driving a Porsche with an elaborate sound system. The cassette deck replayed the tape over and over without any effort from me. Rachel's voice sounded scratchy and far away, not the rich full sound I remembered from the Wild Hall. I would sing along, my own voice rusty and off-key after years of disuse.

I spent two days in the small town of Moscow, Idaho. Moscow was an oasis of culture set in the rolling wheat fields of the Palouse. Home to the University of Idaho and host of one of the largest jazz festivals in the nation, Moscow had good restaurants, good bookstores, and friendly people. As I sat in an outdoor cafe, listening to street musicians improvise a jazz riff, I thought about giving up everything —the house, the money, the women—and living there, in that small town, eating vegetarian food and fighting for causes almost no one believed in. The thought seemed so attractive that I scanned the paper for apartments, and did odd calculations on a napkin to see if I could live off my savings.

Then I remembered that I had been listening to Rachel Long on the way into town, and a shudder ran down my back. I only thought about changing my lifestyle when I listened to Rachel's music. Perhaps she had put some sort of subliminal message in there, some way that she had planned to change the world. Or perhaps a part of me really did want to change.

I left the newspaper and the street musicians and returned to my car. I had finished my work half a day ago, and had been hanging out in the town just because I liked it. I drove to the Best Western on the far end of town and checked out, feeling the same kind of urgency I had felt in Seattle a year before.

Rachel's voice eeked out of the stereo system and I switched it off. I still had other places to go, new accounts to see and a new rep to hire. I wanted to get a new couch for my living room and one of those large screen, oversized t.v.s. I had goals and obligations, things I couldn't chuck for a teenage vision of life in a college town.

The hitchhiker at the side of the road stood out against the checkerboard swatches of rolling wheat field. She was thin, a guitar strapped over her back, and a green duffel at her feet. I pulled over before I thought about it and eased the passenger door open with my right hand.

"Where're you going?" I asked.

"I don't know," she said, her soft, musical voice sending a chill through me. "Some city where they like music. This town is a bit too small."

"Get in." I leaned away from the door and put both hands on the steering wheel. The words had come out before I could stop them and I knew that I would regret them sometime down the road.

She got in, put her guitar and duffel behind the seat, and slammed the door. She was even smaller off stage, the bones in her hands and arms showing like knobby limbs of a starving child. "I'm Rachel," she said.

"I know," I replied.

149

*   *   *

That night, in a hotel room in Boise, she allowed me to touch her guitar. It had the warmth of a live thing. I sat on the edge of one of the queen sized beds, holding the guitar, and she sat behind me, her arms wrapped around me, her thin hands over mine. She pressed my fingers to the strings, and helped me pluck a tune. I had never made a guitar sound so rich or so fine. We seemed to form a conductive loop: the music flowed from her to me to the instrument to the air and back through us again. The feeling was more than erotic; when she finally let me go, I vibrated with an energy I had never felt before.

"How do you do it?" I asked, setting the guitar down.

She didn't answer.

I turned. She was asleep on the bed, a rosiness to her cheeks that hadn't been there before, a glow that had not been present in the car. I caressed her face, then pulled away. She was too young, too fragile to make love to. I didn't want to shatter the illusion of beauty and magic in a single act of sweat and release.

So I picked up the guitar and retreated to the plastic chair near the curtained window. The instrument's warmth seemed to have left it and it felt almost brittle to my touch. I played a few chords; they sounded off-key and jangled to my ears. Frustrated, I set the instrument down, and stared at Rachel, too wired to sleep and to exhausted to do anything else.

*   *   *

The sound of a guitar woke me. The large black-out curtains were open, and through them, I could see Rachel sitting on the balcony overlooking the pool. Her feet were braced on the rail and she was almost supine, guitar resting on her belly. I didn't recognize the song she played and she didn't sing the lyrics. It almost seemed as if the music flowed through her instead of from her.

I slid out of bed, slipped on my jeans, and walked through the open glass doors. The air outside was cool—the sun hadn't yet had a chance to add the blistering heat of midday—and goosebumps rose on my bare chest. I pulled over the other balcony chair, a white plastic thing stained with dust, and sat beside her.

"I was thinking—" I said, only semi-truthfully. I had awakened with the thought and hadn't had the chance to comtemplate it fully "—that you need a promoter. I'm doing well for myself. I could afford to take some time, get you jobs, help you work your way to Los Angeles and a recording contract."

"Fame and acclaim," she said softly. Her words sounded like part of the vocal track for the guitar piece she continued to play.

I heard the subtle sarcasm in her tone. "And a chance to get your message out."

She smiled and continued to play for a few minutes. Below, a child screamed as he dove into the pool. Water rose in the air and splattered on the edge of the balcony, cool against my bare feet.

"I think you're good," I said, "and I don't care how—" I stopped myself before I added *how strange the circumstances of your existence are* "—how long it takes. I know we could get you a measure of fame."

"And fortune." Again, her soft words had that edge. She stopped playing, set her guitar down and sat up. "You don't understand, do you? I am a folk musician. If I play for profit, if I go out into the mechanized world, I become something other."

"Tracy Chapman, Joan Baez, Michelle Shocked, Bob Dylan, Peter, Paul and Mary—they all perform and record. How else does a musician sustain his art?"

"The old way." She didn't look at me as she spoke, but stared straight ahead as she had when she played. I glanced that way and saw nothing but blue sky dotted by a few very white clouds.

When I didn't respond, she smiled and picked up her guitar. "I made this guitar a long time ago," she said. "It has parts of me in it, as does my music. I am a *folk* musician, a musician of the folk, of the people. My music arises from the people around me and becomes something else for those people, a reflection of dreams, of hopes, of to-bes. The kinds of things that never die."

"You're not real, are you?" The question slipped out, sounded strange on that brightly lit morning, with the slender woman at my side.

She smiled and looked at me, truly looked at me, for the first time. "I'm as real as you are," she said. "I have just found my own inner strength."

*   *   *

151

At her request, I left her in Salt Lake City and drove on. In the silence of the car, I sang the songs she taught me and my fingers itched for a guitar made from parts of me. By the time I reached San Francisco, I was shaky and woosy, and a fear had settled in the base of my belly. I knew of a guitar-maker in Santa Cruz, but I didn't drive down. Instead, I haunted bars and nightclubs, searching for Rachel's kind of music and finding only snatches of it, floating in the center of a song, at the end of a note.

I went to the library, did more research, and discovered an unsettling fact: Andrew Slescher, the man who had killed her in Tacoma, had owned the Wild Hall when Rachel sang and died there. He had influenced her career in the same strange way that Neil Stebbons had, and like Stebbons, he had killed her in her next life.

That news didn't stop me from seeing Rachel each time I drove through Salt Lake, although her music made that fear in my stomach grow stronger. I found myself giving away money to homeless people, to charity organizations, to anyone who appeared to be in need. I pushed textbooks on social trends and reforms to my buyers. Still the fear remained. I had been right all those years ago. The little efforts of one person were not enough to make the kind of difference that I wanted to make.

About three months after I had dropped Rachel in Salt Lake, I stopped at the coffee house where she had been playing and felt the fear intensify when I saw the police tape blocking the entrance. Two police cars parked outside. Inside, I saw people moving. A man leaned against a telephone pole, hands shoved into his pockets, watching. Other people stared as they passed by, but they didn't stop.

I walked over to the man. He looked vaguely familiar, and it took me a moment to remember that he owned the restaurant. He didn't move as I approached.

"Let me guess," I said. "Rachel Long."

Slowly, he turned and looked at me. His eyes were haunted, an expression I recognized. "How did you know?" he asked.

"It's happened before." Another policeman crossed under the tape. I wondered if they had removed her body yet, and then decided that I didn't want to know. I would wait for her to return before I saw her again.

"You knew her?" His voice sounded rusty, unused. It had a musical quality that had almost faded away.

"I brought her to Salt Lake."

He nodded. I studied him closely. The haunted look had latched onto his eyes, centered in the worry lines on his forehead. Neil Stebbons had had such an expression, only it had been accented by time and deterioration. Andrew Slescher probably had the same kind of countenance. And so, I would wager, did the person who killed her that night.

"You gave her a job, supported her, helped her?" I asked.

"Yeah." The hands in his pockets balled into fists.

"Then don't search her out."

He frowned, glancing at me as if I were crazy—and maybe I was. I was discussing Rachel's fourth death with a man who was seeing such tragedy for the first time. I was calm, unworried. I knew that she would be back.

"Leave music alone for a little while," I said, trying to make myself sound a bit more sane. "Just let Rachel ease into the back of your mind. I've seen this kind of thing before. You could obsess on it if you let yourself."

"I already am," he said softly. "I've been dreaming her music, listening to its words, wondering if I should change—you know, give up things."

"I know," I said. "But as far as you're concerned, Rachel's gone. Let it stay that way."

A police officer waved from the door and beckoned the man inside. He waved back and turned to me. "I appreciate the talk," he said. "You're welcome here anytime if I can keep this thing open."

"Thanks."

"I'm Ricky Stubs. Just ask for me when you come in."

"I will," I said. I watched him walk, head down, back to his restaurant, and wondered what made me refuse to give him my own name.

*   *   *

The waiting began. I sold my house and went to work at the Mission. I joined the city task force on the homeless. I found a small house with a vegetable garden on the far side of Bay Area, and ate only naturally grown, naturally produced things. In my spare time, I took voice lessons.

My voice teacher told me of her return. "There's a singer you must hear," he said one afternoon in early summer. "Her name is Rachel Long, and she just started playing at the Wooden Nickel."

I thanked him and stayed away. I had helped her too, in her last life. She had as much to fear from me as she did from Ricky Stubs.

But she didn't think so. She showed up at the Mission late one afternoon and found me dishing out a vat of rich vegetable soup to the people shuffling through the line. She had lost her beauty, and she was thin as a famine victim, only without the characteristic distended stomach. Her guitar, slung over her back, shone in the florescent light. She waited until I was finished, then sidled up beside me.

"You haven't come to see me, Devon," she said.

I took her arm and led her into the office. I leaned against the edge of the paper-covered desk and gave her the only chair. "You know why not."

She didn't sit down. Her smile was wistful, almost sad. "You still don't understand, do you?"

I frowned and waited for her to explain.

Her thin hand brushed mine. "All the very best folk tales have an inevitability to them. That inevitability gives them their power and their strength."

"I don't want to hurt you, Rachel," I said.

Her nod seemed wise. "I know," she said.

* * *

The Wooden Nickel was a coffee shop that served beer and wine, and brought in musical attractions from all over the West Coast. I hovered near the rustic, Old West exterior for nearly forty-five minutes, watching people enter and not leave. I carried nothing. She wanted me there to play out some kind of drama, and I wasn't sure if I would be doing us both a favor by leaving and refusing to accept the inevitable. Finally I decided that she knew more about mysteries than I did.

I went inside.

The interior was lighter than I expected. The entire restaurant had been decorated in unstained pine. Real kerosene lamps flickered on the tables and walls. The place was full. Rachel stopped singing, glanced at me, smiled and nodded. I nodded in return, pulled an empty seat from a crowded table, and sat in the middle of the aisle. A waitress came to serve me, but I waved her away. I wanted to hear Rachel. I didn't want anything to disturb that.

She had become all voice and guitar. Her songs were different, more militant, with talk of struggles even after death. The haunted look I had seen on Ricky Stub's face was also on hers. The messages of love and hope were still there, not as an end, but as a salvation. *Only love and hope survive*, she sang, *for in them lies the best of us.*

The crowd sang with her on the songs they knew, clapped with the ones they didn't. Finally, a woman in a long print dress stood up front and began to dance. Others stood and swayed too. The waitress tried to stop them — saying something about fire code — but no one listened. I stood on my chair so that I could see Rachel. The fear had returned to my stomach, fear for her, and I glanced around the room, looking for familiar faces. I didn't see any. I clenched my hands into fists and trapped them under my arms. My hands were the only weapons I had. I wasn't going to free them to hurt Rachel.

The smell of smoke started it. Two kerosene lanterns had fallen to the floor. Maybe the dancing had loosened them or maybe it was deliberate. All I know is that someone screamed and people ran as little rivulets of flaming kerosene ran across the floor. Rachel kept singing, the words lost in the screams.

I ran for her, but the crowd caught me, moving me toward the door in their panic. I pushed against them, reaching for Rachel, alone on the stage floor, her guitar in her hands. Her voice lilted as she sang. She did nothing to save herself, smiling as if she were receiving an ovation. My feet swept out from under me and suddenly I was on the floor, protecting my head as people stepped on me, over me, around me. In a stampede, anything on the floor got trampled to death. Rachel and I both would die. I tried to pull myself up, but couldn't. Smoke filled my lungs and water streamed from my eyes. The room had grown unbearably hot. I crawled toward the stage. Flames danced at the edge of it, licking Rachel's feet. Finally, a hand reached under my armpit, yanked me to my feet. Ricky Stubs pulled me against his left side, his right hand still clutching his gun. I struggled against him, but he was stronger. He pulled me into the fresh air and held me there as I gulped it like water. A fire crew had arrived, but behind me the building had already become an inferno and all they could do was splash water from outside.

Ricky stayed beside me until I could breathe easier. "Why?" I whispered.

"I owe you," he said. "I should have listened to you."

I shook my head. My throat felt raw as if the fire had gone inside and destroyed it. "No," I said. "Rachel."

"Oh." He sat on the wet ash-covered curb, dangling the gun from his hands. "I couldn't get her out of my head."

*　　*　　*

The fire burned too hot to retrieve Rachel's body. No one else died. They took me and about 100 other patrons to the hospital and they took Ricky to the police station at his own request. The next morning they let me out, with a caution about overdoing, and some creme for the minor burns I sustained on my arms and legs. I didn't go home. I went to the Wooden Nickel instead.

The familiar police barracade surrounded the still-smouldering ruins. I hugged myself as I stared at it and remembered the night in Boise as she showed me how to play the guitar. Neil Stebbons had found her guitar in Chicago and his desire to hear her music again brought her back, just as my desire brought her back in Moscow almost a year before. Each return ate up more of her, and yet she continued to give. Only this time, no one killed her. Her personal cycle had ended. All that remained of Rachel was a scratchy tape made on a hand-held tape recorder. Something other. Something not folksy at all.

I took a plastic bag and a metal gardening trowel from the car, then I climbed under the police tape to the edge of the ruins. I stepped lightly toward the spot where the stage had been. Then I scooped up charred and ash-covered wood, and placed it in the bag. I was tampering with evidence, but I didn't care. I climbed back out, got into my car and drove to Santa Cruz. I stopped in front of the guitar maker's and asked him to teach me how to make a guitar.

He did. And I use that guitar every night, as I sing for the people in the Mission. I watch for half-crazed eyes, knowing one night I'll see a face I recognize, a haunted face that wants to silence me. I may let it try, knowing that it won't succeed.

My grandmother would probably say that Rachel Long has walked in and replaced my soul.

But she would be wrong.

Merlin and the Hitman

Teri White

Farrow knew that he was losing his mind.

He could not quite remember when the knowledge of that fact first came to him, but over the last six months or so, it had become clearer every day.

He was going crazy.

There was no way of knowing why this was happening to him. Maybe it was something physiological. Like a brain tumor or cancer. Or perhaps this was a purely emotional thing, although Farrow didn't like to think that; he was a man who had always prided himself on his ability to keep his emotions under strict control. Had to, in his line of work or else you'd . . . freak out.

His best guess was that it was all in the genes. Hereditary. Now that he actually stopped to think about it, his mother—who died when he was fifteen—must have been a little schizo, not just the looney drunk he always assumed. And who the hell knew what he'd inherited from the father he'd never known?

When you came right down to it, *why* he was losing his mind wasn't the important thing anyway. What mattered most was what he could do about it. No doctors, that was for damned sure, and no shrinks either. There were too many secrets in his life that couldn't be spilled under anesthesia or therapy. He'd even come to the conclusion that insanity wasn't the worst way things could end for him.

And over the last few weeks, he had even managed to come up with a solution to his problem. Once upon a time, he'd spent a vacation on a small and unpopular island in the Carribean. Empty beaches and lots of water, along with a population of pleasant, non-curious inhabitants. It seemed like a nice enough place for a man to go crazy.

Of course, as always, money was a sticky detail. In order to live the way he wanted to, he would need quite a lot of cash. Enough to last him until . . . well, until whatever.

In light of that, Farrow decided to take on one more job. It was something he'd never done before, but now the risk seemed acceptable.

Farrow was going to kill a cop.

*   *   *

"I must be going crazy," Spaceman Kowalski muttered. "What the hell business do I have getting married again? At my age?"

His partner, Blue Maguire, had been listening to that or similar remarks for most of the past week, as the day for the planned nuptials drew even closer. By now, he was mostly just ignoring the complaints. He could afford to be nonchalant, because all he had to do was show up on time and remember to bring the ring. A best man had all of the fun and none of the pressures.

Blue was only sorry that the wedding wasn't going to be formal, because he hadn't worn his tux since transferring out of the department's public relations office. It would have been nice to dress up again. But Spaceman had drawn the line at that, so Blue had to settle for getting a new blazer.

He'd offered to throw a bachelor party for the groom tonight, his last as a free man, but Spaceman even passed on that honor. So they just had one drink at a bar near the station house, and then they went their separate ways.

Blue stopped at Yves St. Laurent to pick up his blazer from alterations and then browsed along Rodeo until he decided on an Austrian cut crystal wine carafe and glasses as a wedding present. Spaceman, of course, was more the beer-from-the-bottle type, but

Lainie would appreciate a touch of class, he thought.

Finally, he had a steak at Carroll O'Connor's Place and then went home.

* * *

Farrow never got nervous before a job.

Some people called him The Iceman. Even the prospect of killing a cop didn't seem to be shaking him up too much. But, still, he couldn't deny that his edge wasn't as sharp as it once had been. He could only suppose that going crazy did that to a man.

The cop lived way up in the hills above the city. Farrow parked on the next block over, down below the house, then climbed through the lush jungle until he was crouched next to the driveway. He smoked a couple of cigarettes, carefully shredding the butts and scattering the remains.

It seemed to be a very long time before a car turned into the drive. The driver's door opened and a tall, slender blond man got out. That was Maguire, all right, looking just like the picture provided by the client. He was carrying a box in one hand and a garment bag in the other.

Farrow shifted the gun to his left hand and stepped out of the bushes. "Here's a message from Owens," he said.

Maguire turned, surprised, started to speak, and Farrow fired once. Maguire hesitated and then crumpled to the ground, dropping the things he was carrying. There was a crash as the box hit the driveway. Farrow was getting ready to pull the trigger again, when he saw the eyes watching him. Yellow cat-eyes staring, unblinkingly, right at him. The animal was sitting on the porch.

Farrow was gripped with a sudden, altogether unprecedented sense of panic. Fear, in fact, such as he had never known before. He shifted the aim of the gun, intending to shoot the cat, but before his finger could tighten on the trigger, the porch was empty, the cat gone.

Farrow, still scared although he could not have explained why, turned and headed quickly back toward his car.

Damned cat.

* * *

The next awareness he had was of pain. It washed over him in unending waves, bringing him to the brink of blackness. Well, pain meant that he was still alive, and that was something. But he could also feel a warm wetness spreading across the front of his shirt and that was frightening. He might bleed to death right here in his own driveway.

Blue realized that he had to do something and quickly.

The house was too far away and he would never make it up the steps anyway. But there was a phone in the car. It was new, a birthday gift to himself, and Spaceman had made a lot of nasty cracks about it. Well, this pretty much proved him wrong, didn't it?

Blue managed to roll himself over and, using the car as support, finally stand. The blood seemed to gush even harder now and again dizziness seized him. Pass out now, he told himself firmly, and you probably won't wake up again. Except in heaven or hell or someplace in-between. He shook his head to try and clear away some of the fuzziness.

It took precious seconds to get the door open. Once it was, he fell inward across the seat and reached for the phone. There was a number, right? A number you were supposed to call when there was trouble . . . he couldn't remember the freaking number.

Instead, his bloody finger began to automatically punch out the only number he *could* remember. Instinct had taken over.

Spaceman answered with a distracted, "Yeah?"

Of course he was distracted; he was getting married in a few hours. Obviously pre-wedding jitters had really set in, Blue thought sympathetically. It was too bad to have to bother him with something like this right now. Except that I'm bleeding to death, Blue reminded himself.

"Who's this?" Spaceman said, now sounding impatient and more like his usual self.

"Me," Blue said, surprised at how weak his voice sounded. "It's me," he said again. "I need help. Some bastard just shot me. I'm at the house."

"What?" Spaceman said.

"I'm dying," Blue said.

The next wave of pain drew him down into the blackness.

*   *   *

162

Farrow signalled the bartender for another drink. He kept thinking that each additional jolt of whiskey would calm his jangled nerves. But it didn't seem to be working.

Most aggravating was the fact that he didn't even know what the hell he had to be nervous about. The cop was dead, must be, even though he hadn't stayed around long enough to deliver the second bullet, the insurance shot. But Maguire had been very still, bleeding all over the place, and nobody was around. Yeah, that cop was a goner.

So, then, what was making him so uptight?

Farrow swallowed half the new drink.

It was the cat.

And that, he knew was stupid. What the hell could a cat do? Squeal to the heat? It was absurd. A cat couldn't do anything. So why then was he so . . . unsettled about this?

All he had to do now was wait twenty-four hours for the rest of his fee to be deposited in the safe drop, and then he was out of here. He'd be on a plane to the Carribean, where a man could relax and quietly lose his mind.

Except that there was that damned cat, who saw him kill the cop.

Farrow signalled the bartender again.

The hooker who had been watching him from the far end of the bar moved closer. She was young, early twenties, he guessed, and not bad looking, for a whore.

Maybe this would help take his mind off the cat.

Farrow smiled at her and went into his charming persona. It took more effort than usual. Well, this would be his last lay in the good old U.S. of A., so he might as well try to enjoy it.

That called for another drink.

He resolved not to think about Maguire or the cat for the rest of the night.

*　　*　　*

The ambulance was already there by the time Spaceman arrived at Blue's place. He parked at the end of the driveway and propelled himself toward the flashing lights.

Two men in white were bent over a very still figure on a stretcher. "How is he?" Spaceman asked.

163

"Not good," was the answer.

"Can he talk?"

"Not until he's conscious," the other attendant said somewhat sarcastically.

Spaceman stepped back a little to give them room and glanced around. A team of uniforms had also arrived and was already searching the yard. "Find anything?"

"Nope," said one, a young woman whose name Spaceman couldn't remember at the moment. "Looks like somebody just walked up and shot him when he got out of the car." She gestured toward the ground. "Those things, we figure he was carrying."

Spaceman bent down for a closer look. A blood-smeared garment bag and a box wrapped in fancy paper and tied with silver ribbon. The box rattled and clinked when he lifted it. "Shit," he said to himself.

He stood again when the doors of the ambulance slammed closed. The siren began to sound as the vehicle hit the street.

There was a dark, wet patch that had to be blood on the driveway. Spaceman stared at it as he listened to the wailing of the siren disappear down the hill.

*　　*　　*

Farrow had no idea how many hotel rooms just like this one he'd been in over the last twenty years. Too many to count. But they all looked alike, so it didn't really matter. They all smelled the same, too. It made him a little tired to think of all those rooms and all those years.

He stopped pacing finally and went into the bathroom to splash some cold water in his face. Despite all that he'd had to drink during the evening, he still wasn't drunk. Farrow rarely got drunk, actually. Inebriation brought with it a loss of control which was unpleasant at best and which, in his line of work, could be fatal at worst.

Lately, however, his sense of control seemed to be slipping away anyway. Slowly, irrevocably, it seemed, he was losing touch. Not so much with the outside world, which had only ever been his tenuously, but with himself. With his sanity.

A perfect example was what had happened with the hooker hours before.

There had been no reason to kill her. Hell, pay her off and she'd be gone. But there was something odd about her or, more precisely, about the way she looked at him. Funny eyes. Almost like cat eyes.

It was crazy to kill her because she looked at him funny. But Farrow had done it and now he was irritated at himself.

Stupid things like that could get a man in a lot of trouble.

He was still bent over the sink as a shudder ran through him and he gripped the cool white porcelain for support. When he had the strength, he straightened and gazed at himself in the mirror. What he saw was a man just past forty, with brown hair starting to thin a little, pleasant eyes, and a forgettable face.

Farrow had never really thought that he looked like a killer. Now he peered closely at the face in the glass, wondering if any signs of his craziness could be seen there yet.

Everything would be all right, he told himself firmly, everything would be fine once he was on the beach.

If only that damned cat hadn't been there.

* * *

Lainie wanted to come over to the hospital, but he talked her out of it. "All right," she said finally, "but I'll start making some calls."

"Calls?"

"To postpone the wedding until he's better."

Spaceman was reminded of why he loved her. He told her that and also that he would be in touch as soon as he knew anything.

Lieutenant McGannon was waiting in the lounge when Spaceman got back there. "Any ideas?" he said briskly.

Spaceman was glad for the businesslike attitude; it made it a little easier for him not to give in to the rage waiting to break loose inside. He sat down next to McGannon and shrugged. "You know as well as I do what we've been working on. I don't think anybody felt threatened enough to do this."

McGannon just looked at him.

Spaceman grimaced. "But obviously somebody did. Unless this was just an act of random violence like they're always talking about on the news."

"Which you don't believe."

"Which I don't believe for a minute, right."

They stopped talking for a moment.

Spaceman leaned back in the chair and closed his eyes. He wasn't tired; he was just running a mental image of their desks. Case files. What were they working on? A couple of ordinary homicides. Some major league truck hijackings. A hit and run.

But why whack Blue over any of those? Or why not shoot both of them?

He had to be missing something.

"Did the canvas of the neighborhood turn up anything?" he asked.

"Not much. Couple people saw a strange car parked in the area. A tan Toyota. No plate number, though."

Spaceman tossed that around for a few moments, but it meant nothing. Impatient, restless, he crashed the chair to the floor and stood. "Damnit," he said.

McGannon didn't ask what he meant by that; McGannon had been a cop a long time.

Others were starting to arrive—cops, the press, some flack from the mayor's office, and in a suit that cost significant bucks, a lawyer that nobody knew. He introduced himself; he was, it seemed, in charge of Blue's millions. For the first time in a long while, Spaceman was reminded that his partner was a very, very rich man.

Maybe he could buy himself recovery from a bullet in the chest.

"I gotta get out of here," Spaceman said to McGannon.

"Keep in touch."

He nodded and pushed his way out of the increasingly crowded lounge.

What was he missing? What piece of the puzzle?

*　　*　　*

Farrow woke early, feeling as if he hadn't slept at all. He peeled off the sweaty, wrinkled clothes he'd worn to bed and stood under the shower until all the hot water was gone. As he started to shiver from the cold spray hitting his body, he stepped out and dried himself slowly.

The mistake he'd made was in breaking a lifelong rule. The rule was: You don't hit cops. He'd learned that, if not at his mother's knee, almost as early in life. Joe Herndon, the man who taught him the trade, drilled that message into Farrow every day.

You didn't whack a cop, because it was bad luck. It always got messy.

166

If he hadn't decided to break that rule, then the cat wouldn't have seen him.

Farrow was dressing carefully, because crazy people frequently let their appearance go to hell, and he didn't want that to happen to him.

That cat.

Of course, he knew that the cat couldn't really do anything. How could a dumb animal burn him? Maybe a *dog* could do something, like Lassie always used to, but not a cat.

He shaved and combed his hair.

The phone rang.

He let it ring twice more before answering. It was Owens. "Maguire isn't dead," he said in a cold, clipped voice. "What the fuck happened?"

"Not dead?" Farrow said, bewildered. "I shot him. He has to be dead."

"Well, he's not. All I want to know is, what are you going to do about it?"

Farrow tried to think quickly. "I'll handle it," he said to Owens. "Don't worry."

"You should be the one worrying," Owens replied. "If this isn't straightened out fast, you better start worrying big time."

Farrow hung up.

He sat on the edge of the bed and leaned forward, resting his head in his hands. It felt as if his skull might explode. He had to do something.

But first he had to get a rein on himself.

Then he had to go out and finish killing the cop. It was a job he should never have taken on, but now that he had, it must be finished.

He stood up and started strapping on his gun.

Whack the cop for good this time, yes. But first of all, he had to rid himself of the curse. He had to get that damned cat.

It was all the cat's fault.

*   *   *

Spaceman was downing his tenth or so cup of coffee as he pored over recent arrest reports. Nothing seemed to point him in the direction of a cop killer. Every thirty minutes, he broke off reading long enough to call the hospital, only to be told that there was nothing new to report. The surgery was over and had gone well, they finally told him, but nobody seemed to know how Blue was really doing.

He leaned back from the desk and rubbed his eyes with the heel of one hand. This was dumb, really dumb. He might as well be home in bed for all the good this was doing.

He left the office, but didn't go home, of course. Instead, he cruised the streets of the still-awakening city.

The constant chatter of the police radio kept him company as he drove. A call was put out about a dead body found in an alley not far from where he was and more out of habit than anything else, Spaceman headed over to the scene.

It was a dead woman, probably a hooker according to the beat cop who'd stumbled across her body when he'd slipped into the alley to take a quick leak.

Her throat had been cut.

Spaceman watched the commotion for a few minutes and then, restless, drove away to resume his pointless cruising.

It occurred to him that this was supposed to have been his wedding day. Maybe he was a little relieved not to be getting married, but he didn't think so. His mind wandered back to the hospital and everybody hanging around the lounge waiting for some word. Cops and reporters and that fancy lawyer.

A sudden thought struck him and he braked too sharply at a red light. He kept forgetting that Blue Maguire was more than just another cop. He was also rich. And follow the money was a primary rule of detective work. Follow the money. Maybe, just maybe, the shooting had nothing to do with department business. Maybe, instead, it had to do with all of Blue's money.

He made an illegal U-turn and headed for the hospital again, hoping that the fancy pants lawyer was still there.

*   *   *

You couldn't really find a cat if that cat didn't want to be found. Farrow, who had never known a cat before, hadn't been aware of that until now. He figured a couple minutes of "here, kitty, kitty," and the damned thing would come running. A dog would do that, right?

168

But not, it seemed, a cat.

After an hour of walking around the yard, calling in his kindest voice, Farrow retreated to his car again to think things over.

This was crazy.

And what was even crazier was that he *knew* it made no sense to be out here stalking a cat. But still, he couldn't quit. That cat could bring him down, even if he didn't know how.

He went in search of a store where he could buy a can of tuna fish or something to use as bait.

*　　*　　*

The lawyer's name was Goldblum and he didn't understand, at first, what Spaceman was trying to get at. Spaceman struggled for patience and askd him again. "Has there been anything unusual happening recently? Any problems?"

"What kind of problems?"

He sighed. "Whatever kind of problems multi-millionaires have. Some-thing that would get someone else mad enough to kill."

Goldblum looked as if the very thought left a bad taste in his mouth. "We are not dealing with street thugs. And Mr. Maguire is not involved in the day-to-day management of his holdings."

"I know that," Spaceman said. He rubbed a hand along his unshaven jawline. "But when a lot of money is involved, things don't always go the way they should. Sometimes even rich people kill each other, if you hadn't noticed."

Goldblum pursed his lips.

"Think, man," Spaceman said urgently.

After a few moments, Goldblum looked at him. "There was a corporate take-over about six weeks ago."

"A corporate take-over?" The words might as well have been in Chinese for all they meant to Spaceman.

"An unfriendly take-over," Goldblum amplified. "A small computer software firm."

"When you say unfriendly, does that mean somebody wasn't real happy about the whole thing?"

"I suppose it could mean that."

"Who, exactly?"

Goldblum thought again. "William Owens."

"Owens?"

"Founder and president of Owens Compu-Data. He fought the take-over with some bitterness. He even made what might be construed as threats."

"Against Maguire?"

"Against everyone involved. But no one took him seriously."

"Great. Where can I find William Owens?"

"I'll make a call."

Before Goldblum returned, a doctor walked into the room. "You're Kowalski, right?"

"Yes." He couldn't read anything in the other man's face. "What's happening?"

"Sergeant Maguire is conscious and would like to see you."

"Is he going to be okay?"

"His condition is satisfactory."

That was all the doctor seemed inclined to say, so Spaceman walked in the direction he pointed and found the room. A nurse was monitoring various lights and beeps, but Blue Maguire didn't look half-bad for a man who'd been shot only a few hours before.

"If you didn't want to be my best man," Spaceman said, "all you had to do was tell me."

Blue's mouth twitched. "You . . . married?"

"Without a best man?"

Blue stirred a little on the pillow. "I've been trying to remember . . . he said something . . . before he shot me."

"What?"

But Blue just shook his head.

Spaceman patted his arm. "Okay. Does the name Owens mean anything to you?"

After a moment, the foggy eyes cleared a little. "That was it . . . he said something about Owens. I don't know any Owens."

"He knows you, though. Well, don't worry about it, because super-cop Kowalski is on the case."

"Uh."

Spaceman figured it was time to leave. "I'll let you know how it all comes out," he said, starting for the door.

"Spaceman, wait."

"What?"

"Do me a favor?"

"Sure."

"Go by the house and feed Merlin."

"Feed who?"

"Merlin."

Spaceman frowned. "That cat of yours? You want me to take the time to go feed a cat? When I'm about to close in on the bastard who shot you?"

"Yeah, I want you to."

He sighed. "All right. But if he tears into me with his claws like he did the last time I fed him, I won't be responsible."

Blue almost smiled again and then, in the very next instant, he was asleep.

Spaceman stopped by the lounge to get an address from Goldblum and then he headed for the parking garage.

* * *

Farrow crouched in the bushes and stared at the open can of tuna fish that he'd set on the top step. His gun was at his side, but there was nothing to shoot at so far. Soon as that furry little bastard showed up, he would be history. Then Farrow would finish off the cop, collect his money, and head off into the sunset.

A happy ending.

Suddenly a car appeared in the driveway and stopped only a few feet away from where Farrow was. He ducked lower in the bushes. Damn. Couldn't anything go right on this job?

A man got out of the car. "Hey, Merlin," he called. "You wanna eat?"

Farrow couldn't believe his eyes: the damned cat ran across the yard and right up to the man. Maybe he hadn't come before because Farrow hadn't known his name.

Of course, now he couldn't do anything but sit where he was and watch the cat and the man go inside the house together. Unless he wanted to off the intruder, too, and Farrow didn't really want to do that. It was messy and, anyway, the big slob just about wore a sign reading COP. Killing one of them was trouble enough.

So he waited.

* * *

Spaceman saw the open can of generic tuna on the porch. "Somebody already feeding you, Merlin?" The cat didn't seem interested. "Guess whoever it was didn't know you only eat the high price stuff."

They went into the house and through to the kitchen. As Spaceman stood at the sink and opened a can of something that smelled better than a lot of the things he'd fixed for himself over the years, his gaze went out the window, across the deck, and down toward the street below. He almost dropped the can of food.

A car was parked there. A tan Toyota.

Very carefully, he dumped the catfood into a bowl and set it on the floor. He even remembered to put out clean water. "You stay here, Merlin," he said quietly. "I have to do a little work."

He left the house by the front door and got into his car without glancing around at all. His hand rested inside his jacket, on the gun there, but he didn't pull it out.

Instead, he just got into his car and drove away.

*   *   *

Farrow waited for several minutes after the car had disappeared before he crawled out of the bushes. At least now he knew that the cat was inside the house someplace. If he had to burn the whole freaking place down, he was going to eradicate that animal.

He forced the door open and slipped inside. After pausing a moment to listen, he followed soft sounds coming from the rear of the house. It sounded like water being lapped up.

Farrow smiled a little. Pussycat, pussycat, where have you been?

He walked silently into a bright kitchen. The cat looked up at him with absolutely no interest at all. "Bye-bye, Merlin," he whispered, raising the gun.

"Cats have nine lives," said a quiet voice from just behind him. "You probably only have one."

The gun barrel that was jammed against the back of his head paralyzed Farrow. He stared at the cat, who was licking its whiskers.

"Gimme that gun, you bastard." A hand reached around and took the weapon from him. Then his arms were yanked behind him and cuffs were clamped onto his wrists.

Farrow was spun around and saw the man he'd thought had left.

"You came back," he said. "Very clever."

"Thank you. I climbed up the hill, just like you. You're under arrest for attempted murder of a police officer and probably a lot of other things." He rattled off the standard spiel, which Farrow only half-listened to.

When all that was done, Farrow just smiled and shook his head. "I should tell you," he said, "that I'm going crazy."

"Right," the cop said. "Well, you can save it for the judge, because I don't give a damn."

"The cat gave me away, right?"

The cop just looked at him.

*　　*　　*

The hospital room was a little crowded, what with the witnesses and the judge and Lainie's maid of honor, not to mention the bride and groom. Maguire was lucky, of course; he didn't even have to get out of bed to perform his duties as best man.

Spaceman didn't complain about the mob scene. At least nobody expected him to dress up for a wedding being held in a hospital.

And so far, none of the nurses who had dropped in uninvited had spotted the cat under the blanket.

Anytime I Want

Andrew Vachss

She didn't answer my knock. I used the key she gave me to open the door. When I saw her lying on the bare hardwood floor, I knew he'd finally taken her. Like he always told us he would.

I went next door, rang the bell. The people there called the police, like I asked. I didn't scare them, didn't panic. I was polite, like I always am.

Two detectives came. I told them Denise was my sister. My big sister. They were all my big sisters, four of them. Denise was the baby girl, twenty two years old when he took her.

The cops asked me a lot of questions. It was okay—I'm used to questions. They asked me where I'd been, before it happened. That was the easy part—I work the night shift, plenty of guys at the plant saw me.

I gave them the names: Fiona, Rhonda, Evelyn. And Denise. My four sisters. I have one brother, Frankie. He's sixteen. I wasn't worried about an alibi for him—he was in the last month of a one year jolt with the state. Frankie's a big kid, and he's got a bad temper.

I'm nineteen. I work nights, go to college in the daytime. Weekends, I'm a thief. A careful, quiet thief.

Denise's face was all swollen, slash marks on her hands, trying

175

to stop the knife before it went in the last time. All her clothes were off, thrown around the room. He left her like that.

"Did you love her?" one of the detectives asked me.

"I still love her," I told him.

I went home, changed my clothes, put on a nice suit. I drove down to Pontiac. The guards like me there. I'm always polite, always respectful.

They brought Frankie out, left us alone.

I told him.

"Don't kill him until I get out," he begged me, looking at me with those big dark eyes.

"Can I count on you?" I asked him.

"Count on me? He's dead, Fal. On my honor, he's dead. You just make sure you got yourself a place where you can be seen, first night I come out of here."

Frankie calls me Fal—short for Falcon. Most of the kids in our club did. Because I was always watching. I leaned over close to him, talking quiet. "You remember, Frankie? Remember how it was . . . before we got out?"

His face was chiseled stone, big hands clenched the table. Scars all across his knuckles.

Our house. A terror zone. No locks anywhere, not even on the bathroom door. The basement, where he'd take the girls. One at a time. The leather strap, the one with the brass studs. I can still feel it across my back.

I was just a baby when he started with Fiona—Frankie wasn't even born. One after the other. His property. Mom tried to stop him once. I remember—I was eight, Evelyn was about thirteen. He made her suck him, right at the kitchen table. He made us all watch. "Anytime I want," is what he said. "My property—anytime I want." I tried to go after him—Denise held me back. It didn't do any good. He beat me so bad I woke up in the hospital.

Mom told them I fell down a flight of stairs. Into the basement, onto the concrete floor.

He never got Denise. She wouldn't do it. He broke her arm once, twisted it hard behind her back. I heard it snap.

I don't know what Denise told the hospital, but some social workers came to the house. The older girls, they all said Denise was a liar . . . she was staying out late, smoking cigarettes, drinking. Messing with boys. The social workers said something to him about counseling.

When they left, he punched me in the face. I lost two teeth. Then he took Rhonda down to the basement.

Denise tried to stab him once. With a kitchen knife, when he was holding my hand in the flame from the stove burner. I threw up on myself but he didn't stop.

The girls moved out, one by one. Fiona is a whore. She works in a club downtown, dancing naked. Rhonda killed herself with drugs. Evelyn went off with a biker.

He still sees Fiona. Anytime he wants.

Denise worked as a typist. For a lawyer. She was the smartest one, Denise. She was going to go to law school herself, someday. He picked her up once. Told her Mom was in the hospital. Drove her into an alley and went after her. Denise fought him to a standstill. She told the cops. They picked him up. He said it never happened—he was home with Mom all night. Mom was never in the hospital. But Denise was. Once before. A psychiatric hospital. When she tried to kill herself.

When the cops found out about that, they closed the case.

He always said he'd take her. She was his. They all were. Fred is his name. The girl's names were his brand. Fiona. Rhonda. Evelyn. Denise.

Frankie's name didn't matter. Neither did mine.

"Can I count on you?" I asked Frankie again.

He got it that time. Reached out his hand. "It has to be right," I told him. "For Denise. Blowing him up, it wouldn't be good enough. You understand?"

He nodded.

"No more nonsense, Frankie. Do the rest of your time, no beefs, got it?"

He nodded again.

I waited and I watched.

Mom said he was with her the night Denise was killed. It's an unsolved homicide.

Frankie got out on a Monday. I picked him up. He came to live with me.

Friday night we went in. The locks only took me a couple of minutes.

He never woke up. I left Frankie at the head of the stairs while I went down into the basement. Frankie had a tire iron in his hand. "If he comes downstairs, you can do it," I said.

I know where he keeps his trophies. In this little back room he built in the basement. Under a loose brick in the corner. A red silk scarf, a faded corsage from a dance, a pair of little girl's panties, white. And the pictures: Fiona on her knees, with him in her mouth, Rhonda bent over, something sticking out of her. Evelyn nude, lying down, a mirror between her legs. He didn't have any little girl pictures of Denise . . . just a Polaroid of her lying on the apartment floor. Naked. A knife between her breasts.

I took everything. Left him a note.

He's a creature. Needs his blood. After the girls left, whenever something went wrong, when he got stressed, he'd go down to his room, take out his trophies, say his prayers.

Saturday morning, I called the house. Mom answered, like she always does.

"Put him on," is all I said.

"What'd you want?" he challenged. Hard, aggressive. The way he told us you had to be . . . to be a man.

"Revenge," I told him, quiet-voice. "Revenge for Denise."

"Hey! I didn't have nothing to do with . . ."

"Yes. Yes, you did. You're going down. Soon. Very soon. Maybe a fire while you sleep. Maybe your car will blow up when you start it. Maybe a rifle shot. There's no place you can go. Nothing you can do. I'm good at it now. Stay there and wait for it, old man. It's coming."

I hung up the phone.

He called the next day. Frankie listened in on the extension. He told me how he was a sick man. How the girls had led him on, how Mom wasn't any good for sex anymore, what with all her plumbing problems. How he was going to see a psychologist, get all better. It wasn't his fault.

I told him I didn't know what he was talking about.

When Frankie called later to tell me the old man went out with Mom, I drove over there.

Frankie and I went in the back door, quick and smooth. I popped the fuse to the basement lights and went downstairs. I opened my briefcase, took out the sheets of clear soft plastic, like cloth. We wrapped the plastic around ourselves and we waited.

It was late when he came downstairs. We heard the click of the light switch. Nothing. He came back with a flashlight. Made his way into the little back room.

We heard the sound of the brick being moved. He made some beast-noise in his throat and ran out. Frankie and I took him before he got to the stairs.

We left him there on the concrete floor. He was just bloody pulp, no face left. A corpse, clutching the suicide note he wrote years ago.

Anytime I Want.

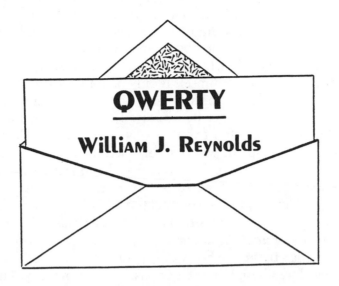

QWERTY

William J. Reynolds

It was Alexander Grimm's first "signing party." Also, he felt with certainty, his last. Grimm had signed a number of books in the eight months since publication of *The Killer Inside*, his account of how he and his special investigation team solved—or "cracked," as Grimm's editor like to say—a string of serial killings not quite two years ago. But those signings had been small, even cozy affairs in various bookstores here and there, consisting of nothing more than Grimm, a table bearing a dozen or so copies of *The Killer Inside*, and people who were interested enough to come in and meet him, some of whom even shelled out $18.95 for the book.

But tonight's "signing party" was something else again; Grimm was still working on making a positive identification. Half a dozen local authors of various degrees of renown, plus perhaps 50 times that many "civilians," all crowded into the overdone opulence of the Embassy Hotel's Ambassador Room, where they vied for soggy hors-d'oeuvres and cheap champagne as if they were the greatest delicacies imaginable, when in fact all they were was free. There were tables of books, too, *The Killer Inside* among them, but as far as Grimm could see, no one was showing them the slightest interest. Certainly no one was buying them. And no one, including Grimm, was signing them. Leaving Grimm to wonder why it was called a "signing party."

Reflecting on this, Grimm risked another mouthful of the alleged champagne—produced by a method that generated an enormous quantity of bubbles, and almost no flavor—and surveyed the room. Grimm had been approached by three or four well-wishers, and one fast-talking glad-hander who wanted him to ghost the "sure-fire" bestseller he would write himself if only he had the time, but otherwise Grimm had spent most of the last ninety minutes almost unnoticed—which was how he preferred things. He was fifty-eight now, widowed, retired after twenty-five years with the police department, and past the point where he needed or wanted to be always at the center of attention. If he had ever been at that point at all.

Clearly the show had two stars. One of them was an overweight woman with frizzy red hair who was the author of a dozen or more bestselling romance novels with names like *Love's Haunted Heart* and *Passion's Purple Fury*, whose cover art featured young women with gravity-defying figures who were about to be consumed by, presumably, love's haunted heart or passion's purple fury. The other was a man with craggy, pink features and an annoyingly loud voice. Grimm couldn't seem to keep a fix on the red-haired woman's name, but he knew the man. Everybody knew the man. Everybody knew Colman Howell.

Nobody liked Colman Howell, but everybody knew him.

For nearly thirty years Colman Howell had produced the thrice-weekly syndicated newspaper column "One Man's Opinion." And in those three decades Howell had honed to a lethal keenness his journalistic technique: Choose a popular cause, issue, or individual and oppose it, or an unpopular one and support it. Devil's advocacy, and so successfully plied that Colman Howell had created sworn enemies within both the Pro-Life and Pro-Choice camps; among environmentalists and industrialists; communists and fascists; the NAACP and the KKK.

Every year or two, a number of Howell's more flammable columns were assembled into book form—which, Grimm thought, must be a little like finding money on the sidewalk: the only work you had to do was bend over and pick it up—and the most recent of these, *Points of View,* was on display in copious quantities. For fear that people might miss those towering stacks, Howell's publisher had enlarged by roughly 500 percent the book's dust-jacket photograph of the unsmiling author sporting a go-to-hell look, and mounted it to the flocked wallpaper behind the *Points of View* table. In front of the table the author himself, as unsmiling as in his portrait, but pinker in the face, was holding forth to eight or ten seemingly fascinated men and women.

"These people have been fighting with each other for so long, nobody even remembers what it is they're fighting about," Howell was saying. "The people over there plain don't want peace — if they did, they wouldn't have been *killing* each other for the last four thousand years. There's nothing — but nothing — in that whole corner of the world that's worth a dime . . . except oil. What you need, then, is a bomb that will take care of the population and not harm the oil fields . . ."

"I don't understand why anybody gives that jerk the time of day," said a low voice in Grimm's left ear.

Grimm turned and looked up into the face of Michael Barrett. Curly haired, tall, and skinny as a table fork, Barrett had been a member of Grimm's team, the special squad that "cracked" the murders recounted in *The Killer Inside*. Although only thirty-four, Barrett was one of the finest detectives Grimm had ever worked with. When Grimm had put in for retirement, he also put in a good word for Barrett, strongly urging that Barrett be put in charge of the squad. That didn't happen — like all bureaucracies, the police department was wedded to the idea that seniority is a good indicator of competence — but the younger cop had appreciated his ex-boss's efforts. Appreciated them more than Grimm had realized: Grimm had put half a dozen of his former colleagues on the invitation list for tonight's event, but Barrett was the only one to show.

"The gainsayers, fault-finders, and bad-mouthers have always had their day," Grimm said in a response to Barrett's comment. "But usually it's been a short day. Howell's been carping about everything and everyone for about thirty years now, and he only gets more popular. That's what *I* don't understand."

"Colman Howell is one of the few people in the world with enough guts to say what *most* people really think," said a serious-looking young woman standing not far from them. She was slender, with dark hair that she wore short, and pale skin set off by a black evening-dress.

Grimm, who hadn't thought anyone was near enough to overhear him and Barrett, was embarrassed. He opened his mouth to speak, though he didn't know what he was going to say, when the woman's serious demeanor melted into a beautiful smile. "It's on the front cover of the book," she said with a chuckle. "Colman wrote it himself." She put out a slim hand. "I'm Francine McAdams. I work for Colman Howell."

"This is Michael Barrett. I'm Alexander Grimm." The two men shook hands with her.

"Alexander Grimm," she said reflectively. "Yes, I have your book. I'm afraid I haven't had time to start it . . ."

"That's all right," Grimm assured her. "I get paid for copies sold, not copies read. I hope we weren't too offensive, what we said about your employer . . ."

Francine laughed. "Listen, you guys are candidates for his fan club, by comparison," she said. "I've lost track of the number of death threats he's gotten since I came to work for him—thirteen months ago. Most of his mail is hate mail, to put it politely. A lot of it consists of just two words, the second of which is 'you.' He doesn't even have a phone in his office, because it's ringing all the time with complaints from this group or that."

"Hell of a way to make a living," Barrett said.

"I suppose. But it's great experience. Most women my age, twenty-three, a year out of journalism school, are interviewing prize-winning gardeners for the *Plotsville Courier-Ledger* or whatever. Me, I'm editorial assistant to the famous, or infamous, Colman Howell. And I'm on a first-name basis with most of the bomb-squad boys to boot." She laughed. "It'll look great on my résumé. Unless one of those mysterious packages with no return address really does contain a bomb someday. In which case it'll look great in my obituary."

From across the room, they could still hear the drone of Howell's stentorian voice, although crowd-noise drowned out the lyrics to his latest jeremiad. Francine McAdams watched her employer for a few minutes and then said quietly, almost as if she didn't realize she was speaking aloud, "It's probably only a matter of time before someone does do him in."

*   *   *

"On TV, someone predicts that so-and-so's about to get his, and you know it's going to happen before the next commercial break. But I never saw it happen in real life before." Michael Barrett's voice was breezy, bemused. Some people mistook this seemingly casual attitude for a lack of serious-mindedness. Those people, Alexander Grimm knew from experience, underestimated the young detective.

"Maybe it's because real life doesn't have commercial breaks," Grimm said.

Barrett chuckled. They were standing in the wide entryway of Colman Howell's huge Tudor-style house. The circular drive in front of the house was clogged with official vehicles representing half a dozen city and county offices, departments, and agencies. People in various uniforms prowled everywhere, intent on their individual tasks. It was noisy, confusing, almost overwhelming. It was to Grimm what water is to a guppy.

When Barrett had called, just over an hour ago, he told Grimm only that Howell was dead—murdered—and that Grimm might want to interrupt his retirement long enough to come have a look. He had said Grimm would "get a kick" out of what the crime-scene unit had found upstairs. Grimm knew there was no point pressing for details. When Barrett acted like this, clams became envious of him. If Grimm wanted to know what his friend was talking about, and he did, his only recourse was to rouse himself from his cluttered two-bedroom apartment and hope his old Grand Prix would hold together long enough to get him to Howell's place, out in darkest suburbia.

They climbed a wide staircase, passed down a short corridor, and went through a mahogany door guarded by a uniformed officer.

The room was large. Grimm presumed it had been intended as a bedroom, but in more recent times it clearly had been Howell's office. A large cherrywood desk dominated the room, which had floor-to-ceiling bookcases along two walls, high windows and a windowseat in the back wall behind the desk, and a connecting door in the side wall to the left. A burgundy leather sofa and matching armchairs were arranged around a low table near the hallway door.

The desk was strewn with papers, file folders, notepads, pens, books, and magazines, scattered in an apparently haphazard manner. A green-shaded lamp was positioned so as to illuminate a big, pale-red IBM Selectric typewriter on the return that jutted from the lefthand side of the desk.

"Run it down for me," Grimm said to Barrett, just as he would have in the old days.

Must be like riding a bicycle, Barrett thought, grinning to himself. "Assault took place last night," Barrett said, "probably between eleven p.m. and two this morning. Weapon was a pewter letter-opener, about as big as a sword. It's the victim's—he usually kept it on that mess of a desk. One strike, right side of the neck, opening the carotid."

"Ouch," Grimm said. He was studying a section of bookcase near the furniture arrangement. "This must be where it happened. Looks like a spray of blood on the spines of these books, at what would be neck-level for Howell." He looked down at the soft, pale-gray carpet. "Droplets indicate he staggered over to the desk . . . around it . . . and into the chair." Grimm was moving as he spoke.

"Careful," Barrett said, "that's still wet." He was referring to a puddle of dark, sticky looking blood on the desk chair's seat and arm rest. "That's where his assistant—you remember Francine McAdams from the other night?—that's where she found him when she came in at eight-thirty this morning. Cold as a tuna."

Grimm was peering over the back of the desk chair, careful to avoid getting blood on himself, and studying the big typewriter. In the machine, behind the roller bar, was a sheet of flimsy yellow paper. The paper bore two lines of typing, obviously part of a column that Howell had been writing. Below the typing was a couple of lines' worth of space, and then a single word:

fram

"No," he said, straightening up. "A 'dying clue'? It doesn't happen, it just doesn't happen."

Barrett laughed. "Why not? Because it's been done to death in books and movies? That's probably where Howell got the idea. Anyway, consider the facts. No sign of forced entry, no sign of a struggle— some of those books over there are messed up, but we think that's from Howell staggering into the bookcase when he was attacked. If the killer was right-handed, then he struck Howell from behind—if they were facing, the wound would have been in the left side of Howell's neck. Nothing was stolen, as far as we can determine. All of which says that Howell knew his assailant and didn't fear him."

"Or her," Grimm said.

"Or her," Barrett agreed, nodding. "Coroner says the wound could have been inflicted by any woman of ordinary strength. Anyway, the killer does his dirty deed and splits. Howell staggers to his desk. The nearest phone's in the next room—Francine McAdams's office, through that connecting door. Maybe Howell realizes he can't make it that far. Maybe he knows he's not going to make it at all—the doc

186

put his odds at no better than fifty-fifty, *if* Howell had gotten immediate attention. There's no one else in the house. No way for him to get help. But he can at least finger his killer. There's already paper in the typewriter. Instinct of a lifelong scribbler: Get it down on paper." Barrett beamed proudly.

"Get what down?" Grimm said irritably. "What does *fram* mean? That he was killed by someone who sells oil filters?"

"Hey, you're the mystery buff."

Grimm turned down the corners of his mouth. He had always been a little ashamed of his enthusiasm for murder mysteries. As a cop, he knew what a complete crock most of them were. Exotic poisons, elaborate schemes, locked rooms.

Dying clues.

He stared again at the yellow sheet. *fram*. Obviously no kind of message in itself. Had Howell—injured, confused, dying—simply gotten his fingers on the wrong keys? Grimm spread his own blunt-tipped fingers over the machine and rested them lightly on the "home keys"—a, s, d, and f on the left, j, k, l, and ; on the right. Then he moved them up a row and tried to imagine what one might *think* he was typing if he thought his fingers were properly positioned. *r4qi*. Wonderful.

"Except Colman didn't know touch typing."

The two men turned. Francine McAdams was standing in the doorway between the two offices. She looked wan, and Grimm noticed that she clutched the door jamb as if afraid it might go somewhere, but on the whole she seemed to be in pretty decent shape— considering what she had encountered when she reported for work that morning.

"Miss McAdams," Grimm said. "I'm sorry we aren't renewing our acquaintance under pleasanter circumstances."

She smiled weakly, and gestured toward the typewriter. "Colman was a two-finger typist. Well, maybe four." Again the smile. "He was fast, but sloppy. His copy was always full of strike-overs, transpositions, misspellings. He refused to worry about 'trivialities,' as he called them. So my job was to decode his typing, know that he meant 'roll' and not 'rool,' that 'unclear war' should be 'nuclear war,' and so on. I'd clean it up on my computer, then run out a copy on the laser printer for him to look over."

"Funny he didn't use some kind of word processor himself." Grimm, no kind of typist himself, had invested in a computer when he was less than fifty pages into the first draft of *The Killer Inside.* At the rate he had been going, he knew whole forests would have to die in order to produce enough paper for him to clean-type a measly five-hundred-page manuscript.

"Ah, that was another of Colman's bugbears—how computers were going to be the undoing of us all. He wouldn't even have one in the house, until his editor, Morrie Waxman, explained how he could send his columns down to the paper by modem. Colman always cut his deadlines close. The modem let him go until the last possible minute before sending his copy."

Grimm regarded her as she spoke. She was young and healthy, and Grimm would have bet she fit the coroner's definition of "ordinary strength." Had Howell been trying to type *Francine,* making it only halfway through and, as he expired, missing the *n* and hitting the *m* key by mistake?

Aware that Francine had finished rhapsodizing about the wonders of the electronic age, and that something was expected of him, Grimm said, "Tell me about yesterday."

She shrugged. "It was just a day. I came in around eight-thirty and started working on some copy Colman had left on my desk. He didn't keep regular hours, and it wasn't unusual for him to work into the evening and leave things on my desk for me to work on when I came in. Colman came down around ten. The mail came—"

"Was there anything usual in the mail?" Barrett interrupted.

Francine shook her dark head. "Hate mail, junk mail, business mail. No personal mail—almost never is. Was. I threw away the junk mail, filed the hate mail—no death threats in yesterday's batch—and took the rest in to Colman. At around noon, as I was getting ready to go to lunch, Gary Bauer stopped in. He was in with Colman when I left, gone when I got back at about one-thirty."

Grimm looked at Barrett. "Gerhardt Bauer," he said, suppressing a snicker. "Howell's research assistant."

Francine nodded. "Gary does background research, preliminary interviews, that sort of thing."

"Really," Grimm said, surprise in his voice. "I would have thought 'One Man's Opinion' was just that—one man's."

"Well, pretty much," Francine said. "Colman did all that actual writing, and the opinions certainly were his and his alone. There's more to an opinion column that just writing down whatever happens to be on your mind when you roll out of bed in the morning; there's

188

a lot of homework to be done first. I guess that's what Gary was for, although it never seemed to me that he really had all that much to do. I guess that's why Colman refused to let Gary have a credit line on the columns. According to some of the rumors I've heard, they were at each other's throats over that. Not that it matters now, I guess."

Grimm and Barrett exchanged looks.

At Grimm's urging, Francine continued: "Around three or three-thirty, Colman came into my office with a list of people he wanted to receive copies of *Points of View*. Morrie Waxman showed up just before five. Colman's contract with the syndicate was ending, and they were in the middle of negotiating a new contract. Poor Morrie. Colman was really putting him through the hoops. It's no secret that Colman *is* the syndicate—they built it around 'One Man's Opinion,' and without it there's nothing except a couple of comic strips and a few second-league columnists that no one would run except the syndicate bundles them in with Colman's column. They were in there talking when I left at around five-thirty." She looked from one man to the other. "And that was yesterday. Nothing noteworthy about it. I thought today would be just like it, but when I came in . . ." She broke off, staring at the bloodied chair behind the big desk.

"Thank you, Miss McAdams," Grimm said. "Unless Lieutenant Barrett needs you for anything else . . ."

Barrett said, "I can have someone drives you home if you like."

"Thanks," Francine said. "I'm okay. I just— Poor Colman. No one's going to cry at his funeral, you know."

*   *   *

When he returned to the room a few minutes later, Barrett said, "Nice girl. Smart, good-looking, funny."

"You think she did it, then," Grimm said.

Barrett shrugged. "Maybe *fram* was supposed to have been *fran*, as in *Francine*. She had access. And she could, physically, have done it."

"Motive?"

"She wanted more money and he wouldn't come across. He wanted more than just a business relationship and she wouldn't come across. Or they had something more than just a business relationship, and it had gone south. Two of them alone together in a big house like this . . ."

"You'll need more than just a dirty mind to convince a D.A.,"
Grimm chided. "Besides, Miss McAdams has given us food for thought
regarding Messrs. Waxman and Bauer, too."

"True enough," Barrett said agreeably. "I've got Herr Bauer cooling
his heels downstairs. You want to be there when I talk at him?"

"You know damn well I can't just walk away now and say, 'Let
me know how it all turns out,'" Grimm said with mock irritation.

Barrett laughed, and the two went downstairs.

Gary Bauer turned out to be in his early thirties, blond and slim,
with a kind of pained look in his eyes that suggested perhaps his shoes
were too tight. He wore a pale mustache that did not succeed in
making him look older, as Grimm presumed it was supposed to do.
He seemed jittery, but both Grimm and Barrett knew not to place
undue importance on such things as that. Some people are simply
jittery. Most people are jittery when someone's been murdered and
the police wish to talk to them about it.

In response to Barrett's question, Bauer said, "I came to Colman
a little over a year ago, looking for work. I was with a medium-size
paper back in Wisconsin, and that was all right. They were owned
by one of the big chains, so if I'd stuck with it they'd probably have
moved me to a bigger market eventually. On the other hand, they
might not have. I heard Colman speak in Milwaukee, and figured what
the hell. I sent him my résumé, we talked a few times, he offered
me a job . . . there you have it."

"According to Francine McAdams, you were here yesterday
around noon," Barrett said.

Bauer nodded. "Colman planned to do a short series of columns
about environmental issues, and I was doing some research. That's
how we'd work. We'd meet, he'd tell me what he was interested in,
I'd go off to do the digging, touching base with him now and then
as I went."

Grimm said, "We understand there was some bad feeling between
you and your employer."

"I don't—"

"We hear you wanted credit on the columns, Howell wouldn't
allow it," Barrett said. "That's kind of crummy, isn't it? Other research
associates working for other columnists get that much, why shouldn't
you? You have a key to the house?"

Bauer was momentarily confused. "Of course I do. Francine, too.
We're in and out of here all the time at odd hours. What's that got

to do with anything?"

"No sign of forced entry," Barrett said. "Suggests Howell's killer might have had a key."

"Or Howell let him in himself," Bauer said forcefully. "Listen, I wasn't here last night. I didn't kill him. I know there's a rumor going around that Howell and I were at each odds over my wanting credit on the column, but I don't know how that got started. I mentioned it to him once, a few months ago, and he was dead-set against it— 'One Man's Opinion' was his baby, period, and no one else's name went on it. So that was the end of it. I figured, everyone in the business, at least, knows my contribution, and Mr. and Mrs. America probably don't even read credit lines anyway. It wouldn't make sense for me to kill Howell: it wouldn't get me a credit line, and I'd be out of a job besides."

Barrett contemplated this for a moment. While he did, Grimm said, "What will happen to the column now that Howell is dead?"

Bauer frowned. "I don't know. We worked on a four-week lead time, so there's a month's worth left to run . . . After that, I suppose the syndicate will find someone else to continue it. They'd be foolish to let it die with Howell. 'One Man's Opinion' is the only hit they've got."

"And what are the odds the syndicate will ask you to continue 'One Man's Opinion'?"

Bauer stared at him. "I get you," he said after a while. "I killed Howell, figuring the syndicate would give me the ball. Well, I'd say my odds are no better than even on that score. True, Morrie Waxman and the boys might figure I was close enough to the old man that I can step into his shoes. On the other hand, they might say I'm too young and inexperienced, and opt for a well-known writer. Any way you look at it, no sure thing. I don't think it'd be worth my taking the risk, do you?"

"No," Grimm admitted. "But, then, I've never met a murderer whose potential reward was worth killing for."

*   *   *

Morrie Waxman was in his late fifties, balding, graying, and thirty-five pounds overweight. He had a habit of massaging his considerable belly, and Grimm didn't know whether the man was trying to smooth away the flab there or was nursing a gnawing ulcer.

"Yeah, Colman Howell was a smug, egotistical, opinionated son of a bitch," Waxman was saying, "and I'm gonna miss the heck out of the guy. Knew him for damn near forty years. I was assistant city editor when he started at the paper as a general-assignment reporter. Then I became city editor, and put Howell on special assignment, poking around into all the corruption at city hall. This used to be a big machine town, you know, back in the forties, fifties, early sixties. Dirty as all get-out. Today you'd call what Howell did investigative reporting. He was good at it," Waxman added reflectively. "Damn good."

"How'd he get from that to 'One Man's Opinion'?" Grimm asked.

Waxman took a minute to answer, time he spent looking at mementos on the walls and shelves of his large but untidy office. When he spoke again, his voice had changed, as if coming now from a distance. "Howell threw a lot of light under a lot of rocks down at city hall, and the people didn't like the looks of the bugs and worms he found there. There was a hoo-hah." He looked at his visitors. "You're too young to know about any of that," he said to Barrett, "but you might remember," he said, looking at Grimm.

Grimm nodded.

"Howell had a source downtown," Waxman went on. "A middle-level guy, no one important—except that he knew important stuff. He gave Howell a lot of good dirt, and Howell made it stick to some pretty big shots. Finally, the machine boys figured out Howell had to have someone on the inside. And late one night, they paid Howell a visit."

Waxman sighed, and turned his eyes, which had been focused on the past, back to his visitors. "You can guess it: Howell caved, gave them the name they wanted. Less than twenty-four hours later the poor schmuck was found dead in a drainage ditch just outside of town.

"Howell was not the same after that," Waxman continued. "He'd been an okay guy before—not bad, not great—but after that business with the political goons, it was like something in him was dead, and he became the antagonistic know-it-all we all loved. It was bluster, I think—a way to compensate for having chickened out when it counted."

"What was the name of Howell's source?" Grimm asked.

"I don't remember, after all these years," Waxman said. "I can go back and find out, if you think it's important."

"You never know," Grimm said.

Waxman nodded and jotted a note on a yellow pad near his elbow. Then he sat back again and grew reflective. "After that," he said, "Howell was kind of gun-shy. He was afraid to tackle the big guys, afraid to hit them hard for fear they'd hit back. His work lost its punch. Finally I had to put him back on general assignment, which was a come-down for him. But he'd started doing little opinion pieces now and then, thumb-suckers, on his own. We'd run 'em when we needed filler. Eventually he worked it into a regular column, which became 'One Man's Opinion.'" He shook his head. "Doesn't seem very long ago at all," he said.

"We heard something about Howell's giving you a bad time about renewing his contract with your syndicate," Barrett said. "Is that what you went to see him about yesterday?"

"Oh, I see," Waxman said, smiling. "Did I get mad and kill Howell because he wouldn't sign on the old dotted? Well, look. The industry press always liked to make a big deal about how Colman Howell was entertaining this or that seven-figure offer from one or the other of the big syndicates. But here's how it really played: Every syndicate in the country would like to carry 'One Man's Opinion'—it's one of the hottest newspaper columns in the world. But it wasn't always. In the early days, when we decided to try to take it nationwide, this newspaper approached every syndicate in existence, and they all turned us down flat. That's the only reason we started our own syndicate. So it tickled Howell no end that the people who'd shown him the door back then were wooing him now. That's half the reason he'd string 'em along—the other half was to needle me, the old bastard. In the end, he and I both knew he'd sign with us again. Here, he was the biggest frog in a very small pond. Anyplace else, he'd be one of several big frogs in a big pond. The money would be great, but his ego wouldn't have been able to take it. He knew it, I knew it, and that's all there was to that.

"As to your question—yes, I went out to the house yesterday to discuss the contract with him. I wanted to know if the order was important in the clause where we promised him the sun, the moon, and the stars." He grinned. "We kicked it around, came up with some stuff to keep the legal department busy, had a drink, and I went home to dinner with my wife."

"What happens to 'One Man's Opinion' without Howell?" Barrett asked.

Waxman drew a deep breath. "Wish I knew. I suppose we'll try to keep it going with another writer—what other choice do we have? But I wouldn't want to bet my pension on our chances for success."

"Which would be worse," Grimm said ruminatively, "trying to continue 'One Man's Opinion' without Howell, or losing him and the column to the competition?"

The balding man frowned and massaged his stomach. "I don't think I like what you're implying, Mr. Grimm."

"I'm not aware that I'm implying anything. I merely asked."

"Got an answer, too, I think," said Barrett.

*   *   *

Grimm was sitting in front of his Macintosh computer when Michael Barrett called him the following afternoon.

"Got the read-out on Colman Howell's bank accounts," Barrett said without preamble. "They indicate a lot of cash withdrawals, at irregular intervals, over the past year. Always just below the limit where you have to report it to the government, but all together they total up to about twenty thousand."

"Interesting," Grimm said, his mind on a paragraph flickering on the Mac's screen, a paragraph that refused to gel properly and say what Grimm wanted it to say. "But not necessarily significant."

"Not *necessarily* significant," Barrett emphasized, "but there's enough of a possibility that I'd like to talk to Francine McAdams about it. The withdrawals started shortly after she came to work for Howell; she has a key to the house; and there's still the matter of that *fram*-maybe-*fran* in Howell's typewriter."

"Yes," Grimm said slowly, tugging his mind away from the letters on his screen to the letters in Colman Howell's IBM Selectric. "I think those four letters are significant. I just don't know how, exactly."

"I'm on my way over to her apartment right now," Barrett said.

Grimm sighed.

Ten minutes later Michael Barrett pulled up to the curb in front of Grimm's building.

"The other odd thing is this," Barrett said when he'd pulled his LeBaron back into the traffic lane. "I've been doing a little poking into Francine McAdams's background, including talking to her journalism school adviser in Washington state. According to him, Miss McAdams was a top-notch student, best he's had in twenty years. Woodward and Bernstein all rolled into one."

"So?"

"So I asked him how's come this ace reporter is working as a glorified secretary," Barrett said. "And he was stunned. He thought the job was a bigger deal than that. In fact, I don't think he believed me when I said it pretty much boiled down to correcting Howell's typos and opening his mail."

"I don't suppose it would be the first time a job didn't live up to its description," Grimm said. "Perhaps Miss McAdams felt the experience would be worth it in any event."

"Yeah," Barrett said. "Maybe there were great perks."

Francine McAdam's building was not far from Grimm's own, but traffic was heavy enough that it took Barrett and Grimm nearly twenty minutes to reach it.

There was no response to Barrett's rapping on Francine's door.

"That's funny," Barrett said. "I talked to her an hour ago, just before I called you, and she said she'd be home all afternoon. I didn't tell her what I wanted, just that I needed to ask her some more questions about Howell. Maybe that was enough to spook her . . ."

"I doubt it."

"Me too." Barrett tried the door. It was unlocked.

Francine McAdams lay on the living-room floor.

The two men rushed to her, but there was no need for haste. She was quite dead, having been strangled with a length of brown lamp-cord.

*　　*　　*

The safe-deposit box contained the usual sorts of things you'd expect to find in a safe-deposit box, plus half a dozen neatly rubber-banded three-and-a-half-inch computer disks in Tyvek sleeves, and $10,000 in hundred-dollar bills.

"This is even better than I promised the judge it would be," Barrett said when he had finished counting the money.

"You said Howell's accounts showed cash withdrawals of roughly twenty thousand," Grimm reminded the younger man. "If your angle is that Francine McAdams was shaking down Howell in some fashion, where's the other ten thousand? And who killed Miss McAdams, and why?"

"Maybe she spent it," Barrett said, filling out an inventory list.

"Or maybe she's got another hidey-hole that we don't know about yet. Or maybe only *some* of Howell's withdrawals were for her. But I think it's interesting as anything that a woman who's only a year out of college, carrying student loans and car payments, making nineteen grand a year and having less than two thousand bucks between her checking and savings accounts, has ten grand in cash in a safe-deposit box. What have you got there?"

Grimm had been looking over the floppy disks, which were unlabeled and unmarked. Now he was holding one of the Tyvek sleeves just so, angling it to catch the overhead flourescent light. "There's something written here, in pencil, very faintly. Numbers. Looks like a phone number. 232-8537, I think." He passed the small square of paper over to Barrett.

"Yeah, 232-8537," Barrett said. "Anything else?"

"As far as labeling, no. We'll have to boot up these disks and see what's on them."

"All right. I'm done here. Let's go upstairs and try that number."

Grimm pocketed the disks and the two men left the cubicle in the safe-deposit room. Upstairs, in the lobby of the bank, Barrett dropped a coin into a pay phone and dialed the number Grimm had spotted on the floppy disk sleeve. A moment later he held up the receiver so Grimm could hear:

". . . call can not be completed as dialed. Please hang up, and if—"

Barrett cradled the receiver, reclaimed his money, tried again, and got the same recording. "No such number," he said, hanging up.

"Try it dialing '1' first," Grimm suggested. "Maybe it's outside the calling area."

"I'll take it back to the station and let one of the clerks work on it," Barrett said. "We're pulling the McAdams woman's telephone records, too, and maybe it'll turn up there—if it's an out-of-state number, it'd take us till doomsday to try and guess the right Area Code. You want to go try those disks?"

Grimm nodded.

The McAdams apartment already had that closed up, musty feeling to it, only two days after its tenant had been killed. The forensic team had been over the place like a sweat, but come up with nothing of significance. There was no sign of forced entry. No sign of a struggle. The coroner's opinion was that Francine's killer had taken her by surprise, knocked her down, and then strangled her with cord torn from a nearby floor lamp. Fingerprints had been lifted, but prints alone are seldom any use until you've caught someone to compare the prints to. Fingerprints are evidence, not clues.

The apartment was sealed, but Barrett ignored the yellow tape and went on in, Grimm right behind him.

"While you play with the computer, I'm going to see if that telephone number appears in her address book. It was in the kitchen . . ."

He moved off, and Grimm turned his attention to Francine McAdams's computer. It sat on a tidy little desk, under a shelf bowed beneath the weight of a tiny stereo unit and collection of tapes and compact disks. The computer was a Macintosh—a more expensive and therefore more sophisticated model than Grimm's rather basic set-up, but he still felt comfortable working with it. He powered up and waited for the machine's built-in hard-disk drive to boot. It didn't. Grimm shoved one of the disks in his hands into the floppy-disk drive, but the machine spit it right back out: it wasn't a start-up disk, obviously.

Frowning, Grimm rummaged through a plastic disk-file on the desk next to the Mac, and came up with a disk labeled *System Disk*, which he popped into the machine. At last the familiar Macintosh "happy disk" icon appeared on the screen, and in a few seconds the disk had loaded and the Macintosh's "desktop" appeared. An icon labeled *Hard Disk* appeared just below the icon for *System Disk*, and Grimm realized why the hard disk hadn't booted when he powered up the machine: all of its files had been erased. He checked the directory, which showed the hard disk had last been modified yesterday— the day Francine McAdams had been murdered—less than forty minutes before Grimm and Barrett had arrived to find the body.

Shaking his head, Grimm inserted one of the floppy disks he had brought from the bank. It loaded promptly. It was named, unhelpfully, *Disk 1*, and contained what appeared to be a number of standard word-processing documents. Unfortunately, with the hard disk erased, so were the programs with which Grimm might have read the documents. He went back to the plastic file box and came out with Francine McAdams's original master disk of MacWrite. Using floppy disks would involve a fair amount of disk-swapping, Grimm realized, as the Macintosh read information from three disks rotating between two disk drives, but for the time being he didn't want to copy anything onto the speedier hard disk.

Eventually Grimm got MacWrite launched. But just as the

document he had selected was about to be displayed, a small box appeared. It contained one word and a blinking cursor in a smaller rectangle. The word was *Password?*

Grimm stared at it.

Finally he typed *Francine.*

****Incorrect Password**** appeared in another box.

Grimm hit the Enter key and was returned to the box with the blinking cursor. He typed *McAdams.*

****Incorrect Password****.

He tried a few other guesses, with the same results, and then, disgusted, picked up the phone next to the computer and dialed a number.

Barrett came back to the room a few seconds after Grimm had hung up. "No luck with the address book," he said. "Did she keep an address file or anything like that on that computer of hers?"

"Hard to say," Grimm said. "The hard disk has been erased, and these disks have been encrypted in some fashion. I just called my friendly computer dealer, who says that he *might* be able to restore the hard drive, but that we should forget about cracking the code on these password-protected disks. Apparently there are half a dozen or more security programs for the Macintosh, and what they all have in common is that it's next to impossible to defeat them."

Barrett had begun shaking his head midway through this, and didn't stop until Grimm had. "If you say so," he said when his friend had finished his explanation, which explained nothing to the cheerfully computer-illiterate Barrett. "Do whatever you need to do. It could be important, and we haven't much to go on so far."

"I'll need to get this computer to my friend. Also, I want to make copies of these disks to give to him, to see if he can crack them."

"Fine," Barrett said. He acted as if he was about to say more, but the telephone interrupted him. Since Grimm had no official capacity, he let Barrett answer it. "Yes? Oh, good, put him through. Hello, Mr. Waxman. Really? Huh. Okay, thanks."

Barrett put down the phone and looked at the older man with a funny half-grin on his face. "This is interesting," he said. "You remember that *fram* in Howell's typewriter?"

"Dimly, yes."

"Well, Morrie Waxman went back and dug up the name of Howell's city hall contact, the one Howell gave up? His name was Farmer. Will Farmer."

Grimm nodded slowly. "It works. A notoriously poor typist starts to type *farmer*, transposes the second and third letters, and dies before he can finish the word."

"Problem is, Farmer's been dead for thirty years."

"That is irritating. But he may have had survivors—"

"According to Waxman, just a widow."

"Brothers? Sisters? Cousins? Close friends?"

Barrett had the phone to his ear and was dialing headquarters.

* * *

It was late. Alexander Grimm stared at his computer screen, on which that afternoon's troublesome paragraph still twinkled serenely, mockingly. His mind was not on his work. He had hoped his computer-expert friend would have been able to restore Francine McAdams's hard disk by now, but the program Grimm's friend was using for the chore was "very thorough"—words that Grimm realized translated to "very slow" when applied to computer matters. As he waited, Grimm tried not to let his hopes rise. There was, he knew, a chance that whoever had taken the time to erase the disk had been smart enough to "zero" it, using a program that would write a meaningless string of zeroes and ones to the disk, effectively eradicating the previous information forever.

On top of that, as Michael Barrett had pointed out, who was to say Francine hadn't encrypted the files on her hard disk, too, in which case any recovered data would be useless to them. There was no good reason for her to have done so—she lived alone, minimizing the likelihood of anyone else accessing her computer—but anyone who was cautious enough to protect disks that were locked away in a bank vault was liable to be cautious enough to protect data from even nonexistent prying eyes.

Irritatingly, Barrett was right.

Barrett was reluctant to let go of Francine as his primary suspect in the murder of Colman Howell—after all, there was nothing to prevent a murderer from being murdered—but Grimm, who had never seriously suspected her in the first place, felt that her death removed her from the list of candidates. His belief, as he had told Barrett, was that someone else killed Howell, and Francine McAdams found out who. To protect himself, the murderer had murdered again.

Grimm further believed—*knew*—that the computer disks contained Francine's evidence, or at least her suspicions, and that they would lead them to her and Howell's killer.

If they could only *read* the damn things!

Muttering a mild oath, Grimm quit his word-processing program and loaded in one of Francine's disks. He made no further headway with it than he had that afternoon at the dead woman's apartment. It being common knowledge that most people set combinations, passwords, and other codes based on information important to them, Grimm tried spelling Francine McAdams's name backwards and "sideways." He tried her initials, forward, backward, and jumbled. He tried simple number-letter substitution codes. He tried Francine's mother's maiden name, gleaned from information in the file Barrett's people has assembled. Birth dates. Addresses.

Incorrect Password.

Grimm jumped out of his chair, feeling a sudden need to put as much space as possible between him and the computer. He would never under-stand how cryptographers could do this sort of thing for a living. Grimm didn't even like to work crossword puzzles.

He went out to his living room, dropped into his broken-down old easy chair, and fired up the television set. The late news had gone to one of its interminable commercial breaks, so he picked up the evening paper and began to give it a slightly more thorough skim than he had earlier.

His mind thus occupied, it was only out of the corner of his ear that he heard the tail-end of one of the TV spots: "Have your credit card ready. Operators are standing by. Dial 1 800 4 MY DOGS. That's 1 800 4 MY DOGS. Quantities are limited. That number again—1 800 4 MY DOGS . . ." Grimm lowered his paper and stared at the screen. He always wondered what sort of people ordered things from 800-number TV ads. Apparently they were people who couldn't remember a telephone number for ten seconds, even if it did spell something clever—

Grimm turned his attention from the TV set to the telephone at the side of his chair. He stared at the Touch Tone dial for a few minutes, then got up and went back to his computer. The TV was still prattling away, but he didn't hear it.

His first few attempts failed. But less than five minutes after having returned to his computer, Grimm sat back in his chair and smiled at the screen.

*   *   *

"Francine McAdams was doubly clever," Grimm said. "Not only did she encrypt data that she never expected anyone else to see, but she left herself a clue to ensure that *she* would remember how to decrypt it. It's easy enough to outsmart yourself on something like that—come up with a password that no one could ever guess, including you if you forget what it was." He looked at Michael Barrett. "We thought that 232-8537 was merely a phone number she'd jotted down, and that's what she meant it to look like. In fact, it's the key to the password to those disks of hers. The number itself isn't the password; nor did it work when I tried to convert it using a number-letter substitution—A equals 1, B equals 2, and so on. But by accident, thanks to one of those annoying 800-number TV ads, I discovered the key to the password. I assume that when Miss McAdams was encrypting her disks, hunting for a password, she looked around her room and her eyes settled on the tapes and CDs over her desk. If you spell out 232-8537 on a telephone dial, you get the password: *Beatles.*"

"Yes, that's very clever," Morrie Waxman said brusquely, "but what was *on* those disks once you could read them?"

Grimm smiled at the men assembled in his little apartment—Barrett, Waxman, and Gary Bauer. "Several things," he said mysteriously. "One of which I should have realized yesterday, Mr. Waxman, when you talked to Lieutenant Barrett."

Morrie Waxman's head came up as if someone had yanked on a string fastened to the top of his head, and he began to massage his belly.

Grimm, though, had already turned his attention to Michael Barrett. "I should have paid more attention to you when you were telling me about Miss McAdams's college instructor, and wondering why such a promising young reporter would be willing to work as a 'glorified secretary,' as you put it. For the experience, she told us, and I rather naively accepted that. In fact, she had an ulterior motive."

"Blackmail," Barrett said triumphantly.

"Biography," Grimm corrected him. He held up Francine's computer disks. "Mainly these contain notes and collected research for a biography of Colman Howell, which Miss McAdams intended to write. The reason she took her job was to get close to the man, in order to be able to add her first-hand impressions and observations to her account." He frowned at the little squares of plastic in his hands. "I do not think Miss McAdams was blackmailing Howell—although it's obvious from her notes that she knew his secret, the one you told us about the other day, Mr. Waxman."

Waxman opened his mouth, but Barrett spoke first: "But if she wasn't blackmailing anyone, what about the ten thousand dollars?"

"Yes, what about that?" Grimm turned his head. "Mr. Bauer?"

The blond man looked up from studying his hands, which rested in his lap.

"Is there nothing you would like to say at this point?"

Gary Bauer sighed. "How much do you know?"

"I know a fair amount, and I think I can guess at a fair amount more. But we'd like to hear your account."

Bauer nodded, and drew a breath.

*　　*　　*

"I suppose you know that my father was Will Farmer," Bauer said in a low monotone. "He was killed, thanks to Colman Howell, six months before I was born. After my father's death, mother moved back to Milwaukee, where her family lived.

"I had always known about my father and Howell. My mother made no secret of her hatred for Howell, and his success and fame—at my father's expense, in her view—always enraged her.

"But I never shared her outrage. To me, my father was only a face in some old pictures. Having never known him, I never seemed to be able to work up any anger that he was dead.

"That changed two years ago.

"Howell came to Milwaukee to address a journalists' society. Out of curiosity, I decided to go and see in person the man my mother had decried for as long as I could remember. I wish I hadn't. Howell was so . . . so arrogant, so full of himself, so *smug*—and suddenly all I could think of was how this man owed everything—*everything*, including his very life—to the fact that he betrayed my father's trust.

"That's when I decided to kill him."

Bauer paused, and looked around the small room, into the faces of each of the men there. "I bought a gun, practiced, planned. Worked

202

up my courage. A little over a year ago, I took a week's vacation and came down here. My plan was to simply blow Howell off the map, but I needed to let him know first who was killing him and why. I expected him to plead for his life—you always think the arrogant ones will turn out to be the biggest cowards—but to my surprise he didn't. He acted like people came into his house waving guns at him every day of the week. I wouldn't be surprised if they did. Anyhow, Howell said he wouldn't blame me for killing him, but he proposed an alternative. He said that he always knew that he should have at least tried to get money to my mother after what happened to my father, but that he had been too intent on trying to forget the whole business. He claimed that, had he known my mother was expecting, he certainly would have contributed something to her, somehow. Now he suggested that we establish a position that was little more than a no-show job, through which he could make what he called restitution to me. He said he knew it didn't make up for my not having had a father, but didn't it make more sense to take his money than to ruin my life by killing him?"

"Hold on," Barrett said. "You mean Howell *suggested* you blackmail him? That's crazy!"

The young man shrugged. "Was I blackmailing him, or was he bribing me? Either way, I went along with it—to my shame. I told myself that my father would be just as dead whether Howell lived or died . . . and I took the money." His eyes were red and wet.

It was some time before he could resume: "As the months passed, I grew more and more disgusted with myself, and I felt more and more strongly that I had betrayed my father and myself by allowing Howell to buy me off so easily. I no longer wanted to kill Howell—I realized that it would accomplish nothing—but I felt that something had to be done. I confronted Howell last week. I told him I wanted him to go public with the story of what he had done to my father, or I would.

"He laughed at me. He said he certainly wasn't about to wreck his reputation over an old 'mistake'—his word—that no one cared about any more. He also said that no one would believe my version—there was no proof, and everyone would write me off as a disgruntled employee trying to get back at Howell for not giving me a credit line on the column. It turns out Howell had started that little rumor himself, anticipating that I might try exposing him.

"I was furious. I left, knowing that Francine would be back from lunch soon. But I came back that night, with my gun, and let myself in. I hadn't planned to kill him, just to force him to do the right thing. Howell surprised me, and took the gun away. We argued. I grabbed the letter opener from his desk and—" Bauer paled, and swallowed hard. "He dropped the gun. I scooped it up and got out. I didn't know whether he was alive or dead, how badly I might have hurt him . . . I considered running away, but when I thought about all the blood, it seemed to me he couldn't possibly live, in which case I'd put myself in a worse fix by running."

He looked at Alexander Grimm with his red, tearing eyes. "But I wish I had."

"Because Francine McAdams realized almost immediately what had happened," Grimm said, and Bauer nodded mutely.

"She knew about Howell and your father," Grimm went on, "from her research into Howell's life. She didn't know about you, who you were, but I suspect she figured it out based on the clue Howell left in his typewriter the night he was killed. As *I* should have done," he added ruefully. "She did a little checking to verify her guess—her notes are on the disks—and then confronted you. That's where the ten thousand came from. You tried to buy her off just as Howell had tried to buy you off."

Bauer nodded. "I gave her the ten thousand, which was all I could get my hands on at short notice, and promised her another ten. She agreed. But when I met with her the other day, she said she'd reconsidered. She said she realized that Howell's death, and the circumstances of his death, made her book worth more than I could ever pay her. She had already talked with a couple of publishers, and they were talking in six figures—more if she could finger Howell's killer. I begged her not to, for my mother's sake if not mine, but she was insistent. She said she was certain I could claim self defense, temporary insanity, all kinds of things. I threatened her, and she ordered me to leave her apartment. She said she had all of her notes written down in a safe place, and if anything happened to her it would be all the worse for me. I thought she was bluffing, so I took the only way out I could see. I hit her and she fell. She was semi-conscious. I broke the cord off a lamp and used it to . . ." He swallowed hard. "I figured she'd have everything on her computer, so I erased the hard disk and went through the floppy disks to make sure there was nothing that could harm me." He closed his eyes.

"I guess she wasn't bluffing," he said in a small voice.

*　*　*

Some hours later, Grimm sat slumped in a hard straight chair across from Michael Barrett's cluttered steel desk. He had tried to get comfortable, failed, and given up on the idea. Now he merely waited for the younger man. Gary Bauer had been taken into custody without incident, and was now languishing in the Public Safety Building awaiting his bail hearing.

Barrett entered, edged around the desk, and collapsed into his chair. It tilted back dangerously, but Barrett seemed unfazed by it. He crossed his ankles on a corner of the desk. Grimm had wondered why that one corner alone was free of débris.

Barrett considered his friend wordlessly for some little time, then said, "Somebody kill your dog?"

Grimm attempted a smile, and had just as much luck as he'd had trying to get comfortable in Barrett's visitor's chair. "I keep thinking that Francine McAdams would still be alive if I'd figured out Colman Howell's final message on day one—as I should have, and as she obviously did."

"That's one way of looking at it," Barrett said. "Another is, she'd still be alive if she had told us about it when *she* figured it out, instead of holding back in the hopes of a fat book-contract or whatever. But you know, I still don't get it. I mean, I understand that Howell was trying to type *farmer* when he typed *fram*, but how do you get from that to Gary Bauer? No one knew that Farmer's wife was pregnant when he was killed, and with the son using the name Bauer—"

"He wasn't 'using' it," Grimm interrupted. "It's his real, legal, honest-to-Godfrey name." He nodded at the cop's desk. "You have it there—somewhere—in your files. Gerhardt Bauer, mother Karla, father Wilhelm. That's why your people didn't make the connection to Farmer when they checked Bauer's background. Obviously when Farmer was killed and his wife went back to Milwaukee, she reinstated the family name." Grimm sighed heavily. "Naturally, it would have been more helpful if Howell had tried to type *bauer* instead of *farmer*, but in his condition—dying, scared, probably in pain—his confusion is understandable. What's not understandable is how I, being almost one-hundred percent German, with two sets of grandparents who always spoke German at home, could fail to put that together from the start."

"I still don't—"

"Isn't it obvious?" Grimm said. "'Wilhelm,' of course, would have been translated to 'William,' or 'Will'; and 'Bauer'—"

"Means 'farmer,'" Barrett said with sudden understanding.

A Bunch of Mumbo Jumbo

Jan Grape

Nathan Foster walked back from the bathroom just as his wife Sara awoke. He'd heard her moans and saw her thrashing when he walked through their bedroom, but hoped the nightmare would quickly subside and she'd slip back into a deeper sleep. It was not to be, he saw, when he reached the bedside, for she was staring wide-eyed at him, perspiration causing her pale brown hair to curl around her face. The sheet and bedspread were tangled around Sara's left arm and both legs.

"Sara?" he asked, "are you all right? You must have had a bad dream. Your cries woke me up." Nathan was lying, he'd only walked into their house a few minutes ago. He slipped quickly onto the bed, beside his wife of twenty-four years and hoped Sara wasn't awake enough to realize he'd not been there before.

"Oh, God. Nathan. It was horrible."

Sara turned to him for comfort and he put his hand on her shoulder, patting clumsily a moment before removing his hand. "Sara, was it about your Mother again?" He felt a small pang of guilt because he really didn't care about hearing her answer.

If she hadn't been so wrapped up in all that metaphysical stuff, he thought, none of this would have happened. Dammit all . . . she'd even taken to wearing crystals, some of them two and three inches long and talking with some "entity" she claimed had been her mentor and teacher for the past two thousand years. Channeling she called it.

Nathan's world focused on mathematics; numbers were so precise and absolute. He had great difficulty understanding Sara's psychic leanings.

Nathan, born during the depression years into a family fathered by an alcoholic, remembered being five years old and going to bed hungry. He swore an oath that he'd have all he wanted to eat when he grew up. There would be no help from anyone, he'd have to depend solely on himself.

In junior high school, his aptitude for mathematics was noted by a conscientious teacher and he soon excelled. He learned to set goals based on the application of numbers and figures. Step by step, he attained his goals and now owned a highly successful CPA firm in Houston, Texas. The exact science of dealing with numbers was so far removed from Sara's ESP that his mind could never grasp her clairvoyance.

His wife, Sara, was a warm, caring person and a good mother to their only child, Kimberly, now twenty-two. Yet her "gift" as she called it, a strong ability for ESP and predictions, set her apart from other people, even Nathan. When she was small, she had "movies" which played in her head of events that would happen later. More than once she had "seen" a friend or family member lying in a casket and invariably, that person had died. Nathan laughingly called Sara's gift; *mumbo-jumbo.*

Nathan yawned and closed his eyes, but Sara insisted on telling him all about her dream. "Nathan. I don't know what's happening. Ishtar says I'm only going through a growth change, brought about by mother's death, but it's so . . . so horrible. The dreams are getting more . . . well, violent and bloody and this nightmare seemed so real."

Ishtar was the name of Sara's spirit guide and she claimed to believe all he told her, but sometimes she was frustrated by what "he" said.

Nathan sighed and didn't speak, knowing all the time Sara would continue even if he feigned sleep.

"Mother and I were at her house, sitting on her sofa and talking. A man wearing a ski stocking mask and carrying a baseball bat broke in; and before I could stop him, he started beating her on the head. It was awful. Bone cracked and blood was everywhere and I ran at him to stop him. I was beating him with my fists and mother was lying on the floor. Blood was pumping out of her and covering my feet and legs, but somehow I . . . uh . . . I was able to get my fingers under the bottom part of the mask. Before I could pull it off though, I woke up. I want to know who he was, I've got to know."

"Sara, you shouldn't talk like this."

"But he murdered my mother. I know it was Jack who killed her. I didn't see his face, but I know it was him. And I'm in danger now, too."

"Sara, it's just a dream you're talking about. Jack didn't kill Maudi. Her death was an accident." Sara's mother had died in a fall while on her honeymoon in the Greek Islands. "You know Maudi wouldn't want you acting like this."

While it was true Maudi's skull had been crushed, the police said the older woman had sustained the type of injury you'd expect from falling down a steep staircase.

"Stop thinking about the nightmare, Sara. Try to go back to sleep if you can."

His wife's visions and dreams had intensified after Maudi's death. Nathan was sure it was only the grief causing her to have nightmares and behave like a woman obsessed. Sara used all of her energy to try and convince people that Maudi had been murdered.

Murdered by her new husband. The motive? Money.

Sara's father had made a fortune, running whiskey into Galveston during prohibition. He'd invested in real estate and in the 1940s and 50s had made another fortune when oil had been found on much of his West Texas land. When he died fifteen years ago, his estate had been worth an estimated ten million dollars.

Sara closed her eyes and breathed deeply, hypnotically.

Nathan turned away from her abruptly as he felt the flush coming over him. Thinking of Maudi's death had reminded him of Allison. Strange how Maudi's death had led to new life for him.

Allison Neely. Three weeks ago, Nathan's whole world changed when the beautiful young woman touched his arm in a gesture of sympathy over his mother-in-law's death and seared herself into his soul.

She'd been working in his office for three months, and although, he'd noticed her, he'd not really seen her. Allison, the most beautiful, voluptuous woman he'd ever encountered, with raven colored hair and sparkling green eyes, had taken him into her bed that same night and he'd been with her every day or night since.

Every moment he could snatch from work and home, Nathan would take, and take Allison and spend hours, lost in the scent and taste and the flesh of her. He had been with Allison again tonight and the memories of what had happened in her bed with her, wiped out Sara's nightmare and even erased the realization that Sara was now lying beside him, unable to return to sleep. Nathan's sleep and dreams were filled only of Allison Neely.

The next morning, Sara bustled around fixing breakfast, but it was obvious she wanted to talk about her mother's death again. "Nathan, it's quite clear you, and everyone else thinks I'm losing it, that I'm crazy or heading that way, but I know Jack had something to do with mother's accident. That courtship and marriage was entirely too quick. And remember when she called to tell us they were getting married—how giddy she sounded. Like she was on a champagne drunk."

Sara's mother had met Jack Clifford, while on a trip to Europe. Two weeks later, they were married and three weeks later Maudi was dead. Maudi had never returned home. According to instructions in her new will, Jack had her cremated and her ashes sprinkled around the Greek Isles where they met.

"Honestly, Nathan. Mother sounded worse than some sixteen year old over that man. In fact, our Kimberly never was that giddy over any boy." Sara sat down, but didn't touch her food.

Nathan was weary of the whole discussion, but he tried to reach Sara once again. Tried to make her see how wrong she was. Tried to reach her intuitive nature. "Maybe Maudi knew she didn't have much time left. Maybe she only wanted to grab a little bit of happiness. Can you blame her for that?"

"No . . . I guess not. But I didn't get to see her or be with her. The happiest weeks of her life in years, and I didn't get to share in them. That hurts.

"And we never got to meet Jack either. That's something that really puzzles me, him not showing up for the memorial service we held. No one has heard from him since either. Isn't that proof of his . . ."

"It is odd, but not exactly sinister."

"Well, it is to me. After all, she did leave him a million dollars . . ."

"Yes. And the other nine million to you and Kimberly, but that doesn't mean that you or I killed Maudi."

"Well, he got her to change his will, but you can bet he didn't know she made one more change the day before she died. I'll bet he thought he was going to get it all."

Nathan drained his coffee, eager to be on his way. Eager to see Allison. "Sara. You've got to put this all behind you. And you've got to stop thinking this non. . ."

"Nathan? Do you have to go? I wanted to tell you my other dream. The one after my nightmare. It was a bad dream, too. I can't remember exact details, but you and I were in extreme danger. There was water all around me and . . ."

"Sara, I've told you and Dr. Simms has told you. You're letting grief cloud your judgement about everything." He started to get up when he thought of a new argument to try to get through to her. "Listen, you've never had dreams like this before, have you? I mean, all these years you've always been wide awake when you see whatever it is that you see?"

"Yes, but . . ."

"That should prove to you that what you're dreaming is something grief induced."

Sara's anguished look made him guiltily think he should stay home with her a few minutes longer, but then, Allison filled his mind and the guilty thought vanished. He got up and picked his briefcase up from the kitchen counter.

"Even if you're right about Jack, there's nothing you or anyone can do about it now." He turned and left.

Nathan discovered later that Sara's obsession was stronger than he'd even imagined. She hired a private investigator, sent the man to Europe, all expenses paid, in an effort to determine what really had happened to Maudi.

Sara reported the P.I. could find no evidence of foul play and two witnesses placed Jack at a hotel bar a mile away when Maudi's accident occurred.

Nathan, who was totally wrapped up in *his* new obsession, in the form of Allison, stopped listening to Sara's news or lack of it.

Once, just before he moved out of the house, Nathan did listen to Sara complaining that the P.I. was making little progress in locating Jack. He tried to make Sara see the investigator was taking advantage of her. "He's milking you for thousands, Sara."

"I don't care. It's my money, to spend as I please."

Nathan didn't answer. Nothing of his old life mattered anymore. His daughter, Kim, was the only thing from his past to linger briefly in the back of his mind. Nothing else was important. Not Sara with her metaphysics nor Maudi nor the missing Jack Clifford.

Nathan's every waking thought was filled with thoughts of smoothing Allison's dark silky hair away from her eyes and kissing her warm, sensitive mouth.

Allison was totally intoxicating; she never seemed to have enough of him nor was his desire for her ever satiated. Her slightest touch electrified him and turned his legs to rubber. And each time he crawled into her bed and pulled her fabulous body up close to sear his flesh each place they touched, Nathan felt certain he knew what paradise was like.

Allison was like having champagne and lobster every night, a new sports car every day and she was as addictive as heroin; he knew he could not rest until she would be with him every moment, in his life and in his home as his wife.

Sara did not protest when Nathan moved out. She was in a mostly unresponsive world of her own, filled with "entities and ethereal planes." When Nathan asked for a divorce, she quickly signed the papers and all of Sara's dreams and visions and mumbo-jumbo faded from Nathan's mind.

The day after his divorce was final, Nathan and Allison were wed in Las Vegas.

To the newlywed's surprise, Sara remarried also, a month after their wedding, but two weeks later she was found dead; floating face down in her newly installed swimming pool.

*　　*　　*

Allison followed Nathan into the living room, "Clifton gave Sara a nice send off, don't you think, dear?"

Nathan didn't answer as he loosened his tie, slid out of his jacket, throwing it across the back of the sofa, then headed to the liquor cabinet and mixed a pitcher of martinis. Psychics and ESP, he was thinking, was it really a bunch of hogwash?

Ever since he'd heard of Sara's death, all her doom and gloom predictions, all her mumbo-jumbo warnings of danger came swirling and rushing back to him as quickly as a Gulf Coast hurricane. He still couldn't believe Sara was dead. He had seen her body lying in the bronzed casket, but even now, the actual thought of Sara dead and gone made him queasy and nauseated.

He took a slow, deep breath to clear his head and walked slowly to the sofa and sat, leaning back into its softness. Nathan lifted the glass and drank half of the gin and vermouth, feeling the warmth spread through his abdomen. God. What a nightmare. Sara's funeral. His first thought was not to go, but he felt obligated for Kim's sake. How would it look to his daughter if her father didn't attend her mother's funeral? "Wonder if Sara had a premonition of how or when she'd die?"

"What dear?" Allison, as usual, hadn't been paying attention.

We don't communicate anymore, he thought, except in bed. The emptiness in her head somehow made their twenty year age difference seem greater. "Never mind."

Beautiful Allison, so sexy and voluptuous, but oh, so selfish and greedy. If Nathan wasn't talking about money or giving her money or telling her to go spend money, Allison wasn't interested in what he said.

She spent money as if she thought he was churning it out of the basement. Nathan deplored waste. Allison never understood and when he tried to talk to her about cutting back, she would laugh and call him "Old Scrooge."

Sara, on the other hand, had always understood about being careful with a dollar, even though she had been born into money. They had lived on his salary, in the early years and later, when he made a good six figure income, she would account for every dollar. Right up until they divorced, at least, Sara's only splurge had been hiring that private detective and she had paid for him out of her inheritance.

But Sara had changed, too. After her marriage to Clifton, she changed completely. She'd bought her new husband an expensive sports car and new clothes and that fancy house where she built that damned swimming pool.

Thinking of the pool, reminded Nathan of what had happened. Sighing, he got up and poured another martini. If Sara actually could have foretold her own death, why then, did she go swimming at night when she was all alone? The idea that she had somehow been right about being in danger made Nathan's head roar like a jackhammer digging out concrete.

Allison kept flitting around the room, her mind obviously on money. Eventually, she lit beside Nathan on the sofa. "I don't understand why I couldn't buy a new dress to wear to Sara's funeral."

"A funeral is not a fashion parade. Honestly, Allison, sometimes I think you're sick . . ."

"Just because I wanted a new outfit?"

"You have a closet full of clothes. Anyone who's a compulsive shopper like you are—is definitely sick."

"Speaking of money," Allison said, turning the conversation from herself, but staying on her favorite subject, "I'll bet ole Clifton spent plenty on that service."

Nathan ignored her.

"He couldn't afford not to, though. Not with all of Sara's money. His fancy friends would have laughed at him behind his back if he'd been stingy."

Nathan shook his head, "Mr. Jackson does not inherit. Oh well, Sara left him a tidy lump sum, but Kimberly gets the majority."

"But I . . . I thought Sara left him everything or gave him control or something. Isn't Kim too young to handle that much money on her own?"

"Sara rewrote her will, the day before her death. The money will be in a special account until Kim reaches twenty-five. I'm her trustee and Sara's executor."

Allison was listening intently, but Nathan didn't notice. "I didn't know Sara changed her will, did you know? And what does being the trustee mean? Do you have actual control?"

"It wasn't something Sara would discuss. And no. She didn't talk to me about it. She just went to Poindexter's office and had him make the changes. And yes, the trustee has some control and also gets a salary for taking care of things."

"I see." Allison tapped a fingernail against her front tooth. "Sara was kind of a suspicious person, wasn't she? She always thought all those awful things about me and now it looks like she didn't trust her new husband either."

"Maybe she suddenly came to her senses and wondered where in the hell Clifton came from."

"Well. Who would really care? A sexy hunk like that. And a versatile athlete; plays tennis, sails, rides horses, flies airplanes, and gliders. I adore his British accent. And so handsome, so dashing . . ."

"So gigoloish, if you ask me. He'd do anything for money."

"Speaking of money, Nathan. What happens if you should die

before Kim reaches twenty-five? I mean . . . not that I . . ."

"Don't worry Allison. You'll be well cared for."

Allison slid across the cushions, closer to Nathan and pulled his head into her lap. "Let's not talk about Clifton or Kim or anything else tonight, okay?" She snaked her arms around his neck, smoothing his salt and pepper gray hair back from his forehead, then, rained teasing, little kisses onto his eyelids and face and mouth.

Nathan couldn't deny the desire that arose, his blood pounded as he automatically began caressing her warm, firm breast with his right hand. Instantly, he felt the response of her nipple underneath his fingers.

*   *   *

Nathan shook his head to clear away the grogginess of sleep and answered the ringing telephone.

"Daddy?"

"Kim? What's wrong, Baby? Why are you crying?"

"I'm sorry, but I . . ."

"Honey, what is it? What's wrong?"

"I, uh . . . I got a letter from Mother, written before she died. Mr. Poindexter was to send it if anything strange happened."

"What does it say?"

Kim snubbed and blew her nose. "I can't read it over the phone. Can you meet me for brunch?"

Nathan reached The Glass Hut in a little over an hour. The hostess led him to a corner table in the back where Kimberly was already seated. He was shocked by his daughter's appearance. Her face was devoid of make-up and her hair had been hastily pulled back into a pony-tail, giving her such a vulnerable little girl look, that his heart tightened in his chest. He remembered how she'd worshipped him; looking to him for every answer.

Kim could barely wait until he sat and the hostess left. "Daddy, I'm so afraid." Fear clouded her eyes.

"Honey, what on earth? What did Sara say?" When did he lose Kim? he wondered. She was part of him; of his blood.

"Mother said she'd had this dream."

"Oh. Hell. You know your mother and her ESP. It's all a bunch of malarkey. Is that all?"

215

"Look. I happen to believe Mother was psychic." Kim jumped up, anger tightening her face and forcing her words out through clenched teeth. "I should have know better than . . ."

Nathan was overwhelmed by his feelings of love for his child. If he turned her down now, she might be lost to him forever. He reached out his hand, gently taking his daughter's arm. "I'm sorry, Kim. Let's not argue. Sit back down. We'll eat and then you can tell me what your mother said that frightens you."

Kimberly hesitated, but only for a second, then sat. They made small talk until their food came and they had eaten.

"Now," said Nathan. "Tell me about your mother's letter."

"Mother said for us to be *very* careful. You and I. Something terrible's going to happen. That we could be saved, but not her."

"She saw something about her own death?"

Kimberly nodded her head, slowly. "She dreamed Clifton hit her in the head with a hammer." The girl stopped, biting her lip and fighting back her tears. "She saw herself falling . . ." Kim sobbed. "Falling into water and sinking like a rock." The tears rolled down the girl's cheeks and dripped onto the table.

"Kim, honey, Clifton was in Dallas, uh . . . when your mother, uh . . . the coroner said Sara hit her head on the diving board." Nathan pulled his chair closer and put his arm around his daughter's slim shoulders. "I do wish Sara had kept all this psycho stuff to herself. You know the police found nothing suspicious. I believe it was a horrible accident."

"But Daddy. There's something else. That's why I'm so afraid. Look at this newspaper clipping."

Nathan took the clipping from his daughter and read:

BEAUTY BLUDGEONED TO DEATH

Twenty-two year old Kimmie Foster was found dead yesterday in her apartment near Rice University. Houston homicide detectives have no suspects and no clues. When questioned they also had "no comment."

"But Kim, this newspaper is from the 1960s, this isn't you."

"No. But mother's letter said that's how I died before and if I'm not careful it would happen again. The exact same way."

How ridiculous. Kim living before, with the same name—and,

being murdered? Nathan couldn't take it seriously. He almost laughed, but one look at Kim's face sobered him. "Honey, it's just a coincidence." Yet, suddenly, something felt almost spooky about the situation.

"But let me tell you what she said about you. She dreamed she saw Allison pushing you out of a boat." Kimberly buried her face into her hands.

Nathan stared at the top of Kimberly's head. Migod. Just last night, Allison *begged* to be taken on a Caribbean cruise. He'd objected strenuously, not really knowing why, but finally had put his foot down and had eventually talked Allison into a trip to The Grand Canyon. No, he thought, that's utter nonsense.

Logical, practical Nathan, with a new awareness of the trust Kim always had in him, was determined to calm her fears. He mentally shrugged off his uneasiness, but it *was* weird. "Believe me. None of this is going to happen, Kim. Your mother's dreams were unusual, but they're not real life."

It took some doing, but Nathan eventually saw Kim's composure return. Before parting, he mentioned the trip he and Allison were planning. "No boats there," he teased, "but your old Dad will stay on his toes." Her trusting smile warmed him.

* * *

Nathan supervised the loading of the luggage while Allison checked to make sure all the doors were locked.

The telephone rang and was quickly answered.

"Is everything set?" the caller asked.

"Signed, sealed and delivered."

The couple climbed into the limousine which would take them to the airport.

"Who was it?"

"Clifton. He called to wish us a pleasant trip."

Two days later in a remote forested section of the north rim of the Grand Canyon, and after a brief struggle, Nathan pushed Allison out of the single engine Cessna. He turned and tapped the helmeted pilot on the shoulder. "Okay, Clifton Jackson, that's one million dollars I owe you. Aren't you glad you decided to deal with me instead of my wife?"

"Shit, yes. You pay a lot better. Besides, that damned Allison was one greedy bitch. She was going to be more trouble than Maudi or Sara put together. The best part though, this time, I don't have to split the take with anyone."

Clifton had told Nathan how Allison had figured out his scheme of marrying rich women and then killing them. She convinced him to work with her. Together the two had planned Nathan's demise; hoping for a bigger prize.

Nathan smiled as they headed back to the airport in Flagstaff. Of course, it was too late for Sara and her mother, but he'd managed to outfox the murdering schemes of Allison and her hired killer. And more importantly, both he and Kim would be safe.

Clifton would never be as greedy as Allison. Especially, after he turned the man over to the police. That private investigator had finally turned up two previous women in Clifton's background who had also been murdered for money.

Nathan's testimony that Clifton and Allison had tried to murder him and she'd fallen from the plane during the struggle would be believed. He couldn't help mumbling aloud the thought which deepened his smile. "I always told Sara her psychic abilities were just a bunch of mumbo-jumbo."

THE BODY BEAUTIFUL

JUdiTh KElMAN

A bell tinkled as Marna Alexander entered the Slim-arama Weight Loss Center in the Eastgate Mall. The sound reminded her of the Good Humor truck. Then, most things did.

The waiting room was festooned with nutritional pamphlets; posters featuring high-fiber, low-flavor foods; and a scatter of overweight women. After whispering her name to the receptionist, Marna settled on one of the saggy blue leatherette sofas and picked up a copy of *Calorie Conscious* magazine.

The table of contents boasted such scintillating articles as: "Sprouts: To Gnaw them is to Love Them" and "Tofu or Not To-Fu." Marna pretended to read anyway. A veteran of many such facilities, she was conversant with the unspoken rules. One did not make small talk or eye contact. Women in reduction salons, no matter how corpulent or conspicuous, prized their anonymity. Marna had learned to feign interest in some virtuous reading material while stealing secret glances at the competition.

To Marna, such surreptitious evaluations and comparisons were irresistible. They made her feel somewhat better about herself, though not nearly better enough.

The Junior League type with the Bermuda bag had thunder

thighs severe enough to merit storm warnings. The upper arms on the redhead in the corner would serve nicely as built-in hang-gliders. Across the room was a Betty Boop clone inflated to the size of a Macy's parade float. Poor thing could probably pinch an inch of flab on her forehead.

Marna's heart really went out to the freckle-faced girl near the receptionist's desk who, at about ten, looked as if she'd spent the majority of her formative years chewing and swallowing. Marna had slogged through childhood in similiar condition, and she knew it was not anyone's notion of fun.

According to her mother, Marna had been born two months ahead of schedule, scrawny as a sale chicken at the A & P. Her parents' efforts to see her thrive had been entirely too successful. At a year, she'd weighed in at a hefty thirty-five pounds. By two, she'd been virtually too stout to toddle. In school, she'd been the mammoth butt of cruel teasing, reviled by all but her fellow outcasts: buck-toothed Barbara Biggerstaff, Zack "The Zit" Morris, Nerdy Paula Lassover and, of course, Elaine Dribben, who had no eyebrows and could curl the leaves of a healthy plant with her breath.

All those years, Marna had dreamed of having a beautiful body. Alone at night on her reinforced Sealy Posturepedic, she had invented a svelte alter-ego named Marilyn who was blessed with a belly flat as Texas, a twenty-one inch waistline, and perky little breasts with perfect posture. The imaginary Marilyn weighed a constant one hundred and three pounds, wore a size four, and had hip and cheekbones you could actually see without having to perform major surgery. Musing about Marilyn had often filled Marna with the sort of desperate longing that could only be alleviated by an emergency dose of Sarah Lee chocolate swirl pound cake a la mode.

"Marna Alexander."

Marna turned at her name. A Lycra-clad program assistant stood at the entrance to the fitness area sporting Marna's chart and a towel. Marna stood, and the woman flashed a curious smile. Slender people never quite understood, Marna thought. And this one even had thin lips and hair.

"Come along, Miss Alexander. I'll get you started."

For the next two hours, Marna sweated and groaned her way through a watercize class, step aerobics, buns and abs, and a programmed round of full-body tortures on the Nautilus machines. This was followed by the infamous Slim-arama massage, which combined elements of Swedish, Shiatsu, and pounding veal for scallopini. When it was finally time for her consultation with Slim-arama's medical director, Dr. Toner (his *real* name,) Marna was exhausted.

Waiting for Toner to arrive, she decided to lie down on one of the massage tables for a second and rest her eyes. Marna fell asleep instantly, but she was soon jolted awake by a sound across the room. Following the noise, she was startled to see a woman on a nearby table who was built exactly like her imaginary thin self, Marilyn.

Astonished, she surveyed the woman's gorgeous body from the firm turn of her trim little feet to the lithe, muscled legs to the wispy waist to the buoyant bosom capping a xylophone of ribs.

Marna flushed with embarrassment as her eyes drifted without permission to the woman's face. Incredible. She even had Marilyn's perky chin and prominent cheekbones. And there was Marilyn's chiselled nose. Marna tried to contain herself, but she simply had to violate the edict against eye contact. She had to get to know this woman, this dead ringer for her imaginary Marilyn.

This—*dead*—ringer.

It took a minute for reality to pierce the cushion of shock. The woman's eyes were stretched beyond human limits, frozen with shock. Unblinking. Unseeing.

The scream erupted from deep in Marna's gut as she bounded off the massage table and raced to the hall.

"Help! There's a skinny dead girl in the consultation room. God, help me! Someone, anyone."

In seconds a curious crowd of rotund women and their paid tormenters had gathered. Marna, shocked nearly speechless, pointed at the door of the massage room.

"In there. Oh God, it's horrible."

Dr. Toner instructed the throng to remain in the hall while he ventured inside to investigate. The man looked pale and shaken. Then, sudden deaths could not be very good for business.

A beat later, he emerged. His expression had hardened and taken on a reproachful edge.

"Miss Alexander, will you come in here?"

Marna's knees felt like unset Jell-o. "I can't, Dr. Toner. Please."

He flung open the door. "Then look from where you are, Miss Alexander. See for yourself. There is nobody in the room."

Startled, Marna peered inside. Cringing, she forced herself to glance at the massage table. No body.

"But you don't understand. She was right there a minute ago."

Everyone was staring. Heads were shaking, eyes rolling in contemptuous rebuke. One woman in tent-sized sweats and a turban twirled a pudgy finger near her left temple.

"Crazy," someone else whispered in agreement.

"But I saw her," Marna protested. "You have to believe me. She was slim and gorgeous and dead."

Dr. Toner led her to his office, took her pulse, shook his bald head disapprovingly, and ordered her to compose herself and see herself out.

"Perhaps you should consider counseling, Miss Alexander," he huffed as he took his leave.

Over the next two days, the incident faded from Marna's consciousness, displaced by pressing issues at work.

Marna was an associate director in the art department at Pennysworth Publishing. After graduating from the Rhode Island School of Design, she'd landed an assistant's post and quickly ascended to the associate directorship in charge of cover art for Pennysworth's ribald romance line: "Wild Weekend."

During her ten-month stint in that slot, she'd become very adroit at tossing off wisp-waisted women with bosoms that heaved in two dimension and dashing Clark Gable clones with thick hair and sinkhole dimples.

For her efforts, she'd been promoted to the team assigned to Pennysworth's newest venture: "Diamonds in the Rough." The imprint featured books with a great deal of sex and violence by authors willing to work for the glory and a mid three-figure advance. Marna's mandate was to give these Pennysworth dreadfuls a "class" package.

She was working on *Hog Tied*, the charming tale of a sadomasochistic romance on a Virginia farm, when the phone rang. Welcome interruption. Marna was having a great deal of trouble deciding between the cattle prod and the bullwhip as the central cover motif.

"Marna Alexander?"

"Speaking."

"This is Dr. Cheng's office calling. We had you down for an 11:30 appointment today."

Marna cast a desperate eye at her watch. Noon. "Oh no. I can't believe I forgot. Listen, I waited two months for this appointment. There must be a way you can squeeze me in if I come right over. Please."

"Well . . ."

"I'll be right there."

She sprinted out of the Pennysworth Building on Forty-fifth and Third and tried to flail down a cab. After five minutes of futile gesticulating, she started jogging toward Dr. Cheng's office on West Twenty-eighth Street.

She arrived less than ten minutes later, breathless and beet-faced. Perspiration had pasted her white blouse to her back, and her navy pumps had raised screaming blisters on both feet. Small sacrifice, she thought as she hobbled through the lobby.

Cheng's office was a converted ground floor apartment. The receptionist buzzed Marna in, nodded coolly, and cast a pointed look at the wall clock.

"I know," Marna said. "I'm really sorry. It won't happen again."

The waiting area reminded Marna of her grandmother's living room in Brooklyn. It was furnished with heavy upholstered pieces in sensible shades with doilies on the arms and backs to catch the body oils. The needlepoint pillows were exactly like Granny's also, except that Granny's stitched aphorisms were not in Chinese. Marna settled on a brown leather recliner and prepared herself for a long wait. The receptionist, an officious little woman with a crossbite, did not look like the forgiving type.

Marna leafed through a prehistoric *National Geographic*. Disappointed to find no nude pictures of primitive tribesmen, she set the magazine aside and mused about the wonders of Dr. Simon Cheng.

Cheng was a holistic nutritionist whose methods combined ancient Eastern practices with elements of contemporary Western biochemistry. After suffering through every imaginable diet, Marna had found his prescribed regimen both palatable and easy to follow. Basically, she ate a lot of take-out from Ho Chi's East washed down by large glasses of Dr. Cheng's weight control elixir. The bottle listed forty tongue-twisting ingredients, but it tasted for all the world like a chocolate egg cream.

Marna was frankly hooked on the stuff, which was amazing given that it contained neither whipped cream nor fudge. The only problem was Dr. Cheng's insistence that she come in for a check-up every six months before he'd consent to replenish her supply.

She cast a longing look at the receptionist.

"Soon, Miss Alexander," the woman said sharply.

Nearly an hour later, the receptionist nodded for Marna to step into Cheng's hallowed examining room. Marna undressed, slipped on a paper gown and sat on the examining table.

More waiting. More old *National Geographics*. Her mind drifted back to *Hog Tied*. Closing her eyes, she envisioned Manny, the escaped arsonist and feed salesman, and Fiona, the farmer's daughter, a nursery school teacher and erstwhile nymphomaniac. The cover design should probably include the Virginia ham in that incredible hayloft scene after which Fiona agrees to give Manny the kidney he needs for the transplant.

The door rattled, and Marna snapped alert. She expected to see the compact form of Dr. Cheng, but instead, she found herself face to face with the dead woman from the Slim-arama.

Marna swallowed back a rising scream. Slowly, carefully, she slipped off the table and made her tremulous way to the door. In the hall, she spotted Cheng coming out of his office. As he approached, she gestured at the examining room. Her mouth was chalk.

"Marilyn. In there . . ." Unable to get out the part about the deplorable state of the woman's health, she made a throat-slicing gesture.

"You all right, Miss Alexander? What's wrong? You choking?"

"She's—dead," Marna finally managed. "There's a dead woman in there."

Cheng peered inside and then at Marna. "No one in there, Miss Alexander. Must be you imagined it."

He escorted her to his office, sat her down, and drew a glass of water off the Crystal Rock cooler beside the desk.

"Better now?"

Marna nodded, but she didn't feel at all better. Something was terribly wrong. Maybe someone was trying to drive her crazy. Maybe she *was* crazy.

The rest of the day passed in a blur. She left work early, unable to concentrate on *Hog Tied* or anything else. From long habit, she stopped at Ho Chi's East on the way home and picked up her standard order of Buddha's delight with a side of vegetarian lo mein. But, for the first time in memory, Marna was not the least bit hungry.

Her only appetite was for answers. Who was that dead woman? How had she died? Why was someone using the body to torment Marna? Could it be some kind of sick warning? Maybe Marna was next on the murderer's list.

The thought set her pulse racing like a caged hamster. Plenty of lunatics in New York City. What if one of them had targeted Marna?

Maybe she should call the police.

But what would she tell them? She knew the whole thing sounded preposterous, and she had no witnesses. Even if the police took her seriously, what could they do? They weren't about to offer her protection from a disappearing dead girl or a possible serial murderer with a really tasteless way of advertising his services.

Marna considered her options. Like it or not, she knew her best shot was to discuss the whole business with Phoebe Kalisher. True, Phoebe had been avoiding her. True, the woman was petulant, stubborn and unreasonable. But she also happened to be a problem-solving genius. If there was a way to deal with this horrendous situation, Phoebe would figure it out.

Half an hour later, Phoebe bustled in and wrinkled her nose. "Stinks in here."

"Buddha's delight," Marna said.

"Smells like Buddha's outhouse. So what's up? I'm sure you wouldn't have called unless you needed a favor, Marna. I have to tell you, if I didn't find you needy and pathetic, I wouldn't even have come."

"I'm not needy and pathetic, Phoebe. You're the one who's needy and pathetic."

"You called me, Marna. So get to the point."

Marna decided to put off fighting with Phoebe until she'd picked her brain about the peripatetic dead girl. From long experience, Marna knew that Phoebe was not at her best after a battle.

The two had met in their freshman year at the Rhode Island School of Design. As seasoned obese misfits, they'd naturally been drawn to one another.

Through four years of school, they'd had a close, if prickly friendship. After graduation, they'd taken apartments within blocks of each other in the Yorkville section of Manhattan. They'd continued to get together several evenings a week to overeat and exchange insults. Their relationship had flourished on a solid foundation of mutual antipathy and a shared adoration of extra rich ice cream.

But in the last six months, things between them had deteriorated. Phoebe had grown cool and distant. She'd taken to walking out after a good fight, instead of making up over dessert as was their tradition. Soon, she'd taken to avoiding their dinners altogether, making up improbable excuses like needing the evening to wash her hair. Phoebe's hair was a porcupine bob that took four minutes maximum to wash and dry. Six when she deep-conditioned.

Marna has tried once to discuss the problem, but Phoebe refused to admit there *was* a problem. So the two had simply drifted apart. Though she hated to admit it, Marna regretted the breach. There were not all that many socially undesirable people who lived within walking distance.

Fortunately, Phoebe was still willing to hear Marna's harrowing tale. She listened intently, her face set in that rodent-like expression that meant she was paying close attention.

"And she looked exactly like Marilyn?" Phoebe asked when Marna finished her monologue.

"Same body, same face. Same everything. Isn't it the weirdest thing you ever heard?"

Phoebe frowned. "Can I ask you a personal question?"

"If I said no, would it stop you?"

"Have you been feeling like yourself lately, Marna? I mean, maybe the strain is getting to you."

"What strain?"

"All the dieting, the exercise, the special foods, special drinks, doctors, trainers. Maybe you should just give it up already. It's enough to make anyone nuts."

"I'm not nuts. I saw the woman, and she was dead. What's nuts is that you refuse to believe me, and you weren't even there. *I* was there, Phoebe. And that's the truth."

Phoebe went grim. "You asked for my read on this thing, so I'm giving it to you. I think you should see a head doctor. And I think you should give up all the dieting business and get on with your life. You've taken this thing far enough. Too far, if you ask me."

Marna shook her head. "I expected more from you of all people, Phoebe Kalisher. You of all people should understand."

"I do understand. I understand you're several cards short of a full deck, Marna. So good night." She paused at the door. "And one more piece of advice, get rid of that Buddha's boo boo stuff. Smells like low tide in here."

After Phoebe left, Marna spent a couple of hours sputtering and fuming. Wearying of that, she ate half a box of dietetic cookies, slugged down a bottle of Cheng's elixir and went to bed.

Sleep was elusive. It finally arrived bearing sackfuls of grim imaginings. First, Marna dreamed Phoebe Kalisher was trying to drown her in a gigantic vat of Rocky Road ice cream. That was followed by a horrific nightmare in which the imaginary Marilyn's dead twin came alive and was working out beside Marna in Intermediate Step Aerobics.

She awoke at dawn, shaken and sapped. How much more of this could she stand? How could she possibly make it through another day of worrying that the dead girl might turn up without warning. What if the corpse was waiting for her at work? What if someone had planted that gorgeous body somewhere right here, in Marna's own apartment?

That thought sent her turtling under the covers. She couldn't shake the feeling that the corpse might be in her bathtub or propped at the dinette table or sprawled on the sofa in front of "Good Morning America."

Marna knew she was running late for work. And she knew that would not sit well with her new boss at Pennysworth, who was not all that happy to have her in the department in the first place. But for the next half hour, she remained a prisoner of her own dread.

Finally, in desperation, she snaked her hand out of the covers, retrieved the phone from the nightstand and phoned Phoebe Kalisher.

"Please, Phoebe. I'm a wreck. You've got to come right over and help me."

Phoebe used her spare key to let herself in. Without a word, she separated Marna from her covers and helped her dress. Clutching Phoebe like a life preserver, Marna managed to make it out of the apartment and down to the street. Phoebe hailed a cab and barked an address on Central Park West and Eighty-first.

"I called my cousin Harold, the psychiatrist," Phoebe said. "I said it was an emergency, and he agreed to squeeze you in right away. Harold's a genius, Marna. You'll see."

Marna took slow, measured breaths. She wanted desperately to believe the whole thing had been a figment of her imagination. Maybe a psychiatrist was the answer. Something had to be. She was such a mess, Phoebe practically had to carry her out of the cab and through the posh lobby to the elevators.

Harold Kalisher greeted them at the entrance to the fourth floor apartment that doubled as an office. He was a striking young man with a warm smile and firm, reassuring handshake. "Marna? Come on in. Cousin Phoebe, there's coffee in the kitchen if you like."

Harold put Marna instantly at ease. Lying on his leather couch, she told him everything, from her first run-in with the body at the Slim-arama to the awful fright of Dr. Cheng's office to the terrifying depths of her current incapacity.

He listened with minimal comment. When Marna got teary, he handed her a Kleenex. "It's okay," he said.

When she finished the whole sordid tale, she drew a hard breath. "Do you think I'm crazy, Dr. Kalisher?"

"Not at all."

"What then? What's going on?"

"It's complicated, Marna. But I think . . ."

A buzzer sounded on his desk. Harold crossed and picked up the phone. "Yes? All right, Betty. I'll take it inside." He turned to Marna. "Sorry, it's an emergency. You relax. I'll be right back."

Drained from the awful night and the difficult confession, Marna let her mind drift. Why had Phoebe kept this hunk of a cousin such a big secret?

Maybe Phoebe was just ashamed to introduce her to anyone. Who'd want to introduce a handsome, accomplished relative to a lump like Marna after all?

A wash of weariness overtook her. Marna yawned and rubbed her eyes. This time she refused to fall asleep and wake up to the sight of that dead woman with the drop dead body. No way.

Struggling to stay awake, Marna looked around Harold Kalisher's office. On the wall beside the couch were diplomas from Yale and Downstate Medical School and Harold's diplomate certificate from the American College of Psychiatry. Directly ahead was a cluster of artful underwater photographs. Tracking the wall toward the door, she spotted several smiling family portraits. No one who looked at all wifely. Then maybe the wife or girlfriend's picture was on Harold's desk.

Turning in that direction, Marna froze. Poking out from behind the desk was a pair of feet. They were the dead girl's feet. No question. Marilyn's dead twin was back there, behind that desk.

Marna couldn't move, couldn't think. Panic looped around her neck. A blade of a scream coursed through her and escaped to shatter the silence. The screams took her over. She became a huge, wrenching scream.

Suddenly, arms caught and subdued her. A hand stroked her back. A calming voice reached in and started pulling her back from the brink. Her screams gentled to a syncopated whimper.

"Sssh now, Marna. What happened? Tell me what's wrong."

"She's there, Harold. Over there behind the desk. I saw her feet."

"Come, Marna. Show me."

Panic gripped her tighter. "No! Don't make me."

"Come. It'll be all right. I'm right here. Right with you."

Trembling, leaning on Harold, Marna managed to make it across the room. Sparks shot off in her mind as she found herself face to face with Marilyn's moribund twin. The dead girl was standing now, a startled expression on her face. Looked as if she'd seen a ghost. But it was Marna who'd seen the damned ghost.

"There," she said. "That's her. Make her go away. Make her stop."

Harold moved a step closer. Suddenly, Marna saw him standing beside the dead girl. But how the hell?

"It's a mirror, Marna. That's no dead girl. That's you."

"Me? But it can't be. Look at her. She's slim, gorgeous. I'm a fat tub of lard. Always have been."

"It's what I suspected. It can take a long time for the self image to catch up with a major change. I still find myself thinking aboout the big man's shop when I need clothes, and I lost the hundred pounds ten years ago."

"You were fat? I don't believe it."

"Well I was. And in a way, I still am. At least, in my head I am. Just like you."

Dumbfounded, Marna stared at her incredible image. She pinched herself to make sure she wasn't dreaming, and, given her total lack of extra flesh, the pinch actually hurt. "That's me? I mean, hey, that's me. Marna Ackerman, the body beautiful."

For several minutes, she stared at her new shape. It was a body to behold, but she couldn't quite believe it actually belonged to her.

"Thank you, Harold. Sorry for all the commotion."

"No problem. I'm glad it was as simple as that."

She crossed to leave. "I pay the receptionist?"

"No charge."

At the door, she hesitated. Emboldened by her incredible new form, she cleared her throat and took the plunge. "How about I take you out to dinner then? Any night's okay."

Harold smiled warmly. "That'd be nice, Marna. Why don't I check with my wife and let you know what's good for her."

"Yeah, why don't you?"

Phoebe was in the reception area. "So, Cousin Harold? You straighten out my loony friend here?"

He shot her a look. "Say hello to your mother, Phoebe. Nice meeting you, Marna."

As soon as they were in the elevator, Phoebe started pelting her with questions. "So what was all the shrieking, Marna. You freak out and see that dead woman again?"

"No, I didn't."

"So did Harold help you figure out what all the lunacy was about?"

"Yes."

"So what was it about?"

Marna strode across the lobby and out to Central Park West. She crossed the street and headed into the park with Phoebe yapping at her heels. "So tell me, Marna. I didn't bring you all the way here to play games."

"I'm fine, Phoebe. I understand now."

"You understand what? Don't be this way, Marna. I mean it. I'm warning you, Marna. Cut it out."

Marna hardly heard her. Her mind was tuned to the tinkle of approaching bells. This time it really was a Good Humor truck. Flagging it down, she fished in her purse for the change.

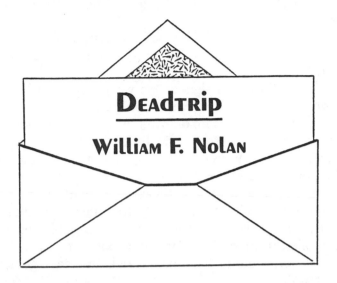

Deadtrip

William F. Nolan

It was murky in Bubble City. A blowing mist of sand had spread like a dark red shroud over the streets and buildings, reminding me of the way Frisco used to look in the fog before the Big Quake put the whole berg under several zillion gallons of saltwater.

But every planet has its problems, and if you live on Mars, you put up with a helluva lot of blowing red sand. It comes with the territory.

I was in a mood as murky as the weather. I'd just been stiffed out of my fee by a crooked Mercurian pork stuffer who'd skipped the galaxy before I could bill him for my services. Worse yet, he'd run off with Hildy, my new solid-state electronic secretary. I figured I couldn't afford to replace her. I'd just have to get Edna, my old battery-operated office model, out of storage. The whole sorry affair was a real pain in the assola — and I was taking it out on my hovercar, yelling about how slow he was going.

"Hey, Space, I'm practically *blind* in this shit," the car replied defensively. (He had a dirty mouth.) "Can't see my own frigging jet fins."

"Then use your sensors."

"They went out two months ago and you've been too cheap to replace them," the car growled.

"Not too cheap, too *broke*," I snapped back. "You should have my bills."

"Hah!" snorted the car. "It's bad enough having to fulfill your requirements in basic transportation. I certainly don't need a stack of unpaid bills to make me peevish."

"All right, all right," I sighed. "So we're *both* in a lousy mood."

When the car let me out at my coapt I decided it would be a good idea to drink myself into oblivion. At least until morning. Then I wouldn't have to deal with the fact that I was an aging, overweight, sex-starved, jobless private dick who was all out of future. Being an alcoholic helped me get past days like this.

I palmed the door and it flipped open with a cheery "Good evening, boss!" I *hate* cheerful doors, but this one came with the coapt.

Inside, I stripped off my coat and shoulder rig, placing my loaded .450 Lansdale-Puechner twingrip pinbeamer on the coftabe and immediately activated the bar. I had to kick it twice to get it to come out of the wall.

"What'll it be?" asked the bar.

"Dogstar Stinger," I told it. "Double, no ice."

"Hit me," said the bar.

I took out my credcard and slotted it into the bar's nearwood top.

The Stinger appeared and I gulped it down, ordering another.

"Better take it easy on these babies," warned the bar. "They're potent."

"When I need your advice about my drinking, I'll ask for it," I said. "So butt off."

"So screw you," said the bar, grumpily folding itself back into the wall.

I took my Stinger and headed for the bedroom, intending to stretch out and float into shuteye.

That's when I found her.

A deadtrip. Flat on her back in a glowzip flarecoat and pink transpants, her three mouths gaping, her three sets of eyes glazed and staring.

She'd been a beaut. Lovely skin, full thrusters, flat tummy, great legs. What a waste!

I saw that the bedroom coolvent had been forced open, so I knew how she got inside, but I had two big questions for myself: Why did she come to *my* coapt? And who snuffed her?

I'd known my share of Venusian tripleheads, but I'd never seen this particular beauty in Bubble City.

What was I going to say to the law? Hey, fellas, I just found this deadtrip in my coapt. Don't know her. Don't know who killed her. Don't know nothin'.

Which wouldn't cut it. Not with Lt. O'Malloy hating me more than his mother-in-law. Nothing he'd like better than seeing me cool out in the local jug. Obviously, I had to get this little sexpot out of my coapt.

I checked her for cause, and could find nothing. No cuts, holes, skin punctures, or bruises. Not a mark on her. Weird!

I wrapped her in a nearblanket, heaved her onto my shoulder, and left. The car was waiting in its hoverslot on the roof, and when I dumped the corpse inside I got what I expected. Sour grapes.

"It is illegal for me to transport a dead body," the car said. "I refuse to engage power until it is removed."

"Look, I don't intend to argue with you about this," I said flatly. "If you don't engage power on your own, I'll switch to manual and drive you myself."

"Okay, Space," said the car, "but I want you to know something. I think you're a creep. You make me *sick!*"

"Just shut your gob and take me to the Boneyard," I snapped. And he did.

The Boneyard is at the edge of the bubble, the last cemetery on Mars. The new deathregs on Big Red require cremation. The Boneyard is a relic of the past, reflecting a period when people were actually buried in the ground. In 2090 they dug up all the caskets from various gravesites and moved them here to this one central yard. Closed all the others. If you have a dead relative in the ground you come to the Boneyard to pay your respects. What better place to bury my stiff?

I had the deadtrip over my right shoulder when the seven-foot robo graveguard stopped me at the gate.

"What's in the bundle?" he asked.

"What's it look like?"

"Dead body."

"Bingo! You get the cigar."

"Can't take it in here. Against the law."

I put down the body and used my Straub .410 on the big lug.

The charge was strong enough to stun an Earthelephant, and when he was out cold I opened his chest and fiddled with his memory circuits. Once he woke up, he wouldn't remember a damn thing.

I buried the triplehead in a shallow grave (since if I needed to check her bod again I wouldn't have to do a lot of heavy digging). Then I had the car take me back to my office. A slow trip with the sand still blowing.

She hadn't been carrying any body ID on her, but all Venusians have a skull number implanted on their middle heads at birth. Hers was 66224-95, which gave me something to work with.

I ran the number through my compudesk and got the stats I wanted.

Name:	ROBERTA SASHONON
Age:	29
Employment:	LAB TECH, GEEVER INDUSTRIES, LUNA
Residence:	DARKSIDE ARMS, UNIT 412

An hour later I was on an express Mooner heading for Darkside. When a stiff pops up in my bedroom, I take it personally. I had to find out what the hell was going on.

The Darkside Arms was strictly high gloss—way too rich for a lab tech's salary. Which meant somebody was helping Sashonon pay her rent. Maybe the same bozo who iced her.

I got to 412 with no hassle, but by the time I'd laser-keyed the door I had a vampire house dick on my neck. He was big, three hundred pounds of Mercurian beef, with a set of fangs long enough to suck the life out of an Earthwhale. And right now he had those fangs buried in me up to the gums.

I keep a buzzblade strapped to my right leg and I got this one into action, sinking it into his fat belly. Then I hit the blade stud and electrocuted him.

He danced into a pile of black ash on the nearcarpet.

I didn't mind killing him since I'd never met a house dick who wasn't on the take. And I don't like vampires.

Unit 412 was a mess. Broken flowcabs, smashed glowdrawers, overturned bodlamps. Even the wallbed had been gutted.

Somebody was looking for something, and that somebody wanted that something real bad. But what? And had they found it?

My next stop was a natural. Geever Industries at Luna Base. A huge sprawl of boxbeam labs surrounded by a force fence that *nobody* gets through.

I talked to the robo at the main entrance dome.

"I'd like to see Mr. G.," I said.

"Do you have a confirmed meetdate?"

"No, but he'll want to see me. I'm his cousin Oscar from Bubble City and I have some urgent family biz to discuss with him. Emergency."

The robo didn't look impressed, but since he had no face, it was hard to tell. He vidded Mr. G., who told him to admit me.

A quickbelt took me directly to his den. It was so freaking fast I didn't get more than a flash of Geever Industries, the labs passing in a silver blur at the edge of my vision. Then I was inside Mr. G's private workden, facing the old boy.

I'd read a lot about him in *Forbesfax*. Born on Venus, he'd made his fortune as a young tad mining Titan's moons, and was now rich enough to buy his own solar system. Brilliant, cruel, avaricious, and highly sexed. He was also, of course, triple-headed. Two of his heads had mustaches; the middle one was bearded. It did most of the talking.

"You are not my cousin Oscar," he said. He wore a zircon zipsuit with tuckered cuffs. Classy.

"I'm Samuel T. Space, a private investigator from Bubble City. But I'm sure you already know that."

"Ah," and his right head smiled. "And just how would I know your real identity?"

I sat down in front of his classy desk.

"Body scan. The dome robo's got a unit built right into his deltoids. You didn't buy my cover story, but you wanted to see me."

"And why would I want to see a cheap, ill-clad, impoverished peeper from Mars?"

"You keep asking me questions with obvious answers," I said. "You want to see me because you had Roberta Sashonon followed to my coapt. When she died there, you were smart enough to figure that I was smart enough to trace her to you."

"And why would I have one of my lab techs followed to Mars?"

I decided to keep answering. I was making some wild guesses, but he wasn't denying anything.

"Because she was more than a lab tech. She was one of your numerous sexual diversions. You set her up at the Darkside and played bed-a-bye with her there. Until she double-crossed you, taking away something you wanted real bad. You had your goons trash her unit looking for it, but they didn't find the gizmo. So you had her followed."

"Let us assume that all of this is true," said the mustached head on the left. "Why, then, did she come to you?"

"To hire me to protect her—or the thing she'd taken away from you. Or maybe both. But she died before she could offer me the assignment."

"And did I kill her?"

"Indirectly. You put her under so much stress her heart exploded. Happens with tripleheads—as I guess you know."

"And why, Mr. Space," asked the middle head, "if I'm the guilty party, did I admit you to my workden?"

"To find out if I know where the gizmo is. You figured she just might have lived long enough to tell me. She didn't."

"Ah," said the bearded head, "and how do I know you're telling me the truth?"

"This chair I'm sitting in is equipped with a body temp detector. If I lied, you'd know it by my body's emotional response."

"You are very observant, Mr. Space."

"It's my job. I try to keep up with what's going on around me."

"Well," and all three heads sighed, "I suppose there's no real reason to torture you to death for the information I'm seeking."

"Thanks," I said. "I've never enjoyed being tortured to death."

"But what am I going to do with you? I cannot allow you to return to Mars knowing as much as you do, now can I?"

"Sure you can," I said. "My desk knows I was coming here to see you. If I don't get back okay, it will relay that info to the law and *you'll* be the one answering all the questions. Since I don't know what the gizmo is that you're looking for, and since I don't know where to find it, you're safe in letting me go back to Mars with a little buy-off money in my kick."

"Buy off?"

"To insure that I'll keep my yap shut." I held out my hand. "Ten thousand creds should take care of my big mouth. So fork it over, chum."

All three of his faces went red. Mr. G. was one sore dude. What he wanted to do was kill me. What he *did* was pay me.

"Obliged," I said, pocketing the creds.

Of course it was blackmail, but with a prime scuzzball like Geever, I didn't mind putting the blocks to him.

"Let me warn you, Mr. Space," he said through his beard, "if you wish to remain alive, you are to forget what you know and drop this entire situation from your mind. Is that clearly understood?"

"Yo," I nodded. "I get your drift."

And I was out of there.

Back on Big Red I headed for the Boneyard again, feeling stupid. The reason I felt that way is because I had failed to run a complete bodcheck on the deadtrip. Sure, I had sense enough to get her skull number, but I hadn't checked her body for what I now suspected was there: info on where she'd hidden the gizmo.

This time I decided to short out the electrofence and go in that way, avoiding the guard robo. Once inside, I dug out my triplehead. She was a little the worse for wear, but before putting her into the ground I'd given her an injection which delayed organ decay for 36 hours, so at least I didn't have to contend with a rotting stiff.

I checked her bod and hit the jackpot when I found a fake molar in the middle head and removed it. Inside the hollow tooth was a foilslip with the info I needed. Loc 29-Z, Subbase, DArms. Which told me she'd stashed the gizmo in Locker No. 29, Row Z, in the sub-basement of the Darkside Arms. And I kept the foilslip, knowing the locker wouldn't open without it.

On the express Mooner back to Luna I figured I was playing a very dangerous game, double-crossing Mr. G. and going for his gizmo. I got the first indication of trouble when a spider assassin attacked me in the ship's john.

He was a real pro, with enough arms to do the job on three or four of me. He had one arm around my throat, another was crushing my ribcage, a third was going for a crotch-crush (really painful!) and a fourth was battering my kneecaps. I managed to activate my buckle, which released a swarm of nitrodarts from the back of my belt. They took out the assassin in a single explosion and parts of him rained down on me in a gooey shower. Took me a while to clean myself up.

When we touched down on Luna, I was in a depressed state, realizing how dumb I was to be going up against a solar kingpin like Mr. G. The spider man had undoubtedly been instructed to blitz me for the info on Mr. G.'s missing gizmo.

How did he know I had the info? Well, I wouldn't be coming back to Luna this soon without it, would I?

So what chance did one antiquated private eye have against a multizillionaire with half the goons in the System working for him? Space, I told myself, this time you've gone round the bend. You're wacko! And all because I'd found a deadtrip in my bedroom.

Okay, I reasoned with myself, once I find out what the gizmo is, then maybe I'll let Mr. G. have it back. I told myself I just wanted to satisfy my curiosity. That's what I *told* myself.

I got into the locker area at the Darkside Arms with no sweat. All I had to do was flash the foil. I asked for privacy and got it. Opened Locker 29-Z, and there was the gizmo. I took it out, looked it over.

A shiny silver orb the size of an Earth grapefruit. With metalloid plugs at one end.

It reminded me of something familiar, but *what?* I couldn't get a mindfix on it. I decided to hang onto the thing until I could ID it. Which meant I had to take some immediate precautions.

I had my identiswitch kit with me, and I made sure that Sam Space did not walk out of that building. Oh, sure, I left—but with a new nose, altered cheekbones and skull configuration, fresh body hair, and a change of clothes. (I simply reversed the outfit I was wearing.) The disguise would get me back to Mars at least, and from there it would be touch and go, with all the odds in Mr. G.'s favor.

But I was willing to take the risk.

Actually, I didn't go back to Mars. Not yet. Instead, I booked a warper for Earth.

When I walked into Nathan Oliver's workshop under the Art Museum in Old Chicago my fat friend was waiting for me. I'd vidphoned from the landing port to tell him I was coming.

We embraced. I had a warm spot in my heart for this bell-shaped, pink-jowled little man. We'd been linked on a lot of wild capers, and

Nate had saved my life more than a couple of times.

"Sam, Sam, Sam," he said, looking at me. "Is it still you under all the gook?"

I took off my fake nose, retroaltered my skull and cheeks, and got rid of the excess body hair. "It's me," I said.

We embraced again. Nate loved to give bearhugs to people he cared about. Then we sat down on Marlon Brando.

"I made him into a couch," Nate said, smiling.

Nate's hobby was making furniture out of film legends. He'd done a fine job with Marlon.

"I can't wait to find out why you're here, Samuel," Oliver said, smacking his thick red lips. "It's bound to be exciting. Always is!"

"I found something I want you to try and identify," I told him. "With all the nutty inventions you work on, I figured you might be able to tell me what this is."

And I handed him the round silver object.

"This is an oversized android's left testicle," he said matter-of-factly.

"Huh?" I blinked. "You mean . . . it's a robot's nut?"

"In erstwhile slang, yes."

I leaned back into Brando, more than a little stunned. "But what's it *for*?"

"What any testicle is for," said Nate. "It supplies a sexual substance which travels through the penis and is expelled at orgasm. In this case, from a *robotic* penis."

"Robo semen?"

"I'll have to analyze it in my lab before I can tell you the exact nature of the substance."

"Then *do* it," I said. "I want to know what's in there."

I paced the room nervously while Nate worked in his lab. I tried sitting down to relax, first on Al Pacino, then on Barbara Walters, but it was no good. So I just paced. Somehow, I knew that whatever was in that robot's nut was of major importance. Call it instinct, but I *knew.*

Nate returned with the testicle.

"Well?"

"It's pipium," he said.

"What's pipium?"

Nate didn't answer. Instead, he slowly raised his arms in the air, staring fearfully at someone behind me. It was Mr. G. Holding a Freebish-Etchison .620 Magrifle in his manicured hand. Two other armed goons were in the doorway.

"I shall be delighted to show you exactly what pipium is, and what it does," said the smiling Geever, letting his bearded head do the talking. "You shall both accompany me back to Luna as my personal guests for a special demonstration."

"How'd you know I was here?" I asked him.

"I've had you followed ever since our little talk," said Mr. G. "I knew it was simply a matter of time until you led me to the testicle."

"But I took your money and agreed to quit the case."

"Of course, but I knew curiosity would force you to continue. All I had to do was be patient."

"And the spider assassin?"

"I allowed you to kill him. To give you a false sense of security." He prodded me with the barrel of the Freebish-Etchison. "And now . . . shall we, to use your quaint slang, split out of this joint?"

We split.

I was really in the soup. I'd played myself for a prime sap all the way down the line. Maybe if I'd turned over the nut to Geever I wouldn't be in this fix, but no, Geever would have iced me no matter what I did. Still, Nate wouldn't be taking the fall with me if I hadn't involved him in all this.

Damn!

We were taken straight to Geever's main lab on Luna. Vast and impressive. State-of-the-art equipment. I got the feeling he could build anything here. But I wasn't ready for what he actually *had* built.

His goons kept us continually in their gunsights, leaving Geever free to conduct the grand tour. He escorted us to the far end of the cavernous chamber—to a tall, alum-covered object which extended halfway to the high ceiling.

"Before I unveil my masterwork," Geever said, "I shall keep my promise as to informing you about pipium."

"That's real kind, Mr. G.," I said.d "You're a sweetheart."

I knew he intended to kill us, that he was simply playacting for his own amusement. But there was nothing I could do about it.

"Pipium is extremely rare. In fact, this testicle," and he held it up, slowly turning the silvery orb in his hand, "holds the last grains of it known to exist in our galaxy. It acts in the same manner as plutonium did on the atomic bomb back in your twentieth earth-century."

"You've built a super bomb!" breathed Nate. It was the first time he'd spoken to Geever since we arrived on Luna.

"Not exactly," said Mr. G. "I think that as a fellow-inventor, Mr. Oliver, you'll agree that what I *have* built is far more sophisticted and, one could say, *inspiring.*"

He gestured to a goon, and the alum covering slid away from the giant object in front of us. My jaw fell. I was gaping. Nate's eyes were bugging.

"Ah, I see that you are both properly awestruck at my little creation," he said.

And we were.

Looming above us were two giant, cunningly-fashioned nude robots, a male and a female, their shining metal skins relfecting the lab lights as they leaned into one another's arms in a frozen embrace. Their heads were close together, lips almost touching.

"They are poised to make love," Geever told us. "All I need do to activate them is plug *this* into its proper place." He held up the robot testicle.

Now I could see that the left nut was missing on the genitals of the male robot.

"So you've built yourself a couple of sex toys to get off with," I said. "What I don't fathom is what these two tin lovebirds have to do with the atomic bomb."

"Once they begin to make love, Mr. Space," Geever said, "you will find they are capable of far more than sexual amusement."

He walked over to a massive screen to the left, pressed a stud at its base. My home planet hovered to life on the screen like a giant blue and white marble. Beautiful! Good old Earth. No matter how long I lived on Mars, I was an Earthling to my blood and bones.

"You will have the unique privilege of watching the demise of this miserable planet," Geever said.

"What the hell are you saying?" I snapped at him.

"The testicle activates what I call my Doomsday Device," declared Mr. G. "When the robots' lovemaking reaches climax, their double orgasm will set off a cosmic vibration powerful enough to detonate the Earth. You will be able to see it blown apart on the tri-dim screen. In fact, I shall set the screen at slow motion, so you won't miss any of the explosive details." And he chuckled at his word play.

I knew he wasn't kidding. This guy had the power and the money to do almost anything.

241

"But why destroy Earth?" I asked.

"Because I loathe and detest that pale ball of clay," he replied, mouth twisting with anger.

I wasn't going to argue with him. Geever was totally crackers, that was clear. But I did want to keep him talking. I needed to stall for time, to try and think of a way to stop him . . .

"What did Roberta Sashonon have to do with all this?" I asked. "How did she end up with your testicle?"

"I trusted her!" raged Geever, giving full vent to his anger. All three of his faces were red. "I told her I loved her, set her up in a unit of her own, gave her expensive gifts—and she *betrayed* me. She unplugged the testicle and made off with it. I couldn't kill her, as much as I wanted to, not until I'd regained my testicle."

"But why did she steal it?" I wanted to know. "For money?"

"No, no, not for that. She knew I'd provide her with all the money she wanted. She told me she did it to save Earth."

"But why risk her life for Earth? She was a Venusian."

"She was in love with an Earthman. Imagine—falling in love with a man with just *one* head! It's revolting. She wanted him to leave Earth and live on Venus with her, but he refused—so she visited him regularly in New Old New York. When I thought she was visiting her sister on Venus, she was actually screwing this miserable Earthman. When I found out about the affair, I built the Doomsday Device. I intended to make her watch as I destroyed Earth, and her lover along with it. That's when she made off with my testicle, knowing that I needed it to activate my creation."

"And you had her followed to my place in Bubble City?"

"Yes, but I told my goons not to harm her. I was hoping she'd reveal the location of the testicle. I had not counted on her heart giving out. We tripleheads are far too emotional for our own good."

"If you're an example, I'd have to agree," I told him.

"Enough of this chatter. It's time to eliminate Earth. I can't force that dead bitch to watch, but at least the two of you can fill in for her. Sorry I can't be here to share the fun."

"You're going to miss your own show?" I asked.

"Oh, no. I'll see it all from my ship's port window," he said. "Naturally, I can't stay here. When Earth disintegrates, it will take Luna with it. When that occurs, I shall be on my personal warper for Venus. Homeward bound."

"And we'll die here?" Nate asked.

242

"Of course," nodded all three of Geever's heads, "but you'll live to see Earth die first. And now, gentlemen, let us allow our two metal lovers to have at one another. I'll stay long enough to witness their erotic progress, but I'll have to be leaving when they reach their pre-orgasmic state."

I watched Geever walk over to the giant love robots. Mounting a small ladder, he reached the male's genital level, leaned forward, gave us a triple smile, and plugged in the left testicle.

The two big robos began to glow.

A pair of Geever's goons slammed me into a chair and tapewired my hands behind my back.

"This doesn't look good, Samuel," Nate said.

"I've had better days," I admitted.

Then they went for Nate, but he seemed to go suddenly berserk. He charged the first goon, bringing him down with a head-butt. Then he grabbed the goon's laserweapon.

"Kill him!" shouted Geever's three heads.

A sizzle of laser fire sliced into poor Nate and he staggered back, falling to the polished nearfloor. His eyes fluttered . . . closed . . . and then he didn't move anymore.

They'd killed my best friend!

"That was very foolish of him," said Geever, gazing down at the motionless corpse with two of his heads.

"You lousy three-necked bastard!" I shouted, lunging against the tapewire. But it held, and there was nothing I could do.

Meanwhile, the two big robot lovers were heating up, fondling one another, deep-kissing, writhing together in a sensuous tangle of arms and glowing metal flesh.

"Amazingly erotic, is it not?" asked Geever, licking all of his lips.

Their lovemaking had become a light show of rippling auras and bands of shimmering color as the metal bodies radiated intense heat. The male had penetrated the female and his pistoning movements were speeding up.

"Ah, they have reached the pre-orgasmic state," Geever oserved. "As much as I hate to leave before the climax, I had best be moving along. Goodbye, Mr. Space. I'm sure you'll enjoy the remainder of my little show."

I found myself alone in the vast lab, watching in numbed shock as the two big robos approached orgasm. The ground was beginning to tremble, and I could see a few cracks opening across the ceiling. On the screen, good old green-hilled Earth still floated in space, but how much longer did the planet have? Hell of a way to see it go!

I was totally frustrated. Was there no way to stop these infernal robots?

There was.

Nate Oliver stopped them.

He materialized next to his own corpse, wearing a visored helmet and a pair of long heat-resist bodygloves.

"Hello, Samuel," he said, his pink jowls quivering. "Sorry it took me so long to get here."

He then mounted the ladder, reached forward, and calmly unplugged the male robot's left nut. "There. That should do it."

It did it.

The two big robots were instantly frozen in mid-screw.

No orgasm.

No disintegration of Earth . . . or of Luna . . . or of me.

Nate stripped away the tapewire and I stood up, rubbing circulation back into my wrists.

"I don't get it," I said, nodding toward the stiff on the nearfloor.

"Quite simple to explain, really," said Nate, taking off his helmet. "When I was in my lab room during your visit, analyzing the testicle, I spotted our three-headed friend and his goon squad on the premises."

I started to ask how, but he said, "Vision screens. I have several placed at strategic points. Thus forewarned, I sent this android duplicate of myself back with the testicle and remained hidden until the pair of you were taken away."

"Since you saw Geever grab us, what took you so long to get here? You could have used your time-snatcher."

"I wanted to try out my new materializer—so that I could dematerialize in Old Chicago and materialize here, using your body coordinates to home in on."

"Okay, fine. But how come you—"

"I discovered that the machine had a few glitches in it. When I materialized the first time I found myself next to a freckled Zubu on Pluto. I had to send myself back to Old Chicago and start over."

"Well, at least you finally got it right," I said. "What about the helmet and gloves? How'd you know they'd be needed?"

"My meter reading on the heat factor was so high I assumed I'd need them."

"Okay, let's cut the gab," I said. "Got us a warper to catch."

The rest of this is anticlimax, if you'll pardon the pun. I caught Geever before he reached Venus and blew him out of the sky.

Then I sent Nate home, went back to my office in Bubble City, and got out a bottlle of Old Turkey. Sitting behind my desk, eased back in my swivchair, I raised the bottle. I was thinking of Roberta Sashonon.

"Here's looking at you, kid," I said softly.

And took a deep swig.

Outside, in the thick Martian darkness, the red sand continued to blow.

Still Life With Gold Frame

Rex Miller

The dreams brought with them the cascading illusion of a waterfall crashing down through his mind engulfing the thought processes, coming always without warning, each dream with its own distinctive voice, and each more intense than the last.

The voices were spactacularly true: hard-edged Hammett, haunted Woolrich, Craig Rice at the top of her form, perfect impersonations at first—like representational portraits fused with wit and an undeniable authenticity. Then they became like caricatures and parodies. Some of the voices were totally alien to Durrell's subconscious.

Take Jonathan Latimer: he'd never had the pleasure of reading the man's work. Durrell didn't know "Solomon's Vineyard" from Martha's Vineyard. He didn't know Crime Club from Canadian Club. But his Latimer caused even the dyspeptic critic Von Baumann to gush "not since Latimer's best work have we been treated to such an intoxicating potion of hardboiled gags and authentic pulp-age prose." Open the Latimer-style book to a random page and read . . .

"The fat man got out of the car. He had a big red face and eyes full of busted vessels. Then I saw the flossy dame. She gave me a gander at her beautiful legs and I could see creamy flesh where her nylons stopped."

"Are you packing a roscoe, big boy?" she asked, eyeing the bulge in my suit.

"I'm packing," I said, "but his name isn't Roscoe."

Durrell thought the word flossy sounded like something out of a dental hygiene manual. The dreams came complete with their own vocabulation. But then they began to change. They became frightening, murderous things that burnt their way through the brain like coarse bar whiskey.

Durrell was a writer and he was dying. His brain was doing it to him; killing him slowly. Inch by inch, step by step, slowly Durrell's brain was taking him down—not gently—but in a ferocious, unyielding nightmare. His illness, madness if you prefer, had unlocked the room where one's imagination lives.

In four years Durrell wrote forty-some books, pounding them out on the keyboard of an ancient typewriter, one of the early electric models, and when that would momentarily break down he'd carry on with his word processor until the old faithful machine was operable again. He was not a writer, he told people; he was a typist. And each novel was in a different auctorial voice.

The daymares, as he called them, came to him in measured, nightly dreams, at first. Violent, most of the time. Steaming with perversions and unspeakable depravity. Each morning at seven sharp he'd been typing. Six or seven hours laters, shaking and covered with perspiration, he'd force himself to quit for the day. That was at first.

Of course the editors loved it, his agent loved it, and—truth be told—he loved it. The books were successful, relatively, and he was making a very good midlist living. He was making a living dying.

But as the brain disorder worsened so did the dreams. They came more and more frequently, coming in the day as well as during the time he was asleep, coming even while he pounded out purple prose on the antique typewriter.

The old typewriter finally went up in smoke. Durrell had to buy a new one. Then three more. His fingers ached constantly from the typing, and he began using recording devices—talking one book into a recorder to be transcribed as he typed his latest stream-of-consciousness inspiration. He even hired a couple of secretaries and temporarily abandoned typing the stories himself. He'd take turns dictating two or three novels simultaneously, but that didn't work. It only aggravated the daymares.

They were growing worse: more intense as well as more

numerous. Durrell's specialty had been tough mysteries, dark fantasies, violent crime yarns, horror and suspense, and an extreme sub-genre of speculative cyberpunk science-fiction. The daymares were becoming so bloody and horrific that he could barely stand to imagine them. His head was becoming a terror-filled swamp of the most depraved, terrible acts. And the voices were growing wilder—crazier.

It helped some to get rid of the secretaries. He discovered that by dreamtheming he was able to exert some measure of control over his imagination. He could sometimes force his mind to stay on a single story as he typed, and when he would begin to dreamtheme a super-jacent storyline, he could mentally force the other thoughts away by imagining—within the text of the dreamtheme—that the details of the daymare were happening in realtime.

These thwarted daymares became fragments which he saved for his short story anthology, which was an ongoing script of vignettes. This was what he was typing, writing if you prefer, when yet another of the murderous daymares came clawing at his brain.

"Dreamthemes," he wrote "are accessed by a personal dreamkey." Durrell indented and began a new graph as the thing hit.

"Following the breakthroughs in neural communication and thought transmission, mankind learned to alter certain physical realities with a type of instantly-induced self-hypnosis. The military and industrial applications of dreamtheming included—" and the thing smashed into him.

Overpowering this time. An instant vision of a dead girl that took over everything—even his fingers. He ejected the paper from the machine, put in a fresh sheet, and wrote:

"Mary was only twenty-three but she had one hundred and twenty-three fine hatreds.

"Small, wiry, compact, a seductive she-devil in her fetish heels and fishnets, she had tiny Panaflex features, Steadicam eyes, and a wide-angle chest. She was born to boogie, raised on candy from strangers, mini-waisted, high-bottomed, with the devil in her glance and stardom in her pants. This lady was a painmaker and a heart breaker.

"She was wrong as week-old fish, tough as iron, sneaky as a mother snake, and badder than twenty-three kinds of slow death. She had a checkered past, a bloodstained now, and a screaming future."

As he wrote he heard the words come to him in the pulp-gonzo beat, but—language aside—the voice was old-time episodic radio:

"New York Is My Beat—the loneliest mile in the world."

"This honey was as counterfeit as homemade twenties, more guaranteed bad news than an airline crash, and twisted to the ultramax. But she had a way of coming up to a man and putting her hand on his shoulder, leaning into him and whispering in her breathiest happy-birthday-Mr.-President voice

"Wanna see me touch my nose with my tongue?"

Preceding transcribed.

"This is why she had to die." He wrote. "This is why I killed her. Because she—" The jarring ring of the telephone interrupted him and he picked it up and said hello. He hated the machines even worse than the sound of a ringing telephone, and had so far resisted putting one in place to answer his calls.

"This is Mary at Doctor Carroll's clinic. Just reminding you that you were supposed to be here twelve minutes ago for your appointment."

"Oh, my God! I'm sorry, Mary." It was 9:12 a.m. He'd completely forgotten. "I'm really—"

"That's okay. His eight-thirty is running over. Could you come on in by, say, nine-thirty?"

"You bet I can. Thanks, Mary. Be right over."

"Okay." His shrink had a practice less than ten minutes away. The money he paid Doctor Carroll he could wait for him once in a while. He typed the rest of the sentence.

"—needed killing. To her we were nothing but tricks." He noticed he was dreamtheming Mary the receptionist at Doctor Carroll's clinic, near nude, in a thin chiffon thing, sprawled dead in her apartment. He forced his mind back to reality, got up, and hurried outside to his car.

He was used to this stuff now, seeing the dreams and fantasies and horror images intrude on realtime, and using realtime to anchor his thoughts, or to yank his imagination back into low gear. The thing was it became like a multi-dimensional painting with an infinity perspective: you stare down into the pool and see the reflection of a man staring down into the pool seeing the reflection of a man staring down into the pool seeing the reflection of a man staring down into the pool seeing—aaah.

The next one hit when he touched the ignition key. His world turned over as the engine started and it was the wildest one he'd ever had.

It was nighttime! He glanced at the clock on his dashboard and it was not in the right place—it was centered now in a chrome instrument panel, and the figures were no longer luminous. He popped the door back open and saw a small version of the timepiece in The Big Clock, and it read 9:21. But it was 9:21 at *night*.

He started to pull out into traffic and he realized he was on a strange street, driving fast, like Ralph Meeker in the opening of the film "Kiss Me, Deadly", and he could sense that a woman was running toward him, and that she would come running out of the night, blinded by fear and the bright glare of his headlights.

He saw her. She was on him in an instant—or the reverse. He slammed on the brake, somehow knowing to hit the clutch at the same instant, and a woman with Mary's face vanished into the night. He knew the dreamtheme had firm hold of him so he just settled back and drove, letting the images flow over him.

The dark downtown area was lit up with lights. Glowing, continuous, curved neon in the shape of bubbling cocktail glasses, ringed planets and stars, enormous lipsticked kisses, and tall spiked fetish heels like the dead girl was wearing.

The skyline architecture was a montage of classical silhouettes: the Wrigley Building, Radio City Music Hall, Theo Van Doesburg's movie auditorium in Strasbourg, the Johnson's Wax building, a Voisin X-block designed by Le Corbusier and Jeanneret, the Chrysler building; a city etched by Henri Sauvage on acid.

The town was a dazzling, soaring fantasy of orbital arches, rocket-ship tailfin shapes, Dick Calkins nose cones. Massive lightning bolts in concrete, and tesla-coil death-ray rings were mirrored in the store doorways of aluminum fluting, as Durrell drove past silver-bullet trailers, Cords, and improbable-looking adventure caravans.

Small storefront businesses were shaped like hats, hotdogs, donuts, and dancers. A hundred-foot dimensional sign of a girl carhop served from atop a chrome-striped diner. Institutional buildings towered like the William Cameron Menzies sets of the 30s, or the Metropolis-like shapes of the 20s.

High overhead the night air was alive with the shadowy configurations of speedy midget biplanes and triplanes with streamlined wheel boots and scalloped batwings. Marvelously clunky-looking tin zeps and pencil-slim skyrockers vied with enormous monocoque-fuselage airliners for a flight path in this busy sky. The clouds and stars appeared to have been drawn by Ub Iwerks.

An immense, cutaway mobile fortress on tracks, bristling with cannon, chugged across his field of vision on mighty, armored tank treads. Blue-mirror-enameled cars with hood ornaments as big as table lamps could be seen.

The whole thing was like an art deco movie concocted by some insane Busby Berkeley, and as Durrell dreamthemed the image he passed the all-glass wall of a huge nightspot where a descending staircase of identically-attired dancing girls tap-danced. Neon signs blinked words and numbers across the immense background, and he caught glimpses of "Jazz", "1933", "The Continental", "42nd Street", and "Cocoanut Grove."

Just as the words winked out at him in blue neon he rubbed his eyes and flipped the radio knob on, hoping to pull his mind out of this.

"From high atop the beautiful Melody Room, it's Ray Roscoe and his Cocoanut Grove Melodiers, asking the musical question— Am I Blue?"

The voice over the speakers was slightly adenoidal, one of those old time announcers whose vogue passed with the Boy Tenor, a sound meant for megaphones and white wicker lawn furniture.

"As we drift along, in the gentle corridors of moonlight, we welcome the velvet throw of night's soft cloak." The sing-song litany sounded like it had been frozen out there in the ether, caught for a century in an elctro-magnetic time warp, then beamed back to earth.

The music had that uniquely bittersweet sound that a trained adult ear finds so charmingly dated, and yet—often as not—poignantly appealing. The voicing of the horns so quaintly out of tune with Industriels Modernes, as it were. The strings almost embarrassingly and hopelessly schmaltzy, the beat metronomic Mickey-tick.

"JEEZUS!" He almost hit another woman, getting a quick flash of a face like Mary's but with bee-stung limps and flapper-girl hair. He flipped the dial from the cloying music and heard a young boy's voice talking about how "for only a dime and a box-top from Quaker's Oats, you can get your own exact model of Dick Daring's Secret Underground Headquarters." Savagely Durrell twisted the tuner knob.

"—so tune in tomorrow for Backstage Wife, the story of Mary Noble, and what it means to be the wife of a famous Broadway star, dream sweet-heart of a million other women." The woman's voice was replaced by a man's deep baritone.

"This is the NBC Blue Network." The sound of a train jolted Durrell as an incredible art deco shape materialized beside the downtown traffic, a streamlined express train rocketing through the night on invisible parallel tracks, as the radio voice intoned,

"As a bullet seeks its target, shining rails are aimed at Grand Central Station, heart of the nation's greatest city." He remembered that show from childhood. His Mom and Dad had been fans. "Drawn by the magnetic force of the fantastic metropolis, day and night great trains rush toward the Hudson River," he seemed to be driving closer to the big train, as the parallel lines appeared to converge in the distance. He couldn't see any crossing signs.

"—sweep down its eastern bank for 140 miles, flash briefly by the long red row of tenement houses south of 125th Street," My God! He was very close to the train now and he tried to brake but nothing happened when he tapped the pedal. He tried to turn the wheel and it wouldn't move. He was going to hit the train.

"—dive with a roar into the 2½-mile tunnel which burrows beneath the glitter and swank of Park Avenue and then—" SCREEEEEE! The brakes took just in time, grabbing and slowing the fishtailing Hupmobile seconds before it slammed into the train. As he looked up in terror he saw the face of Ava Gardner. Ava as she looked in 1946, when "The Killers" was released.

"It's Mary!" he heard himself say aloud.

"Yes, sir?" she said, rather taken aback by the forcefulness of Durrel's greeting.

"I apologize again for being late."

"Hello," Dr. Carroll said, coming around the corner with a woman he'd seen before in the waiting room of the clinic. "See you next week," he said to her, turning to him with a smile in place. "Right this way." A different office this time. The clinic had several doctors.

"How have you been doing?" he asked, when Durrell had taken a chair.

"*Damn!*" Durrell said, leaning forward, obviously troubled. "You can't imagine what this one was like. I was in the car. And it was night. Art deco buildings. Old time stuff everywhere." He looked around at the doctor's office, which was covered in the artifacts of the Golden Age: bubble front Wurlitzers and Rainbow-cascade Rockolas, outrageous Bally pinballs and gothic Atwater-Kent cathedrals, rectilinear wall sculpture, and lithos of gull-wing dihedral Squeegees. The breath just went out of him, as he collapsed, still inside the dreamtheme.

"—hear me? Yeah. He's all right." The doctor and one of his nurses, a girl who slightly resembled Veronica Lake in "The Blue Dahlia"— in the face—but with legs reminiscent of Barbara Stanwyck's in "Double Indemnity", watched him anxiously.

What—?" He wanted to ask Where Am I? What the victim always said upon resuming consciousness in those old B-mysteries. "Is this real or is it Memorex?" he said, trying to keep his sense of humor.

"—still hallucinating," the doctor told Veronica Stanwyck, whose face was beginning to appear distorted as if reflected in a fun house mirror.

"I'm going to give you a mild sedative." Doctor Carroll said, "But don't take it till you get home. It isn't safe to drive when you've had one of these." Drive? He doubted whether he could walk, much less operate a car. Apparently he'd fainted as soon as he got to the doctor's office and remained unconscious for an hour or so.

"I want you to go home now," he told Durrell, helping him out of the office chair. The fantasy jukes and pin balls were gone. Behind the desk there were a few diplomas, and a small print under a museum portrait light. The silhouette of a man in a wide-brimmed hat and voluminous black cape, standing in front of a yellow field.

He put the pill in his pockets. As Carroll and the nurse helped him to the door he tried to read the caption under the print. It was imprinted on a small brass tag and in tiny letters it read:

"To her we were nothing but tricks."

It felt very cold in the room. He was glad to leave the austere, chilly clinic. As he reached the receptionist area Dr. Carroll bid him farewell.

"See you next week," he said with a big smile. "Show him a good time, Mary," it sounded like he said to the receptionist, as he turned and went back in his office. Durrell realized he'd probably instructed her to "give him a time."

"Would next week be all right? A week from today at nine?"

"Fine," he said. Why was the doctor letting him leave in this condition? He could feel himself coming unglued again. The receptionist was very lovely. In her early twenties. One of those women whom men find extremely provocative. He wondered if she might be a wanton woman under her businesslike demeanor.

All the clinic employees wore nametags. He tried to read hers but his vision, like his concentration, had become unfocused again. It was irresponsible of Doctor Carroll to allow him to leave in this

254

state—perhaps he should say something. "Mary (space)" a four letter word. The name took nine spaces. He couldn't read it. Maybe the nametag read "Sternwood." Sternwood was nine spaces.

"Could I ask a big favor?"

"Sure," she said.

"Could I borrow your pen for a moment?"

"Here you go," she said with a smile, assuming he was going to write a check to pay for the office visit.

But Durrell's disorientation had triumphed. He turned the appointment card over and started writing on the back, just as if he were in his office typing:

"It was about ten thirty with the sun not shining and a look of hard wet ink in the clearness of his footnotes. He was a writer and he was dying."

"Do you know what they call someone who supplies provisions to ships? Or a merchant who specializes in wax candles?" he asked, aloud.

The receptionist looked up for a beat, thinking perhaps he was talking to himself, but he was looking at her so she smiled—a bit too brightly—and shook her pretty head.

"No."

"A chandler," he told her, giving her a wink.

"A chandler," she repeated. "Hm," she said, tilting her head as if to tell him that was certainly interesting trivia.

He returned the pen. Put the card in his pocket.

"Thanks very much," he said.

"You bet." She looked back down at her paperwork. Hoping the phone would ring. Durrell started out the clinic door.

"Goodbye," he called out.

"Bye," she said.

"He's a very sick man," Doctor Carroll said to his receptionist, hovering over her, after Durrell had left the office.

"Yes. I know he is." She pulled away. She hated the feel of his soft hands on her.

Doctor Carroll looked down at Mary, who was seated at the receptionist's desk in the outer foyer. From his vantage above her he could see her beautiful legs in the short skirt she wore. Creamy flesh showed where her nylons stopped.

"The disease he has," the doctor whispered to her, unprofessionally, "it is like looking into a mirror and seeing yourself looking into a mirror and seeing the reflected image of yourself looking into a mirror and seeing the reflected image of yourself looking into a mirror and seeing the reflected image of—"

"Yes," she said, cutting him off, "I see. It must be very difficult for him." To her they were nothing but tricks.

"Fortunately he's dying."

"Um."

"Of course we ALL are, in a manner of speaking."

Durrell snapped out of the dreamtheme when he hit the air, but for a second he wondered if the old Hupmobile would resemble a Chandler, instead. It was his regular car, thank goodness, and he made it home virtually without incident—although when he drove by a club called The Dancers a man in a Rolls Royce Silver Wraith waved at him.

He was so exhausted by the time he arrived back at his home he fell asleep, and when he woke up it really was nine o'clock at night. He forced himself to eat a bite of food. Stayed up long enough to watch the Ten O'clock News and Nightline, and went back to bed. The pounding on his door awoke him at six-thirty in the morning, shortly before his alarm was set to go off.

"Who is it?" He said, through the closed door.

"*Police! Open the door!*" a man's voice commanded. He instantly began unchaining the door and turned the bolt. Four armed officers entered.

"Durrell?"

"Yes."

"Turn around, sir. Put your hands on the wall. *DO IT.*" He started to ask what it was all about but he was being horsed over to the wall, his legs forced apart, and two cops had him frisked before he could get his wits about him.

"Look here. Found this in his pocket."

"Aha," he heard the ranking officer say, as one of the cops handed his superior the sedative.

"My doctor gave me that yesterday. It's just a mild sedative. I forgot to take it."

"Yeah. Right." The officer said, sarcastically, "You wanna take it now?" The other cops snickered.

"You have the right to remain silent," they began informing him of the post-Miranda information. He listened, waiting to hear the reading of his rights. Then he asked them.

"Am I being arrested?"

"Yes, sir."

"What charge?"

"Murder."

"Who'd I kill?" He half-smiled. It would be like his nutzoid agent to pull something like this.

"Mary Earl."

"Who?" The name was unfamiliar. Who the heck was Mary Earl?

"Come on, Mister Durrell. You're under arrest." They started leading him out the door.

"Can't I get my wallet? My keys?"

"You won't be needing any money or car keys," the police officer told him. "We'll be furnishing your transportation as well as room and board for a while." Mary *Earl*.

"That's not the Mary who works for Doctor Carroll is it?" he asked, as they took him away.

"Congratulations, another winner."

"But I just saw her yesterday."

"Yeah, we know," one of the cops said with a humorless chuckle. "You saw her and *poisoned* her with that same stuff we found in your apartment."

"HEY!" another cop called to the ranking officer as they walked toward a police car. "Check this out." He had a sheet of paper sealed inside a large plastic evidence bag. "In his typewriter," he told the head cop as he handed it over to be read. The officer glanced at it and looked at Durrell hard, then read from the page of script aloud, in a rough voice:

"This is why she had to die. This is why I killed her. Because she needed killing. To her we were nothing but tricks."

"That's a STORY! FICTION! It's part of a new novel I'm writing. I'm a writer!"

"Yeah, Durrell, we know you're a writer." Another cop spoke up.

"We've got a witness who heard you threaten to kill Mary Earl at the place she worked yesterday. THAT wasn't fiction." The man in charge glowered at him and he shut up.

It appeared to be a fairly incriminating body of evidence, and clearly someone had framed Durrell rather carefully and ingeniously. There was even a note about his needing to "get rid of the secretaries" that someone found. Taken out of context it appeared like an ominous prophecy, even though it could easily be explained away.

The woman he was "murdering" in a story was named Mary. Mary

Earl was dead. His dead girl was 23. Mary Earl was 23. Each had been killed in their apartment. Poisoned. The toxic agent was an obscure poison called Latoxivil, which he'd written about in his novel "1939." Mary Earl had been moonlighting as an expensive call girl. His fictional Mary had been a call girl. He's written about a dead girl sprawled on the living room floor, wearing nothing but a thin chiffon peignoir, the way Doctor Carroll's receptionist had been found.

The police had received an anonymous phone tip. The call came in at a few minutes past five a.m. A whispered voice saying they heard a fight in the apartment, that the caller had overheard a man yelling "I told you I'd kill you if you kept this up." That they'd seen a man leaving the apartment a few minutes later—a man who looked a lot like Durrell, the author.

They'd called Durrell's publisher to find his address, and had been told about the writer's illness, and that he was seeing a psychiatrist. They called the doctor, Dr. Carroll, who admitted that Durrell was a violent, disturbed individual. And that he'd heard Durrell *threatening* his receptionist only the day before. They obtained Durrell's address and placed him under arrest.

After two hours of interrogation and nearly four abominable hours in the local drunk tank, Durrell's lawyer was finally allowed to post bail and he was back on the streets.

That night he went home and slept without medication, and dreamthemed the girl's murder in great detail. He even imagined a fairly credible scenario to explain why the good doctor had decided to frame him.

Then, around two a.m., Durrell awoke. He went to the bathroom. Puttered around in his office. Finally decided it was too early to do any writing, and he padded back toward the bedroom. Coming down the hallway he saw a framed photo of his family—a picture that sat on the nightstand. The photo was framed in gold. The images covered with No-Glare Plexiglas.

In the daytime, in sunlight or bright electric light, you could not see the Plexiglas. But at night it reflected light like a mirror, and as Durrell padded down the hall he could not see the photo in the frame, only the reflection of himself moving into it.

The image was the perfect metaphor for a writer, and just as he began to dreamtheme, moving a bit closer to the object, he saw himself moving closer. But his image moved *BEFORE* he did! He was seeing, in this golden frame, which had held a moment of the past captured in the present, a moment of the future just as it was about to happen.

He saw himself come even closer, and repeated the scene. Saw his face fill the frame and imitated the vision. Went over and flopped back into bed and let the dreamtheme swallow him up in it.

* * *

In his dreamtheme he was a trick. But he hated the hold Mary had over him. She was only twenty-three but she had one hundred and twenty-three fine hatreds. Born to boogie, raised on candy from strangers, she was a painmaker and a heart breaker. Inside his mind a script read *ANNCR READ COLD:*

"And that's why Broadway is the loneliest mile in the world. I should know. New York Is My Beat." *SPFX: ORGAN STINGER.*

The organ stabbed like a jolt of high octane into his C.N.S. "New York Is My Beat," a radio show notorious for turgidity and over-writing, was one of his favorite tongue-in-cheek fictional voices. It was the voice of the story about Mary's death.

"This is why she had to die," he dreamed. "This is why I killed her. Because she—" the jarring ring of the phone shook him awake and he picked it up but there was no one on the other end of the line. Only a dial tone.

A loud, persistent knock on the door was followed by another ring of the doorbell. And Durrell struggled out of bed and into his bathrobe, calling out in a cracked, morning voice—

"Yeah! Just a second."

It was the cops. Two of them. One he hadn't seen before.

"Morning," the cop who'm he hadn't seen before said. "We wanted you to know Dr. Carroll confessed to the murder of Mary Earl." It had no real meaning to him.

"He'd fallen in love with his receptionist—she was tricking—and he figured out a way he could frame one of his patients for her murder—because of your illness he knew he could—prescribe a powerful drug—acting on the eighth cranial . . . extremely hallucinogenic . . ." He was beginning to dreamtheme even as they explained that he was no longer a suspect in this real murder case. He was already working out the first chapter of his new book inside his head. He only wanted them to go away so he could start typing.

Later he would learn about the mysterious properties of the medication Carroll had been prescribing for Durrell's rare malady. How the synergistic combination of that drug and his biochemical disorder produced hallucino-genic reactions, using Durrell's own twisted fantasies together with random visual, aural, tactile, and olfactory images from his "unlocked" memory.

One of the cops who'd been there when Dr. Carroll had claimed he'd heard a patient threaten his receptionist, which had made Durrell a murder suspect, also happened to hear the whispered voice of the anonymous phone tip. The similarities of the language or the sound of the voice touched a chord. They took a closer look at Dr. Carroll and discovered a relationship between the doctor and his receptionist.

A court-ordered search warrant resulted in the police finding incriminating photographs and more documentation about the dead woman.

Then they discovered the audio cassettes. Dr. Carroll had found a perfect subject—a man whose runaway nightmares could be accellerated by hallucinogenic medication, and whose oeuvre in fact had been fueled by those aberrant thoughts. Such a subject, Durrell, could be further manipulated by post-hypnotic suggestion, and all of this managed within the context of a weekly office call. Carroll would set Durrell up for the moment when he could destroy the woman whom he felt needed killing. After all, why *not* use Durrell? He was dying anyway, wasn't he? It was like one of those perfect insurance scams Carroll was fond of running—it could be a crime without any innocent victims, in a sense. Hadn't Durrell made his living by pandering? Perfect justice for a whore and a panderer.

Then Carroll would give Durrell the same poison he'd used on Mary, as a "mild sedative", hoping that it would later appear to be a murder-suicide.

"Mary *Earl* was murdered by Dr. *Carroll*. His *vanities* were so—" the cop was saying, and as he told Durrell about how the doctor had forced the woman to ingest poison, Durrell saw the chorus line of Earl Carroll's Vanities of 1933, tap-dancing down the spiral lucite staircase of the Cocoanut Grove. His fingers itched to type.

"Yes. Well. Glad it's all over. Appreciate your help. Thank you," he said, pushing the police out the door rather unceremoniously. They let him do so. A dying man can surely be permitted a few idiosyncracies. And time was sliding down.

He rushed back to his office, put paper into the machine, and began typing, not looking at the typewriter, typing on auto-pilot.

From where he sat he could just see the gold frame on the nightstand in his bedroom, down the hall. It glittered like a shiny, gilt-edged rectangle the size of a postage stamp.

He knew that if he gazed into it he would see the face of a man gazing into the face of a man gazing into the face of a man gazing into the face of a man gazing into the face of a man gazing into the face of a man gazing into the face of a man gazing . . .

As fast as one can type the most familiar phrase, such as "now is the time for all good men to come"—his fingers struck the keys.

"Mary was only twenty-three," he typed, "but she had one hundred and twenty-three fine hatreds."

Who What When Where Why

Barbara Paul

Chickie's eyes recorded everything: the high-ceilinged warehouse space with its ambiguously-shaped storage crates looming tall in the shadows; the one cleared spot in the center captured within a cone of harsh white light; the immaculately attired man sitting on a folding chair, one elegant leg crossed over the other. Chickie quickscanned the shadows: four figures, all of them armed.

She approached the elegant man slowly, giving the figures in the shadows time to use whatever scanning devices they had; Chickie had come unarmed, as she'd said she would. The man looked at her without speaking. She ran a quick read of his body signs: rapid pulse, surge of adrenalin. He liked what he saw, but he was surprised, too. The usual response.

"You're much younger than I expected," the man said. "How old are you?"

"Twenty-two," Chickie said. "How old are you?"

He smiled humorlessly. "The message being, 'Don't mess with me?' How subtle."

"Subtle enough to get the job done. You sent for me, remember." She said no more, daring him to make up his mind without any attempt at persuasion from her. He knew her credentials.

Finally he gave an almost imperceptible nod. "Very well. We already have a man inside Hightower Electronics. All you have to do is get him past internal security and he'll do the rest."

"I'm not to bring anything out?"

"No. Melville will take care of it. That's his name, Todd Melville. He'll meet you tomorrow noon at the fountain across the street from the Hightower Building. You can make your plans then."

Forty blocks away, a woman named Kara Pope tried to decide what to do. Did she have enough? No, she didn't.

Chickie put one hand on her hip. "Not satisfactory. For all I know, your Todd Melville could be planting a bomb. I don't do murder."

The elegant man was irritated. "You have my assurances that no violence is planned."

She just smiled at that. "Your assurances."

"Do you wish to go in with him? Would that satisfy you?"

Chickie pretended to think. "If you tell me what to expect."

"You can expect an Olafsson 940 security vault. Inside is the prototype of a new tissue-layer microchip designed for subdermal implantation. Don't ask me what it's programmed for because I won't tell you. Melville will take the chip and leave nothing. No bombs."

Kara Pope exulted; *now* she had enough. She sent commands; forty blocks away Chickie tossed her long blond hair and smiled. "That is satisfactory."

The elegant man was growing skeptical again. "The Olafsson 940 security vault has never been breached. Are you sure you can do it?"

"It's been breached once. Carlotta Cosmetics has one—which they *think* is still guarding their skin-dyeing formula while they wait for FDA approval."

"They *think*?"

"They don't know the formula's gone. I left a substitute."

He smiled. "Excellent." Then he looked amused. "Carlotta doesn't have an arrangement with the FDA?"

Chickie shrugged, as if not interested. But Kara Pope was interested. The FDA could be bought? She made a note.

"Half your fee will be deposited to your account before you leave the building," the man said. "You'll get the other half when I have the microchip in my hand."

"Also satisfactory, Mr. Tyrell."

He did a good job of hiding his surprise. "So. You know who I am."

"Of course. I never work blind." Chickie turned and started to walk away, in a casual lope that looked especially interesting from the rear.

Tyrell called after her, "Perhaps when all this is finished . . .?"

She threw him a look back over her shoulder. "Perhaps." She left the warehouse, never once having glimpsed the four henchmen hiding in the shadows.

Kara Pope breathed a sigh of relief. She had what she needed and Chickie had got out safely. Kara downloaded the scene in the warehouse from her simulacrum's memory, then put her in a cab and sent her home.

But before she disconnected the wires running into the base of her skull, Kara logged onto the newsnet and put her story up for bid: *Handley Tyrell, CEO of KRJ Systems, Inc., caught in the act of hiring industrial spy to steal from Hightower Electronics.* The bidding was vigorous, the story ultimately going to UP/AP Combine. Kara signaled acceptance and duped the story to potential victim Hightower, as required by law.

She shut down her system and unplugged with a feeling of satisfaction. A good night's work.

*　　*　　*

Kara Pope owned two state-of-the-art simulacra, the best bio-engineering available. Only a half dozen of the topline models existed, each one custom-made; the other four belonged to rich men too old and frail to leave their homes. Kara decided to give Chickie a rest and the following day activated Jocko. She logged him on to the public records net and set him to looking for pharmaceutical and cosmetic companies that always seemed to get quick FDA approval for new products.

Kara had bought separate condos for her two supercyborgs; it had proved easier than she'd imagined to maintain the fiction that Chickie and Jocko were human beings, living normal human-being-type lives. Guaranteed undetectable by any known scanning system, the manufacturer had said proudly. That was only temporary, unfortunately; sooner or later somebody would come up with a way to distinguish the sims from the reals. Then the sim-makers would come out with a new generation of Chickies and Jockos to beat *that* scanning system; and if Kara didn't have enough in her account to cover the new models, she'd be out of work. Newsgathering had become too dangerous to undertake in person.

While Jocko searched for companies that might have bribed some FDA official or other, Kara checked her credit account. UP/AP Combine had paid up quickly—as they always did, godblessem. Kara made big money, but she had big expenses.

The constantly running news channel on the big screen caught her attention: there was her story, as seen through Chickie's recording eyes. No question, Handley Tyrell was guilty of attempted industrial theft; he'd already been picked up by Hightower Electronics' private police force and turned over to the civil authorities.

Then a live telecast caught Tyrell right after he'd made bail. Even in these circumstances he still managed to look cool and elegant, peering down his elevated nose at the gatherers yelling questions at him. "It was entrapment," he said in an attention-commanding voice, "entrapment pure and simple. A woman pretending to be a security expert set me up. The fact that there were pictures means that at least one of her eyes was a camera. And *that* means either police or a newsgatherer."

"Do you know which?" someone asked.

"Not yet. But I have a line on her. This story isn't finished yet."

A sudden chill. Kara thought back to last night: had she had Chickie change cabs or do anything at all to make sure she wasn't followed? No. She hadn't. Appalled at her own carelessness, Kara plugged in and got to work.

Across town, Chickie came to life. She assembled the equipment necessary for some instant cosmetic surgery and sat down before a mirror. One last time Kara ran Chickie's hand through her long blond hair. Then Chickie opened a thermosealed aluminum case and took out a new head.

Kara/Chickie worked quickly. The new head had altogether dissimilar features and short, curly black hair. The voice was different, and, more importantly, so were the eyes; no retinal scan would identify *this* Chickie as the one who set up Handley Tyrell. The new head in place, Chickie the Brunette carefully applied a layer of false skin to her neck; it would take about an hour to grow in place.

The job done, Chickie stored the old head and the rest of the equipment in a hidden vault Kara had had installed—an Olafsson 940, as a matter of fact. Chickie activated the vault's security system, and Kara at last relaxed. Tyrell didn't know it, but he'd been right last

WHO WHAT WHEN WHERE WHY

night; the 940 had never been breached.

Her investment protected, Kara took a moment to examine her remodeled simulacrum more carefully. The new Chickie was truly beautiful, with a saucy look to her that Kara liked; she was sorely tempted to take the sim out for a little fun and games. Both Chickie and Jocko were what the manufacturer called stimulus-responsive; from the safety of her home Kara could taste what they tasted, smell what they smelled, feel what they felt. And the sims could feel *everything*. The best love affairs of Kara's life had been the ones where she'd used Chickie as her surrogate. The men never knew, and Kara couldn't think of a better way to practice safe sex.

Once Kara found herself strongly attracted to a man Chickie had recently met. His name was Austin, and he was beautiful. A rather worldly man with a ready laugh and the sense to know how to listen when Kara wanted to talk, Austin had been pure delight. But when he and Chickie eventually ended up in bed, Kara got suspicious; something about his skin, the texture of his musculature—they didn't feel quite right. She ran an internal scan and learned that Austin, beautiful Austin, was also a simulacrum. One of the earlier models; still quite good, but not adequately shielded against Chickie's advanced scanning system. So Austin was as phony as Chickie; someone else was doing the same thing with his sim that Kara was doing with hers. She'd laughed out loud at the idea of making whoopee with some stranger somewhere in the city, neither of them knowing what the other looked like. One time she'd even used Jocko for the same purpose, curious to know what it was like for a man. She'd quickly returned to Chickie.

But fun and games could wait; Kara sent Chickie to bed and checked in on Jocko, who'd compiled a list of companies that had gotten suspiciously fast FDA approval of their products. Jocko picked out a couple dozen at random, identified the FDA officials whose signatures had appeared on the approvals, and ran credit checks on them. Seventeen had larger balances than their salaries alone would account for. Six of those had no investments to explain the extra income.

Kara had a choice. She could send Jocko in as a blackmailer or an IRS investigator. Better still: as an accountant working within the FDA, hinting that someone had been diddling with departmental funds, and where did this extra moolah in your account come from, Mr. X? Even so, no one was going to come right out and admit to taking kickbacks; Jocko would have to play it by ear.

But he'd need credentials. Kara sent a coded message to her contact, a man whose true identity she'd never been able to learn. For some reason he used the codename CreamAss; but whoever he was, he was always able to come up with whatever forged credentials she needed. CreamAss charged an arm and a leg, but no one ever challenged the Employee I.D. or the net data or anything else he fabricated. And come income tax time, Kara had no qualms about putting down his fee as a legitimate business expense.

*　　*　　*

Six hours later the new credentials were ready. Since they were for Jocko, Chickie would pick them up — a little extra precaution Kara always took: obscure the trail as much as possible. Kara had stopped making pick-ups herself three years ago, when two of her fellow gatherers were set upon and beaten in a similar circumstance. Chickie and Jocko would meet at a restaurant some distance from the pick-up site. Jocko left, looking stiff-backed and a bit stern — exactly like a disapproving accountant — and Kara activated Chickie.

Or tried to. For the very first time, Chickie failed to respond.

Puzzled, Kara ran systems checks on both her home equipment and on Chickie herself. Nothing was wrong at Kara's end, but from Chickie's there was no response at all. Nothing. That didn't make sense; there should be at least an error message. Irritated and a bit uneasy, Kara switched back to Jocko.

A few blocks away, Jocko pressed the speaker button in the back of the cab. "I've changed my mind. Take me to 1074 Glendover Street."

He checked to make sure he had the keycard to Chickie's place with him. When the cab stopped, he paid the fare and climbed the one flight of stairs to his sister sim's condo . . . where he saw he wouldn't need the keycard. The door was slid open a few inches.

Still not suspecting anything, Jocko pushed the door all the way open and called out, "Chickie?" He headed straight for the bedroom, where Kara had left her. And that's where he found her, lying in bed.

With a laser-burn hole in her head. And another in her chest. Jocko bent over the bed for a closer look. The pseudoflesh had cauterized, but the real destruction was inside. All that expensive

WHO WHAT WHEN WHERE WHY

bioengineering, irreparably damaged. Chickie had shut down completely. Completely and permanently.

"Hold it right there!" a loud voice rang out. "Put your hands out to the side and turn around slowly. *Slowly!*"

Jocko straightened up and held his hands away from his body. Slowly he turned to see three black-helmeted figures in body armor pointing needle guns at him.

"You're under arrest," one of the helmets said. "The charge is murder."

*　　*　　*

Kara was so shocked that her system's automatics had to cut in. Chickie "murdered" and Jocko accused of the deed? Kara watched unbelieving through Jocko's recording eyes as her only remaining sim was taken in and charged with homicide, levels one and/or two. This couldn't be happening. She was going to lose both her sims?

Then common sense returned. That's what simulacra were for, weren't they? To take the heat. That could have been Kara Pope herself lying in that bed; her insurance policy had paid off. Kara told herself to count her blessings.

As to losing Jocko—that wouldn't happen. Chickie might be shielded against every known scanning system, but she'd yield up her secrets to the autopsy surgeon's laser. Since the wrecking of a simulacrum wasn't murder, Jocko would eventually be released; it was just a matter of time. And in the interval, Kara could get a story out of it: what it's like to be falsely accused of a crime, etc.—feature stuff, always good for weekend newscasts.

Jocko was taken to an interrogation room where two cops who didn't introduce themselves were waiting to question him. Full name first, Jocko Watchman. (Kara had thought Watchman an appropriate name for a newsgatherer's sim; Chickie's last name was Shield.) Address, occupation, ID, etc., all accounted for.

One of the cops said, "All right, Watchman, who was she? Who's the dead girl?"

"I have no idea," Jocko said.

"We know she's not the woman who lived there—the neighbors told us that. Why'd you kill her?"

"I didn't kill her. I came looking for Chickie—"

"Chickie Shield?" the other cop interrupted, reading from a computer screen.

"That's right. We were supposed to meet for lunch, but she didn't show. I tried calling her but got no answer, so I went to see if anything was wrong. I'd just found that other woman when the three troopers burst in on me. What were *they* doing there?"

"Neighbor saw the door open and thought the place was being burglarized," the first cop said. "So you never saw the dead woman before. You expect us to believe that?"

"Yes," Jocko said evenly. "I expect you to believe that."

"Where's Chickie Shield?"

"I wish I knew. I'm worried about her."

"Yeah, sure you are. Maybe you killed her, and this other woman saw you do it."

Kara cut into the newsnet and offered a story for sale: *Unidentified corpse found in missing woman's apartment.*

The cops kept on haranguing Jocko, but quick body scans suggested they believed his story. Easy to guess why: he'd had no weapon on him. But there was no other suspect, so the grilling went on a bit longer before Jocko was finally locked into a holding cell. Kara put him on automatic so she could think.

Handley Tyrell, you lousy son of a bitch—you killed my beautiful simulacrum!

Even if she could prove he'd done it, Tyrell would no more stand trial for murder than Jocko would. She could get him for destruction of property; but to do that, Kara would have to come forward and identify herself as the sim's owner . . . thereby targeting herself as the next object of Tyrellian ire. No, she'd have to get him some other way.

Obviously, Tyrell had not done the deed himself; he would have known the brunette sleeping in Chickie's bed was not the one who set him up. He would have *thought* she wasn't the one. Kara remembered the four figures hidden in the warehouse shadows during her talk with Tyrell; but they too knew what Chickie looked like. They had to be private police employed by Tyrell's company, KRJ Systems; one or more had followed Chickie home and passed on her address to Tyrell. But they wouldn't have killed the "wrong" woman, unless KRJ had an especially bloodthirsty constabulary in its employ. More likely, KRJ didn't know anything about the murder.

So Tyrell had had to go outside the company to find his hit man; that suggested his authority within KRJ was not absolute. But he'd found his man, handed him the address, and said kill the woman who lives there. Yes, that's the way it would have happened. And once Kara's story appeared on the news, he'd realize the mistake his hitter had made.

Which meant that Tyrell would think Chickie was still alive.

There had to be a way she could use that. Chickie's head was still locked up in the hidden Olafsson 940; the police had been scouring the place for clues, not sounding the walls for concealed rooms. But the police would have sealed the scene of the crime . . .

Message interrupt. From CreamAss: since she failed to pick up the credentials she'd commissioned, the price had just doubled.

Shit.

Kara wondered how long before the police autopsy report would kick Jocko loose. She wondered where Tyrell was right now. She wondered how long CreamAss would wait before cutting her off entirely.

She could see no way around it. She was going to have to go out herself.

✳   ✳   ✳

The streets were always changing—distending, decaying, putting on new coats of paint. Having facelifts, or not bothering. *Growing* people, Kara sometimes thought, right from the cracks in the sidewalks. And such strange people they were, somehow menacing just in the way they looked at you. The man CreamAss had sent with Jocko's new credentials wore a diamond stud in one nostril; he had his greasy hair pulled back in a pony tail, and he was dressed in a fashion Kara was sure had not been invented yet. He hinted strongly for a tip; when she refused, he called her a name. Kara grabbed the credentials and fled.

The tape the police had used to seal off the door to Chickie's place had wires running through it; an alarm would sound in the nearest station if the seal was tampered with in any way. Kara checked her watch. Then she broke the seal, headed straight for the Olafsson 940, picked up the aluminum case containing Chickie's head, and left. She was down on the street in under a minute.

Kara took refuge in a restaurant across the street, curious to see how long it would take the police to get there. She took a swallow of coffee and chewed on a bagel, then turned on her table vid. The news showed what was left of a house in New Jersey after it had been bombed; the entire family had died in the explosion. The owner had been a newsgatherer.

Kara yielded to a moment of despair. *We don't deserve this! Why do they hate us so?*

The bleating sound of an approaching police van brought her out of her funk. Kara checked her watch. It had taken the overworked, underpaid, understaffed civil police twenty-two minutes and fourteen seconds to answer the alarm. A company-employed private police force would have had people there within seconds.

Kara left the restaurant; she had one more stop to make before she could go home. A cab took her to KRJ Systems, where she waited until she saw Tyrell leave the building. Then she went in and asked for the Personnel Director. Kara applied for a programming position under the name Chickie Shield, using some old credentials CreamAss had provided; it didn't matter if they stood up or not. When asked for a personal reference, Kara gave the name Handley Tyrell. The Personnel Director said she'd check with Mr. Tyrell and get back to her. Kara said that would be fine.

Then she went home.

*　　*　　*

Jocko was out; the police told him goodbye the minute they learned the dead woman was a simulacrum. Kara had beat the other gatherers with her story to the newsnet.

The timing was perfect. She'd given Tyrell twenty-four hours to stew; Kara wanted him to think Chickie was after him. She plugged in and put her remaining sim to work.

Jocko went shopping. First he bought a curly black wig. Then he bought a laser gun—easier to find than the right kind of wig. Then he went hunting for a second-hand simulacrum, the cheaper the better. He found one, a poorly maintained early model that could perform only the simplest of tasks; it was little more than a robot. And it was an "It"; those first models had been genderless. But It could still walk, and that was all that was required.

272

Jocko led It to Chickie's condo and checked the time; he had a maximum of twenty-two minutes and fourteen seconds before the police came roaring in. He broke the newly replaced seal around the door and hurried inside. Jocko put the curly black wig on It's head and bundled the old sim into Chickie's bed, arranging the covers so that the face was mostly hidden. Carefully he hung a sheet over a nearby mirror so he wouldn't accidentally record his own image. Time elapsed: one minute and forty-seven seconds.

Then Jocko went back to the front door and pulled out his laser gun. His recording eyes showed him searching for his victim and finding "her" in the bedroom. He fired one blast into the simulacrum's head, another to the chest. Jocko stood over poor dead It and muttered to himself, "It's done, Tyrell. What you wanted." He made his way back to the front door.

And that's a wrap, Kara thought happily.

Jocko went back one more time, to hide It in the Olafsson 940 and to take the sheet off the mirror. Then he left the building and strolled casually away. Total time elapsed: thirteen minutes, nine seconds.

The police were nowhere in sight.

*   *   *

Kara had positioned Chickie's head in front of the vidphone so that nothing below the chin showed. Then she plugged in and called Tyrell. The look on his face when he saw who it was was downright delicious.

"You've been naughty," Chickie said mockingly. "Trying to kill me! Is that any way to do business?"

He looked as if he couldn't believe what he was hearing. "Do business? Is that what you said, do business? You set me up! Hold on — is your carrier secure?"

"Check it yourself." She waited until Tyrell had satisfied himself their conversation would remain private. "Do you have any idea how much it's going to cost me to replace that simulacrum your hit man killed?" Chickie went on. "Or cost *you*, rather."

Tyrell raised one elegant eyebrow. "Now, what makes you think I'm going to pay for your expensive toy?"

"This." Kara blanked the screen and ran the playlet she'd just

273

staged in Chickie's condo. She wished she could watch Tyrell's face as he took in the scene, seeing exactly what Jocko had seen.

When Tyrell came back on the screen, all the blood had drained from his face. "He . . . he recorded it?"

"Yup. Can't trust anybody these days."

"But, but he doesn't have a camera eye! Both his eyes are natural!"

"Probably used a microcam strapped to his forehead."

"How did you get the recording?" Tyrell barked.

"Highest bidder," Chickie said blandly. "You get the picture, Tyrell? I show this to the civil police and you head straight to the organ banks. Attempted murder is still a capital offense. Resign yourself, this one is going to cost you." She named a figure that was four times what she'd paid for Chickie.

Tyrell let out a loud, inelegant yelp. "That's absurd!"

"Not nearly as absurd as the sight of you lying frozen in an organ bank. You want to give up your liver to some cirrhotic sot?"

"I want the recording."

Chickie just laughed. "Don't push it, Tyrell. I'm having trouble with this already. I don't like the idea of a would-be murderer running around loose. For all I know, you've already killed before. And will again. So don't give me any crap about the money, d'you hear?"

He glared at her with contempt. "I hear."

"You have one hour. If the funds aren't transferred within an hour, this recording gets duped straight to the police." Confidently she gave him the coded deposit sequence to her A-Prime account. Tyrell could never trace her that way; those A-Primes were the apotheosis of financial anonymity. Even the banks didn't know the names behind the numbers.

"All right, you'll get your blackmail money," Tyrell said bitterly. "Within the hour." He pressed his lips together. "One thing—which one is it?"

"Which one what?"

"Which eye is the camera?"

Chickie winked her right eye. "That one." *Both, dum-dum.* "By the way, don't bother looking for me at my old address. I'm not there any more." Kara blanked the screen.

She waited the full hour before checking. And hallelujah, the funds were there in her account; Tyrell had made the transfer. Kara let out a cheer. This called for a celebration; Jocko was going to have himself one high old time tonight.

But a chore needed tending to first. Kara logged on to the newsnet. For sale: *Eyewitness evidence implicating Handley Tyrell in attempted murder.* Stupid sim-wasting bastard, thought he could buy his way out.

Tomorrow Jocko would get to work on the FDA story. And Kara would call the sim-manufacturer, to find out when the new-model Chickies would be ready to go.

Snow Angels

Loren D. Estleman

They were the unlikeliest visitors I'd had in my office since the time a priest came in looking for the antiquarian bookshop on the next floor.

She was a comfortably overstuffed sixty in a plain wool dress and a cloth coat with a monkey collar, gray hair pinned up under a hat with artificial flowers planted around the crown. He was a long skinny length of fencewire two or three years older with a horse face and sixteen hairs stretched across his scalp like violin strings, wearing a forty-dollar suit over a white shirt buttoned to the neck, no tie, and holding his hat. They sat facing my desk in the chairs I'd brought out for them as if posing for a picture back when a photograph was serious business. Their name was Cuttle.

I grinned. "Ma and Pa?"

"Jeremy and Judy," the woman said seriously. "Ed Snilly gave us your name. The lawyer?"

I excused myself and got up to consult the file cabinet. Snilly had hired me over the telephone three years ago to check the credit rating on a client, a half-hour job. He'd paid promptly.

"Good man," I said, resuming my seat. "What's he recommending me for?"

Judy said, "He's a neighbor. He sat in when we closed on the old Stage Stop. He said you might be able to help us."

"Stage Stop?"

"It's a tavern out on Old US-23, a roadhouse. Jeremy and me used to go there Saturday night when all our friends were alive. It's been closed a long time. When the developers gave us a hundred thousand for our farm—we bought it for ten back in '53—I said to Jeremy, 'We're always talking about buying the old Stage Stop and fixing it up and running it the way they used to, here's our chance.' And we did; buy it, that is, only—"

"Dream turned into a nightmare, right?"

"Good Lord, yes! You must know something about it. Building codes, sanitation, insurance, the liquor commission—I swear, if farming wasn't the most heartbreaking life a couple could choose, we'd never have had the sand for this. When the inspector told us we'd be better off tearing down and rebuilding—"

"Tell him about Simon," Jeremy snapped. I'd begun to wonder if he had vocal cords.

"Solomon," she corrected. "The Children of Solomon. Have you heard of it, Mr. Walker?"

"Some kind of Bible camp. I thought the state closed them down. Something about the discipline getting out of hand."

"A boy died in their camp up north, a runaway. But they claimed he came to them in that condition and nobody could prove different, so the charges were dropped. But they lost their lease on the land. They were negotiating a contract on the Stage Stop property when we paid cash for it. Solomon sued the previous owner, but nothing was signed between them and the judge threw it out. They tried to buy us off at a profit, but we said no."

"Took a shot at me," Jeremy said.

I sat up. "Who did?"

"Well, someone," Judy said. "We don't know it was them."

"Put a hole in my hat." Jeremy thrust it across the desk.

I took it and looked it over. It was stiff brown felt with a silk band. Something that might have been a bullet had torn a gash near the dimple on the right side of the crown. I gave it back. "Where'd it happen?"

"Jeremy was in front of the building yesterday morning, doing some measuring. I wasn't with him. He said his hat came off just like somebody grabbed it. Then he heard the shot. He ducked in through the doorway. He waited an hour before going back out, but there wasn't any more shots and he couldn't tell where that one had come from."

"Maybe it was a careless hunter."

"Wasn't no hunter."

Judy said, "We called Ollie Springer at the sheriff's substation and he came out and pried a bullet out of the doorframe. He said it came from a rifle, a .30-30. Nobody hunts with a high-powered rifle in this part of the state, Mr. Walker. It's illegal."

"Did this Springer talk to the Solomon people?"

She nodded. "They denied knowing anything about it, and there it sits. Ollie said he didn't have enough to get a warrant and search for the rifle."

I said he was probably right.

"Oh, we know he was," she said. "Jeremy and me know Ollie since he was three. Where we come from folks don't move far from home. You'll see why when you get there."

I hadn't said I was going yet, but I let it sail. "Can you think of anyone else who might want to take a shot at you?"

She answered for Jeremy. "Good Lord, no! It's a friendly place. Nobody's killed anybody around there since 1867, and that was between outsiders passing through. Besides, I don't think anybody wants to hurt either one of us. They're just trying to scare us into selling. Well, we're not scared. That's what we want you to tell those Solomon people."

"Why not tell them yourself?"

"Ed Snilly said it would mean more coming from a detective." She folded her hands on her purse in her lap, ending that discussion.

"Want me to scare *them*?"

"Yes." Something nudged the comfortable look out of her face. "Yes, we'd like that a whole lot."

I scratched my ear with the pencil I used to take notes. "I usually get a three-day retainer, but this doesn't sound like it'll take more than half a day. Make it two-fifty."

Jeremy pulled an old black wallet from his hip pocket and counted three one hundred-dollar bills onto the desk from a compartment stuffed full of them. "Gimme fifty back," he said. "And I want a receipt."

I gave him two twenties and a ten from my own wallet, replaced them with the bills he'd given me, and wrote out the transaction, handing him a copy. "Do you always come to town with that much cash on you?" I asked.

"First time we been to Detroit since '59."

"Oh, that's not true," Judy said. "We were here in '61 to see the new Studebakers."

I got some more information from them, said I'd attend to their case that afternoon, and stood to see them out.

"Don't you wear a coat?" I asked Jeremy. Outside the window the snow was falling in sheets.

"When it gets cold."

I accompanied them through the outer office into the hallway, where I shook Jeremy Cuttle's corded old hand and we said good-bye. I resisted the urge to follow them out to their car. If they drove away in anything but a 1961 Studebaker I might not have been able to handle the disappointment.

*   *   *

I killed an hour in the microfilm reading room at the library catching up on the Children of Solomon.

It was a fundamentalist religious group founded in the 1970s by a party named Bertram Comfort on the grounds that the New Testament and Christian thought were upstarts and that the way to salvation led through a belief in a vengeful God, tempered with the wisdom of King Solomon. Although a number of complaints had been filed against the sect's youth camp in the north woods, mostly for breach of the peace, the outstate press remained unaware of the order's existence until a fourteen-year-old boy died in one of the cabins, his body bearing the unmistakeable signs of a severe beating.

The camp was closed by injunction and an investigation was launched, but no evidence surfaced to disprove Comfort's testimony that the boy died in their care after receiving rough treatment Solomon only knew where. The Children themselves were unpaid volunteers working in the light of their faith and the people who sent their children to the camp were members and patrons of the church, which was not recognized as such by the state.

There was nothing to indicate that Comfort and his disciples would shoot at an old man in order to acquire real estate in South-eastern Michigan, but before heading out the Cuttles' way I went back to the office and strapped on the Smith & Wesson. Any place that hadn't had a murder in more than 120 years was past due.

* * *

An hour west of Detroit the snow stopped falling and the sun came out, glaring hard off a field of white that blended pavement with countryside; even the overpasses looked like the ruins of Atlantis rearing out of a salt sea. The farther I got from town the more the scenery resembled a Perry Como Christmas special, rolling away to the horizon with frosted trees and here and there a homeowner in Eskimo dress shoveling his driveway. The mall builders and fast-food chains had left droppings there just like everywhere else, but on days like that you remembered that kids still sledded down hills too steep for them and set out to build the world's tallest snowman and lay on their backs in the snow fanning their arms and legs to make angels.

Judy had told me she and Jeremy were living in a trailer behind the old Stage Stop, which stood on a hill overlooking Old US-23 near the exit from the younger expressway. At the end of the ramp, an aging barn she had also told me about provided more directions in the form of a painted advertisement flaking off the end wall. I turned that way, straddling a hump of snow left in the middle of the road by a county plow. Over a hill, and then the gray frame saltbox she had described thrust itself between me and a bright sky.

As it turned out, I wouldn't have needed either the sign or the directions. The rotating beacon of a county sheriff's car bounced red and blue light off the front of the building.

I parked among a collection of civilian cars and pickup trucks and followed footsteps in the snow past the county unit, left unattended with its flashers on and the two-way radio hawking and spitting at top volume, toward a fourteen-foot house trailer parked behind the empty tavern. A crowd was breaking up there, helped along by a gangling young deputy in uniform who was shooing them like chickens. He moved in front of me as I stepped toward the trailer.

"We got business here, mister. Please help us by minding yours."

I showed him the license, which might have been in cuneiform for all the reaction it got. "I'm working for the Cuttles. Who's in charge?"

"Sergeant Springer. Until the detectives show up from the county seat, anyway. You're not one of them."

I held out a card. "Please tell him the Cuttles hired me this morning."

He looked past me, saw the first of the civilian vehicles pulling out, and took the card. "Wait." He circled behind the trailer. After a few minutes he came back and beckoned me from the end.

The sergeant was a hard-looking stump about my age with silver splinters in the black hair at his temples and flat tired eyes under a fur cap. The muscles in his jaw were bunched like grapeshot. He was standing ankle-deep in snow fifty feet from the trailer with his back to it on the edge of a five-acre field that ended in a line of firs on the other side. A few yards beyond him, a man and woman lay spreadeagled side by side on their faces in the snow. The backs of the man's suitcoat and the woman's overcoat were smeared red. More red stained the snow around them in a bright fan. They were dressed exactly as I had last seen Judy and Jeremy Cuttle.

"Figure the son of a bitch gave them a running start," the sergeant said as I joined him. "Maybe he told them if they made it to the trees they were home free."

"Who found them?" I asked.

"Paper boy came to collect. When they didn't answer his knock he went looking.

"Anybody hear the shots?"

"It's rabbit season. Day goes by without a couple of shotgun blasts . . ." He let it dangle. "Your name's Walker? Ollie Springer. I command the substation here." I could feel the wire strength in his grip through the leather glove. "What'd they hire you for?"

"To hooraw the Children of Solomon. Jeremy thought they were the ones who took a shot at him yesterday. Who identified them?"

"It's them all right. I started running errands for the Cuttles when I was six and my parents knew them before that. If Comfort's bunch did this I'll nail every damn one of them to a cross." His jaw muscles worked.

"Any sign of a struggle?"

"Trailer's neat as a button. Judy was the last of the great homemakers. Bastard must've got the drop on them. Jeremy didn't talk much, but he was a fighter. You don't want to mess with these old farmers. But you can't fight a jinx."

282

"What kind of jinx?"

"The Stage Stop. Everybody who ever had anything to do with the place came to no good. Last guy who ran it went bankrupt. One before that tried to torch the place for the insurance and died in prison. I took a run at it myself once—nest egg for my retirement—and then my wife walked out on me. I guess I should've tried to talk them out of it, not that they'd have listened."

"Mind if I take a look inside the trailer?"

"Why, didn't they pay you?"

"Excuse me, Sergeant," I said, "but go to hell."

There was a door on that side of the trailer, but the deputy and I went around to the side facing the Stage Stop. Gordy should have set up his post closer to the road; the path to the door had been trampled all over by curious citizens, obliterating the killer's footprints and those of any herd of Clydesdales that might have happened by. Inside, Judy Cuttle had done what she could to turn a mobile home into an Edwardian farmhouse, complete with antimacassars and rusty photos in bamboo frames of geezers in waistcoats and glum women in cameoes. A .20-gauge Remington pump shotgun, still a fixture in Michigan country houses, leaned in a corner of the tiny parlor. Without touching it I bent over to sniff the muzzle. It hadn't been fired recently.

"Jeremy's, Ollie says," the deputy reported. "He used to shoot pheasants till he slowed down."

The door we had entered through had a window with a clear view to the tavern and the road beyond. The purse Judy had carried into my office lay on a lamp table near the door. The quality of the housekeeping said she hadn't intended it to stay there for long. I wondered if they'd even had a chance to take off their hats before receiving their last visitor.

An unmarked Dodge was parked next to the patrol car when we came out. On the other side we found a plainclothesman in conversation with Sergeant Springer while his partner examined the bodies. Their business with me didn't take any longer than Springer's. I thanked the sergeant for talking to me and left.

So far the whole thing stank; and in snow, yet.

*   *   *

283

Judy Cuttle's directions were still working. A houseboy or something in a turtleneck and whipcord trousers answered the door of a
gray stone house on the edge of the nearby town and showed me
into a room paneled in fruitwood with potted plants on the built-in
shelves. I was alone for only a few seconds when Bertram Comfort
joined me.

He was a well-upholstered fifty in a brown suit off the rack, with
fading red hair brushed gently back from a bulging forehead and
no visible neck. His hands were pink and plump and hairless, and
grasping one was like shaking hands with a baby. He waved me into
a padded chair and sat down himself behind a desk anchored by a
chrome doodad on one end and a King James Bible the size of a hand-
truck on the other.

"Is it Reverend Comfort?" I asked.

"Mister will do." His voice had the enveloping quality of a maiden
aunt's sofa. "I'm merely a lay reader. Are you with the prosecutor's
office up north? I thought that tragic business was settled."

"I'm working for Judy and Jeremy Cuttle. I'm a private investigator."

He looked as if he were going to cry. "I told the officer none of
the Children were near the property yesterday. I wish these people
could lay aside the suspicions of the secular world long enough to
understand it is not we but Solomon who sits in judgment."

"I notice you refer to it as *the* property, not *their* property. Do
you still hope to obtain it for your camp?"

"Not *my* camp. Solomon's. All the legal avenues have not yet been
traveled."

"It's the illegal ones I'm interested in. Maybe you've got a rebel
in the fold. It happens in the best of families, even the God-fearing
ones."

"The Children love God; we don't fear Him. And everyone is
accounted for at the time of yesterday's unfortunate incident."

"Yesterday's yesterday. I'm here about today."

"Today?"

"Somebody shotgunned the Cuttles behind their trailer about
an hour ago. Give or take."

"Great glory!" He glanced at the Bible. "Are they—"

"Gone to God. Knocking on the pearly. Purgatory bound. Dead
as a mackerel."

"I find your mockery abhorrent under the circumstances. Do the police think the Children are involved?"

"The police think what the police think. I'm not the police. Yesterday somebody potted at Jeremy Cuttle, or maybe just at his hat as a warning. Today he and his wife engaged me to investigate. Now they're not in a position to engage anything but six feet of God's good earth. I'm a detective. I see a connection." I looked at my watch. "It's three o'clock. Do you know where the Children are?"

Again his eyes strayed to the Bible. Then he placed his pudgy hands on the desk, jacked himself to his feet, and hiked up his belt, the way fat men do. "I have Solomon's work to attend to. 'Go thou from the presence of a foolish man when thou perceivest not in him the lips of knowledge.'"

"'Sticks and stones may break my bones,'" I said, rising, "but any parakeet can memorize sentences." I went me from his presence.

*   *   *

Ed Snilly, the lawyer who had recommended me to the Cuttles, lived in an Edwardian farmhouse on eighty acres with a five-year-old Fleetwood parked in the driveway sporting a bumper sticker reading HAVE YOU HUGGED YOUR HOGS TODAY? His wife, fifty-odd years of pork and potatoes stuffed into stretch jeans, directed me to the large yellow barn behind the house, where I found him tossing ears of dried corn from a bucket into a row of stalls occupied by chugging, snuffling pigs.

"One of my neighbors called me with the news," he said after he'd set down the bucket and shaken my hand. He was a wiry old scarecrow in his seventies with a spotty bald head and false teeth in a jaw too narrow for them. "Terrible thing. I've known Judy and Jeremy since the Depression. I'd gladly help out the prosecution on this one gratis. Do you suspect Comfort?"

"I'd like to. Did you represent the Cuttles when they bought the Stage Stop?"

"Yes. It was an estate sale, very complicated. Old Man Herndon's heirs wanted to liquidate quickly and wouldn't carry any paper. Jeremy negotiated to the last penny. I also stood up with them at the hearing with the State Liquor Control Commission. A license transfer can be pretty thorny without chicanery. I'm not sure we'd have swung it if Ollie Springer hadn't appeared to vouch for them."

"I'm surprised he spoke up. He told me the place was jinxed."

"I can see why he'd feel that way. Old Man Herndon was Ollie's father-in-law. The Stage Stop was going to be a belated wedding present, but that ended when Herndon's daughter ran out on Ollie. The rumor was she ditched him for some third rate rock singer who came through here a couple of years back. I think that's what killed the old man."

"So far this place is getting to be almost as interesting as Detroit."

"Scandals happen everywhere, but in the main we country folk look out for one another. That's why Ollie helped Judy and Jeremy in spite of his personal tragedy. To be honest, I thought they were getting in over their heads too, especially later when they talked about digging a wine cellar and adding a room for pool. They were looking far beyond your usual mom-and-pop operation."

"Is gaming that big hereabouts?"

"Son, people around here will go to a christening and bet on when the baby's first tooth will come in. Phil Costa's made a fortune off the pool tables in the basement of his bowling alley out on M-52. Lord knows I've represented enough of his clientele at their arraignments every time Ollie's raided the place."

"Little Phil? Last I heard he was doing something like seven to twelve in Jackson for fixing the races at Hazel Park."

"He's out two years now, and smarter than when he went in. These rural county commissioners stay fixed longer than the city kind. Phil never seems to be around when the deputies bust in."

"So if the Cuttles went ahead and put in their poolroom, Little Phil might have lost business."

"It's a thought." Snilly picked up his bucket and resumed scattering ears of corn in the stalls. "A thought is what it is."

*　*　*

The Paul Bunyan Bowl-A-Rama, an aluminum hangar with a two-story neon lumberjack bowling on its roof, looked abashed at mid-afternoon, like a nude dancer caught under a conventional electric bulb. A young thick-shouldered bouncer who hadn't bothered to change out of his overalls on his way in from the back forty conferred with the office and came back to escort me past the lanes.

Little Phil Costa crowded four-foot ten in his two-inch elevators, a sour-faced baldy in his middle years with pointed features like a chihuahua's. Small men are usually neat, but his tie was loose, his sleeves rolled up unevenly, and an archaeologist could have reconstructed his last five meals from the stains on his unbuttoned vest. He didn't look up from the adding-machine tapes he was sorting through on a folding card table when I entered. "Tell Lorraine the support check's in the mail. I ain't about to bust my parole over the brat."

"I'm not from your ex. I'm working for the Cuttles."

"What the hell's a Cuttle?"

I told him. He scowled, but it was at a wrong sum on one of the tapes. He corrected it with a pencil stub. "I heard about it. I hope you got your bread up front."

"Talk is Judy and Jeremy were going to add a pool room to the Stage Stop."

"How about that. What's six times twelve?"

"Think of it in terms of years in stir." I laid a hand on top of the tape. "A few years back, two guys who were operating their handbook in one of your neighborhoods were shotgunned behind the New Hellas Cafe in Hamtramck. The cops never did pin it to you, but nobody's tried to cut in on you since. Until the Cuttles."

The farmboy-bouncer took a step forward, but Costa stopped him with a hand. "Get the bottle."

It was a pinch bottle filled with amber liquid. Costa took it without looking away from me and broke the seal. "You a drinking man, Walker?"

"In the right company. This isn't it."

"I wasn't offering. This stuff's twenty-four years old, flown in special for me from Aberdeen. Seventy-five bucks a fifth." He upended it over his metal wastebasket. When it gurgled empty he tossed in the bottle. "On their best night, that's what the Cuttles' room might cost me. Still think I iced them?"

"I'm way past that," I said. "Now I'm wondering who takes out your trash."

"You trade in information, I'll treat you. Check out a guy named Chuckie Noyes. He's a Child of Solomon, squats in the cemetery behind the Stage Stop property, the old caretaker's hut. I knew him in Jackson before he got religion. He did eleven years for killing a druggie in Detroit. Used a shotgun."

"Why so generous?"

He tipped a hand toward the adding-machine tapes. "I got a good thing here, closest I ever been to legit in my life. Last thing I need's some sticky snoop coming back and back, drawing attention. Time was I'd just have Horace here adjust your spine, but if there's one thing I learned on the block it's diplomacy. Dangle, now. I open at dusk."

"Seventy-two," I said.

"What?"

"Six times twelve."

"Hey, thanks." He wrote it down. "Come back some night when you're not working and bowl a couple of lines. On the house."

* * *

For the second time that day, police strobes had beaten me to my destination. They lanced the shadows gathering among the leaning headstones in what might have been a churchyard before the central building had burned down sometime around Appomattox. Near its charred foundation stood a galvanized steel shed with a slanted roof and a door cut in one side. As I was getting out of the car, two uniformed attendants wheeled a body bag on a stretcher out through the door and into the back of an ambulance that was almost as big as the shed. Sergeant Springer came out behind them, deep in conversation with a man six inches taller in a snapbrim hat and a coat with a fur collar. The two were enveloped in the vapor of their own spent breath.

"I'll want it on my desk in the morning," said the big man, pausing to shake Springer's hand before pulling on his gloves.

"Will do, Lieutenant."

The lieutenant touched his shoulder. "Bad day all around, Ollie. Get some rest before you talk to the shooting team." He boarded an unmarked Dodge with a magnetic flasher on the roof. The motor turned over sluggishly and caught.

"Chuckie Noyes?" I asked Springer.

He looked up at me, then down at his fur cap. "Yeah." He put it on.
"Who shot him, you?"

"Uh-huh."

"He do the Cuttles?"

"Looks like."

"You're not the only one having a bad day, Sergeant."

"Guess you're right." He fastened the snaps on his jacket. "I came here to ask Noyes some questions, thought he might have seen or heard something living so close. He had an antique pin on his chest of drawers by his bed. Judy wore that pin to church every Sunday. Don't know how I missed not seeing it in the trailer. Noyes saw it same time I did. He tried for my gun."

"Were you alone?"

"What?" He lamped me hard.

"Nothing. You folks in the country do things differently."

"I don't expect to lose sleep over squashing a germ like that, but it doesn't mean I wanted to. Now we'll never know if he was working for Comfort or if he slipped the rest of the way over the edge and acted solo. He had a record for violence."

"So Little Phil said."

"That germ. Guess you'll talk to just about anybody."

"It's a job."

"A stinking job."

"Everything about this one stinks," I agreed. "Sleep tight, Sergeant."

*   *   *

I'd always heard God-fearing people went to bed with the chickens. Another myth gone.

At 11:45 P.M. I was still parked down the road from Bertram Comfort's gray stone house, where I'd been for over an hour, warming my calcifying marrow with judicious transfusions of hot coffee from a Thermos and waiting for the lights to go out downstairs. A couple of minutes later they did. I was tempted to go in then but sat tight. Just after midnight the single lighted window on the second story went black. Then I moved.

I'd brought my pocket burglar kit, but just for the hell of it I tried the knob on the front door. Comfort had the old chruchman's prejudice against locks. I let myself in.

I also had my pencil flash, but I didn't use that either. There was a moon, and the glow reflecting off the snow shone bright as my best hopes through the windows. I found my way to the study without tripping over anything.

I didn't waste time going through the desk or looking behind the religious paintings for a wall safe. During my interview with Comfort his eyes had strayed to the big Bible on the desk one too many times for even the devoutest of reasons.

The book was genuine enough. There were no hollowed-out pages and an elaborate red-and-gold bookplate pasted to the flyleaf read TO MR. BERTRAM EZEKIEL COMFORT, FATHER OF THE FAITH, FROM THE CHILDREN OF SOLOMON, flanked by Adam and Eve in figleaves. A dozen strips of microfilm spilled out of a pocket in the spine when I tilted the book.

I carried the strips over to the window and held them up to the moonlight. They were photographed documents bearing the identification of the records departments of various police organizations. The farthest came from Los Angeles. The closest belonged to Detroit. I read that one. Then I put it in my inside breast pocket, returned the others to the Bible and the Bible to its place on the desk, and left, my sabbatical completed on the bones of another Commandment.

* * *

The next day was clear and twenty degrees. The sky had no ceiling and the sun on the snow was a sea of cold white fire. Breathing was like inhaling needles.

The air was colder inside the empty Stage Stop building with the raw damp of enclosed winter. The old floorboards rang like iron when I stepped on them and my breath steamed around the gaunt timbers that held up the roof. Owls nexted in the rafters. The new yellow two-by-fours stacked along the walls were bright with the anticipation of a dead couple's exploded vision.

"Jesus, it's cold in here," said Ollie Springer, pushing aside the front door, which hung on a single scabbed hinge. "Is the cold locker closed at Pete's Meats?"

"It's a hall. The Cuttles might have appreciated the choice. Thanks for coming, Sergeant."

"You made it sound important over the phone. It better be. The lieutenant's waiting for my report on Chuckie Noyes."

"I've got something you might want to add." I handed him the microfilm slip I'd taken from Comfort's Bible.

"What is it?"

"Noyes's arrest report on a homicide squeal he went down for in Detroit a dozen years ago. Since you mentioned his record yesterday I thought you'd like to see the name of the arresting officer."

He was holding it up to a shaft of sunlight coming in through an empty window, but he wasn't reading.

"The city cops are jealous of their reputations," I said. "When they take a killer into custody they sometimes forget to release the name of the rural cop who actually busted him during his flight to freedom; but a report's a report. Just a deputy then, weren't you?"

"This doesn't mean anything." He crumpled the strip into a ball and threw it behind the stack of lumber.

"Detroit has the original. Bertram Comfort maintains the loyalty of the more recalcitrant members of his flock by keeping tabs on their past indiscretions; that's where I got the copy. I figure when you found out Noyes was back in circulation and hanging around your jurisdiction, you either hired him to kill Judy and Jeremy or more likely threatened to bust him on some parole beef if he didn't cooperate. Then you offed him to keep him from talking and planted Judy's pin in the caretaker's hut where he was living. The simple plans are always the best. As a Child of Solomon he'd be blamed for trying to help secure the Stage Stop property for Comfort's new camp.

"I guess I'm responsible for accelerating their deaths," I went on. "Someone—you, probably—made a last ditch attempt to scare them off the other day by taking a potshot at Jeremy. When he and Judy hired me instead to investigate, you switched to Plan B before I could get a foothold. You're one impulsive cop, Sergeant."

"Why would I want to kill the Cuttles? They're like my second parents." He rested his hand on his sidearm, a nickel-plated .38 with a black knurled grip.

"It bothered me too, especially when I found out you spoke up for them at the hearing before the State Liquor Control Commission. But that didn't jibe with what you told me about thinking this place had a hoodoo. I should have guessed the truth when Ed Snilly said they decided later to expand the Stage Stop. At first I thought it was their plans for a pool room and the competition it would create for Phil Costa, but that was chump change to him, not worth killing over. It was the wine cellar."

"What wine cellar?"

"There isn't one now, but there was going to be. You were right in there cheering them on, in spite of your own bad luck with the place and the wife you said left you, until you found out they were going to dig a hole." I paced as I spoke, circling a soft spot in the floor where the old boards had rotted and sunk into a depression eight feet across. He was watching me, trying to keep from staring at my feet. His fingers curled around the grip of the revolver. I said, "I made some calls this morning from my motel room in town, got the name of that rock singer everyone says your wife ran off with. I called eight booking agents before I found one who used to work with him. He didn't skip with anyone's wife. He died of a drug overdose in Cincinnati a couple of months after he played here. Nobody was with him or had been for some time."

"If you stayed at the motel you know she spent a night with him there," Springer said. "It was all over the county next day. They were both gone by then."

"Your wife didn't go as far as he did. No more than six feet from where we're standing, and all of it straight down. Those rotten boards lift right out. I checked before you got here."

"Plenty of room under there for two." He drew his gun.

"Drop it, Ollie!"

He pivoted, snapping off a shot. The bullet knocked a splinter off the big timber the sheriff's lieutenant had been hiding behind. The big man returned fire. Springer shouted, fell down, and grasped his thigh.

"Drop it, I said."

The sergeant looked down at the gun he was still holding as if he'd forgotten about it. He opened his hand and let it fall.

"Thanks, Lieutenant." I took the Smith & Wesson out of my coat pocket and lowered the hammer gently. "Sorry about the cold wait."

He holstered his own gun under his fur-lined coat. "Ollie was right about this place." He shook loose a pair of handcuffs.

I left while he was reading Springer his Miranda and went out into the cold sunshine of the country.

0 4695 c